PRAISE FOR
THE NOVELS OF DAKOTA CASSIDY

"Serious, laugh-out-loud humor with heart, the kind of love story that leaves you rooting for the heroine, sighing for the hero, and looking for your own significant other at the same time."

—Kate Douglas

"Dakota Cassidy is going on my must-read list!"

—*Joyfully Reviewed*

"If you're looking for some steamy romance with something that will have you smiling, you have to read [Dakota Cassidy]."

—*The Best Reviews*

"Ditsy and daring . . . pure escapist fun." —*Romance Reviews Today*

Berkley Sensation titles by Dakota Cassidy

THE ACCIDENTAL WEREWOLF

ACCIDENTALLY DEAD

ACCIDENTALLY DEAD

DAKOTA CASSIDY

BERKLEY SENSATION, NEW YORK

THE BERKLEY PUBLISHING GROUP
Published by the Penguin Group
Penguin Group (USA) Inc.
375 Hudson Street, New York, New York 10014, USA
Penguin Group (Canada), 90 Eglinton Avenue East, Suite 700, Toronto, Ontario M4P 2Y3, Canada
(a division of Pearson Penguin Canada Inc.)
Penguin Books Ltd., 80 Strand, London WC2R 0RL, England
Penguin Group Ireland, 25 St. Stephen's Green, Dublin 2, Ireland (a division of Penguin Books Ltd.)
Penguin Group (Australia), 250 Camberwell Road, Camberwell, Victoria 3124, Australia
(a division of Pearson Australia Group Pty. Ltd.)
Penguin Books India Pvt. Ltd., 11 Community Centre, Panchsheel Park, New Delhi—110 017, India
Penguin Group (NZ), 67 Apollo Drive, Rosedale, North Shore 0632, New Zealand
(a division of Pearson New Zealand Ltd.)
Penguin Books (South Africa) (Pty.) Ltd., 24 Sturdee Avenue, Rosebank, Johannesburg 2196, South Africa

Penguin Books Ltd., Registered Offices: 80 Strand, London WC2R 0RL, England

This book is an original publication of The Berkley Publishing Group.

This is a work of fiction. Names, characters, places, and incidents either are the product of the author's imagination or are used fictitiously, and any resemblance to actual persons, living or dead, business establishments, events, or locales is entirely coincidental. The publisher does not have any control over and does not assume any responsibility for author or third-party websites or their content.

Copyright © 2008 by Dakota Cassidy
Cover art by Katie Wood
Cover design by Diana Kolsky
Text design by Kristin del Rosario

First edition: July 2008

Library of Congress Cataloging-in-Publication Data

Cassidy, Dakota.
    Accidentally dead / Dakota Cassidy.— 1st ed.
        p.   cm.
    ISBN 978-0-425-22159-4
    1. Dental assistants—Fiction. 2. Werewolves—Fiction. 3. Vampires— Fiction. I. Title.
PS3603.A8685A66 2008
    813'.6—dc22   2008009077

PRINTED IN THE UNITED STATES OF AMERICA

10   9   8   7   6   5   4   3   2   1

The words themselves just won't ever have enough meaning, but I'm gonna give it a hella try anyway.

To Kira Stone, Renee George, Michelle Hoppe, Vicky Burkland, Sheri Fogarty, Diane Whiteside, Michele Bardsley, and Erin. Whether it's motherly advice, a read through, the cold, hard truth, or just a shoulder, you all rock the Casbah!

My editor, Cindy Hwang, who gets not just my newbie-ness, but my zaniness.

My mother and my sons, Cameron and Travis. Thanks for not voting me off the island when we're playing Survivor and dinner consists of one granola bar we all have to share, because I'm on deadline and haven't shopped. I love ya, like even more than my collection of shoes.

Jessica Growette, my publicist, who's like God in a tiny Tasmanian devil–like package. She makes stuff so easy on me. You rule, chica!

My agent, Deidre Knight. I'm of the school of thought that *everyone* should have a Deidre Knight. There truly isn't a funnier, smarter, more supportive agent out there, and I'm mad grateful to her for just letting me write while she handles everything else. She rules all things agent-like.

My good friend Laura back in da hood in Jersey—No freakin' way are we gonna let a little thing like this slow us down, baby. We got lots of livin' left to do!

But most especially for Ter, who will never know what her friendship means to me. A phone call, a shoulder, an ear—directions to the bathroom—the path that leads me there—you're all things GPS, baby, and übercool.

Last, but never least, Rob, who knows what it is to lose me to the zone, doesn't care if I look like a bag lady when I do it, and at the end of the day, tells me he loves me no matter what. Soul mates *do* exist—who'da thunk?

Dakota

ACKNOWLEDGMENTS

Kudos to Wikipedia, an online user-based encyclopedia. I spent a great deal of time there, gathering different perspectives on vampire folklore, reading about vampire television shows and movies, too. And please, forgive the artistic license I take when my characters make mention of it—it truly was fun to read the information online users collected and took so much time and effort to record. Also thanks to www.oldandsold.com and www.madametalbot.com, for information about the clothing worn for the time period described in the book and more vampire folklore.

CHAPTER
1

"Marty?"

"Nina?"

"I need to talk to you, and I need to talk to you *now*."

"Do you have any idea what time it is?"

"I know. It's late, and believe me, I wouldn't be calling you at midnight out there in the great beyond if it wasn't like a real 911."

"Okay, so talk," Marty said, yawning so loudly it sounded like the howl of the Santa Ana winds to Nina.

"You know that fucking werewolf thing?"

"Yes, Nina. What about the *fucking* werewolf thing? I know it still seems unbelievable. It is what it is. So do we have to have 'the talk' again? We've only been over it a *hundred* times since it happened."

Nina rolled her eyes and literally bit her tongue. It wasn't like she wanted to go over it again any more than Marty did. However, had she never experienced what she had with Marty Andrews, now Marty Flaherty, she wouldn't have the kind of simpatico she did with this particularly sensitive issue.

Marty—once her regional independent color supervisor at the prestigious Bobbie-Sue Cosmetics—self-proclaimed color wheel of life freak—find your aura and be the best you can be diva—was a *werewolf*.

By accident.

She was a raw beef–eating, bay-at-the-moon, hairy-assed were-wolf. If anyone could give her advice about what to do right now, it was her former color wheel coach, now friend-turned-lupine, Marty.

"Did you hear me, Nina? We've gone over this a hundred ti—"

"How about we shoot for one hundred and one?"

"What are you talking about? God, Nina. It's definitely not like you to beat around the bush. You have such a lovely, direct nature. You know the one where you just say whatever's on your mind, with as many cuss words as you can cram into a sentence, and forget that people around you might find your potty mouth of-fensive? What's the holdup? Did someone yank your tongue out of your head?"

"I need you to listen to me, Marty, and I need you to listen closely."

"Color me listening."

"I'm a vampire."

A snort of derisive laughter, brittle and scathing with a little "poor Nina" thrown in for good measure, crackled in her earpiece. "Sweetie? Are you feeling the green-eyed monster biting your ass? I know the whole werewolf thing caught you off guard, and I un-derstand that, but you don't have to make up crazy stories to get my attention. I'm *always* here for you—even if I do live in Buffalo and you up and dumped Wanda and me for Hackensack. Really, this kind of attention seeking is typical of separation anxiety. You miss us. We miss you too, honey." Marty took a breath, gathering her therapist-like steam.

"Maybe we'll plan a girl's weekend, huh? Like borrow Keegan's little plane and hit a tropical locale. Oh! I know—Cancún. God, this time of year would be perfect. I'll even shut my mouth if you want to Speedo chase. I promise—no matter how disgusting it gets. We'll bring nothing but our bathing suits and sit by the ocean while we drink those pink drinks with umbrellas in them. They're sooo festive. So stop all this silly talk about vampires and such and come to Buffalo. If you pack a—"

Nina's hand clenched the phone. Cheerist, Marty, God love her, could be such a rambling pain in the derriere if given just an inch. "Marty! Shut the hell up and listen to me. Listen to me carefully. This has shit to do with your werewolf-ism and jealousy and men in Speedos." Nina fought a shudder over the mental image that brought to mind. "I am not jealous. Who could possibly be jealous of that tail of yours?"

When Marty had been turned into a werewolf, for a while there, she'd had a lot of trouble shifting fully, as she'd called it. The only time she had even a bit of success was when she was angry. When she was PO'd, a small, nubby tail would pop out on her ass, and the first time Nina had seen it, it had left her speechless.

A rare occurrence indeed.

Though Marty's shifting issues had cleared up, her embarrassment because of it hadn't, and Nina often used that to her own advantage.

Just because she could. Which was probably meaner than shit, but leverage with Marty was leverage.

Marty's gasp was crisp, hurting Nina's sensitive ears. It sounded like a thousand dentist drills screeching in her head. "Don't you dare, Nina Blackman! Do not even remind me of the struggles I've endured over being bitten by a werewolf. The utter humiliation I suffered because I couldn't fully shift was just atrocious. Don't even go there, you potty mouth! I will not be subjugated and ridiculed by you—"

God, if Marty could do anything well, it was yak—at full speed, with nary a pause for breath. Yeah, okay, it had been an accident. They'd been walking Marty's maniacal, overprotective, teacup poodle, Muffin, near an alleyway in the city after a particularly disappointing Bobbie-Sue meeting. Wherein humiliation reigned supreme for her and Wanda Schwartz, Marty's other recruit, because they sucked big man-hooters when it came to selling lip gloss.

On that crazy night, Marty'd been reaming them a new one over their supposed lack of motivation to sell, sell, sell, when they'd spied what they'd thought was nothing more than a big beast of a dog. Muffin, being the whack job she was, took him on like she was David and he was Goliath. In the melee of Marty trying to dislodge Muff from the beast's jaws of death, it had bitten her. Only this beast wasn't just a beast. He was a half human, half werewolf named Keegan Flaherty, and he'd infected Marty with his lycanthropic-ness.

Nina had seen the result of it herself.

That's how she knew what was going on, and nobody was going to tell her differently.

"Nina? Are you there? You listen to me, Miss Potty Mouth. I won't have you mocking me because I was challenged—"

"Marrtyyyyyy! Would you shut the fuck up and listen to me? For once in your life, quit blabbing and listen. I'm in need here, and you're not helping."

Marty's intake of breath was sharp. "I know what this is . . . Is it that you need a deposit in your emotional bank again? Is your cry-for-attention account empty?"

"Marty, save the happy place speech. That's a made-up place that crazy people like you claim exists, so they don't sound crazy while they pretend nothing's wrong. I have some news for you—there is *no* happy place, Marty. It's all made up in your head, and you and all of your breathing techniques and guru crap is just that—crap. So scee-rew the happy place and your bank of hippie-schmippie love child bullshit and listen very closely to me. I'm—a—vampire."

Yep. Yep, she was.

Marty's sigh was long, windy, and put upon. "Fine. Tell me all about your vampire-ness, Nina. I'm all ears."

Nina rolled her dark eyes yet again, watching her fading reflection in the cracked mirror of her small apartment bathroom. It revealed a very fuzzy, distorted image—this couldn't be good. She ran a hand over her teeth—the only thing she could define clearly in the mirror—just to be sure she wasn't seeing things.

She hadn't graduated dental hygienist school for nuthin', and those incisors were definitely not in *any* textbook she'd ever been exposed to.

Nor was the way she could see into the apartments across the street, with eyesight to rival the Green Berets and all their super night vision goggles. She couldn't just see into them; she could actually read the label on the can of creamed corn Mrs. Fedderman had on her worn, yellowed countertop. It had an oval, orange sticker on it marked "Can-Can Sale." Mrs. Fedderman lived for a good Can-Can sale.

She could also see Mrs. Fedderman's Chihuahua, Freddy.

Mean, little, ankle-biting motherfucker.

In fact, she couldn't just see him, she could *smell* him. The lovely, luscious, coppery scent of his blood coursing through his wee little veins. It wafted to her nostrils like paradise on a breeze.

Her stomach growled like a caged, angry tiger.

Gripping the sink, Nina opened her mouth wider.

Jesus Christ.

She really had fangs. Big, white, elongated fangs.

"Nina?"

"Whaaaat?" she hissed, infuriated that Marty kept interrupting her misery. "God, Marty! Can't you see I'm in crisis here?"

"No. I can't see anything, Nina. We're on the phone. Thus, your visual escapes me. So why don't you verbally draw the picture for me?"

"Shit. Okay, here goes. I had my first patient today. Some dude with a last name I can't pronounce. Hot. He was really hot. Anyway, he was having a chipped tooth filed. No big deal, and we only gave him a shot of anesthesia, but he got really, really weird like right away. Like all loopy. Some people react differently to anesthesia, so I didn't give it a lot of thought.

"Anyway, I'm all prepping him for Dr. Berkenstein to come file him, and he's mumbling some nonsensical crap that I don't get. Next thing I know, he jerks and clamps down on my hand. Only for a second, but he pierced my glove. Drew a bit of blood—no big deal. Scared the bejesus out of me, and I have to admit I was a little woozy afterward, but when push came to shove, I was fine. Dr. Berkenstein said I should go home. I mean, he's the boss, but it was my first day, and I didn't want to look like a wuss. But he insisted. So I came home. I got home at two in the afternoon—yesterday, Marty. *Yesterday.* I don't remember anything until I woke up *today*—just a little while ago—with these." She pointed to her incisors, as if Marty could see them.

"Explain *these*. Nina."

"Teeth, Marty. My teeth. I have freakin' fangs!" she yelped into the phone. The realization was settling low in her belly. Like a worm burrowing under the earth, seeking shelter in the dirt.

"Fangs . . ."

"Did I not just say *fangs*. Marty? Yes, by fuck, I have goddamned fangs. Big, long, white fangs."

"Have you been bingeing? I know you're not prone to the lure of alcohol, but well, it's been a difficult transition for you since you left Bobbie-Sue—"

Nina sucked in her cheeks to keep from telling Marty the truth about her Bobbie-Sue matter. It hadn't been difficult at all for Nina to leave her friend's cosmetic supervision. Though she'd come to really dig Marty, despite her bullshit girly crap, she'd hated trying to sell stupid units of eyeliner. She'd answered Marty's ad for Bobbie-Sue Cosmetics in the local paper almost a year ago, after the degradation of applying at McDonald's when she'd lost her stenographer job because of budget cuts.

In essence, desperation had made her consider trying to sell lip gloss and eyeliner for a living. She'd needed a job so badly then, she'd even been willing to take a shot at hawking makeup. Totally not her thing. She hated makeup.

Unfortunately, Nina could never adopt the proper Bobbie-Sue attitude, and instead of gaining clients, she'd been just shy of restraining orders and orange jumpsuits after being turned down time and again.

It'd been a relief to let go of color wheels and palettes of life and all the other shit Bobbie-Sue tried to sell you. Nina had sucked at door-to-door sales—even with Marty's help, she'd failed miserably. Marty was a whiz at it, which was a good thing, seeing as she'd ended up owning a piece of Bobbie-Sue. Now Marty spun her color wheel at regular intervals with the kind of joy contestants took in spinning the Wheel of Fortune.

When they'd all found out Marty was an heir to Bobbie-Sue, Marty had offered Nina a job, but she'd declined. It probably would have been easier, but Nina couldn't fathom a life filled with all that froufrou nonsense and crazy euphemisms about the colors of your life. She also didn't take handouts. Marty knew she sucked big wankers at selling makeup, yet she'd offered her a job anyway, because as annoying and pushy as Marty was, she was good people. So Nina'd decided to take advantage of an unemployment program that helped to school and retrain you in a more marketable field.

And look what that training and nice new job had gotten her.

"Marty, I swear to Christ—I'm warning you. I—have—fangs. I haven't been drinking. I haven't done any drugs since I was sixteen, and I'm not on any antidepressants. Now quit friggin' playing Oprah and listen. I'm a vampire." She knew what was happening. She knew the paranormal existed because of Marty. If there were werewolves floating around the planet, why couldn't there be vampires, too? If you had fangs, there wasn't anything left to do but call vampire.

"A vampire," Marty repeated, sounding vague and distant, and that sent Nina into an angry fit.

"You know what? How come you can be a werewolf, and I can't be a vampire? What's all the skepticism about? I hear it in your voice, Marty. What the fuck makes you so special?"

Marty clucked her tongue. "Oh, Nina, Nina, Nina. It's not like we're playing Barbies and you're left with nothing but Barbie's ratty sister Skipper. This isn't a competition. I'm a werewolf because I was bitten by one. It was an accident. You were there, and it was anything but special—even if now I can't imagine my life before it happened." Her voice grew all breathy and dreamy. Marty and the delish man—werewolf—whatever—who'd bitten her had ended up together. Lifemates or some such crap. Now they were mating and making puppies—kids. Something like that.

Nina's brow furrowed, while Marty droned on.

"So why don't we talk about the real issue here? You're jealous, because I have special powers and you don't."

Nina whipped the phone from her ear and covered it with her hands, jumping up and down to keep from throwing it. While her feet slapped against the cold, stained tile of her bathroom, every muscle in her body fought for restraint. Between clenched teeth she struggled to tamp down the rapid rise of her fury. Placing the phone back to her ear, she spat, "Marty, I never played with Barbies. In fact, I fucking hate Barbie. I always liked GI Joe, personally. At least he didn't have those fake pointed toes—"

"But Barbie had all those glorious clothes and the dream house. Remember the Corvette?"

"I remember, but GI Joe had guns and tanks that could run Barbie's stupid Corvette off the road, hurl a grenade at it, and leave her fancy sports car in a fiery blaze of steaming shit."

"But Barbie had all that long hair and shoes for miles. God, I loved that—"

"Marty!"

"What? Jesus. Quit yelling in my ear. It's sensitive, remember?"

"Could we get to the problem at hand and let the Barbie analogy go?"

"Right. You're jealous because I have superpowers. Because I can shift and like lift a freight train. It doesn't make you any less important, Nina—"

Nina groaned. "I am not jealous, Marty. Who could possibly be jealous over the fact that you're a *dog*? Listen to me. I'm telling you the truth. I have fangs, and if Mrs. Fedderman's pooch, Freddy, doesn't stop parading around that kitchen of hers like he's a corn dog on a stick, I swear I'm going to go over there and bite his little legs off, fry 'em up, and dip 'em in barbecue sauce like little fucking chicken wings!"

Nina heard Marty's distinct gulp.

Ah, now we had the color princess's attention.

"Okay, no biting Freddy. He didn't do anything to you. Do you hear me, Nina? Don't move a muscle. Stay right there. I'll come right away. And for God's sake, move Larry out of your line of vision."

Larry was her pet guinea pig, and, yeah, it would probably be a good thing to avoid, at all costs, watching his wee guinea legs work that exercise wheel . . .

"Nina. Listen to me. Call Wanda for now. She's closer. She'll stay with you until I can get Keegan to find me someone to fly his plane to Jersey. And for God's sake do not tell anyone else about this. You can't trust anyone, Nina. Not a soul but me and Wanda. If this got out—well, I don't know what would happen if it got out, but I know it would be detrimental. That's all I know. If this werewolf thing has taught me anything, it's to keep my mouth shut and blend. The fewer people who know, the better. Now do what I said and wait for Wanda."

"What the hell is Wanda going to do for me? Find me a shade of Bobbie-Sue lipstick to help downplay my fangs?"

Marty scoffed. "To support you, you pain in the ass. Why must you always be so difficult? It's a wonder we've stayed friends with you. You're always so combative. Just once, shut up, stay in your apartment like a good girl, and wait for Wanda. And if I find out you left and didn't listen to me, I *will* kick your ass. Make no mistake. I'm not the Marty of a year ago. I can and will take you," she finished with a deadly calm that let Nina know she meant what she said.

She was well aware of Marty's strength now that she was lycanthropic, but the hell if she'd admit it. "The hell you can. I was raised in the Bronx. I'll wipe the floors of Lord and Taylor with your ass."

"Nina," Marty said with that warning tone Nina was sure was accompanied by the narrowing of her pretty blue eyes. "Do not do battle with me tonight. I can't tell you how important it really is to shut your mouth. I've lived with this werewolf secret for a while now, and it isn't like coming out of the closet or something. There are lots of people who'd far rather stake you through your cold, black heart. Oh . . . wait . . . if all that legend stuff is true about vampires and you really are one, you don't have one of those anymore, do you?"

Nina's hand immediately flew to her chest, pressing against the thin T-shirt she had on. Hellafino . . . nothing. No heartbeat.

"Never mind, it doesn't matter. It wasn't like you used that muscle much anyway," she said, laughing at her own cleverness.

"Marty!"

"What?"

"I have no heartbeat. Nothing. No pulse. Not even a twitch." Blessed hell, what else didn't vampires have? She sank to the floor, curling up against the cool porcelain bathtub, while fleeting memories of an Ann Rice movie flickered through her mind's eye. If she remembered right, Tom Cruise didn't seem terribly happy the entire epic saga. In fact, he'd looked pretty miserable and not at all like his *Top Gun* self.

Fuck. A. Duck.

"Nina, sit your scrawny ass down and do not speculate on anything. Wait for Wanda and me, and whatever you do, leave Mrs. Fedderman's dog alone. Got that?"

Nina pressed the heel of her hand against her head to ease the swirling colors of the bathroom. "Fine. Color me waiting. Hurry up. My stomach is doing all sorts of crazy shit, and I'm telling you, Freddy is looking pretty tasty." She was experiencing a hunger she'd never quite known. Yet it wasn't the characteristic Lean Cuisine, boil-in-a-bag dinner she craved, but she couldn't pinpoint what it was she was hungry for.

The idea of food—frozen pizza—sardines in a can—some of her more typical dining fare—made her want to gag.

Marty gasped again with a brittle inhale of breath. "I'm dialing Wanda on my cell as we speak. *Leave Freddy alone . . .*"

Fine, she'd just wait. She was not going the way of Marty. There'd be no girly freak—no whining about this for a month like her friend had. She'd find the guy who did this to her, and then she'd kick his ass from here to kingdom come.

THREE hours later and after much struggle on her part to keep from hightailing it over to Mrs. Fedderman's house for a taste of Freddy, first Wanda, then Marty had arrived. Wanda remained silent for the entire hour before Marty entered the picture, occasionally cocking her head and reeking of confusion.

Neither looked as freaked as she'd anticipated though, and she wasn't sure if she was disappointed or relieved. "Look." She opened her mouth wide and pointed to her teeth. "Was I fucking lying, Marty? What else could it mean except that I'm a vampire?"

Marty's blue eyes rounded, wide and obviously puzzled. Pinching her fingers together, she tweaked at one fang. "Jesus," she muttered. "You definitely have fangs. I think you might need extra Colgate." Her quip was sarcastic as she headed for Nina's threadbare sofa and plumped a pillow to lean on, brushing imaginary lint from her immaculate black trousers, and scrunching the sleeves up on her bulky, peacock colored sweater. Nothing amazed Nina more than Marty's ability to dress to perfection. No matter how unexpected the occasion, Marty was at all times impeccably outfitted and everything was always totally *in* her color wheel.

"What did you tell Keegan?" Nina asked, wondering exactly how Marty was able to get his fancy private plane without question, but more importantly, how he'd managed to let her leave his side for more than a nanosecond.

"Man trouble," she answered with a sly smile. "I told him you had the boyfriend blues. He'll be fine without me for a day or so."

"Wow, wow, woooow." Wanda exhaled, furrowing her brow and interrupting Marty, finally speaking for the first time since she'd arrived. "How do you talk around those? I don't think I have a shade of lipstick that can help *that*." She was much too much in Nina's opinion.

"And you're so pale. No amount of foundation is going to help that. I don't get it, Nina." Wanda took a place on the couch next to Marty. She looked tired. Her face devoid of makeup left her looking colorless and fragile. She'd let her dark brown hair grow in the past year, and, though Nina would never say it out loud, it suited her in the way it brushed against her shoulders. "How did this happen again?"

"The guy I was prepping for Dr. Berkenstein got loopy from his anesthesia. Most people just get numb, but not this guy. He was mumbling some crap when my hand was in his mouth to suction. All of a sudden he went slack and clamped down. He has to be the one responsible for this, right? I mean, you don't just grow fangs overnight."

Wanda nodded her agreement. "Well, he's as good a place to start as any, I would think. He's at least worthy of a look-see."

"I don't get it. He barely nicked me."

Marty snorted. "Er, yeah. That's what I said, too, and look at me now." She made a pair of ears over her head with her fingers.

"Well, now I have these." Nina pointed to her fangs again with an unpolished fingernail.

"You know," Wanda commented wryly, "it sure would be nice if you both could stay out of trouble for a whole two minutes. If it isn't Marty being kidnapped and werewolf-ized, it's you with teeth like a Halloween costume."

Nina couldn't much blame Wanda for her fed up tone—they *had* been through a lot in the past year as a group. When Marty was bitten, all hell had broken loose. She was kidnapped and all sorts of crazy stuff began to happen. Though, the final result had been a serious color wheel coup for Marty and all had ended well. To say they'd been through the ringer together this past year was putting it lightly.

Nina ran a hand through her long, dark hair, not even bothering to silently curse the curls she could never tame. "I don't like this any better than the color wheel freak did when she became a dog, but it is what it is, and you can't tell me any different."

"I am not a dog, Nina Blackman, and if you don't stop referring to me as such, things could get ugly," Marty retorted sharply, her nostrils flaring.

"Marty, Nina . . ." Wanda's warning was firm. "Do not argue. I'm beat. I worked a long week, and I'm not going to sit between the two of you while you goad one another into a pissing match about who can take who. It's disgusting the way you both behave. Besides, this time we have the chance to do it right. Marty didn't come to us when she turned into a werewolf. So we couldn't possibly help her when we didn't know what was going on. We're three informed women now, and if Nina really is a vampire, we'll get through this together, but not while you two fight. Now go to your appropriate corners and shut your yaps." She sat back on the couch, shooting them a look that screamed one part surprised, two parts smug.

Wanda was big into the "I am woman, hear me roar" scene since her husband had left and she'd found her niche at Bobbie-Sue.

It still shocked Nina that the meek, mild-mannered woman Wanda had been a year ago was the Wanda of today, daring to tell her what the fuck to do. Nina had to admit Wanda wasn't just some rich podiatrist's ex-wife anymore. She was a Bobbie-Sue selling machine. She'd kept her job at Bobbie-Sue, and now she was really making something of her life after that puke of a husband of hers had walked out and hooked up with some floozy chick who reveled in his freaky foot fetish.

"Okay, fine. You're right." Nina made a face of acquiescence. "We're much more informed than we were a year ago about this shit. Let's take a logical approach. I can't see any other explanation for these chops—it has to mean I'm a vampire."

"Shouldn't *you* be like all freaked out?" Wanda wondered out loud. "Don't you remember how Marty was after she was bitten by Keegan? I mean, she totally zoned out for like a week."

Marty giggled. "Nina's not like us, Wanda, she's tough. You know, like grrrrrr. She's not afraid of anyone or anything, remember?"

Wanda nodded her head, sporting a glib smile. "Oh, yeah, right. So, tough guy, what do you plan to do about this? You can't go beating people up over it."

The frig she couldn't. "I've got a plan," she muttered, perching herself on the edge of her worn, leather ottoman, fighting the voracious hunger assaulting her in waves.

Marty lifted a perfectly arched eyebrow. "Oh, do tell, Nina. I'm dying here. How exactly do you plan to beat the information out of a *vampire?*"

Her shoulders moved up and down in a shrug. "I don't know. I mean, there must be a way to fix this, and finding the guy who did this to me is where I should start, right?"

Marty's look was skeptical. "I can tell you this much, there was no going back for me. Once I was bitten, that was kinda that."

Nina frowned at her. "Thanks for the hopeful optimism, color freak."

"Wait, you two. A thought just crossed my mind. Does Lou know?" Wanda asked, referring to Nina's grandmother and another one of the reasons she'd moved to Hackensack.

"Are you kidding me, Wanda? My Nana Lou is more religious than the Pope. She'd have me exorcised quicker than you can say Bela Lugosi. No telling Lou anything yet. Not at all, if I can help it."

"Do you have your laptop around here?" Marty asked, rubbing her hands together, briefly interrupting Nina's worry over what Lou would say about her new set of chops.

"Yeah, why?"

"We're going to look up vampires, that's why. If I'd been in less of a state when Keegan bit me, I'd have looked the folklore of werewolves up on the Internet. I might have been better prepared if I had. Believe me when I tell you, knowing is half the battle with these paranormals."

Nina leaned forward, reaching under the ottoman and pulling out her laptop. "Have at it." She shoved her battered computer at Marty. Nothing about this had her thinking clearly. She couldn't concentrate on Googling vampires right now. The only thing she did know for sure was she was so not going to wander around with teeth like this. And if Bram Stoker slash whatever his name was, really was a vampire, why didn't his fangs stick out like hers did? There'd been nothing about his teeth that suggested he had fangs. And he'd had an *afternoon* appointment. Didn't vampires melt in the sun?

Fuck, she was never going to be able to go to Rockaway Beach again.

An hour later, after endless visits to sites sporting information about vampires, Nina was less optimistic.

"Well," Marty said, tipping her blonde head in Nina's direction and closing the laptop. "I think we have a *situation*. Fangs are the least of it."

"You know, Marty," Nina found herself growling low, "you're a real fucking ray of sunshine."

"Nina—stop *now*." Wanda put a hand up and shook her finger

in Nina's direction. "It's not Marty's fault you're a vampire. Er, might be a vampire. We're only trying to help. If what the Internet says is true, we have to locate Dracula and at least talk to him to find a solution. And that growling your stomach is doing is going to have to be fed, according to www.vampiresarepeopletoo.com. Um, *blood* . . ." Wanda blanched, curling her legs underneath her and worrying her lower lip.

Marty's pert nose wrinkled. "Jesus, and I thought I had it bad having to eat red meat. I mean, I was a vegan before all this were-wolf stuff, but blood? Now that's just icky. How do you know what type to drink anyway? Like what if O neg is too rich for you and you find you're the equivalent of lactose intolerant to it? If what the Internet says is true, you're going to be sucking some serious neck . . ."

Nina tried to gasp to show her displeasure, but it came out in a choked, dry heave. "Shut up, Marty! Could you be just a little sensitive here? I am *not* drinking blood. Not now, not ever—so cut it the fuck out." Thinking a deep breath might be cleansing about now, she inhaled. Sort of.

Fear rippled through her. Her hand flew to her mouth, and she blew.

Nothing.

No air.

Holy immortality.

She couldn't breathe.

What. The. Fuck?

Leaning forward, Nina put her head between her knees and fought for clarity. Her stomach raged, roaring with dissatisfaction. Jesus, she was hungry.

Wanda and Marty were up and on their feet, hovering over her in a matter of seconds. Marty's hand ran along her scalp with a soothing caress. "Nina? What's wrong? Are you okay?"

"I can't breathe," she responded tightly.

"It's anxiety, Nina. God knows I know all about that. Just try and take a deep breath. C'mon, in with the good, out with the bad." Marty's suggestion made her that much more panicked.

Nina waved Marty away and sat back up. Grabbing the hand she'd just dismissed, she blew on it as hard as she could. Nada in the way of air. "No, Marty, I mean I can't breathe. Like *at all*."

Marty's and Wanda's mouths fell open in synchronized drops, making perfect O's of astonishment.

"Hoo boy," Wanda muttered, sending Marty a wide-eyed look of holy shit.

"Okay, so let's look at the bright side of this, Nina." Marty cupped her chin and clearly forced a smile of encouragement.

Nina gave her a skeptical look. "And that would be?"

"Think of all the money you'll save on mouthwash. You'll never have bad breath, of course." She flashed her teeth in another grin.

"Get the frig off me, Marty! I'm not *breathing*, you 'look at the bright side' bullshit artist! I shouldn't even be having this conversation with you. I should be in the flippin' morgue while you guys sob like babies and plan my funeral attire—which better have nothing to do with the color yellow, by the way. But here I am. Walking, talking, and so hungry I feel like I could eat a herd of buffalo, except the idea of food makes me want to goddamned hurl. So what the hell do I do now?"

Wanda's mouth thinned, her hands worrying the edge of her skirt. "I think we find the guy with the funny name from yesterday. If what those websites say is right anyway. He's the only one who would know who can help us, right? He holds the key to our troubles."

"It isn't *our* trouble, Wanda. It's mine, and I'll deal with it." Yeah . . .

Marty gave her a playful shove, but her expression was disapproving. "Stop already, would you? Quit with the 'I don't need anybody' crap. You've done it to death. If you didn't need us, you wouldn't be the first person to make the round of calls to set up karaoke night once a month. You're not as tough as you'd like us to believe, and don't think for a minute we don't know that. Stop bulldozing through everything and let us help. You're stuck with us, like it or not, okay? So knock it the hell off, and let's formulate a plan, got that?"

Her heart would warm to Marty's words because—whether she liked to admit it or not, these women who'd forced their way into her life via nail polish and mascara—had grown on her—but apparently, she no longer had one.

Nice. Very nice.

Nina clutched her thin shirt and nodded, letting the curtain of her hair fall over her face to hide her embarrassment. "Okay. I'm sorry. I just don't want you involved in something that might potentially end up hurting either of you. These vampire people aren't exactly the most upstanding dudes, if what you read from the Internet is true."

Wanda gave them a coy smile and giggled. Twisting a strand of her hair, she winked at them while bouncing her crossed leg. "Oh, I dunno, Nina. I've been reading some romance novels lately. Par-a-normal ones and I gotta tell you, some of the men in these books are downright dreamy. Alpha. They're called alpha males, and I wouldn't mind having one—even if he does drink blood and couldn't do brunch at Hogan's on Sundays because he'd burn to a crisp."

The thought of Hogan's early bird Sunday special—corned beef hash and eggs Benedict for a buck ninety-nine—made Nina's stomach roll with fierce indignation. She covered her mouth with a hand and gagged.

Well, it was more like hacked, because nothing was coming out of her yap but dead space.

Looking her friends square in the eye, Nina said, "Okay, so we find this dude. Good. I'm all in, but to do that I have to get past the Belinda-nator."

"Who?" Marty looked down at her, tilting her head.

"Belinda's Dr. Berkenstein's receptionist, and she guards patient files like they're part of a CSI investigation instead of just a bunch of pictures of teeth. She's a fucking terrorist when it comes to those damned things. You'd think she was guarding Fort Knox. She's the one who has all the patient files."

Marty looked at her thick, gold watch. "Well, it's almost six now. When does the good doctor arrive in the mornings?"

"What the hell day is it, anyway?" Nina pinched her temples, trying to clear the cobwebs from her brain. Wait, did she still have one of those? Wasn't that a vital organ, too? Oh, shit on a shingle. Terror rose in a wave, and she gritted her teeth—her big teeth—to fight back a scream.

"It's Wednesday." Wanda gave her a hesitant smile, oozing sympathy.

Crap, she'd missed an entire day of work and had never called in vampire, er, sick. Those bennies and paid vacations were going to be yanked out from under her like a rug if she didn't figure this out. "Nine sharp. He'll be in at nine sharp. If we get there about eight-thirty Belinda will definitely be there. She's kind of anal that way."

"Then it's a date," Marty confirmed with another one of her falsely cheerful grins. "Now go shower or whatever vampires do to freshen up, and we'll be on our way."

"And don't forget to moisturize," Wanda chirped.

"Yeah, I'll get right on that," Nina said with sarcasm. "While I'm moisturizing, why don't you two angels fire up the Bat Mobile?"

Marty screwed her face up. "Oh, Nina. The Angels didn't have a Bat Mobile—"

"Shut up, Maaarty," Nina singsonged over her shoulder, keeping her tone light to hide her terror.

Shutting the door to her bathroom firmly behind her, she caught sight of her fangs in the mirror again. It was almost the only thing she could see in her distorted reflection.

Christ, she'd better break out the big toothbrush for these bad boys.

CHAPTER 2

"How about some Barry, Nina? He always makes everything better, doesn't he? Maybe a little 'Weekend in New England'—or 'Could It Be the Magic?' Wait, 'Mandy.' You love 'Mandy.'" Wanda's suggestion made Nina groan.

When Marty and Wanda had heard about her addiction to Barry Manilow and his girlie love songs, they'd decided Nina did have at least one feeling, and since then, they'd never let her hear the end of it. Whenever she was agitated, Wanda always broke out the Barry CD's. Music to soothe the savage Nina was what she called it.

She groaned again. "No Barry."

Wanda sniffed. "Fine. Just be cranky then."

"Jesus, it's hot in here. Isn't it hot, Wanda?" Nina nudged her from the passenger seat, messing with the car's controls to try and find the air conditioner. The sun, though weak for this time of year, beat at her skin through the windshield like they were driving through the bowels of bloody Hell. Though Nina was covered head to toe in thick gloves, a scarf, and hat, the sun left her feeling like her skin had been through a hand grater.

Wanda ran a hand over Nina's exposed forehead. "Do you have enough sunscreen? I have more in my purse if you need it."

She had so much sunscreen on, she felt like fried chicken in a vat of oil. They'd slathered her up but good, because the Internet said she was going to be sensitive, as Wanda had called it, to the sun. She sported a mighty fine stripe of zinc oxide across the bridge of her nose, too. Just in case, Marty had said. "I'm fine. Let's just get there before Dr. Berkenstein comes in."

"I'm freezing." Marty leaned forward and poked Nina in the shoulder. "Turn that A/C off, Elvira. Jesus, it's twenty degrees out."

She immediately let go of the A/C dial and sat back, folding her fidgety hands in her lap. Her head throbbed, the glare from the sun making her eyeballs feel like steaks on a grill. "Gimme those fancy sunglasses, Marty. My frickin' eyes are killing me." Nina jammed her hand back at Marty without turning around and wiggled her fingers, waiting.

"I will not. If I don't wear sunglasses I'll develop wrinkles from squinting, and it's *very* bright out today."

No shit, it was bright. Each flicker of sunlight felt like an ice pick to the space between her eyes.

Her head began a steady cadence with a beat reminiscent of the noisiest of nightclubs. All bass, no melody. Nina's voice was tight, her words measured. "Give me the damn sunglasses, Marty, or I'll poke your eyes out, and wrinkles will be the least of your problems." Another sharp stab of pain dug right between her eyes, making her clench her jaw.

"Oh, Nina, just stop. You can't take me anymore, and you know it. Remember? Me werewolf—you? Not so much." If Nina turned around, she knew she'd find Marty with a smug smile of triumph on her face, but it hurt too much to move her head. Tightening the scarf she wore around the lower half of her face to hide her teeth, Nina then clenched her fists to keep from ramming one down Marty's throat.

Wanda's exasperated sigh filled the car. "Going anywhere with the two of you is like taking two children on a long, long, loooong car trip cross country. Knock it off, the both of you. And Marty? I wouldn't be so sure about being able to kick Nina's ass anymore. You held the title for a while, but Nina just might be able to snatch it back and declare a comeback win. Again I say, if the Internet is right, she's got superhuman strength on her side now that she's—well, now that she's—um, possibly immortal. Not to mention daylight could potentially kill her. Now before this turns into Godzilla vs. Kong, give Nina your sunglasses, *please*. The sun is like poison to her." Wanda kept one hand on the steering wheel, while sticking the other back at Marty.

Marty plunked them in her hand with a puff of defeat. "Fine, but you'd better give them back."

"Whoa, daylight can *kill* me?" Hold the fuck on. Nobody'd said a thing about daylight and *death*. How in theee hell did you die if you were immortal? Didn't that take like a stake through the heart? The heart she didn't have? What an assload of contradictions.

Wanda's face grew worried again. That place at her temple, just beneath a lock of hair, pulsed. "Well, we didn't want to freak you out with too many details, but yes. I'm afraid daylight isn't good for you anymore. I guess our girls' trip to somewhere tropical is out. But I hear Alaska's kinda cool when it's dark twenty-four-seven and besides, I like icebergs."

She handed the trendy glasses to Nina, who put them on, feeling relieved. It helped lessen the sting, but by no means was it making her comfortable. "That's just freakin' lovely, and here I am in broad daylight with you two riding shotgun just waiting for me to melt."

"Don't be silly, Nina. You won't melt. You'll fr—"

"Marty!" Wanda stopped Marty with an urgent cry before she could say another word. "Enough, okay? How about we just get to Dr. Berkenstein's office in one piece, and no one is melting or anything else for that matter. Now both of you shut your faces and let me drive. I haven't slept all night, and unlike you two super creatures, I need my sleep!"

Silence, contrite and embarrassed, filled the car. Nina scrunched farther down in the seat, as if doing that was going to actually keep her from frying like so much bacon. That's what Marty was going to say before Wanda had shut her up. She'd fry from exposure to the sunlight.

Oh, shit. This was bad.

Wanda finally made a left into Dr. Berkenstein's parking lot and pulled into a slot. The large brick building loomed over the car, seeming far more intimidating than it ever had when she'd come for an interview just two weeks ago. Though thankfully, the parking lot was fairly empty. The only car in it was Belinda's. She showed up to work early just to make everyone else look bad, according to Joanne, another hygienist in the office.

Ass licker.

She'd rubbed Nina wrong from the get-go, with her Hitler-like organizational skills and her anal filing rules. Nina thought Belinda might incur apoplexy when she'd mistakenly placed a patient's file in the wrong bin on her first day. She'd given Nina "the look." The one that said she was an idiot who didn't know her ass from her elbow.

"Okay, so now what? Do you want us to cause a diversion so you can get past the Belinda-nator?" Wanda's question was filled with eager anticipation, her blue eyes flashing with the hope of intrigue, danger, excitement.

Nina lifted Marty's glasses momentarily and glared at her. "No, Farrah. I don't need the Angels' help today. This is on me. I'm going to have to steal Mr. Unpronounceable Name's file, and believe me when I tell you the Belinda-nator's going to put up a fight if she finds out what I'm up to. Patient confidentiality and all that crap. You two just sit here and keep the car running. I'll be back as fast as I can."

Nina hopped out of the car before her friends could protest, heading for the blue door. Bells chimed when she entered, announcing her arrival. She tugged the scarf farther up, keeping it around her mouth. She was grateful it was cold today. It gave her a reason to hide her teeth—which were becoming an increasingly bigger drag than they had been when she'd first discovered them.

Belinda's head popped up from behind the reception desk like toast from a toaster. Her face twisted into a narrowed gaze filled with condescension. Her neat bleached-blonde updo, molded to her head, thanks to a gallon of sculpting gel, didn't budge, as her long earrings dangled in the fluorescent light.

Nina eyed her guardedly, wondering if anyone had told her frosted blue eye shadow was soooo not this era. Marty would shit color wheels of joy if she knew some of the crap she'd taught her during her stint at Bobbie-Sue had actually stuck with her.

Belinda's tongue clucked with disapproval, dragging Nina back to the sticky task at hand. "Well, look who's decided to come back from her unannounced vacation. Must be nice to just come and go as you please at a job you've had for oh, *two days* without even calling in sick. And what's that on your nose? You look ridiculous." Sarcasm dripped from her words, like melting butter on a hot summer's day. Belinda's hand went to the necklace she wore, and she began to twist it, wrapping the chain around her index finger.

Nina's eyes, still behind Marty's glasses, rolled to the back of her head. She cringed, her feet suddenly like cement blocks.

She squinted from the razor sharp jabs of pain in her head.

What in the hell was going on? Rubbing her eyes with her gloved fingers, Nina finally was able to focus on Belinda's necklace and identify the problem with it.

A crucifix.

Jesus Christ in a miniskirt. Belinda's crucifix was searing her eyes as though she'd branded them with the chain personally.

What a Dracula cliché.

If she didn't do something soon, her eyeballs were going to combust, but she couldn't will her body to move. It was like some invisible force rooted her in place. Panic washed over her, yet she couldn't tear her eyes away from the cross Belinda wore. It gleamed in the florescent lighting, taunting her, dangling with menace.

"Well, hurry up and get your butt in gear, Nina. We have a full day today, and I daresay you have some sucking up to do if you don't want to find yourself fired when the doctor arrives." Smoothing a hand over her already perfect hair, Belinda stared at Nina and tapped on the protective glass encasing her receptionist's throne.

Was it not enough the woman wore a cross around her neck, but did she have to have them dangling from her charm bracelet, too? Nina remained riveted, stuck to the floor like someone had superglued her sneaker-clad feet to it.

Belinda clapped her hands, leaving a sharp snap in their wake. "Um, hello, slacker? Work. You have *work* to do."

When Nina finally found her voice, it sounded three octaves lower and a little snarly to her ears. Had she really used the word *slacker*? Slack this, you oral Nazi. "Did you just call me a *slacker?*"

Belinda straightened and lifted one eyebrow—an eyebrow that to Nina's assessment could use some good old-fashioned plucking.

It didn't match her bleached blonde hair anyway. "I did. You are. Hang up your coat, and move your ass."

Whatever had held her in place, abruptly unglued her. She might have this vampire thing going on, but the old Nina, the one who at one time didn't blink an eye at a crucifix, reared her ugly head. She took two steps closer to Belinda, rolling her shoulders in her thick coat to keep her momentum. "Oh. Got ya. I just wanted to be sure I heard you right, you ballbuster. Funny, I don't remember Dr. Berkenstein leaving *you* in charge. So why don't you go do receptionist-like shit, and I'll do the stuff I got a *degree* for, 'K?" Nina about-faced and headed for the door leading to the offices in back, stopping at Belinda's desk.

Belinda plunked down on her swivel chair and whirled to face Nina. Her large breasts jiggled at the opening of her dark purple silk blouse, oozing like a freshly popped can of dinner rolls. Her face screwed up into a ball of too much foundation and blusher. Clearly someone didn't like to be told what was what. "You *cannot* talk to me like that."

Nina tightened the scarf around her mouth then braced her hands on the Formica overhang of the counter, sticking her face in Belinda's, fighting the nausea and waves of fire licking at her skin. Nearly nose to nose with Belinda, Nina had to swallow hard. Belinda's breath just might rival the smell of a three-day-old dead body left to decay in the desert.

Lawd, who'd had way too much garlic? Nina let her nostrils flare for effect, making a face at Belinda and wrinkling her nose. "Well, I just did." Changing gears, she asked because repulsion compelled her to do so, "Hey, tell me something?"

Belinda sucked in her cheeks. "What?"

"You like Giuseppe's down on Lancaster?"

"Yeah. So?"

"Didja have lunch there yesterday?"

Her face changed from annoyed to leery in seconds. "Were you spying on me, Nina?"

"Uh, no. But here's a little advice. The next time you opt for a meatball parm sub with extra garlic at Giuseppe's, do us all the biggest of favors and use the chronic halitosis mouthwash Dr. Berkenstein gives his *special* patients. You're going to scare away the clientele."

Belinda's hand flew to her mouth in obvious mortification before she jumped up and ran down the hallway that led to the bathrooms.

Nina's smile was sly with victory, but only for a moment. The ache in her gut had begun to gnaw its way up to her throat, sitting there like a lump. Cold chills broke out along her spine, yet not a bead of sweat followed. And she'd been able to tell Belinda had had lunch at Giuseppe's.

Yesterday.

Hell's bells.

She needed to move fast, and these new ailments cropping up left and right weren't helping her.

Now to find those files.

"I got 'em." Nina nearly fell into the front seat of the car, holding a piece of paper with the fanged-one's address on it. She'd been lucky that Belinda still had his file in the insurance claim bin. He'd been easy enough to locate. He was the only chipped tooth the day before yesterday. With a slump, she let her body rest against the door.

Wanda put the car in drive and lurched out of the parking lot, sending Nina a look of concern. "God, that felt like forever. Did Belinda give you any trouble?"

"Belinda is trouble, period, but I fixed her."

"Did black eyes ensue, Sugar Ray?" Marty quipped from the backseat.

Nina ignored her. "His name is Gregori Statleon. I told you he had some crazy ethnic name, and he lives on the Island."

"Staten or Long?" Wanda asked.

"Long." Nina rambled off the address to Wanda.

"Ohhhh, and I like his name. Very alpha. It isn't at all like the names of the vampires I've been reading in those books. They have names like Dimitri, Declan, and Lucien."

Nina cupped her hands over her eyes, rolling her palms over her forehead. "Well, it definitely isn't John Smith. So get me home, and I'll take the train or something out there. I need to straighten this shit out before my head explodes."

"Do you think aspirin would help?" Wanda handed Nina her purse. "I have some in there. God knows I need it when I'm with you two on absolutely no sleep."

"No aspirin. I tried to take some before we left my place, and I think I hacked it up whole. Nothing is staying in my stomach."

Wanda patted her arm. "Well, you're not taking the train. We're going with you."

Nina shook her head with an emphatic no at Wanda. "No, you're not."

"Are."

"Not."

"Are," Marty finally spoke from the backseat.

Nina's voice took on a calm she didn't think she had in her today. "You are not. I can't let you guys get involved. What if all that crazy website shit is true? The vampires will rule the world website? What if this guy bit me on purpose so he could add me to his list of conquests? What if he wants to turn Wanda into a vampire? What if he bites you, Marty? What the fuck will you be then? A were-vamp? A vamp-were? If you think you had trouble getting those crazy dogs in Keegan's pack to accept you before, just imagine what it'd be like to add vampire to your list of whack-job issues." She shook her head, then winced. The mere act of moving but a millimeter was agonizing.

"They like me just fine now, thank you very much, and if I have to tell you one more time, I am not, I repeat, *not a dog*—I swear, Nina, I'm going to choke the life out of you!"

Wanda rolled her tongue over her lips, popping them. A sure sign it meant she was pissed. "Nina, lay off the dog references *this instant.* Marty, before you open that mouth to protest your AKC non-status one more time, shut up. Nina's due a little leeway here. She's a vampire. Or at least we think she is. Whatever the case is, the two of you will knock it off now, or I'll stop this car. Don't make me stop this car. Got it?"

Nina lowered the sunglasses again and glared over her shoulder at Marty, but she kept her mouth shut.

Wanda pinched the bridge of her nose. "Now, technically speaking, I think if what I've been reading in those paranormal romances lately is true, Marty'd be a were-vamp. Because she was a werewolf before she was a vampire. Therefore, her wolfie side takes precedence," Wanda offered, in her typically helpful fashion. "God, imagine that, Marty. You'd be like crazy scary, huh?"

Marty's giggle tinkled in the small interior of the car.

Nina clenched her jaw, ignoring the rub of her new incisors against her bottom teeth. "Wanda?"

"What?"

"Shut up and drive me home."

She shook her pretty dark head, turning onto the highway and away from the general direction of Nina's apartment. "Nope."

Marty poked her again from behind. "Nina?"

"What, Marty?"

"We're going. I'm not afraid of some vampire. I'm a force to be reckoned with, and if anything happened to me, Keegan and the pack would be up this guy's ass so far, he'd be able to brush his teeth with angry werewolves. So knock it off. If push comes to shove, I'll shift and have his little bat wings for lunch. I'm more afraid of what he'll do if he's angry."

Nina was aghast. "Why the fuck should he be angry? He bit *me*, for Christ's sake." Oh, God. If that dude with the ice pick behind her eyeballs didn't stop poking her, she was going to scream.

"How do we know if he's a friendly vampire, Nina? Maybe he's all dark and scary. You know, like the vampires who don't want to be vampires. They just want a stake through their hearts. They wander around all angst ridden, bemoaning their eternal fate, lashing out at the nearest innocent victim."

"Oh! I love those kinds of vampires," Wanda squealed. "I was just reading about one the other night, and he despises being a vampire. Wait, lemme think of the title . . ." She paused, gnawing the inside of her cheek. "*My Beloved Immortal.* Or was it *My Immortal Beloved*—or *My Dear Beloved Immortal*? Shoot, I can't remember. Anyway, he hated being a vampire—until he found the girl of his dreams, of course. Then you know, HEA." Her grin was almost secretive.

Nina fought for control, clutching the armrest between them to keep from socking Wanda in her pretty mouth. "*H-E* who?"

"*H-E-A,* silly. Happily ever after. You know, the couple rides off into the sunset and lives happily ever after." She said it like Nina should know this new world of acronyms Wanda seemed to have found in the pages of some stupid romance novel.

"I think you should quit reading that lame shit written by people with retarded names like Va Va Lamoure. You're living in a fantasy if you think this is anything remotely like a *romance* novel," she said, pointing at her mouth.

Wanda clucked her tongue at Nina. "Stop saying the word *ro-*

mance like it's the equivalent of leprosy. It's *women's fiction*, thank you, and what's the harm in immersing yourself in a place you wouldn't normally be able to go?"

"Look, pay attention. There's not going to be an H-E-A and what about this"—Nina yanked the scarf that was covering her lips and flashed her ever-growing teeth at Wanda—"is at all happy?"

Wanda sank back in her seat and shot Nina a sympathetic look. "Okay, so you're not going to hit the catwalk anytime soon here, but—but—I dunno, we'll figure it out. Obviously the guy who bit you didn't have teeth like that, right?"

Nina shook her head, pulling the scarf back over her mouth. "No. He looked as normal as any other patient."

"So that means there's hope."

Nina slouched against the door, so weary she could curl up in a nest of snakes and sleep without a qualm. "Know what else I don't get? His appointment was *early afternoon*. If he's a vampire, how can he tolerate the sunlight, when I feel like raw hamburger meat just waiting to sizzle? I don't get it. But it had to be him, right? I mean, he drew blood—infected me with his battiness or whatever. But what if we're wrong? Fuck. What kind of dumb asses will we look like if we show up and accuse this guy of being a vampire and he isn't one at all?"

Marty stirred from the backseat. "Believe it or not, I'm actually going to agree with you, Nina. He had to be the one responsible for this. I would have never believed it if not for Keegan biting me, and, well, the Internet did say that's how you become a vampire. A bite. Unless you've been bitten recently by someone other than this Gregori guy? Been in any barroom brawls lately? Maybe a little girl-on-girl Jell-O wrestling?"

Nina whipped around, sticking her gloved hand through the gap between the headrest and the seat, grabbing at a startled

Marty. "C'mere, you German Shepherd. I'll give you a little girl-on-girl—"

Wanda snaked a hand out, yanking the collar of Nina's coat and shoving her back into her seat, shooting her a look so fierce, it stopped Nina cold. "No hands! There will be no hands, miss. Use your words and try some nice ones for a change." She shook off her anger and said, "Okay, so yeah, this guy is probably our perp. I guess we'll just have to be careful. Although I have no clue how in Heaven's name we're going to figure out if he's a vampire unless we ask. If he doesn't have visible fangs, asking might be the only way to find out."

Nina's head clanged like one of those windup monkeys with the cymbals was traipsing around in her head. "Do we even know where we're going, Wanda?"

"I have a fairly good idea. I have a couple of clients out here sort of by proxy. I can tell you, if where he lives is the spot I'm thinking of, it's pretty exclusive. And there's something else to consider. If he lives on the Island, why would he go all the way to Hackensack to see a dentist? Seems like a pretty long trip."

While Wanda and Marty pondered that, Nina leaned her head against the cool glass of the window and tried to block out their chatter. As it became a muted jumble of jabber, her eyes grew heavier and heavier. Maybe a nap would relieve this friggin' head-ache.

THE next thing she was aware of was Wanda shaking her. "Nina. Wake up now. We're . . . um, we're here."

Nina felt sluggish and so drowsy, parting her eyelids was like trying to play Moses and part the Red Sea. "Gimme a sec. I feel like I've been drugged."

"Just wait until you open your eyes." Marty's voice sounded hesitant to her ears.

Nina stuck two fingers under the glasses and pried one eye open.

Okay, yeah. Drugs had to be involved here 'cause there was no way she was seeing what she thought she was seeing. She let her eyelid go and closed it again. Tight.

Wanda popped up the sunglasses she wore, propping them on her forehead. "Open your eyes, Nina."

"Um, no," she muttered. "Not going there."

"If you want to figure this out, you're going." Wanda's lips were surely moving. She heard the words she spoke, but Nina couldn't focus. Wanda took matters into her own hands and used her fingers to hold Nina's eyes open, leaning over her lap and to the right so she could see what they'd apparently already witnessed.

Good gravy.

No, this was much better with her eyes closed. Slapping at Wanda's hands, she slammed her eyes shut again.

"Did you see what I saw, Nina?" Wanda prodded.

No. No fucking way. "No, but I smelled your breath. You should lay off the spicy chicken wings at Woo's. Isn't that bad for your thighs or something?"

"Did you hear that, Marty? She can tell what I had for dinner yesterday, and I've brushed my teeth three times since then. The Internet said vampires are very sensitive to smell. Hoo, boy do we have trouble. Now stop being a sissy and open your eyes, Nina, so we can figure this out. I know you saw what we saw."

"It's impossible," Nina said without emotion, her eyes still closed.

"Does that turret made of stone look impossible to you? In fact, there isn't just one turret, but three. And let's not find ourselves remiss in mentioning the little moat over near the hedge maze."

"Funny, I didn't see a moat." Nina shrugged her shoulders, dismissing the notion.

"Yes you did, and you saw the drawbridge, too. It's a castle, Nina. A *big* castle like out of some scary-tale. Right here in Long Island. Who knew? Now stop hiding from the inevitable and open your eyes."

She really, really didn't want to do that.

"Um, hey, Snaggletooth," Marty chimed from the backseat. "If you hope to get rid of those teeth—which surely will hinder any future dating endeavors—I'd open your eyes."

Nina leaned forward, holding her stomach. That gnawing ache was back again. Okay, it was time to take it like a man. So he had a castle. Lots of people had castles.

Or not.

At least not privately owned in fucking Long Island.

Dude was definitely livin' large.

Summoning the last of her reserved energy, Nina sat back up and popped her eyes open. Sho' 'nuff, there was no denying it was a castle. Its structure, made of stone, reached skyward in all its ominous, dark gray glory. Cast-iron gates surrounded the entire exterior, behind them winding pathways leading to various portions of the grounds. Though it was winter, each bush and shrub was neatly trimmed, and the grass didn't look nearly as brown and dead as some of his neighbors' lawns did.

"This has to be some kind of joke," Nina muttered out of the side of her mouth.

The set to Wanda's lips was stern. "Oh, I don't think so. I think this is very serious, and I think we need to investigate, like now."

"Tell me something, Wanda?"

"Anything, Nina." She smiled all angelic-like.

"When the fuck did you get a backbone?"

Wanda snorted and popped open her door. "When I met you two. Now let's go."

With great reluctance, Nina opened her door, holding the seat forward for Marty, so she could get out, too. Folding her arms over her chest, she looked at them both. "Now what?"

Wanda linked arms with her, ushering her forward. "Now we make nice. You know, knock on the door and say, 'Hello. My name is Nina Blackman, and I do believe we've met via some goofy gas and a suctioning tool.'" Wanda tugged her toward the tall gates.

"Those gates look locked. Maybe we'll have to come back . . ." She was stalling because if this guy wasn't what she thought he was, they were going to end up in the pokey.

Marty skipped ahead of them and used a finger to jar the gate open. Her shoulders lifted, and she smiled. "Easy. One hurdle down—one more to go." She pointed her perfect, red-tipped nail toward the ominous front door.

Wanda pulled her toward the double doors, large, black, and made of heavy steel.

"Wait." Nina dug her heels into the winding pathway flanked with shorter boxwood hedges that led to the front door. "You guys wait in those bushes by the landing. This way, if something goes wrong you can call for help. So keep your cell phones handy."

Marty took Wanda's hand and scurried along the edge of the decorative cement, pulling her into the tall set of arborvitaes by the front door. "Okay. We're in position." She gave Nina a thumbs-up.

Nina sauntered up to the door like she owned the joint, but her legs were like jelly. For all her bravado, for all her big-mouthed, ass-kicking smack talk, she was scared witless. This was the craziest bullshit going. She had absolutely no clue what to do next, but if Marty could survive the transformation to werewolf, Nina Blackman could be a vampire.

Temporarily.

If that's what these fangs meant, anyway.

The arborvitaes rustled, then Marty stuck her nose through them. "Knock on the damned door, Nina," she urged, her lips thinning into a line of disapproval.

"Okay, okay. I'm knocking." With nothing left to do but keep her tough facade in place in front of the two people who lovingly called her "bully," she knocked.

All right, so it was more like a light tap, but maybe he was sleeping or something, and if she pissed him off, God only knew what he'd do.

Wanda's whisper was clearly hushed and annoyed. "Oh, Nina, that was pathetic! Put some gumption into it. Even the Bionic Woman couldn't have heard that."

Sucking in her cheeks, Nina gave the door a sharper rap, just as the breeze began to pick up and that sun that had fried her ass earlier skittered away behind a cloud. The sky grew darker with the kind of gray that threatened snow. The chill wind she could no longer seem to feel brought with it a scent Nina found teased her nostrils with an odd blend of *man*.

Still, no one answered the door.

But she knew, as sure as she knew she was going to pass out if she didn't find a place to sit down, he was behind that door. She smelled him, almost heard the rustle of his hand jamming into the pocket of his pants. She smelled him as succinctly as she had Mrs. Fedderman's Chihuahua Freddy.

Was he hiding from her? Fucktard coward.

Wanda was clearly growing impatient with her. Her head popped back out from the greenery. Her eyes, now glaring in Nina's direction, had dark circles around them, and in the sudden gloom, they made her look more tired. "Knock again, Nina! God, what is wrong with you? Do you want to keep those teeth forever? And we're cold. Some of us don't have special vampire powers to keep us warm. Now hurry it up!"

If there was ever a time to use the balls she was always claiming she should have been born with, now would be it. All right, enough stalling. He had to be the guy who did this, and the fuck she'd not take him to task for it.

With a firm fist, Nina used the side of it to pound on the door. The very effort left her drained. She pressed a cheek to the cold steel door and said, "Um, Mr. Vampire?" *Weak, that was very weak, Nina Blackman. Not at all like you. Whassamatter? Is the psycho in you taking a temporary sabbatical?* God, she was so not herself.

"Mr. *Vampire.*" Marty cackled with a high-pitched keen.

Nina flicked at the bushes, her anger flaring. "Shut up, Marty, or I'll beat the shit out of you."

Wanda caught her hand and poked it. "Nina! Focus and forget Marty."

Focus. Yeah, that'd be great if the call of some much-needed sleep didn't keep getting in the way. Shit, she had to get a grip. With an irritated shove, she pushed up the sleeves of her heavy trench coat and pounded on the door again. All she wanted to do was be changed back to a human and go home and sleep. Christ and a sidecar, she needed to sleep.

She'd deal with the Belinda-nator and the possibility she might have to consider decorating the interior of a cardboard box and call it home once she could think clearly again.

Trying to take a deep breath—one that came out as nothing more than a dry heave—she mentally sought the last bit of energy in her. Rolling her head on her neck, she focused on being as intimidating as she could.

It never usually required much effort.

"Pay attention in there! If you don't open this frickin' door right now, I'll be forced to pitch the hissy fit of the millennium, and all your rich, fancy neighbors will see me. I'm supposing you wouldn't much like that, seeing as you well-to-do folk like to keep your business private. So open this dungeon door and open it *now*. I'll be fucked and feathered if you think for a split-second I'm going to let you get away with what you've done to me. I *know* you, *Gregori*. I know your type—species—whatever. Your spooky-kooky *paranormal* type, that is." Putting her ear to the heavy door, Nina listened again with her fancy new hearing. A slight stirring came from behind the dark steel and then silence. "I mean it. You do not want to mess with me."

"Oh, gawd," Marty mumbled.

Nina narrowed her eyes, lacing her gloved fingers together and cracking her knuckles. "What? What the hell am I supposed to say, Miss Manners? He bit me, and he's going to fix it."

Wanda shoved her way out of the bushes with greenery clinging to her lavender, wool scarf and a twig jutting from the top of her head. "Were you raised at a truck stop? God, Nina, would it kill you to at least be courteous?"

Nina tugged at the twig in Wanda's hair with a hand she couldn't get to stop trembling and made a face. "Courteous my ass. He bit me, and now I have fangs. What was *courteous* about that?"

Wanda's eyes rolled skyward. "Oh, for Heaven's sake, Nina. It was an accident. You said so yourself. Why don't you try to kill him with kindness instead of being such a—a—meanie-butt all the time?"

Nina would've replied. In fact, she was preparing to tell Wanda to get off her back, but Wanda's features, pretty and usually sharply defined, began to swim before her eyes.

The creak of the door startled them all. All but Nina, who felt the ground beneath her shift and give way, as she tumbled back-ward.

Back into a solid wall that seriously could have been mistaken for brick if not for the fact that when her cheek hit it, it wasn't brick at all.

It was a yummy hard chest, thinly veiled in a flash of white T-shirt molded against rippling muscle.

And just before she succumbed to the fan-freakin'-tastic-ness of all that brick-shithouse, she thought, there were definitely worse places to crash.

CHAPTER
3

"Drink, Nina," the dark voice encouraged. A thick liquid, coppery with a salty hint to it, slipped down her throat easier than any apple martini at Phil's House of Brews and Tattoos ever had. The sweet taste of it settled in her mouth, lingering on her tongue with tangy euphoria. Her lips eagerly sought the cool edge of the cup for more.

"C'mon, drink it all. You'll feel better," sinfully husky of voice prompted.

And sure enough, she was feeling better—in a slow, upwardly mobile fashion. A tingle twisted its way along her spine, infusing her with a new rejuvenation.

"Oh, God, Marty. I can't watch," she heard Wanda snivel, but it sounded distant and warbled.

Watch what? she wondered, but couldn't ask for the utter bliss her stomach was experiencing as she gulped whatever the hell was in the cup. It was like an orgasm. It was so close to being better than one, it bordered beating it with a two-by-four. Which again brought to mind—what the frig was Wanda doing watching something so decadent?

"Um, so tell me, Mr. Statleon. Does she always have to do this? I mean, it's so Bohemian." Nina heard the disapproval in Marty's question, but couldn't quite grasp what she was so disapproving of. Nina couldn't seem to find a thing wrong with *this*—whatever this was.

There was a deep chuckle and a shift of big hands beneath her head before the naughty voice somewhere from above answered. "Call me Greg, and if you don't want her collapsing all over people's front porches, yeah, I'm afraid she does."

They were talking about her . . . and Greg was a perfectly nice name. Kinda hot in a Brady Bunch sorta way—even if Peter had turned out to be the real hottie in the closet.

"But *where* is she going to get *it?*" Wanda asked, her tone anxious. In fact, Nina could almost see her worriedly shuffling her feet while folding and unfolding her hands. Wanda always did that when she was nervous.

And *it*. What was *it?*

Nina's eyes popped open with renewed energy. Gazing upward, she lifted her chin to find a pair of very green eyes, fringed with short, dark lashes gazing back. They gleamed with amusement, crinkling at the corners. A square, sharply angled jaw shifted into a semi-smile. His bottom lip, fuller than the top, curved upward in a slow, sensuous movement that she'd score a respectably solid eight-point-five. Wavy hair, the color of milk chocolate, fell to a chin that was chiseled and unrelenting. His skin had a rather eerie sort of pale cast to it, but it didn't deter from the overall brick-shithouse effect of him.

Her head rested on a pair of hard thighs, definitely male thighs, comforting in all their hardness.

Wow. Niiiice. Very nice place to wake up after an all-nighter. No way did she want to gnaw her own arm off to get out of this little bit of one-night-stand awkwardness. But why the hell were Wanda and Marty in the middle of her getting a good groove on? What kind of sick shit were they into, and how come she'd never been invited to play, too?

"Sleeping Beauty's up," the man from above quipped.

Wanda's and Marty's faces crowded together, hovering over her. "Ya okay?" Marty's blue eyes were hesitant, worried.

Okay had many, many variables as far as Nina was concerned. "Um, care to explain?"

Wanda ran her tongue over her lips. "You collapsed."

She'd collapsed? Oh, yeah . . . She'd been really, really tired, and all of a sudden, the weariness had seeped into every pore and she couldn't keep herself from pitching backward. Here was where she must've pitched and *here* wasn't so bad. At least if her stomach was any indication. "And I'll presume this is the hunky paramedic who dramatically saved me from the brink of death?" Nina's question was caustic, but hopeful because there was a vague niggle of something terribly wrong occurring. But how wrong could anything be if it involved the hottie who so carefully held her head in his hands?

Again, she heard the rumble of a chuckle coming from against the side of her head, felt it in every cell of her body. "Hardly." Those delish lips smiled again.

Marty held out a hand to her. "Are you okay enough to sit up now, Nina?"

Who wanted to sit up when they could cuddle up against *this*? "I like it where I am, thanks." And that wasn't a lie. She was plenty happy to linger.

Wanda's face distorted with censure. She leaned down, placing her lips near Nina's ear. "Get up, Nina. Do you want to look like a cheap tart to the nice vampire?"

Vampire.

Right.

How quickly we forget.

Her mortality had been circling like a hungry vulture over a buffalo carcass before she'd passed out. Which meant she wasn't pleasantly napping on some hot guy's lap after a naughty-filled romp. She was napping on some hot guy *vampire's* lap.

He must be Gregori of the chipped tooth.

Tee-rific.

Sweet Jesus.

Her legs automatically swung to the right, jumping up and away from the comfort of Dracula and falling into Wanda and Marty with wobbly legs. A wave of dizzy, disorienting flashes of color and sound assaulted her. She clung to Wanda for support.

While Wanda righted her, Marty dug in her purse. "Here." She handed Nina a tissue, casting a look of distaste. "Wipe your mouth."

Her look of confusion must have said it all. The vampire—oh, my God—the *vampire*—rose from his seat on the black leather couch and pressed a thumb to the corner of her mouth. "Blood." He smirked. "You have some on the side of your mouth."

"Uh, say again?" Nina demanded, taking in the long, lean length of him. He was tall. At least six-foot-two or so. His shoulders were broad, his waist tapered and lean. Legs with muscles that flexed beneath his faded jeans moved in her direction.

His smile was filled with amusement. "I said you have blood on the corner of your mouth." He wet his finger and wiped her lips again for good measure. "There. All better."

Aha. Blood. "Blood you say?" Nina took an immediate, familiar defensive stance, glaring up at him. The look she sent his way typically left most men either open-mouthed or slinking back off to their corners.

Him? Not so much. His position, from where she stood any-way, was clearly resolute.

He crossed his finely honed arms over his chest, obviously not impressed with her fiercest of looks. As a matter of fact, he appeared rather bored. "Yep."

"Wanda, Marty?"

"Hmmm?" their voices answered in vague unification.

"You let him give me *blood*?"

"Him's name is Greg. My name is Greg," he offered with one-hundred-watt charm.

"Okay, you let *Greg* give me blood?"

"Well, yeah," Marty muttered, as if this was as normal a practice as accepting a bottle of Evian from a stranger after being stranded in the desert. "It really is true. You are a vampire. Greg said it's just like the Internet says. You have to drink blood to survive now. You fell like a ton of bricks out there, Nina, and it's because you needed to—to—"

"Feed," Gregori interjected helpfully, rocking back on his heels and winking.

Marty's blonde head dipped. "Yes, because you need to feed. It's also why your fangs were so out of control and you didn't see his at the dentist's office. Because you needed to feed and when you don't get blood regularly, it makes your teeth grow or something like that. Sheesh, and you call us crazy."

Nina's hand immediately went to her mouth, sticking a finger into it to find she no longer had incisors to rival elephant tusks. Anger, swift and furious, consumed her. She whirled around to face Marty and Wanda. "Are the two of you fucking out of your minds? You let him give me blood? *Blood*? From what? From *who*? What kind of friends are you?" Visions of her swallowing some dead person's blood like it was a Starbucks caramel cappuccino

made her want to yark, but then so did the idea of her once favorite flavored coffee.

Wanda's hand flew up in Nina's face to thwart her. "Before you
go on one of your infamous rants, it wasn't like we had a choice,
Nina. It's not like you have a heartbeat anymore, so we couldn't tell
if you were dead. I mean, well, you can't be dead, because technically you *are* dead." She sighed a ragged breath in clear exasperation and pinched the bridge of her nose. "I just mean, we didn't
know if you were of this earth anymore. When we explained what
happened and how you'd been bitten, Greg here was very helpful.
So could you puulease try and at least be appreciative."

Nina's face went slack, her jaw dropping to her chest. "Appreciative? You two are bat-shit and so is he." She thumbed over her
shoulder in the mantasy's general direction. "You're both acting
like this is something that happens every day and I should just get
over myself. Screw that already. He's crazy. This—*this* is crazy, and
I want off the crazy train. Like *now*."

Hands, strong and steady, turned her back around. Greg's green
eyes met hers with a flash of what she'd label defiant. "Tell me, do
you feel better, Nina?"

Yeah, yeah, yeah. She felt great. Just like she had the power of
Greyskull. Very he-man. So-the-fuck-what? This made a difference
how? She'd drunk blood, for shit's sake. Blood! Was no one in the
room sane but her? Peeling his fingers from her shoulder one by
one, Nina brushed him off. "Look, you nut-job, I don't know what
the hell you did to me the other day at Dr. Berkenstein's, but you'd
better fix it and fix it freaking *now*."

He grinned. His white teeth—teeth that didn't look anything like her fangs—flashed momentarily. Gregori eyed Marty
and Wanda. "You weren't kidding when you said she's got a potty
mouth, were you?"

Nina's mouth flopped open. "You not only let him give me

blood, but you told him my life story? What kind of friends are you?" she shouted.

His dark chocolate eyebrow rose, and it was very clear, her fury left him unimpressed. "Obviously the kind that were willing to do whatever they had to in order to save your big mouth. Now from what I understand, we have some things to talk about. Marty and Wanda told me all about what happened at Dr. Berkenstein's. I went for a simple filing of my tooth, and I had no idea I'd have that kind of reaction to the anesthesia. It must be the difference between human chemistry and vampire chemistry. I do know a vampire's teeth can be a very sensitive place to mess with. I ended up in Hackensack because your doctor was the only dentist who'd take me as a walk-in, and he came highly recommended by a friend. However, I don't remember you or what happened."

He pointed a finger to his lavish couch. "So why don't you plunk that cranky butt of yours down, and we'll see what we can figure out." His statement was more a command, filled with domineering arrogance, than it was a generous offer to help.

Like anyone ever told her what to do. Nina shook her head vehemently. "I'm not sitting on anything, Batman. You're going to wave your magic wand—cape, whatever, and you're going to turn me back into a human, and you're going to do it pronto."

"He can't." Marty winced after she spoke, obviously knowing Nina would react.

"He better." No fucking way was she drinking blood to stay alive. Er, not alive. Immortal. Whatever the flip she was now.

Gregori ran a broad hand over his thick head of hair. The gleam of it shone under the soft lighting in his living room. "Your friend is right, Nina. I don't know the first thing about fixing this. I don't ever recall, in all the time since I was turned, it needing fixing before you."

Nina's stomach spiraled downward, disbelief settling in the pit of it like a boulder. "Do you have any idea what you've done? You bit me, you crazy bastard, and now I'm drinking blood, and I have fangs!"

His face remained calm, impassive. "And I accept full responsibility for that. I'll do whatever I have to in order to help you adjust."

Was he a fucking loon? Adjust? Adjust? Oh, no. There would be no adjusting, drinking blood, or reading people's lunch breath anymore. No can do. Her hands tightened at her sides. "Adjust? Oh, no, brother. I'm not adjusting to anything. Especially the blood drinking part of this shit. I didn't ask to be a vampire, and you'd better find a way to make it right."

His eyes glittered, cold and unreadable. "I told your friends, just like I'll tell you. I can't change what's been done. I apologize for what's happened, but that's all I have to offer. I've never heard of a vampire reverting back to human form. Ever."

"And that's it? You just apologize like you did nothing more than accidentally knock me off my Schwinn and your solution is to offer me a Band-Aid? But I have to spend the rest of my life like *this*?" Nina rocked from foot-to-foot, itching to hurl herself all over his indifferent attitude.

Greg lifted his set of broad shoulders in a shrug. "Er, yeah."

Oh.

My.

God.

Wanda and Nina were immediately at her side, each clutching one of her arms. "Ninaaaaa, relax," Wanda cooed. "Take a deep breath. Wait. Sorry. No deep breath because you don't do that anymore. Damn——"

Nina curled her lips inward, displaying her displeasure, fighting the urge to throw them both across the room.

Wanda bit her lip. "Sorry. I just mean, it won't do you any good to yell. It never got you anywhere before, and it won't now. So let's try to be reasonable and figure this out. Maybe you'll be just like Marty and learn to like being a vampire. It's not impossible, you know. Mr.—um, Greg doesn't seem like he's all that upset about being one. Are you?" Her eyes swung to him with the question.

"I've been this way for a long time." His response was affable, lighthearted even.

"Really?" Marty smiled at him. "How long?"

His lips rose in another smirk. "Several centuries."

Nina flicked Marty on the arm, glaring at her. "Helllloooo in there, you chemically enhanced blondie. This isn't the sharing is caring circle, Marty! I don't give a miner's coal digging ass how long he's been a vampire. I—did—not—ask—to—be—one! Got that? Now quit fraternizing with the enemy and making more supernatural friends. Help the one you've got."

Greg cocked his head in Marty's direction. "Supernatural? You're not vampire." His response to the idea Marty wasn't a vampire was confident.

Marty's face flushed, her lips curving prettily. "Werewolf," she answered with a flirty giggle that burned Nina's ears.

Nina exploded. "That's it! Wanda, meet me in the car. I'm getting the fuck out of here. Marty? When you're done with your paranormal tea party, join us, would ya?" With that she stomped toward the front door, refusing to acknowledge the beauty of the room with its ornate furnishings and polished floors.

Her hand was just hitting the doorknob when he said, "I wouldn't run off just yet, Nina."

His warning sent a cold chill of foreboding along her spine. But she was going to ignore that in favor of getting the hell out of Dodge. "Yeah, well watch the sway of my ass as I do just that. Marty, if I turn around and you aren't right behind me, I'll steal your eyelash curler and shred it in the trash compacter."

The shuffle of shoes followed Nina's satisfied ears as she swung open the heavy door and hit the pavement with feet she couldn't seem to keep up with.

Climbing into the car, Nina noted the sun was preparing to set as she slammed the door behind her. With that thought, a calm, peaceful shift began in her chest, replacing the rush of anger she'd experienced over Gregori's final words. Oh, God. What the frig was she going to do?

Wanda's door cracked open, and she slid in sighing in defeat.

Marty squeezed into the backseat, jarring Nina's shoulder and sniffled. Clearly they were displeased with her. Which was just nucking futs as far as she was concerned. Nina's lips thinned into a line of disapproval.

She was the one who was in need here, and that her friends wanted to make nice with the fucktard who'd done this to her was utterly ludicrous.

Wanda turned the key in the ignition and began backing out of Gregori's long driveway. "Nina."

"Don't you Nina me, Wanda Schwartz. You guys were all up in that jack-off's face like he wasn't the enemy. He turned me into a *vampire*. He fed me blood. *Blood*, Wanda. What about that doesn't sound crazier than a one-eyed whore in a monastery?"

"You are the most difficult woman alive, Nina Blackman!"

Was that Wanda screeching at her? Well, well, well. Look who was all assertive these days.

"You listen to me, Nina. You crashed. Like just dropped. We reacted. What would have happened if we had called 911? You have no heartbeat. What kind of explanation could we have possibly provided for *that*?"

Nina's silence was stony.

"Exactly," Wanda said, shaking her index finger at Nina. "Greg knew exactly what to do, while we babbled like two blithering idiots. He said you needed to feed, because newly turned vampires need replenishing often. Until your body adjusts anyway. That you made it as far into the next day as you did is a real testament to your bitchiness, according to him. I won't be sorry we let him do what he had to do to help you. Would you have rather we just let you kick it?"

Point. "Fine, so you did what you had to do. Thanks oodles. But did you have to make friends with the freak? Marty was all batting her eyelashes and cooing, and you—you may as well have just thrown yourself at him."

"I threw myself nowhere, and, well, he is pretty dreamy. Even you, in your hissy fit, had to have seen that."

"Yeahhhh," Marty said on a windy breath. "He's beyond cute. A little pale and definitely not as hot as my Keegan, but cuuuute."

Yes, indeedy. He was hot. There was no denying it. She wouldn't even try to kid herself otherwise. He was smokin'-licious. And a *vampire.* "Could the two of you stop admiring the enemy's wares?"

Wanda's eyes rolled. "Oh, stop. He's not the enemy, Nina. He seemed perfectly nice to me and more than willing to help. He was very cordial. And unfortunately, you're all in this vampire thing. If what he says is really true, he can't do anything about it."

Nina focused on the sky as they drove, her eyes drawn to the purple, frosty clouds moving overhead. "We're awfully quick to assume there's nothing he can do, aren't we, Miss Infatuated? I think he's lying. Don't vampires want everyone to be like them? Don't they take some kind of sick pleasure in making other people vampires? I'm just another notch on his bat wings."

"He doesn't have wings," Marty chided. "Look, one way or the other you're going to have to talk to him, because you'll need to feed again."

"Would you stop fucking talking about me like I'm some animal in a petting zoo? *Feed* . . . Enough already."

The rustle of paper sounded like the roar of an incoming tide in Nina's ears. Marty stuck a piece of paper under her nose. She grabbed at it and shoved it into her coat pocket. "There's your schedule. Your next feeding is at two a.m. I wrote it all down for you, so you'd know. I also wrote Greg's number down. After all, he is your local blood dealer."

"Oh, and he doesn't kill people for blood, Nina." Wanda said it as if he was doing something as magnanimous as curing cancer because he didn't *kill* people.

What a guy—a real rule follower.

"He buys the blood on the black market."

Sweet.

Blood, fangs, vampires, black markets, oh my. She was officially on overload. "Just take me home. I just want to go home."

"We won't let you bury your head in the sand, Nina." Marty's conviction clearly laced her statement. "You have to feed. It's *imperative.*"

Nina grunted, slipping down against the comfort of the passenger seat. "Yeah, that's a big word there, Marty. Imperative. Know what's imperative right now? Me going home."

"Don't be sullen. It's unattractive and not at all like the Nina of last night, who wasn't going to behave like Marty and cry about her new lot in life."

Marty's gasp of astonishment was prickly. "Did you say that about me, Nina? I can't even believe you. Well, now I guess you know just how it feels when the entire landscape of your life changes, don't you?"

Yeah, she knew how it felt.

Kooky.

That's how it felt.

The rest of the drive was endured in silence, oppressive and thick.

When Wanda finally pulled up to her building, Nina scrambled out with a deftness both women commented on. "You're like lightening fast."

"A total blur." Marty backed Wanda up, swishing her hands in a Karate Kid-like circle.

Nina rested an arm on the passenger door and gave Marty a dirty look. "Remember that the next time you wanna let someone feed me blood, 'cause I'll klunk you over the head *lightening* fast. Now you guys go home. I'm beat, and I just want some peace." She paused, remembering they were her friends and even if they annoyed the living snot out of her, they had helped. "Um, thank you for coming all the way out here. I know I've been a bitch, and I'm sorry." Sort of anyway. She appreciated her friends, kinda got their distorted view on helping her, but she just wanted to be left alone.

Wanda's face changed under the dim car light, sending her a concerned look. "I'm setting my alarm on my watch, Nina. If you don't call Greg by one-thirty this morning, I'm going to do something drastic. Like raid a blood bank or something. Promise me you'll call him. I'm tired, and I haven't slept in over twenty-four hours. That means I'm fragile and I could crack at any second. Who knows the trouble I could get into on so little sleep. Maybe I'll go digging up some fairies and join this club you and Marty have going on."

Nina almost smiled. Almost. "You're very funny these days, Wanda. Very funny, indeed. I'll do what I have to do." It was a vague promise to carry out her wishes, but not quite a lie. No goddamned way was she calling a vampire.

"Promise?" Marty asked once more.

"Yeah. Girl Scout's honor. Now go home to your dog. You've missed the he-man's kibble hour."

Nina threw the borrowed sunglasses in the backseat and

slammed the door before Marty had the chance to croak her tired statement that she wasn't a dog.

She literally flew up the steps of her worn, gray apartment building, jamming a hand into the pocket of her coat for her key, and pushed the door open gratefully.

Blood.

She'd consumed blood.

Shitpissfuck.

Throwing her keys on the cracked tile of her kitchen counter, Nina headed straight for the freezer. She didn't need no stinkin' blood. What she needed was some hot wings and bleu cheese dressing. She ripped open the carton and plunked them with a satisfying thump into the microwave, setting the timer for five minutes.

Larry. She needed to feed Larry.

The click of his little feet in his plastic wheel set her into motion, heading for her bedroom. Larry's multicolored, plastic-enclosed penthouse sat on the scarred dresser she'd found at a tag sale.

Nina bent down and smiled, clicking the plastic with a fingernail. "Dude, what up? Ya hungry?" Flipping open the top of the cage, she scooped Larry's little russet and white body up and held her hand near her face.

Larry's look was pensive.

"Not you, too," she chided with disgust.

He sat up on his hind legs and scratched his jowls. God, he felt wonderfully warm against the palm of her hand. Alive. She could hear the blood course through his veins, his tiny heart beat in quick rhythm.

Nina's lips grew instantly dry. Running a tongue over them, she tried to speak the cutesy words people normally spoke when they were talking to their beloved pets, but her throat clogged. The roar of his blood swishing its way to his heart enticed her, called to her. The mesmerizing throb of life screamed for her to expunge it.

Holy. Shit.

She wanted to *eat* Larry.

Her stomach growled with an ugly rumble.

Mary, mother of God. Who wanted to eat their pet? It was sacrilege. Preposterous. Insanity at its finest.

In one fell swoop Larry was back in his cage safe and sound. She dumped a handful of pellets after him and flew back to the kitchen just in time to hear the timer ding on her microwave.

Nina grabbed for the door handle and clung to it, resting her forehead on her arm before swinging it open and diving for the carton of chicken wings. She grabbed some napkins and dropped them on the table after getting the bleu cheese dressing from the fridge.

Her fingers were frantic in their attempt to gather as many of the wings as she could in her fingers and shovel them into her mouth.

She drank the bleu cheese dressing straight from the bottle, with a gulp to wash them down.

AN hour later, and after much kneeling before the greatness of the Porcelain God, Nina sat at the edge of her bed, pressing a cold cloth to her forehead. Christ, had that chicken wing spree ever been a mistake.

An unwilling glance at the clock told her it was just midnight. She needed to get her shit together if she was getting up at six for work. If she still had a job after the Belinda-nator tattled on her like the sorry sissy she was. Another quick glance told her she had no messages on her machine—so, so far, Dr. Berkenstein hadn't called to fire her. This was a good thing.

So sleep. She needed to sleep. Yet she couldn't seem to slow her body down. Everything around her was a stimulant. The colors of her frayed coverlet danced like sun streaming through stained glass.

And it was pitch black in her bedroom.

The incessant rat-a-tat-tat of Larry's plastic exercise wheel clacked in a cacophony of sound.

She'd never sleep like this.

Her iPod. Music always soothed her. She rose, pulling her jeans off along the way and dug around her dresser drawer, locating her MP3 player. With shaky hands, she jammed the earphones into her ears and clicked on her playlist.

Barry. Barry would get her through this. Hopefully, it would help with her sensory overload tonight.

Nina sprawled out on the bed, closing her eyes and singing along with her most favorite crooner of all time. "At the Copa-Copa Cabanna. Music and passion were always the fashion at the Coooooopppaaaaaaaaaaaaa—"

"Somehow I never would have taken you for a Fanilow, Nina. You just don't strike me as a 'Can't Smile Without You' kind of girl. Not with your mouth anyway. Barry Manilow's a pretty sensitive guy. Some might even say sentimental. I had you pegged for Alice in Chains or Mettalica. Or maybe speed metal."

Nina sat bolt upright, pulling the coverlet over her half-naked body in surprise. A shiver of the unknown skittered up her spine. It was the vampire. Fabulous.

When she found her voice, it had a tone that had a "none too happy to see him" ring to it. "What the hell are you doing in my apartment? How did you get in here?"

Greg's smile, the one she wanted to knock off his face with a good right hook, lit his eerily pale face in her darkened room. "We're crafty, us vampires. Don't get excited. I come bearing gifts." He held up a Starbucks coffee cup. "Call it my peace offering."

Her stomach howled at the very idea of coffee. She covered her mouth to keep from yarking whatever might be left in her bleu cheese dressing-coated stomach.

God, how could it be that the beverage she would most opt to have fed to her intravenously made her want to hurl? The injustice . . . "I don't want any coffee, and I don't want you here in my apartment. I don't give a shit if Marty and Wanda like you—I don't. So take your weirdness elsewhere." She waggled a finger in the direction of her bedroom door as a signal for him to hit the bricks, hoping he wouldn't read the flicker of fear in her eyes. Yet for a brief, crazi-fied moment, she stopped to agree with Wanda and Marty.

Dude *was* hot.

How dare he break into her apartment and be so off the chain hot while he did it?

The fucking nerve.

Setting the coffee cup on her dresser, he shot her a cocky smile filled with a compelling charm, and she just couldn't grasp why it was sucking her in.

Greg cleared his throat, eyeing her with a hint of amusement. "Now, Nina. Is that any way to talk to one of your own?" His tone crooned. "And this isn't coffee. I just put it in a Starbucks cup because your friends said you liked their coffee, and I thought it might comfort you to have something familiar when you feed."

Nina curled her lips into a sneer, yanking her earphones off and tossing them on the bed, scooting to let her back press against the headboard. "How considerate of you. Very sensitive. Very in touch with your warm, fuzzy side. Now get the frig out of my house. I'm not drinking any more blood, or sucking on someone's neck so I can live to have longer fangs. I'm not doing any of that crazy shit I read on the Internet. Now get—the—hell—out!"

He plopped down on the edge of her bed casually, leaning back on his arms and allowing her a real gander at his form in all its vampire-ness. He shook his dark head. "They really ought to ban Wikipedia. Most of the crap on there is only loosely based on my lifestyle—yours now, too, by the way, and the information is provided by online users who I bet aren't even vampires. Now, stop all this crazy talk and chugalug. C'mon, you know you like it." He pointed a finger at the cup and winked a green eye framed with sooty lashes at her.

Her fury overrode her fear, forcing her off the bed in a stumble of tangled sheets and iPod wiring. Forgetting she only had panties on beneath her T-shirt, Nina confronted him with her best bad-ass 'tude. "Go to hell!" Grabbing her jeans, she jammed her legs into them, grunting.

His gaze narrowed, while he assessed her standing in front of him, hands firmly planted on her hips. "I think I'm losing my patience with you," he had the audacity to say with the calm collectiveness of Gandhi.

"You're losing patience with *me?* Are you cracked? You turned me into a vampire, you nut. Whose patience should be on its last leg here?" she spat. "Now I said, get out!"

His jaw clenched just before he spoke. His big arms flexed when he clenched and unclenched his fists. "That's it."

Wow. That sounded like really final. Like all fed up and shit.

With a speed that not only caught her off guard, but would have taken her breath away had she had any left, Greg scooped her up, hauling her over his hard shoulder with a hand firmly planted on her butt and headed for the bedroom door.

She bounced against his back with hard smacks, her eyes level with his ass.

Wow.

If not for the situation—and because of the fact that she was slapping against all his hardness like a helpless sheet in the wind—she'd spend more time admiring the sculpted genius of it.

'Cause he was ass-tastic.

"If you don't put me down, I'll bite you," she yelped as she bounced. Not that that would be a bad thing, given his ass was so bitable . . .

He stopped at her living room window, shoving it open with one hand while getting a firmer grip around the bend in her knees. "Yeah? I dare you." His tone was smug, a challenge.

Rearing up behind him, she tried to get a better view of what they could possibly be doing at her window when he stuck one of those muscled thighs out of the opening and onto her rusty balcony. He pulled them both out to the flat surface with nary a grunt.

"What the fuck are you dooooing?" She fought the roar of the wind as she yelled up at him, alarm and disbelief clinging to her words.

"If I were you, I'd shut my yap, though I know that's not an easy task for you. Oh, and hold the hell on." His suggestion was spoken with a tight voice while climbing over the railing and seating himself there.

Nina pummeled his back with little effect. "Let go of me, you crazy freak!"

He swatted at her hands impatiently. "Cut it out, Nina. For Christ's sake, I have to concentrate in order to fly and you do *not* want to break my concentration—because this is anything but easy, and some nasty shit could go down if we drop like we're hot."

Fly? Did they have wings, too? Marty had said no wings . . .

Omigod. Did she have wings?

"Whoa there, Batman. Fly? *Fly?*"

"Yep. Fly," he reiterated coolly, leaning forward and again tightening his grip around the backs of her knees.

"But that's flippin' crazy, you can't flyyyyyyyyyyyyyyyyyyyyyy . . ."

Her words were lost in the soar of their swoosh off the balcony and the gust of air blowing around them, lifting them into the deep purple of the night sky.

Hookay, so, yeah, he could fly.

CHAPTER 4

"You crazy motherfucker! Are you out of your friggin' miiind?" Nina bellowed when Greg dumped her without ceremony on the ground. Spitting what she could only assume with a cringe were bug guts from her mouth, she ran a hand over her fly-blown hair.

Fly, flew, flown.

To Long Island.

Omigod.

Her stance was the "looking for a fight" kind when she confronted him with a wave of her finger under his nose. "You could have dropped me, you paranormal flying Wolenda, and then what?" She paused for a moment, mentally reassessing this new affliction of hers, then answered her own question. "Wait, nothing would have happened, right? Because I'm now blessed with super immortality, I'd have bounced like some kind of beach ball, yes?"

Flown. They'd just *flown* from Hackensack to friggin' Long Island.

To his castle. With the moat and the turret. Three turrets, if one were to split hairs.

Which would be kinda crazy-cool if it weren't for the fact that in order to find out this undoubtedly sensitive, classified information one had to be a vampire.

Not so cool. Crazy, but sooo not cool.

Greg smirked, his green eyes glistening in the dark night, while opening the front door to his not-so-humble abode. "Something like that, yeah." Holding out an arm, he motioned her inside, making his way to the kitchen without looking back.

Nina trailed behind him with heavy feet, reluctant to follow, but unable to stop herself. Her stomach screamed, rumbling and protesting its lack of sustenance, while her brain slammed around in her skull like a Ping-Pong ball again.

Greg's broad shoulders flexed when he reached out a lean, tapered hand to open the door of his ultra-modern, stainless steel fridge. Packets of blood lined the shelves, and once again Nina winced as her mouth watered. Greg yanked out a package of the gleaming crimson and threw it on the sleek gray granite countertop. "Drink," he ordered, without turning around.

She made a face at him behind the wide expanse of his back, crossing her arms over her chest defiantly. "The hell I will. I'm not drinking any more freaky cocktails with people who can fly. And speaking of flying, get those bat wings a-whirring again, because I'm going home, and since you flew me here, I guess I'm going to rack up some frequent flyer miles when you fly me the frig back."

Looking over his shoulder with an expression that screamed bored, he said dryly, "Not until you drink. I think I've only told you and your friends this ten times now. You absolutely must not miss a feeding. Now *drink*." He pointed a finger over his shoulder at the counter.

"And I said no, or did your überhearing miss that? I'm not

drinking anything unless it's caffeinated, carbonated, or dripping in alcohol." God knew she could use some dulling of her pain, and a bottle of Jack Daniels might do it. Maybe two, just to err on the side of totally blitzed.

In seconds he spun on his heel, looming above her, whipping her around to press her spine to the fridge. The cool steel might have been refreshing since her body was suddenly flaming hot from his touch, but the feeling was muted and dull. Gregori's gaze was many things, one of which she was sure equaled fed up, but there was something else there she couldn't quite define. Amused? Yeah, he thought this was pretty funny.

Ha and ha again.

Greg moved in closer, so close their bodies touched, her hips firmly planted against his. A bolt of heat shot up her spine, leaving her uncomfortable and irritated that his hunky body was so fucking hunky to begin with.

His scent surrounded her, enveloped her senses, the faint smell of his cologne swishing under her nose, making her knees shaky. The impact was like a punch to her gut. Whatever he wore, it was clean, crisp, and wreaking some serious olfactory havoc. Goddamn it all to hell and back. How on earth she could find him so appealing after what he'd done to her was unfathomable.

Unthinkable, unconscionable. Un-everything.

But she couldn't deny what Marty and Wanda had said with those long, breathy sighs in the car on the way home.

He was the *shit*.

B-e-a-uuu-tiful.

Delish.

A ten on the wet panty scale.

Maybe if she just admitted it like a mental mantra over and over in her head it would go away. Sort of like a Gregori exorcism.

Admitting it was the first step to recovery.

"You find me attractive, don't you?" His words, low, husky, confident, were just the cold douse of water she needed to regain her perspective. What an arrogant son of a bitch.

Oh, Nina . . . Was that Wanda in her head, taking the "tone" with her? *You do find him attractive. There's nothing wrong with that, and it isn't like you haven't taken care of your, ahem, "womanly needs" when you set your sights on some guy you want to boink, then discard like so much trash because you're a pansy-ass and afraid of commitment. He's just validating your thoughts in clear, articulate sentences—which really is something to be commended for, considering most of the men you hook up with are Cro-Magnon knuckle draggers. Embrace your truths.*

I've only known him for a day! she mentally protested.

Uh, yeah, and the guy you met on karaoke night about six weeks ago was what you'd call a long-term relationship? You knew him for two rounds of Barry Manilow karaoke, dated him twice, and slept with him once, before losing him like so much luggage.

Okay, enough. He was her assailant. He'd accosted her. He was the perp in a heinous mortality stealing sting. The bitch in her railed against the very idea that she found him attractive. Marty didn't call her a turbo bitch because she gave people warm fuzzies. She called her a turbo bitch because she was one. No one scared people away better than Nina did.

But oh, Jesus Christ on a roller coaster, he smelled good, good, good. Never before had she ever reveled in someone's scent the way she did his. Her nose was picking up the smallest of nuances and luxuriating in them. It was like rolling around in a bowlful of something silky and decadent, letting it caress your skin as it washed over you in cascades of satiny waves.

Breathless—that's what she'd be if she were still human.

And there was the crux of the matter. She wasn't human anymore, and she didn't want to be a vampire. Manning up now instead of snarfing up his yumminess like a Butterfinger she could no longer eat was in order. Nina straightened her spine, lifting her chin to give Greg an angry gaze, faltering when he arrogantly gazed back, lifting one eyebrow. God, his eyes were green.

And green isn't in your color wheel—not his shade of green, anyway. So tell your overactive libido to shut it.

When she finally had the ability to answer, it was to reassure him he didn't turn her on even a little. Not even a *little*. So there. "I don't find you anything but bossy." Her reply was shaky to her ears and far from honest, but worth it just to throw him off track.

Greg continued to stare back at her, his eyes going wide for a moment before they set in stone once more and his jaw tightened. "If you don't drink, you'll regret it."

"Yeah, how so, Wing Man?"

"You'll wither away and die."

Yeah, she could see regretting something as big as that. But if she was immortal, how could she die? Why couldn't these vampire people keep a story straight? "Wither away? Well, how can that be? I thought I was immortal, and the last time I checked, that meant I was going to live forever."

"If you don't properly nourish your new immortality, you'll turn to *dust*. I think it's obvious from the package of chicken wings you upchucked that your dining habits will have to change. Much the way a human needs food and water, you, fledgling, need blood. For the most part you're infallible, but there are things you'll need to do to maintain that infallibility. So in the interest of me not having the maid vacuum you up, I say you drink."

Dust. Huh. "So let me be sure I'm clear on what you've done to me. If I don't learn to fly, adjust to the fact that I'm going to live forever, and drink blood, I turn to dust?"

His eyes scanned hers, crinkling at the corners. "None of the former, just the latter. Yes. If you don't drink the blood, you'll expire, and you don't want to do that before you learn to fly do you?

You thought it was cool, and don't deny you did. Now, *drink*." His lips curved upward when he finished the words.

Her eyes darted to the package of blood on his counter. Its coppery scent and vivid color screamed for Nina to just give in and drink, already. She gulped, averting her face only to find herself staring at the sinewy length of Greg's throat. The muscles along it were tight, clenched, hard. The pale skin of it enticed her. Her fangs approved, too, apparently. They began to elongate, almost itch with the desire to sink them right into that tender flesh.

As Nina bowed her head, her hand flew up to cover her mouth.

His chuckled response to her fangs echoed in the stark kitchen. "That's another problem. If you don't feed, your fangs will become unmanageable. Unsightly, even."

Well, this was a fine bunch of options. Drink blood, or have teeth that looked like elephant's tusks, then wither away and turn to dust. Suh-weet.

Anger for this new discovery ripped into her, and she was just about to say so when she was interrupted. "You're such a fucktard—"

"Gregori? I trust you're making our guest welcome?"

Greg's arms, arms that had bracketed her body while he leaned against the fridge trapping her, dropped. He stepped away from her, as though he'd been burned, all smiles and Gregori charm. "Uh, yeah. Consider yourself welcomed." He looked at Nina, giving her a wink.

Nina took in the woman who'd scolded Greg. He had a girlfriend, the fuck. How many of these vampires were running around planet Earth? Where did they find each other? A year ago, before Marty and her lycanthropic adventure, she'd have never friggin' believed this shit was real. But apparently, they ran around the universe hither and yon, going completely unnoticed. And they came in pairs like some kind of paranormal Match.com.

Not to mention, they weren't exactly weighing in on the ugly side of things either. Jesus, whoever this woman was, she was really good looking, in a totally not-so-common way. Everything about her screamed cool and collected, without winging her refined aura in your face. From her black hair with a splash of gray to her fashionably full, but not overblown lips, she was pretty fierce in Nina's estimation. Her trousers had a pleat down the legs that was crisp and sharp. Nina couldn't accomplish that if she used a ruler. The woman's slim-fitting shirt hugged her waist, flaring out to sit smoothly on her svelte hips. A classic hourglass figure that made Nina's rather skinny one seem pale by comparison.

Nina's hands self-consciously went to her faded jeans and worn-thin T-shirt, sliding them over her thighs and settling for wrapping her arms around her waist.

As sophisticated as the woman appeared, her smile was warm when she asked, "I'm Svetlanna, and you are?" She held out a pale hand that sported shortly trimmed nails, buffed and shiny and a big, honkin' diamond ring glistened brightly from the hand that rested at her side.

Were they married?

And Svetlanna . . . Nina rolled the name mentally on her tongue. Wow. Hot name. Russian? Figured the winged freak would hook up with a chick named Svetlanna. It was almost predictable. Gregori and Svetlanna . . . They sounded like a couple from *Dancing with the Stars*. Nina wiped her hand on her stained jeans and held it out to meet Svetlanna's. "Um, Nina. Nina Blackman."

Her eyes sparkled, black as coal and warm as a tropical night. "What brings you to us, Nina?"

"Your husband."

"My what?"

She did genuine surprise well. Nina's eyes rolled skyward. "Your husband. He bit me when he came into the dentist's office I work at. Seems Gregori here had a bad reaction to the anesthesia we gave him and sorta wigged out. I'm a product of his weak constitution." Nina fought hard to keep the sarcasm out of her tone. It wasn't Svetlanna's fault she had a tard for a life partner.

Greg's irritated guffaw filled the room, but Svetlanna nodded her understanding. "I'm not Gregori's wife, dear. I'm his mother."

Oh.

Hookay then. Relief flooded her belly, but that didn't make any sense. Who gave a shit who this Svetlanna was? Instead Nina opted to dissect this mother thing. She didn't look a day over thirty, but then neither did the Wing Man. It would only figure somebody as hot as Greg would have a MILF for a mother.

Svetlanna went to the countertop and fingered the packet of blood, directing her gaze at Greg. A gaze filled with fond warmth. "So, Greg, what seems to be the trouble here? I'm not sure I fully understand."

Greg rolled his tongue over the inside of his cheek. "How about I let 'Oh Big of Yap' tell you," he offered, shooting Nina an antagonistic glare before backing up against the edge of the counter and crossing his arms over his chest, waiting.

Nina scrunched her face up at him. "There isn't much to explain. Your son bit me, and now he has to fix it. I don't want to be a vampire today, thank you. I liked being a human. Your son says that can't happen. Or it's never happened, at least not that he's heard of. But you've been around longer, I assume, because you're his mother and all. Maybe you have some suggestions about how we can do that, and then I'll get out of your hair." Nina's smile was brief, just to let Svetlanna know she bore no grudges because her son was a fuckhead and all.

Svetlanna's face held sympathy, and then a fleeting turn upward of her mouth in reassurance replaced it. "I'm afraid I can't help you, either. Like Gregori, I've never heard of anyone who's reverted back. I know this must be hard for you, Nina, but it's a matter of acceptance. I choose to look at it with an optimistic view. I'll never miss anything newsworthy." She chuckled at her joke, her laughter as warm as her entire aura.

But Nina wouldn't be swayed. Yeah, living forever and liking it or turning to dust was definitely an overly optimistic view of shit. Fucking Pollyanna. This was the second person who'd told her there was no getting your mortality back, and it was beginning to smell fishy. If what she'd read was accurate, vampires bit people without misgivings all the time. Had he done this on purpose? So he could . . . so he could . . . so he could what?

Well, duh—*rule the world.*

Alrighty then, it was time to set the record straight, but carefully, so as not to upset the vampires, sending them on a biting rampage. "Um, no, see, here's the thing. I'm a victim of this, and I don't want to hear the crap about how it was an accident. If you're carrying around lethal weapons in your mouth, all parties involved in digging around said mouth should be able to opt out. Yanno? I didn't have a choice, and I don't want to drink blood forever. It's ooking me out, lady. I want to eat sardines from a can and not yark them all over my bathroom. I want to have pizza and Hogan's Sunday Brunch Special with my friends. So I say we all put our vampire heads together and figure this out."

"Nina's freaked about drinking blood. I told her she has no choice." Greg held up his hands like white flags. "But she's not hearing me—despite her new hearing abilities."

She ignored Greg's input—too tired to do combat with him. What had weighed her down earlier today began again, full throttle. "Not to mention the new job I just started the day Dracula showed up. It was my first day, and now I've missed two because of this. That doesn't look so good. I don't know how you people make your living, but I gotta work, and I work during the *day.* I can't do that if I have to slather myself in SPF and wear twelve layers of clothing. It's just not conducive to a good working environment. Not to mention, I stole file information from my office to find Batman here. I can't afford any more trouble, or I'll get my ass fired. Besides, I'd be a crappy vampire. I like daytime TV way too much. So call up whoever's in charge of this vampire soiree and hook me up. I'll take it from there."

Svetlanna smiled again like she had all the answers to her problems. "But you no longer need a job, Nina. You'll join the clan here and work with us."

Clan? *Clan?* Like Jim Jones? Like the Hari Krishnas? Wait, they were cults. Whatever . . . Oh, hell, this was a whole lot like Bobbie-Sue. Oh, no, no. There'd be no clan joining. This shit was sounding more and more like the crap Marty'd had to endure with the dogs and their packs. No clans. It was also sounding more and more like the take-over-the-world plot she'd begun to surmise was at the root of this. Maybe Greg biting her was no accident at all. Dread formed in the pit of her belly.

Yeah, because dental hygienists are soooo valuable when taking over the world. They can remind all of their new vampire friends to brush and floss.

Nina fought to keep her wild thoughts in tight check with a crack of her knuckles.

She didn't want to rile these people. They *were* vampires, and from what she gathered in Wanda's reading, some bad-assed dudes. So she'd play nice—or as nice as she knew how to be without looking yellow. Where she came from you just didn't show the enemy the chicken in you. Even if the enemy was lip-smacking and his mother was like June Cleaver in a whiter shade of pale.

"Yeah . . . yeah, I'll do that right after I participate in the human sacrifice. Um, no. Here's the thing. I don't want to live with you, and no disrespect, but you're all crazy to think it's okay to live for an eternity drinking blood. So thanks, but no thanks. I want out, and I want someone—*anyone* to tell me how to do that." Had that sounded persecutory? Defensive?

Svetlanna cocked her head, scanning Nina's face.

Nina was sure she'd burst into a fit of anger for Nina giving her such a hard time and being so sarcastic, but it was quite the opposite. She was downright kind and not at all as condescending as her devil spawn. "I wish I could help. You can certainly be assured if I had any information at all to share, I'd do it. However, for now and if you wish to maintain your immortality until this is figured out, you *must* drink. You're a new vampire, dear. The immortality you now possess must be nurtured. Unfortunately, as distasteful as the blood drinking is to you, it's simply a fact and something you'll have to accept for at least the time being. We really are being honest with you when we say no one has ever turned back. So come," she held her hand out, "come and drink with me."

Nina gave another yearning glance to the packet of blood on the counter. The urge to snatch it up and gargle with it before guzzling every last drop like a piña colada was killing her. Svetlanna was wooing her, and she was swaying. Was this some kind of reverse psychology? Win over the new vampire with kind words and blood, so she'd do your evil bidding?

Nina gave them both a stubborn glance. No blood. Her refusal to drink it was denial, plain and simple. If she didn't acknowledge she wanted the blood, it couldn't exist.

Svetlanna went to one of the many dark cherry stained cabinets lining the walls and popped a door open, pulling out a wine glass that sparkled under the dim recessed lighting. "Tell me about your job, Nina. Do you enjoy it?"

Well, she couldn't say for sure. She'd had it for all of a day before some loon came and turned her into a vampire. Nina voiced just that sentiment to Svetlanna. "Like I said, I've only had it for a day. You know, that brings to mind a question. How is it that you can go to Hackensack in broad daylight, but I feel like crispy fried bacon even when its overcast?"

His eyebrows knitted together, but his smile was smug, making his dimples stand out. Like he had the newest X-box 360 and she didn't. "Tolerance. I've built up a tolerance to sunlight, and that day my tooth was driving me crazy. I couldn't find anyone who'd take me as a walk-in, until I found Dr. Birkenstein. It bothered me enough that I was willing to risk traveling so far."

Her gaze in Greg's direction was almost hopeful. "So what you're saying is if I stay like this I'll eventually be able to go outside when the sun's up?"

"It'll be a long time before that happens, Nina. A long time. I can't tolerate it for long, but it's manageable. There are some small compensations for my immortality. But they take patience and time. Something it's very clear you lack. Oh, and I can also eat a slice of pizza from time to time," Greg said, showering her with another glib smile and cracking his knuckles back at her.

Time. How much was the question? Never-the-fuck-mind. She didn't want to know. No wait. Yeah, she did. She could take it. "What kind of time are we talkin'?"

"Sometimes a couple of centuries."

Her stomach took another nosedive. "Centuries? Um, how old are You?" That research Wanda had done said vampires lived a loooong-ass time. But Greg had told her not to believe everything she'd read on Wikipedia. Still, she was sorry she'd asked.

"I'll be five hundred in a couple of months."

She snorted. "Oh, you so are not."

He snorted back. "On the contrary. I so am, too."

"Bullshit," she shot back, then gave Svetlanna an apologetic look. "Sorry. I swear in tense situations."

Greg glared at her. "You swear in all situations, Nina, and it's not bullshit. I've been around a very long time."

"Hookay, that's enough crazy for me. I'm having a conversation with a man who thinks he's five hundred years old. I want to go home, and I want to go home now. If you won't take me, I'll find my own way." She sought the edge of the island countertop for support. That discombobulated feeling she'd had earlier was taking hold again.

Greg's eyes narrowed, and his lips tightened, but Svetlanna's chuckle thwarted the response Nina was sure he was preparing to spew.

Svetlanna's laughter tinkled like a wind chime. "You're a hoot, so full of fire. I like spirit, and you have plenty of that, but you're not going anywhere until you drink. Now come sit with me and nourish yourself. I won't take no for an answer." Turning her eyes back to the wine glass, she poured the blood into it and then set her gaze patiently on Nina. "I can tell you're slowing down. It isn't good to delay feedings, Nina, and already it's been several hours since you last fed. And it shows, by the way."

Yeah, it probably did. Nina could feel it in her sluggish responses, in the way she was kinda digging Greg's mother and not fighting it tooth and nail. Her body felt boneless and so damned weary. Her eyes were grainy; the world had grown fuzzy and muted.

But her hearing hadn't. Sweet mother of God, just hearing the slosh of the blood pouring into the glass made her tremble with anticipation. Nina clenched her fists to her sides and bit the inside of her lip.

Svetlanna patted the breakfast bar chair that sat beside her own. "I say we look at it this way. You want to figure out how to be human once more. If you're going to do that, you'll need your strength. You won't find the path to mortality again if you turn to dust. I assume Greg told you what will happen if you don't nurture your immortality?"

"Yeah, he told me," she said with tired reluctance, each word becoming a supreme effort.

"Then it's settled. You'll drink." Svetlanna tipped her glass toward Nina, grinning at her over the rim.

Svetlanna couldn't have made more sense, and while that bothered Nina, the truth of her statement couldn't be ignored. Without any more hesitation and probably because her will of iron seemed to have turned to mush, Nina grabbed the glass and threw down, wiping her hand across her mouth to hide the burp bubbling in her throat.

Instantly everything in the kitchen became crystal clear, textures were redefined, smells doubled in intensity, Greg got hotter.

Niiiiiice. Way to want the freak, Nina.

But she couldn't deny how refreshed she felt.

And ashamed that she was clearly unable to resist a little thing called blood. It was like handing a junkie crack and asking them to just hold on to it for you till they came back.

That thought smacked of past instances best left in the dark recesses of her childhood memories, making Nina's feet anxious to hit the bricks.

Backing away from the island countertop, Nina gave Svetlanna a distracted nod. "Well, fellow night dwellers, it's been real."

"Ahhh," Greg drawled with chocolate tones as silken as midnight. "Look, Mother, Nina's back to her old sarcastic self. See how a little blood'll do ya?"

Nina clutched her fists together to keep from giving him a good right hook. "I'm going home now."

"And you plan to get there how?" Greg's "I've got something you don't have" tone rankled her.

"Maybe I'll click my wings three times and fly home," she quipped, moving to exit his fancy-schmancy kitchen.

Svetlanna's laughter filled her ears, but it wasn't mocking her. It was just warm and friendly, and that made Nina even more anxious to get the hell out. She was uncomfortable actually warming to her perp's familial relations, because it could be nothing more than an evil ploy. "We don't have wings, dear. Flying is simply mind over matter for us. A skill you'll no doubt acquire—in time, that is. Greg will take you home for now."

What-the-fuck-ever. "Um, yeah. Hookay, well, it was nice to meet you, but I have to figure out a way to earn a living without roasting like a rotisserie chicken, and it isn't going to be easy on just a couple of hours' sleep." Nina nodded her head in the direction of the stove's clock. "It's four in the morning, and I have to be up at six. So let's get this show on the road, *Greg*." The last she sneered as she made her way to the front door. "Better warm up your wings."

Svetlanna commented that she'd see her soon, but the look on her face was the last thing Nina saw before she went out the door. It was a mixture of confusion and sympathy she read, and she didn't like it. She didn't need anyone's pity.

Stopping at the end of Greg's decorative stone pathway, she waited on jittery feet for him to get his wings a-whirring.

His dark figure, large and tall, exited his big front door, making Nina gulp. Just seeing him was enough to give her now nonexistent intestines a good yank. Whatever it was about him that made her feel all wishy-washy was burning her hide.

"Well, what are you waiting for?" Her impatience to grab some shut-eye grew, while he diddled around.

Greg held up a finger to his lips to hush her, cocking his head as he did, swiveling it to the left and to the right. His nostrils flared momentarily, while his eyes scanned his massive grounds.

Nina sensed his uneasiness, his discomfort, capturing it in her nostrils, but not understanding it one iota. How odd that she could feel what he was feeling. And what the hell kind of vampire was he if he was uneasy? Seemed sorta pansy-assed to her, but that didn't strike her as the right label for him either. His discomfort became hers suddenly, and it left her disturbed on a million levels. Was this like some kind of Patty Hearst syndrome, where you identified with your assailant? How fucking loony tunes.

The atmosphere grew thick, hovering for what seemed interminable hours, then let go like air from a compressor when he shrugged his shoulders and approached her.

Two hands planted themselves on her waist, and for the merest of moments Nina experienced a giddy, light-headed ripple of excitement, then mentally cursed it.

"Let's go," he said curtly. He'd dismissed whatever was troubling him when he'd first come outside in favor of ditching her difficult ass, she guessed.

Her fingers brushed his away, and it wasn't just because she didn't want to be hurled over his shoulder again while he *flew* her home. Suddenly, the very thought of his hands on her, his shoulder pressed to her breasts became intolerable and not in the bad kind of intolerable way. "There must be an easier way . . ."

"I suppose you know an easier way to get from Long Island to Hackensack that doesn't take long hours on some filthy public transportation? Though, come to think of it, you could run. You have the ability—you just don't have the strength."

She faltered. Running was out of the question, when she still felt a bit weak and holy sheeit—she could run from here to Hackensack? No. That was just too much to absorb right now. Instead, she gave in. "Uh, no. But can we not throw me over your shoulder like a sack of potatoes this time?"

Greg's eyes flashed in the dark, glittering with accusation.

"Only if you promise not to squirm around again or open your yap. God save me from your mouth. This *flying*, as you call it, takes concentration, and your constant carrying on could break even a man like me."

Ugh. This man. "What-everrr. Let's just do it. I need sleep." She turned her back to him and held up her arms, hoping his chest pressed to her spine would be somehow less—less sinful than her ass in his face and his in hers.

He met her request with silence, lifting her off her feet with ease. Their landing in front of her apartment was just as smooth and the trip was over in the blink of an eye.

"You're like the Concorde," she joked, feeling much more affable after feeding.

"Indeed" was his only response, dry and without a hint of the chuckle she'd expected to illicit from him.

Okay, so he'd had enough of her. She wouldn't blame him if it weren't for the fact that he'd done this to her in the first place. She knew she could be a lot—especially if she was stressed. Greg not being able to deal with her made him no different than the majority of the opposite sex who'd come long before him. Most men found her difficult and abrasive at best, and she'd smiled secretly while mentally agreeing.

And who gave a Flying Dutchman if he'd had enough? She was of the mind he'd intentionally bitten her, and she was worried he'd find her difficult?

Hellllooooo, in there. Nut who wants to take over the world here.

Yet the sense of Greg's impending exit left her feeling very alone. It almost made her want to tentatively ask if she'd see him again—*ever*. He was the keeper of all things plasma, and if what Svetlanna and Greg said was true, she'd need more to survive. What stopped her from asking if he'd be back was her pride.

Which she totally planned to hang on to like a bargain bridal gown at Filene's Basement.

And her fear that he'd turned her with malice.

Nina folded her hands together in front of her, letting them dangle at her waist, twisting her head from side to side.

So was this it? Maybe if she left quietly, he'd let her be and not make her join his kooky clan. In fact, that'd be just fine. He might be pretty sweet to look at, and her only known source of blood, but he wasn't exactly remorseful for snatching her mortality. That would keep her warm tonight when she blew him off and help her to forget she'd had a weak moment, thinking he was all hot and not some twisted psychopath.

Might as well get this over with and be clear as day while she did it. "Well, thanks for trashing my life. Guess I'll be seeing you."

Greg stared at her for a long moment, his feet firmly planted on the pavement, his expression hard and unyielding. The wind picked up, dragging her long hair across her face, gluing it to her mouth. Clouds gathered above, swooshing to mash together, then bounce away like bumper cars.

Spooooky.

A chill coursed along her spine.

Enough with the glare of death already. She refused to let him intimidate her, but you sure wouldn't have known that from her lame, shaky parting shot. "Um, b-bye."

His smile was as sly as his response. "I'll be seeing you." His words rippled along the evening air almost seductively, making her turn and fly up the stairs to her apartment without saying another word.

When she pushed open her door, she just as quickly slammed it with a solid thunk, leaning against it for support. Like she was locking out the bogeyman. Jesus, he exhausted her, she thought, stumbling to her bedroom to the tune of cool sheets and a soft pillow.

The red light of her answering machine blinked angrily. Wanda . . . she'd promised to call at one-thirty and check on her. Pressing the button, Nina didn't even bother to undress. Dragging the comforter up over her, she listened as Wanda asked if she knew where her blood was.

She'd laugh if she had the energy, but she only had enough left in her to make a quick call to Wanda's voice mail and reassure her she'd fed before she slumped over her fluffy pillows and literally passed out—the pungent scent of Greg still in her nose.

GREG approached Svetlanna from behind with caution. She sat in her favorite chair, facing the trio of windows in the library. The vibes she sent out were complex, but one emotion was infinitely clear.

She was tweaked.

"Don't skulk, Gregori. It's not terribly commanding in presence."

He chuckled, placing his hands on the back of the recliner and dropping his head around the corner of it. His mother only called him by his full name when she was irritated. Over the years they'd learned to blend with others, paying close attention to popular slang, television, and news, so as not to arouse suspicion. She rarely used Gregori because of it. "I'm not skulking. I'm treading lightly."

She shifted positions, peering over the arm of the La-Z-Boy. "Well, if you're not, then you should be. You do know what you've done, don't you?"

His teeth clamped together. The sharp sting of the tooth that had brought him this shitload of trouble was all but gone, yet the phantom pain remained. It nagged him with irritating pangs. "Of course I know what I've done. It certainly wasn't intentional."

Shit. Did he ever know what he'd done. Turned a mouthy, opinionated, smart-assed, difficult woman into one of his own. His
brilliance astonished even him. "I had a chipped tooth that needed
filing. I still don't know why it wouldn't heal like any other ailment
we come across, but it didn't. If I had known I'd react the way I
did to something as simple as anesthesia, I'd have yanked it out
with rusty pliers myself, before I'd have gotten mixed up with that
woman." He couldn't hide the scathing tone lacing his words. Nina
Blackman was a pain in the ass. A loud one.

Svetlanna's look of understanding met his heated one. "I realize
it was an accident, but we have things to deal with, and this devel-
opment with poor Nina won't help an already tense situation."

Greg's eyebrows flew upward in indignation, his jaw grinding
down to clamp the twinge in his tooth he knew logically was gone,
but was, in his mind anyway, a pain by association. He made his
way to his desk, pulling the chair out and dropping into it before
he asked, "Did you just say *poor Nina*? You're kidding, right?"

Svetlanna rose, facing her son with an amused look in her eyes,
as she made her way to his desk, bracing her hands on it for support and leaning in toward him. The twinkle in her eyes caught his
attention. "Yes, *poor Nina*. Her anger is justified, or are you forgetting yours after all this time?"

"Have you heard the mouth on her, Mother? It's big." He held
up his hands, widening them for emphasis, then grinned at her to
soften his words. Yeah, he knew where Nina was, but it'd been a
long time, and acceptance hadn't been nearly as hard for him as it
appeared to be for her. Of course, he hadn't had Wikipedia and the
Internet to fill his head with crap back then, either.

The admonishing cluck of Svetlanna's tongue grated on his
nerves. "It's feisty and that's not something you're used to, I imagine. The women you dabble with don't have enough comprehen-
sion to converse in complete sentences."

Oh, for Christ's sake. He should have known he wasn't going to get off with just an apology to Nina, if Svetlanna had anything to say about it. If his mother had her way, she'd move Nina in here, nurture the hell out of her, teach her how to be a vampire, and that just wasn't going to happen. No matter how sweet her ass was.

Fuck. Had he just given her ass a label? Sweet, no less. What a contradiction.

"So you'll help her." It wasn't a request, it was a statement.

"I tried to help her, or didn't you hear how little she wants my help?"

Her face grew sympathetic. The few lines she'd accumulated over the centuries stood out, reminding him of the kind of woman his mother was. A bleeding heart. A good one, but one nonetheless. "She's in shock, Greg. She's frightened."

Right. "I doubt much frightens Nina."

"Then you'd be wrong. All that smart talk is a way to disguise her fear. Yesterday she was a human, today she's a vampire. Had words like the ones she uses existed back when we were turned, I'd have used them, too. Fucktard has such impact." She followed that with a chuckle.

Greg shook his head, ignoring her attempt to lighten the situation. "I can only help her as much as she lets me, and she obviously isn't in it to win it. I dragged her back here literally kicking and screaming, so I could see to it she fed. And she did. And then she yapped with that out of control mouth of hers some more. So I'm done." He rose from the waist and leaned over his desk to kiss her cheek goodnight, ending their conversation. Sleep, deep and dreamless, called to him. The nagging guilt he felt over Nina would wash away with some solid snoozing.

Svetlanna ducked, avoiding his lips and chucking him under the chin. "You know, Nina's showing up might work in our favor."

He squinted for a moment, and then Svetlanna's intentions

dawned on him. "Um, no. I know exactly what you're thinking, and you can forget it. Not a chance in hell will that ever happen." No way. Period. End of. Not when eternity was at stake.

Svetlanna's slender shoulders shrugged, the worry returning to her face. "She beats the alternative. This won't just go away, Greg, and I don't just mean Nina and her issues."

Grabbing her hand, Greg squeezed it. "Nope. It won't."

Svetlanna switched topics abruptly, which was her way whenever they talked about his future being in such dire straights. "Her job is in jeopardy. We could give her one at Fango, you know. I'm sure I could find something for her to do. Obviously she's fiercely independent, and it would probably make her feel even more like a charity case if we offered, but she won't just accept our help. Maybe, in her mind anyway, she'd feel like she was earning it instead of simply being handed what she's due as a part of the clan."

Greg snorted. "Yeah, maybe."

"Though you realize, it is her right as one of us to live and benefit from the clan, whether you like it or not."

His lips thinned. Oh, he realized. "Does Nina really seem like the kind of girl who'd thrive at a place that designs clothes for a living, Mother? I don't want to sound like a total jerk, but Nina doesn't strike me as the kind of girl who's into fashion . . ." He let his words trail off. The hell he'd let Nina come in and disrupt the only thing that had kept his mother happy since the twentieth century, with her foul mouth and hot temper.

Svetlanna leaned her hip against the mahogany desk where Greg handled her investments from the profits of Fango. "She could learn."

Greg threaded his fingers through his hair, forcing the impatience he felt with his mother out of his words. "Nina doesn't want to be a vampire, Mother. I'd have to err on the side of caution when I say I doubt she's going to want to work for a bunch of them on a clothing line she wouldn't buy as long as Wal-Mart exists."

Svetlanna arched an eyebrow at him. "It's just something to think about."

He pushed away from his desk and strode toward the stairwell. "Stop thinking so much. I'll handle Nina. Now let's get some sleep," he suggested before taking the stairs two at a time to his bedroom.

Greg stripped his clothes off and slid between the sheets of his big bed without looking back at the mess strewn on the floor. It had been one helluva day. The rise of the sun sent out a siren's song for all good vampires to rest, rejuvenate. His eyes were heavy, but his head spun with the day's events. He'd told his mother he'd handle Nina.

Strangely, he had the odd premonition that "handling Nina" might not be such a bad thing.

If he had a roll of duct tape anyway.

CHAPTER
5

Nina woke as if she'd slept the sleep of the dead. She cringed, gathering the sheets around her. Technically, that was true. She had because she was. Dead.

Dead, dead, dead. Doornail dead.

Waking up as a vampire had a whole different meaning, and it wasn't the "omigod, I'm a vampire" deal. Daily she'd struggled to open her eyes. She was a champion palm smacker when it came to the snooze button on her alarm clock. No morning went by without swatting at it at least five times before contemplating putting her feet on the ground to trudge into the bathroom.

Not so much today. Today her eyes popped open like a pair of Pop-Tarts in a toaster, fully alert and aware of everything around her. Each color was again vibrant and new. Each texture felt like she had a thousand fingertips instead of just ten.

This new awareness brought with it the realization that it was dark out and she'd missed another day of work. Missing another day of work reminded her it was now Thursday.

Lou would be waiting for Nina to join her for their weekly pot roast and bottled gravy feast. She made pot roast and red-skinned potatoes every Thursday, and Nina was expected to show up at seven sharp.

Lou accepted absolutely no excuses unless you were calling to cancel from the morgue.

Her grandmother was, in a word, immovable.

The light of her answering machine caught her eye. It blinked furiously with a red, consistently paced rhythm. She fell back on the bed and pulled a pillow over her face, inching her fingers over her nightstand to find the square blue button and pressed Play.

"Nina? This is Beliiinda. You know, from Dr. Berkenstein's. The place you show up at occasionally?" Her annoying, breathy voice filled the air with a squeak.

Nina shoved her cotton pillowcase into her mouth to keep from screaming—she didn't need a degree in rocket science to know why Belinda had gleefully placed this particular call, and she didn't need the gift of clairvoyance to know what her message would contain.

"You're fired." Her voice hitched, probably on a maniacal giggle, and then she cleared her throat. "Seeing as you weren't here long enough to even fill up a pencil holder with personal items, there's no need for you to make a personal appearance, because there's nothing to collect. So . . . um, good luck."

The dial tone greeted Nina's sensitive ears, buzzing harshly with an echo in her small bedroom. She reached over and ripped the answering machine from the tabletop with a hard yank, throwing it across the room, and letting it hit the wall, then clatter to the floor, leaving behind a big, honkin' hole. She looked at her hand with amazement as if it belonged to someone else.

Whoa.

Her new vampire strength was matched only by her fury when she screeched, "Biiiiiiiiiiiitchhhhhh!"

Christ on a cracker. What the frig was she going to do without a job? Not so silently Nina cursed Vlad the Impaler as she flung her legs over the edge of the bed and stomped into the bathroom to prepare for Lou's. Her eyes instantly sought the cracked mirror, blissfully relieved that these new chops of hers seemed to be appeased for the moment. Unfortunately, she couldn't see much else either. Her image remained blurred around the edges and distorted in the middle. It was like looking in a funhouse mirror.

Thank God Marty had taught her how to apply lipstick when she was sans a compact. She'd need at least that much to keep Lou from noticing how pale she was. Oh, she'd sunk so low as to be grateful that Marty's cosmetic advice was working in her favor.

Whipping back the shower curtain, Nina flipped the taps with the snap of her wrist and prayed tonight she'd at least have lukewarm water. Upon entry to the shower, it would seem the water temp didn't really matter—she couldn't much feel it anyway. How odd that some sensations were downright making her jump out of her skin, magnified to epic proportions, and others left her indifferent. The almost below-freezing temperatures when Greg had flown her home last night hadn't troubled her in the least. Yet last night, the press of his rockin' hard body had been so exaggerated, so defined, she could almost still feel the heat of it now.

And feeling what she'd felt last night, experiencing what she'd experienced, left her jobless today.

Throughout her shower, and right up until she tied the laces of her sneakers, Nina raged to herself about the total glee Belinda had taken in firing her. Then when she wasn't satisfied to rant at no one, she railed at poor Larry. Larry, who once again was tempting her like Eve tempted Adam.

Her stomach responded.

How in the hell was she going to feed tonight? There was no chance in Hades she was going back to Greg's house. No matter how down his mother was with her.

Nuh-uh.

Svetlanna seemed like a nice lady—even if it might all be some act to keep Nina coming back so she could brainwash her. It still wasn't her fault her son was a fuckwit.

You don't either think he's a fuckwit, Nina. Yeah, this is your conscience calling, and you think Wing Man is daaaa-reeammy. Not just hot, but hawt. So knock it off.

Yes, that was true. He was hawt.

Hawt and a fuckwit. Never the twain shall meet.

He wanted to make her join his clan and be a part of some plot to take over the world—which meant that while he was indeed smokin', he was some kind of maniacal nut.

Maniacal nuts beat sexy to the point of ridiculous vampires every time.

Threading her fingers through her hair, Nina pulled it back into a ponytail, wrapping an elastic band around the thick base to secure it. She'd have to think about feeding and hot bloodsuckers later. Right now Lou waited, and she wasn't about to have to explain to her why she was late.

Blood-fest 2008 would just have to wait. If she stopped to think too long on how she was going to find blood of all things, she'd be fucked.

Grabbing her purse, Nina yanked open her door.

Out of nowhere, Greg appeared. Her stomach did that nervous jump, and her skin tingled when she took in his snug black jeans and beige pullover sweater. The buttery leather of his jacket made the tone of his skin seem almost ruddy instead of quite so pale.

"Ding-dong. Plasma calling," he joked with a good-humored tone and that luscious grin that this time reached his eyes.

Nina flipped him the bird and pushed her way past him, seething. No way was he talking her into being one of his crazy minions.

He positioned himself alongside her and mimicked her pace, the muscles of his thighs bunching together as he walked beside her. "Go the fuck away already. Jesus, what is it with you? I don't need your help, and I have somewhere to be." *And when you stand this close to me, I want to tear off all your clothes and ride you like the fine stallion you are—which leaves me wanting to sleep with the ememy. Christ, couldn't he see that?*

Shit, could he?

His smile was amicable, yet reserved. "Cool, where're we going?"

Tugging on the tip of her ponytail, Nina curled the ends of her hair around her fingers in a nervous gesture. Now she was nervous? Over *him*? Like some stupid girrrrl? How ludicrous. There was nothing to be nervous over. She'd had a hunky guy or two in her life, and just because he was the hawtest yet, didn't mean he was allowed to make her fucking nervous. Oh, God. "*We're* not going anywhere. *I'm* going somewhere. You're going back to wherever vampires go when they wake up at night."

"But I have something for you," Greg enticed, holding up the packet of blood under the loose, swaying bulb on the ceiling. He offered it to her like he was giving her the friggin' Hope Diamond. All smiles and mentally patting himself on the back.

Nina swatted at the package with fast hands, pulling the edge of his jacket over it to shelter it from view. "Are you crazy? Put that shit away! I don't need any more trouble than I already have, thanks to you. People talk in this neighborhood. I think it's obvious I don't live in some swanky castle like you. Everyone knows everyone else's biz here, and if they see you with that, they'll hang my Kentucky fried carcass from a traffic light."

His brow furrowed, creating a line on his forehead, and he clucked his tongue. "But it's feeding time. We've talked about this until I'm blue in the face, Nina. You have to feed."

She pinched the bridge of her nose and massaged it, pushing the strands of dark hair that escaped her ponytail out of her face. "You don't get blue in the face and, whatever. Look, I don't need you skulking around reminding me I'm a vampire and that I need to feed. I don't want to be a vampire, and I don't want to feed, and if I don't get the hell out of here right now, I'll be late to Lou's. Now scurry on back to the bat cave and let me be."

The slosh of the bag was audible as Greg tucked it back into the inner pocket of his jacket. When it settled against his chest, Nina smothered a groan, licking her dry lips. God, she wanted to tear it from his jacket pocket, pop a straw in it like it was a Capri Sun, and slurp every last ounce, then lick the bag clean. Her hands clenched at her sides, and she picked up her brisk pace while heading down the stairs.

Greg was undaunted. He kept pace with her, opening the door cordially when they hit the bottom floor. "After you."

"Did you put your hearing aid in today? I mean, you *are* really old, if the crazy shit you made up in your mind is really true. I said go away."

"I figure, seeing as this is all my fault, I have to make amends. What better way to do that than to bring you blood? Call it the equivalent of a human courting. I'm just not wooing you with daffodils."

"I don't like daffodils."

"You, Miss Opinionated, don't like *anything*, but I'm overlooking that grave, disturbing character flaw and trying to do what's right."

"I don't need your pity or your blood, and I like things just fine.

I just don't like you. Now, after I'm done at Lou's I'm going to the library or the bookstore, wherever I have to go, and researching this vampire stuff. I don't think I believe you when you say I can't be turned back. In fact, I'd go so far as to call you a bullshit artist, because Wikipedia says you weirdoes like to go forth and multiply by biting people."

"Wikipedia—"

Her palm flicked upward with a sharp snap of her wrist. "I know. They're full of shit. Lemme tell ya a little something. They're not so far off the mark, because nearly every fact they list has turned out to be a little too close to the truth. I *can* live forever if I avoid stakes to the heart that paralyze me while someone chops my head off, etcetera. I *do* have to drink blood to survive. The sun *does* burn my skin like some big, never-ending barbeque. So spare me the crap about the misinformed."

"So who's Lou?" The suspicion in his tone stuck to her ears, striking an odd chord of sensitivity in them.

She sensed his deep curiosity. Knew he wondered if Lou was a man. How fucked up that she could suddenly read emotions she'd never even had a hint about before. "No one you need to concern yourself with. She doesn't want to be a vampire either—"

"She?"

A quick glance at him told her Greg was genuinely curious. She didn't know why she knew that, she just did. Much the way she knew her name or what her favorite color was. "She's my grandmother. I call her Lou, and she's very religious. You showing up at her door in all your hellfire will have her knitting you a garlic scarf and throwing Holy Water like confetti. Now go home to Castlevania and get off my back." Had she paid more attention, she'd have realized he'd hassled her to death for the six blocks it took to get to Lou's. Six blocks that didn't seem nearly as long or as far or even as cold as they had, say a week ago. Shit.

Sprinting up the steps, Nina felt his presence at her back, like one feels Macy's one-day-sale-hungry women nipping at her heels. She was just about to shoo him away for the umpteenth time, when Lou flung open her door.

The smell of pot roast seeped out into the night air, making Nina momentarily gag. She covered her mouth and hacked a dry heave into it, hoping it would sound like a cough to Lou.

Lou pulled her hands from her red and purple flowered house-coat, cupping Nina's face with affection. The pink rollers on her head accentuated the silver gray of her hair. Stray strands of it framed her face in frizzy waves. Her wrinkled features lifted up-ward in a gummy smile as her gnarled hand pinched Nina's cheek. Nina gripped Lou's wrist and squeezed it back. She forgot all about Greg, and for the first time in several days felt a small amount of comfort from her grandmother's touch.

"It's good to see you, Lou. How are you?"

Lou spied Greg hovering behind Nina, and a grin split her face from ear to ear. Her husky cross between Maude and Darth Vad-er's voices was music to Nina's ears. "I'm fine. It looks like you're fine, too. You brought your beau? When did this happen, missy? Jesus, Joseph, and Mary, it's about damn time it did. And I don't have my teeth in. Damn it, Nina, you have to tell me when you're bringing guests. You never bring anyone, and the one time I don't have my teeth in—"

Oh. God. No. "No, Lou. It's not like tha—"

Greg swung around to Nina's left, holding the screen door open with his shoulder, and held out his hand, offering it to Lou. "I'm Greg. Greg Statleon. Nina's told me a lot about you. I'm glad we're finally able to meet."

Lou preened, taking Greg's hand and pulling him into the house in a hug. The screen door slammed into Nina's side with a rusty creak. Lou's smile fairly glowed, and she hugged Greg again, thumping him on the back.

Oh, for fuck's sake. Puuuleease. She may as well just forget it. He was going to charm the open-toed slippers and ankle-length socks right off Lou's feet, just the way he had Wanda and Marty. If Lou was anything, she was desperate to see Nina married off, and if she thought there was even the smallest of chances, just a minute possibility that Greg was her beau, there'd be no stopping her until the wedding invitations were engraved in stone and Nina was dressed in some fucked-up version of the dress Princess Di wore.

Nina braced herself against the screen door, hoping to prepare herself for the hurricane that was her grandmother Lou.

"Come in here, Nina. For Christ's sake, it's cold out there, child!" Lou berated her from inside the door. "Come tell me all about your nice young man." The theme song of *Match Game* played in the background. Her grandmother loved her game shows.

If she could still die, she'd choose this very moment to end it all.

"Nina! Get your hide in here, girl. I said it's cold."

As she stepped over the threshold, her feet turned to cement.

How could she have forgotten?

Lou's was like a tour through Crucifix World with a spontaneous stop in Jesus Country.

How could she have forgotten how many crucifixes her grandmother had? It was a long running joke between the two of them. Lou collected them at flea markets, discount stores, the Dollar Store—friggin' Wal-Mart. She had one in every shape, color, and variation. Statuettes of the Virgin Mary sat in neat rows on the mantel, other versions were on each of her end tables, displayed neatly on doilies Lou had crocheted herself. A picture of Christ hung above the fireplace in a thick, tarnished gold frame flanked by a cross on either side.

A groan slipped from her lips as Nina fought to move her feet, but her eyes burned, her hands shook, and her skin crawled. She said a silent prayer for respite, but the flaming ache was sticking around.

So much for all those years in catechism.

Greg slipped in front of her, blocking her view and pulling at her arms until they wrapped around his waist. He squeezed her hands, hands that shook from the effort it took to continue standing. His broad, leather-clad back sheltered her eyes, tearing them away from the Virgin Marys who taunted her with religious glee from Lou's mantel. "Mind over matter," he muttered. As if that would be the cure-all. Just think it away.

Nina squeezed her eyes shut and bit the inside of her mouth. The cool of Greg's fingers wrapped around hers helping the tremors subside. *Mind over matter, mind over matter*, she repeated mentally.

Lou went to the coffee table and grabbed her dentures, placing them into her mouth. She turned to look at them with another smile. "Hey, girlie, let that man of yours go for two seconds and go check an old woman's pot roast. My knees ache today from the bloody cold," Lou said in her husky, ex-smoker's voice, running her weathered hands along the arms of the thermal shirt she wore beneath her housecoat. "You can let her out of your sight for a few minutes, can't you, young man? I want you to sit down and talk to old Lou. I want to hear your intentions for my Nina." Lou plopped down on the couch and patted the space beside her, shooing Nina toward the swinging door that led to the kitchen.

Fuck. His intentions. I intend to teach your granddaughter the fine art of blood drinking 101, and when we've mastered that, maybe we'll hit the friendly skies and see if we can't practice flying. Oh, and I'm going to brainwash her so she'll turn into a right fine vampire. *If Lou only knew . . .*

When Greg pulled away, Nina found herself almost clinging to his waist, but as Lou arranged herself on the couch, he tilted his neck back and whispered, "Head straight for the kitchen and don't look back. Find something else to think about and keep thinking about it." He unwound her arms from his waist and squeezed her wrist one last time before giving her a shove in the direction of the kitchen.

Over her shoulder, Nina caught him sitting his tall, yummy self right by Lou and heard her comment about how pale Greg was.

She stumbled toward the worn kitchen doors, chipped from so much use, and pushed her way through to be confronted by the gurgling of the pot roast atop Lou's antiquated gas stove.

Her stomach shifted with a violent swerve. On Lou's best day, her pot roast wasn't exactly like dining with Emeril, but it wasn't so bad Nina couldn't pick at it, then grab a cheeseburger on the way home to wash down the glutinous, lumpy gravy. Today her pot roast smelled like a Jersey dump.

As she began to give the roast a good stir with the wooden spoon Lou'd had since she could remember, she pinched her nose with two fingers. Greg's voice hummed in her ears with a buzz, before it adjusted itself like a radio tuner, and Nina could hear every word he spoke.

"My Nina, she's got some mouth on her, huh?" Lou's question crackled in the air.

"Yes, ma'am. That she does," Greg agreed. Nina could almost visualize the smug smile he wore so well, breaking out across his lips.

Tard.

"But she's a good girl, and you must have seen past that mouth of hers, eh?"

Gawd.

Greg's answer was very PC—very evasive. "I saw right past it to her lungs, I think."

Lou cackled, the rustle of her crisp housecoat vibrating against Nina's eardrums. "Has she been yelling at you? She yells a lot, too."

"She has, but I get the feeling her bark is far worse than her bite. Besides, I can yell back."

"That's good to know. She needs someone who won't take her crock of crap. You have to understand where Nina comes from to understand why she's such a toughie, but I suppose she told you already, right?"

Oh.

Hell.

Lou was going to unfurl her business like a flag. Jabbing the pot roast with the spoon, Nina cringed, closing her eyes to fend off what was going to come, whether she wanted it to or not. She was too weak to protest, and who gave a flip anyway? So what if Greg knew her shit?

"I'd love to hear your take on it, Lou." Greg's voice bubbled from his throat, all low and satiny, with a smidge of subtle interest.

God, Nina wished he wouldn't do that. Like he was sensitive or something. He was anything but sensitive. He was a malicious vampire-maker. But she found herself stilling so she could hear Lou anyway.

"She never had it easy, my Nina. My son was a good boy, you know. He worked hard. He was a trucker—which explains her bad language. But he was gone a lot on the road, trying to make a living, and that mother of hers," Lou paused for a moment, and Nina could literally see her grandmother fight not to make "the face" where the mention of her mother was concerned, "her mother was what all you younger people call diseased these days. Yeah, that's it, she had a disease, but I don't care what you kids call it. My generation calls it a druggie." Lou's vehemence where Nina's mother was concerned was well warranted, but it hadn't stopped her from foolishly wishing for things to be different nearly all of her childhood . . .

"Janine just couldn't give up the smack for anyone. Not even Nina. I could never understand how she could leave such a pretty, pretty baby. I remember there was a day when Joe was off on the road, and I'd called and called their house because I promised Joe I'd watch 'em, but nobody answered. I just knew in my gut something was wrong. So I took my lunch break early, and I went to check on them. Sure enough, Nina was in her playpen, soaking wet diaper, balling her eyes out, and Janine was nowhere to be found." The hitch in Lou's voice made Nina's throat thicken, and she gripped the handle of the spoon harder.

"Anyway, she'd taken off again, but she always came back round, begging Joe to take her in. She'd promise to get off the drugs, and she'd do it for a while. Joe'd hold his breath, and when another week passed and she was still clean, he'd call and say, 'See, Ma? I think she's gonna do it this time. And don't think—even if I thought Janine was a crummy mother—that I didn't hope he was right, because he loved her so. Just once I'd have given my eyeteeth for him to be right. But he never was. Janine would always end up right back in the gutter, doin' those drugs she loved more than she loved anything else. I can only thank the Lord Nina was okay, because by some crazy miracle, Nina was unaffected by Janine's drugs."

Lou's sigh was a hiss in Nina's ears, filled with disgust, pity, and the frustration Nina remembered well. "Anyway, I helped Joe take care of Nina when he had to be away. I think the hardest thing for me to watch was how much Nina loved her mother no matter what that woman did to her."

Nina remembered well the hundreds of broken promises to play in the park, go see a movie, go to Macy's makeup counter and get one of those makeovers. Just the two of them, Janine would say. She'd just never followed through.

"Janine'd come around and play at being mommy, after promising Nina they'd do all the things she promised they'd do the last time she dragged herself home, then disappear for a few months, leaving Nina with me while her father worked his tail off. Boy, Joe sure loved her—Janine, I mean. He loved Nina, too, but he was a man, and men aren't any good at raising little girls. Nina didn't have the kind of upbringing she should have, you know? Ballet classes, Girl Scouts, stuff like that."

Nina could hear the rustle of Greg's hair, figuring he'd nodded, yet he remained silent.

"I tried to talk Joe into moving when that neighborhood of his turned bad, but he always said, 'What would Janine do if she came back here and we were gone? How would she find us?' But one day she didn't come back. Not for almost a year, and then the cops called, and well, they'd found Janine's body in some alleyway all poked up with holes and track marks. She'd overdosed, and she'd done it with the good sense to leave her ID in her pocket. And when the cops called, Joe said, 'See, Ma? If we'da left the neighborhood, I woulda never known what happened to Janine.' After that, Joe was broken. Just broken. He worked more, stayed away more, and I moved Nina in here with me. I tried to convince him Nina needed him, but he always said she needed a mother more. He was never the same, and neither was Nina. She got harder and more determined to let everyone know just how tough she was."

There was a slight pause, a moment where Nina thought she might be rid of Greg for good. That he'd just up and hit the bricks hearing this very awkward Jerry Springer retelling of her childhood on his first meeting with Lou.

But he must have only shifted on the couch, repositioning himself, from the sound of his leather jacket crunching. "What happened to Joe?" he asked with absolutely no condemnation in his tone after clearing his throat. It was a tone Nina wouldn't say reeked of the kind of pity she expected, but genuine interest, tinged with a warmth that spread over her in all its unwillingness.

"My poor boy. He'd done a run too many and ran his rig off the road one night. Had to be the worst day of my life, except for when I buried Nina's grandpa. Nina was a rock—she's a good girl. I know she's rough around the edges, but with a little understanding, if you can get past that hoodlum front she puts on, you'll know what I mean."

Nina would never forget that call when she was almost seventeen. Lou had sobbed, wailed for a good day, before dusting herself off and putting together the funeral she thought Joe deserved. Though she and her father didn't see as much of each other as they should have, he'd loved her. She'd loved him, too, for all his faults in loving her stoner mother.

She had a ton of pencils from every state in the country because of him. They were still tucked away with the box of pictures she had under her bed. Pictures of her and Janine, faded from Nina fingering them night after night before she'd gone to bed. Pictures of when she was a chubby infant, sitting on Janine's lap, her mother glassy eyed and only vaguely aware someone was snapping a photo of her. Pictures her father had taken, so she'd always have a little piece of Janine, he'd said.

Janine was where Nina's love of Barry Manilow had come from. She'd loved Barry, playing his albums over and over and singing to Nina. It was one of the few things about her mother Nina remembered fondly.

Nina's shoulders hunched over the stove at the memory, but she gritted her teeth to keep from barging into the living room and shutting Lou up. Lou meant no harm. For her grandmother, it was only natural that she'd share something so personal with Greg.

She thought he was her *boyfriend*, for God's sake. If her mouth ran too much for Nina's—or even Greg's comfort, then so be it.

She'd been nothing but good to Nina when she was a kid. Her fierce affection for her grandmother might not stem from baking cupcakes and reading fairy tales, but came from the solid strength her grandmother represented to her. The unwavering love she'd had for Joe and as a result, for his only child. Lou loved Joe, despite his weakness of loving a woman who'd had severe deficits, and Nina would take that over cupcakes and *Snow White* any day of the week.

Her eyes burned, and she imagined it was because she felt like crying, dredging up all this shit that was far better left buried. Yet she couldn't squeeze a single tear out.

Wow, this vampire thing did have its perks. There were a million nights Nina could reflect back on when she'd wished she could stop crying over Janine.

As she rolled her head on her neck, another of Lou's crucifixes, sitting on the windowsill caught her eye, making her skin crawl. Jesus, they were everywhere.

She aimed the dripping spoon at it, preparing to whack it off the sill, when, Adolph, Lou's beloved parakeet, chirped, flapping his green and yellow wings. Her stomach howled with joy. Blood. Adolph had some zinging through his veins.

The bad vampire in her told her to snatch his chirpy body right out of the cage and gobble him up like he was a Hershey bar. The leftover human in her knew Lou would suffer for her weakness.

Fuck, fuck, fuckity, fuck. "Dude, knock that shit off," she whispered, directing her gaze to the gold varnished cage, hanging from a hook in the ceiling. "I already want to gnaw on your little wings—quit making all that noise, or I will."

"Nina?" Lou poked her head in, raising an eyebrow in question. "You go sit with your young man. I'll finish up. Ask him to forgive a foolish old woman's rambling, would ya, and tell him I think we had a nice chat. I like him."

Nina handed her the spoon and forced a smile. "That's peachy, Lou. Where would I be without your approval?" She followed her words with a snicker of laughter and left with great apprehension to go back to the living room.

Greg sat on Lou's washed-out plaid couch, wearing an expression Nina couldn't read. He looked out of place in Lou's old house, with its floral wallpaper and outdated shag carpeting. Yet, her new senses, tuned into his emotions, didn't get a snobby vibe from him at all. He looked comfortable against the blue ruffled throw pillows. But that didn't mean she couldn't still be pissed at him. Had he stayed the fuck in Castlevania, he'd have never had cause to talk to her grandmother in the first place, and he wouldn't know every last pathetic detail of her life.

Ahhh, righteous indignation was back. This was a much more comfortable emotion for her. It beat the piss out of vulnerable and sentimental. "You're still here," she said with cutting sarcasm.

"Yep."

"Well, go home."

"And miss Lou's pot roast? Not on your life."

"Again, I hate to remind you. I don't have a life anymore. Remember? You took it, you mortality-napper, and if you'd have gone home when I told you to, there'd be no pot roast for you to yearn for. I can't even eat the pot roast, damn it."

He smiled calmly, and Nina had the distinct impression, because of Lou's revelation, that he was thinking he had her all figured out now. "I like Lou, and I won't insult her by leaving after she invited me to stay. If you want to be rude and tell her the truth—I can't stop you. In fact, no one can stop you. So go right ahead. I'll just wait here." Greg stood and made his way to the doily-covered dining room table with the pink ceramic boot in the center that held a spindly fern.

Nina moved in closer, so Lou wouldn't hear her. Standing on her toes, she ground the words out in Greg's ear. His hair tickled her nose. "Ya know, you're really starting to piss me off. Why won't you just leave me the fuck alone?"

Her voice rose several octaves, and Lou's head immediately shot out between the swinging doors. "Trouble in paradise? Lovers' spat?" she asked with a flirty smile at Greg.

"Trouble?" he repeated, flashing a wink and a grin. "No trouble. No trouble at all, Lou. See?" He grinned then, looking down at Nina with a mocking glint in his green, green eyes, just before he hauled her against him, splaying one hand over her spine, and another along the curve of her hip. The rigid width of his hips molded to hers, leaving her to brush the swell of a place she shouldn't be feeling swelling, or *enjoying* the swelling of said place.

And planted his lips solidly on hers.

And made Nina see rainbows and stars and stupid-assed unicorns.

CHAPTER 6

Fantabulous.

Fly.

Dope even.

So Greg was a good kisser. And?

Oh. My. God. Wing Man wasn't just a good kisser, he was like the master of the lip-lock. The Grand Poobah of sucking face.

He molded his lips to hers, creating heat just by the mere touch of them, skimming them, then deepening the kiss until her lips felt pleasantly bruised—taken.

His tongue chased, then captured Nina's, leaving a trail of fire, as she found herself pressing closer to his muscled length, threading her fingers through his hair, melting into him without giving it another thought.

She wanted to envelope him, absorb him, drag him to the floor of Lou's dining room and devour him.

Lou's . . . they were at her *grandmother's*.

"Hey, you two, come up for air. Dinner's ready," Lou chided with a gravelly chuckle.

Nina tore her lips from his with the speed of light, immediately backing away. If breathing were still an option, she'd have had a hard time catching her breath.

Greg smiled like a cat that'd just caught a mouse, the dimples on either side of his mouth deepening, while he arched a dark eyebrow at her, daring her to spew at him now.

Her legs wobbled, but she managed to grab one of the spindleback chairs and grip it to keep herself upright. Greg, on the other hand, didn't look even a little fazed by their tonsil hockey.

Somewhere between Greg throwing himself at her and that—that kiss, Lou had set a place for Greg. She motioned for him to take the seat with the Corning Ware plate lined with brown flowers.

For sure she was sunk. Lou used to tell Nina when she was little—after she'd complained her plate didn't match everyone else's—that it was the *special plate*, made just for little girls who were very important. Now Greg had it, and her grandmother was sending her everything short of smoke signals to let Nina know she liked Greg.

Good, good, good.

Lou sat at the head of the table and passed the pot roast to Greg first. "Dig in, young man. From the size of you, I'd bet you're a good eater."

Nina plunked down in the chair next to Dracula and forced herself to think of something other than food and Jesus statues. Her head began the familiar throb, and her stomach howled its discontent. The smell of dead cow was driving into her nostrils like a jackhammer.

Greg took a huge helping of beef and topped it off with a bigger helping of potatoes, passing the plate to Nina. Her hand shook trying to take it from him, causing a precarious wobble of meat and gravy.

"Let me help you, snooky," he cooed in a warm, silky tone. He forked a small portion of meat onto her plate, smiling.

Snooky this, she thought. Yet she gave him a wisp of a grateful smile despite herself.

How she managed to get through dinner was in and of itself more of a miracle than the Second Coming. As they left Lou's, Greg promising her he'd come back next week and her grandmother making Nina promise she'd eat better next time, Nina literally ran down the wide steps of Lou's porch and hurled herself onto the sidewalk with a jerky lurch. A thousand tons of pressure evaporated from her chest in an instant. No doubt leaving behind the squadron of crucifixes added to her relief.

Greg followed closely behind, like a bad case of crotch rot. She just couldn't shake him. "Haven't you done enough damage? Lou likes you now, but I don't. Or does that matter to you even a little? Have some pride and get off my back already."

"You liked me better on your lips, didn't you?" His question made him laugh, and that laughter grated on her raw nerve endings. She felt vulnerable. Not just because of the kiss, but because he knew way more than she wanted him to about her life. To call it embarrassing was to call World War II a wee squabble. She didn't need Lou to explain why she was the adult she was, and she didn't need some vampire kissing the shit out of her and making her think naughty thoughts when she had some serious de-vampiring to do.

Nina stopped under the streetlamp, digging her toes into the pothole in the uneven sidewalk. She eyeballed him. "I just want you to go home and let me be, okay? I don't want to be like you. I don't. I want my life back, and I'm going to find some way to do that. Now stop following me around, showing up unannounced, and let me be. No hard feelings and all, but I don't want to join your clan."

His face took on a serious slant, the muscles in his jaw and cheek twitched. Jamming his hands into his coat pocket, Greg scanned her eyes. "You have to drink, Nina. I'm not doing this to hassle the shit out of you because I like it, trust me. I have far better ways to spend my evenings. But you do keep reminding me I bit you. It seems I at least owe you what you need to stay upright until you finish this damned stupid quest to find your way back to the land of the mortal. So just take the blood."

Far better ways to spend his evenings, eh? She let go of the rest of his speech, let go of the fact he'd called her desire to be human stupid. What she found gnawing at her was, what *exactly* was a far better way to spend the evening than with her and Lou's pot roast?

Things to ponder . . .

And if he didn't stop winging that blood around like some damned dangling carrot, she was going to scream. A girl could only resist so much temptation. Rather than engage further, she pivoted on her heel and headed home.

With Greg in tow.

Simpleton.

When they reached her apartment building, Greg grabbed her arm, keeping her from stomping up the steps and away from him. "Take the blood, Nina. I'm not kidding even a little when I tell you, you *need* it. Look at the schedule your friend Marty wrote down for you." He looked at the large, square face of the watch on his wrist. "In about five minutes your hunger pangs will hit you harder than they have all night. You really should be having far more feedings than you are, but if you don't want to black out, you'll feed. Not feeding can be a very painful way to go . . ."

Nina turned to look over her shoulder at him. Those lips that had turned her to so much butter weren't smiling anymore. They didn't even have that hint of smug arrogance flitting across them. They were a thin line of oh, so serious. And, as if the maestro had said "strike up the band," her head began to bang like a two dollar whore.

It sort of hit her all at once as she looked at him, his dark hair slick and silky, his face grave and tense, his tall form strong and confident.

She was a vampire.

For now, anyway, and if she continued to make herself suffer because she was a pansy-ass that couldn't come to terms with her reality, she'd kick the can. She couldn't do that if she hoped to find a way out of this. She'd only grow weaker, and the word *weak* just wasn't in her color wheel. Already her knees felt like they might buckle, and her hands shook just from thinking of holding the packet of blood. Cheerist, she was hungry.

Lifting her chin, Nina murmured, "Okay. Give it to me."

He dug in his jacket pocket and pulled it out, plopping it into her hand without another word. "Be well, fledgling," was all he said before he disappeared into the thick of the black night.

The imprint of his hand on her arm, light, but firm, now gone, was replaced by depletion. Going to Lou's with him, pretending he was her boyfriend, had wrung her out. Not to mention the kiss . . . which was now a strictly forbidden thought.

She trudged up the steps with heavy feet and a mouth dryer than the Mohave. Safely inside her apartment, Nina tore open the packet with her teeth and guzzled its contents in two swallows. Immediately the world was no longer like trying to walk underwater, trudging through a sandy-bottomed ocean. It had shape and texture, color and vivid sounds.

And that meant she had work to do.

Nina dragged her laptop out from under a pile of clothes and hit Google.

"MARTY?"

"Jesus, Nina," Marty whispered with a distinctly hushed anxiety. Nina sensed her nervousness even through her cell phone's earpiece.

"Why are you taking the Lord's name in vain with that tone?"

"Because this is crazy."

"Yeah, well call me crazy for not wanting to go begging for blood from a guy who wants everyone to be vampires."

"Oh, you do not either have to beg, Nina. All you have to do is ask, and I know—believe me I know—how hard that is for a mule like you, but it doesn't have to be a big deal. You don't always have to wear your independence on your chest, like some kind of medal. We're all well aware you can hop on one foot while you slap someone around and verbally abuse them all in one free-for-all, but this is far more serious than proving to the world you don't need anybody. Just ask for help. It's easy. You just say, 'Hey, Greg, got blood?' And by the way, you just can't convince me he bit you purposely."

Nina shoved her free hand into the pocket of her trench coat and grimaced. After a long night of scouring the Internet and Googling every bloody paranormal species she could find, she'd come up with nada in the way of reversion. Her choices were limited. This had to be done. "This has nothing to do with my independence and everything to do with not wanting to hook up with a bunch of people that call themselves a *clan*. That word alone should disturb even the biggest loon. If I ask them for anthing, they're going to want something in return eventually, and Christ only knows what that'll be. And it might not be a big deal to you, but it is to me. Forget all of that. Did you get it?"

"Yeah, I got it." Her voice lowered.

"Good deal." Nina lowered her voice, too.

"This makes me really nervous, Nina."

"Marty?"

"Yeah?"

"Why the fuck are we whispering?"

Her response was shaky and rambling. "I don't know! Maybe because I'm aiding and abetting a potential criminal? Don't you ever, *ever* in this lifetime, or however many you end up having, tell me I'm not a good friend to you, Nina Blackman. I wouldn't do this for just anyone."

"Oh, would you just quit with the self-sacrifice speech and give it to me? I know you're doing me a huge solid, okay? I promise to make it up to you by spreading your color wheels of life as far as the eye can see. Now give me the address, so I can get this over with. I'm a friggin' wreck." Nina tugged on her ponytail as she moved down the sidewalk, looking to either side to see if anyone was listening to her conversation.

"Ohhhhhhhh, honey, are you okay? Do you need me? You know I can be there in a matter of less than two hours." Marty's immediate sympathy made her grind her teeth. While Nina knew Marty only did it because her heart was bigger than the Pacific, she didn't want to be coddled. She wanted to be fed. Now.

"No, Marty. I'm okay. Just tired is all, and I really appreciate what you did. Thank the head dog for me, would ya?" If not for Keegan, Nina wouldn't have stood a chance in hell of finding someone to hook her up like this. "Now give me the address, *please*," she tacked on because she realized she sounded completely ungrateful for something so magnanimous.

"It's right by the karaoke bar." Marty rattled off the location, what the dude looked like, and then a warning. "And be careful, would you? I couldn't live with myself if you ended up hurt."

"Puulease. Are you forgetting where I grew up? Not to mention I'm a vampire now. I'll be fine. I'm meeting Wanda right after at my place to do some more research. If I don't show up, I'm sure she'll call you. Now stop worrying about me and go scratch the head dog's ears. Bye." Nina hung up before Marty could make her any more nervous than she was already.

She was going to do something very illegal, but it was her only choice. Asking Greg for any more help was out of the question. Especially seeing as she couldn't seem to erase that kiss from her brain, even if she used a hand sander on it. This strange attraction to the man who'd wreaked havoc in her life was a little too Patty Hearst-ish for her.

The sidewalk was littered with people she couldn't help but eye suspiciously. The air smelled of hot dogs and burritos and the stench of alcohol. It made her stomach do that flippy thing when the scent of so much food assaulted her senses.

Thank Jesus for Keegan, she thought briefly, crossing the street with a purposeful stride. When she'd formulated this plan in her head it had made perfect sense just before sunrise.

Keegan must know others like himself, she'd thought. He was a werewolf. Surely the paranormal must know one another, even if they were a different species, and that meant he must know others like Greg. Wouldn't they have like some paranormal network or something? If Keegan could find someone who knew some vampires, she'd be able to make a connection.

How hard could it be to find some blood? As it turned out, Keegan did know "people" and he'd hooked her up, not quite in the manner she'd anticipated, and begrudgingly, but he just couldn't resist Marty and those big, blue eyes when she'd pleaded Nina's case. He'd even offered to come and watch the deal go down for

Nina's safety. But she didn't want her friends involved more than they had to be.

Anyway, at sunrise this plan had seemed like she'd just reinvented the wheel. Tonight at seven? Not so much.

When she reached her destination, her mouth went dry. God, this must've been what it had been like for her mother. Why she'd compared her experience to her mother's, she couldn't say, other than hooking up to buy blood smacked a little too much of buying drugs.

But Nina didn't need drugs to get through a day. She did need blood to survive, and that soothed her conscience for what she was about to do.

"Hey, you Raquel?" a young, twentyish voice said from behind her.

Nina fought a snort. Raquel had been Marty's brilliant idea for a code name. So she was untraceable and all that covert Charlie's Angels' undercover crap.

She turned around to find herself face-to-face with a guy who was nothing like the greasy-haired, shabbily clothed criminal she'd expected. He looked more like a college kid. His jeans slung low over his hips, and he wore a tall T, red with the phrase "Walk It Out" emblazoned across the front peeking out from beneath his bulky, black down jacket. His dirty brown hair brushed over the left side of his forehead to hang in his eyes, and he had but a wisp of a few hairs on his chin. He was all of maybe twenty. Not nearly as scary as she'd expected. Yet he was selling blood.

Blood.

Fucking hell. She was really buying blood. Blood whose origins were unknown. Blood from a kid who could almost be her kid. Her feet shuffled nervously, and her eyes darted in every direction to see if they were being watched. "Yeah. That's me, um, Raquel. You got the stuff?"

"You got the cash?"

Did she have the cash . . . she had it all right. She'd emptied what she had left in her bank account, money that was supposed to go to her damned rent, just so she could feed. "Yeah, I got the cash. Show me the stuff."

"Show me the cash."

Nina rolled her eyes at him with impatience and dug in her coat pocket to pull out a wad of bills. "See?" She held it up in the light of the neon sign alongside the karaoke bar she, Wanda, and Marty went to, flipping her fingers through it, making the bills fan out. "Now show me the stuff."

He dug in his down jacket and dragged it out. "See?" he parroted back.

"Even swap?"

He held out his hand. "Yeah."

Nina grabbed the blood with hands that trembled, shoving the money at the palm he jabbed in her direction. Her mouth was dry again.

"You think you'll need my services again? I'll give ya my cell number."

Christ and a sidecar, she sure hoped not. This whole deal felt dirty—lowdown. Where did a kid like this get blood anyway? Scratch that. She didn't want to know. She didn't plan on being a vampire longer than she had to in order to find out. For now, she'd ignore the possibility that she'd need more blood—ever. "I hope the fuck not, my friend."

"Can I ask ya somethin'?"

Nina fingered the packet with anxious hands, jamming it into her trench coat pocket. She just wanted to get gone. Experience told her to keep her guard up. "Depends on what you wanna ask."

"What kind of freaky stuff you doin' that involves blood,

anyway?Does it have some weird shit to do with sex or some-thin'?"

Oh, the young and misinformed, still at the stage of his life where everything, even black market blood buying, had to do with sex. "No. I use it for, well . . . for *rituals*, if you know what I mean . . ." She trailed off evasively, whispering the words and nar-rowing her eyes to give them an evil glint. She didn't need anyone knowing what she needed the blood for.

He threw his hands up, backing away from her. "It's coo," he said in the way some kids did these days. Without the letter *L*, and like nothing was a big deal. Not even selling blood. "You know where to find me if you need more. Later." He scurried away and into the darkness, leaving as quickly as he'd arrived.

Nina pivoted on her heel and headed back toward her apart-ment, utterly humiliated that she was so soothed just by the mere presence of the packet in her coat pocket. Like some junkie who was about to get her fix.

Wanda's car was outside when she arrived, adding to her re-lief. She'd never be able to vocalize it, but she was grateful for Wanda and the help she so generously offered without a thought. Wanda was convinced they'd find something if they kept looking hard enough. It just hadn't popped out at them yet.

Her cell phone chirped the arrival of a message. Damn her cell phone company. She could never get a decent signal in some parts of Hackensack. When she flipped it open, the caller ID clas-sified the number as private, and when she called her voice mail, whoever it was had hung up. She wondered with a brief giddiness if it was Greg, then dismissed it. He didn't have her number, and even if he'd somehow gotten hold of it from her crazy friends, she shouldn't be even remotely giddy about it.

On to finding a solution to this. There had to be *something* . . .

Pacifying herself with that thought, Nina dragged herself through her apartment door and waved a weak hand at Wanda in greeting.

Wanda smiled wanly, assessing Nina and clucking her tongue. "Oh, my. You're paler than pale. You need to feed. Did you get it?"

Nina held up the blood and waved it under Wanda's pert nose. She wrinkled it in response. "Okay, I see it. Now put it away, please." She went to the couch and patted a hand on the stack of books she'd brought, which were nestled against the pillows. "I brought every book I have and got a ton from the library. Let's hope we can get to the bottom of this."

Nina began to laugh as she read some of the titles of the books out loud. "*Night Master? Night Warrior? Moons of Desire?* Oh, Jesus, *Nipped by Desire?* Please, please tell me I didn't just read that. I can't believe you read this shit, Wanda."

Her eyebrow arched upward, her face flushing a pretty pink. "Joke all you like, but they have been helpful, now haven't they? I mean, you wouldn't have known about the sun if not for me, and then you would have burned to a crisp the first time you went outside. A *crisp*, Nina. Make fun all you like, but some of the people that write these romance novels are right on the money. Which would freak me out if I let myself think about it too long. Where they come up with some of this and call it *fiction* is beyond me. If they only knew how accurate they really are, huh?"

She shook her head and shooed Nina with a hand, bending her head and grabbing a book. "Now quit with the snarky comments, go drink your dinner, and shut up. I'll start flipping through these to see if we can find out anything else." Plunking down on the couch, Wanda smoothed a hand over her crisp black, pencil-straight skirt and straightened the collar on her emerald green silk blouse while reaching into her purse on the floor and coming up with a yellow highlighter.

"It's cheesy, Wanda," Nina mocked with a snicker over her shoulder, heading for her kitchen and grabbing her favorite mug from the cabinet. She cut the bag open with a pair of scissors and eyed the mug hungrily. "Oh, Sebassssstion, fifteenth Duke slash Lord of the Manor slash King of Yorkshire Pudding, I luuurrve you. Put your hot, hard rocket ship of love in me before I explooooode," Nina taunted with sardonic laughter.

"Oh, knock it off, Nina. It's not like that at all. And stop calling me cheesy. So I like a good escape. Sue me. There's nothing wrong with wanting to experience something you couldn't in real life. Um, er, with the exception of you and Marty, that is. How you two managed this is too surreal for words . . ."

Wanda's voice tapered off, as Nina focused on the cup of blood that so desperately asked to be drunk. Her lips wrapped around the rim of the cup with anticipation, but the first sip had an odd tang to it she hadn't experienced when she'd drunk the blood Greg had supplied her with. She rolled it around on her tongue like the finest of wine connoisseurs. It didn't at all compare to the blood he'd given her. It was rather like drinking a flat Pepsi.

Huh.

Maybe blood was like cuts of beef or brands of wine, and they varied in taste, she thought, shrugging her shoulders.

With one long swig, she emptied it, slapping the cup down on the counter with a satisfied thunk and wiping the back of her hand over her mouth. She made a semisatisfied "ahhh" noise and smiled.

Just as she was turning to head back into the living room, her throat began to feel tight. She rocked her head up and down, trying to relieve it.

But it only grew worse. It felt like a boa constrictor was wrapping its length around her throat, squeezing tighter and tighter.

Her cheeks began to feel tight, too, like someone had found

a valve on her, plugged her in, and was blowing her up like a hot air balloon. Nina's hands flew to her face, knocking the cup from the counter. While she knew rationally she could no longer breathe being all immortal and preserved in a lifelike state, according to Wikipedia, it didn't comfort her when it felt like she was choking.

Panic set in as she felt her cheeks and neck now swollen and so uncomfortably stretched taut, she thought she'd explode, sending bits of herself splattering against the walls. Nina flew from the kitchen to the living room where Wanda sat, still immersed in her books, the yellow highlighter poised over a page.

Nina jumped in front of her and stomped her foot, banging her knee into Wanda's to catch her attention.

She tried to yelp, but nothing came out, increasing her panic.

Wanda looked up, and her face fell like a piano crashing from the window of a high-rise. She hopped up off the couch as Nina circled her throat with her hands to show her the universal sign for choking. "Oh, my Gooooood! What happened to your face? You look like a blowfish!"

Nina rolled her eyes in thanks for the commentary on how horrible she looked and wrapped her hands around her throat more tightly, sticking her face in Wanda's. She opened her mouth and pointed a frantic finger inside.

"Omigod! You're choking!" Wanda immediately circled behind Nina, grabbing her around the waist and pressing her fist to Nina's diaphragm, jerking her upward.

Nina's feet dangled in the air from the force of Wanda yanking her against her slender frame. She struggled against her, pressing her hands down on Wanda's forearms and digging her nails into them, but to no avail. As Nina's throat continued to swell, Wanda's hysteria grew. "Stop—fighting—me—Niiiina!" she spat through teeth that sounded clenched, giving her another upward heave beneath her breasts.

Nina bounced when Wanda gave her another good, hard shake, rattling her teeth. She peeked over Nina's shoulder to the floor and squealed, "Nothing? How can that be?"

Nina's response was to use the heel of her hand to reach behind her and clap Wanda on the forehead, but even that didn't stop Wanda the Warrior.

"Owwwww! Stop hitting me. What have I told you about using your hands to communicate?" she admonished fiercely, gasping for breath, preparing to jerk Nina upright for one more round of Heimlich.

Wanda tried once more, all the while reassuring Nina in a high-pitched, frantic tone that she had credentials in saving lives. "I'm certified in the Heimlich," she grunted. "I bet you didn't know that *and* C—P—R. Crap, Nina, what did you eat? Omigooooood!" she bellowed once more in frustration when she saw no evidence of an obstruction flying from Nina's mouth. "Why won't it come out? Waaaait, how could you have something stuck in your throat? You can't eat? Jesus, Nina! Why didn't you tell me?" She dropped Nina like she was hot, pushing her away and leaving her to land clumsily on her knees, her hands out in front of her, bracing herself for the slam to the floor.

Wanda dropped to her knees, too, prying Nina's mouth open with her fingers and rooting in her purse on the floor with the other. Nina gagged, spitting her fingers out in protest, but Wanda jammed them back in, ripping her mouth open wide. "Damn it, Nina, cooperate!"

Wanda was swearing . . . that meant the shit going down right now was *bad*. Nina vaguely saw something flat, brown, and slim coming at her, but her eyes were so swollen even her super night vision wasn't cutting it.

"Bite down!" Wanda yelled her demand. "My wallet will keep you from swallowing your tongue and where is your phone? My, God, Nina. Clean up once in awhile, would you?"

Swallow her tongue? Holy fucksticks. Nina grabbed at the wallet, but found she was too weak to do much more than let Wanda drag her around like a rag doll.

Wanda hauled Nina up to the couch by the waist, throwing her down. Her head slapped against the back of the cushion like those bobble-heads on the dashboard of a car, her jaw still locked on the wallet. "Damn! Forget the phone. I can't call 911." Grabbing Nina by her shoulders she shook her, fear lining her face, her frustration seeping into her question. "What's happppeeennning to you?"

As the words slipped from Wanda's mouth, pinched with worry, her expression suddenly changed.

It really was true.

You could visually see a lightbulb moment occur. It glowed over Wanda's disheveled head like a beacon in the night.

Understanding washed over Wanda's expression, and then she was all limbs and lightening-fast movement. She hurled her purse up onto the couch and poured the contents out, sifting through them with fingers that Nina saw were shaking.

"Ahaaaaaa!" she cried in victory when she latched onto what looked like a big Magic Marker. Wanda stuck it between her teeth and yanked off the cap, spitting it to the floor, revealing a needle. She took a deep breath, obviously seeking her center. Something she claimed she had to do a lot of when it came to dealing with Nina and Marty when they were together.

Her chest expanded, and her eyes held ferocious determination. "Okay, I know what's happening to you." Her words were measured, only laced with just a touch of anxiety as she clearly attempted to stay calm. "Now just hold still!"

In slow motion, Nina, through swollen eyes, saw the glint of the needle in the lamp light. The tip gleamed manically at her as it swished through the air, aiming in the direction of her thigh.

Uh, no.

Whatever energy Nina had left rose to the surface, and she called on it. Galvanizing all of her strength to her feet, she focused on making them move. No fucking way was she letting Wanda stab her with that. It was the size of a friggin' Dewalt drill bit.

Nina launched herself off the couch in an awkward forward motion, the wallet still hanging out of her mouth, and knocked Wanda out of the way, running for the far side of the living room. Which wasn't far to go, but still . . .

"Ninnnnnnnnaaaaaaaaaaaa! Come back here *noooooow!*" Wanda roared, setting after her, heels clacking on the tile floor like the feet of a thousand elephants.

Nina's head whipped around, the wallet securely clamped between her teeth, to see Wanda coming at her with the speed of Flo-Jo and the hunched shoulders of an NFL pro.

She was like—like some demented warrior Viking.

Wild-eyed, Wanda zeroed in on Nina with a fierce gaze—just like a good bloodthirsty warrior should eyeball her intended prey.

Her hair flowed out behind her in a blaze of chestnut, her breath came in hard, harsh pants, her knees pumped with a thump-thump sound to them. Her left arm sliced the air with a dogged swing, while the other held the Magic Marker above her head like some kind of weapon of mass destruction.

Jesus effin', who the fuck was this woman?

Nina heard Wanda's scream in slow motion, her rebel war cry warbled and distorted to Nina's overly sensitive ears.

Nina faked her out and ran in the other direction. Her eyes but slits in her head left her crashing into the table lamp. Yet the vampire gig was totally helping her evade Wanda. She moved from place to place with the speed of light and that was kinda cooool.

Even if she was choking to death.

"Nina, stop running around like The Flash! I'm just trying to help!" Wanda yelled with a ragged breath, cornering her behind an old wingback chair Lou had given her.

The hell she needed that kind of help. No help involving needles, thank you. She didn't mind administering them, but she didn't at all like being poked with one. Nina fought to keep her head upright, gripping the back of the chair. She rocked to the left and the right, preparing to run as if a pack of women from Bobbie-Sue with makeover kits were upon her.

Wanda stopped suddenly, a few feet in front of the wingback chair Nina stood behind and cocked her head. The bewildered look on her face coupled with her gasping breaths gave Nina pause.

Nina cocked her head in question, too.

"God, Nina." Her voice held disgust. "How long has it been since you washed your curtains. Would you just look at them? They're filthy."

Nina tried to make a face at Wanda just before she found herself compelled to look at her lone living room window. She'd rip Wanda a new one for judging her lack of Martha Stewart-ness. Her face and throat were on freakin' fire, her cheeks were preparing to explode, but she snapped her neck to look behind her anyway.

And that was her first mistake—letting herself be distracted by Wanda.

Actually, it was her second.

She didn't have any fucking curtains.

Nina swiveled her head back—a head that felt like it was the size of a hot air balloon—just in time to see Wanda run over the top of the cushioned seat of the chair, lifting one leg high as she planted it on the wingback and tipped it right over, launching herself at a swollen, off-guard Nina.

Nina vaguely thought Wanda looked like some demented crab,

as her body flew through the air, landing on her with a solid smack. They fell hard to the tile, Wanda throwing her body over Nina's, the puff of air between their bodies making a whooshing noise when they connected. Wanda's heels scraped on the tile floor as she pinned Nina to it.

And it was then that she eyeballed Nina's thigh.

Her mark successfully located, Wanda took action. With the fluid grace of a jouster, she rammed the Magic Marker-like needle into Nina's leg, and looking back a couple of seconds later, Nina wasn't sure why she'd made such a fuss. It didn't even sting.

Wanda peered down into Nina's face and gave her a smile that oozed satisfaction. "Thank goodness." She yanked the wallet from Nina's mouth and tossed it on the table that had cracked in two during their half-assed chase.

Nina pried her lips from her teeth. "Thank goodness what, Refrigerator Perry?" Her tongue still felt thick, but almost instantly useable.

Wanda pinched Nina's cheek, heaving another harsh breath from between her lipstick-smudged lips. "Your face, it's all better, you idiot." She dragged Nina's hand up over her cheek and said, "See? No more swelling. You were in anaphylactic shock. When I finally figured out you couldn't possibly be choking, I realized you'd had an allergic reaction to something. I'm allergic to bees. That was an epi pen I poked you with. I carry one wherever I go in case I'm stung. I took a chance, even if you are dead, that it would work. And I was right." She beamed with pride, patting Nina's cheek with affection.

And Wanda *was* right. Nina ran her hands over her face and neck. The swelling was instantaneously gone. But what the hell was she allergic to?

Nina ran an impatient hand over her face, brushing away the strands of hair stuck to it in wild disarray. "Get off me, Xena. Jesus, who are you anyway? I've never seen you like this, Wanda. You're all fierce and shit lately."

Wanda hiked herself up, straddling Nina's hips and smiling contritely. "I'm not the woman I was a year ago—or even six months ago, that's all. You and Marty seem to think I'm some weakling. I assure you that's not the case. Now how do we go about figuring out what just happened here?" She extricated herself from Nina and stood up, smoothing down her skirt, then her hair.

Nina sat up, letting her palms rest behind her on the floor and drawing her knees to her chest. "It probably has something to do with being a friggin' vampire, and I'm really getting tired of one surprise after the other—"

"It probably does," a luscious male voice said from behind her thin apartment door.

Nice.

Dracula'd come to play.

Booyah.

CHAPTER
7

"Well?" Wanda tilted her jaw toward the front door.

"Well, what?"

"Oh, Nina, stop being such a B-word. Aren't you going to get the door? The vampire's here." Wanda grinned down at her, extending a hand toward Nina, offering to help her up.

Nina grabbed her hand and hauled her body upward, giving Wanda a scathing glance. "Um, no. I'm not going to get the door."

Wanda gasped. "You are, too, and if you won't, I will. I just don't understand, and enlighten me if you will, why you have to be so difficult about this?" Wanda spun on her heel, scooping up the broken table pieces as she went for the door. "He's just trying to help. It could be much worse. He could have just left you to expire, you know."

Expire . . . like she was a carton of milk or something. "He's not trying to help me, Wanda. He's just trying to get me to join his club of fruitcakes, and I don't want to be a part of the club. I'll figure this out alone."

"Stop making him sound like some kind of psychotic vampire on a blood-sucking rampage. Your paranoid delusions are becoming really old. He's offered you what you need to survive. Not a lifetime membership to the vampire nation. Now be nice." With a long breath and a hand run over her mussed hair and clothes, Wanda popped the door open while her smile grew wider. "Hi, Greg. It's nice to see you again, and who's this?"

Svetlanna, serene and smiling, held out a hand. "I'm Svetlanna, Greg's mother. We've come to see how our fledgling vampire is faring."

Wanda stepped aside, allowing Svetlanna and Greg, dressed in a black sweater and jeans, entry, giving some shoes Nina had thrown off a kick to clear their paths.

"Wanda, right?" Greg inquired with that self-assured smile brightened by his deadly charm and not involving a hint of arrogance when he directed it at Wanda. Yet the moment his eyes landed on Nina, they darkened, and his eyebrow rose in that pompous way.

"It is . . . Wanda, I mean. How nice that you would remember." She gave Nina a "see how nice the vampire can be?" look. Nina rolled her eyes back at her.

Wanda's hand encompassed Svetlanna's, shaking it. "Please, come in, and it's so nice to meet you, Svetlanna. I had no idea Greg had a mother. I mean, well, one that was still . . . um, alive, er, here . . . uh . . ."

Svetlanna's light tinkle of laughter crowded Nina's small apartment. "I'm definitely here, though decidedly dead." She lifted her lips in obvious amusement. Svetlanna turned to Nina, the tilt of her mouth growing wider. "How are you, Nina?"

Nina shifted from foot to foot, jamming her hands into the pockets of her faded jeans. While she was pretty sure it wasn't

Svetlanna's intention, just her mere presence, so collected and well put together, made Nina feel like she was fresh off some secondhand thrift store rack. "I'm fine." Her eyes strayed downward, drifting to her couch, which was littered with two weeks' worth of laundry. That she should care that her homemaking skills were less than exemplary struck her as odd. She'd never given a shit before, but somehow Svetlanna's refined presence among the shabby clutter of her apartment seemed wrong. It left her without much to say and rather embarrassed.

Svetlanna, on the other hand, didn't seem to mind at all. She walked right up to Nina, ignoring the broken table, the overturned chair, and the pile of crumpled clothes and grabbed Nina up in a firm hug. "How are you feeling? Have you fed?"

Wanda shut the door, snorting and stepping around Greg, who filled Nina's small apartment with a delicious scent. Not to mention a delicious body that made Nina's stomach react with a jolt. Fuck.

"Oh, she ate, uh, fed all right," Wanda assured them.

"Wanda," Nina warned.

Wanda flicked the air with a finger. "Don't Wanda me. Something isn't right about what just happened, and maybe if you'd stop being such a stubborn B-word about things and started taking the help people so generously offer you, even when you're a total wretch to them, we might find an answer."

"An answer to what?" Greg asked, removing his jacket and laying it over the back of her couch like he planned to stay a spell.

Why couldn't she have just been bitten by some butt-ass fugly vampire? Was it so much to ask that her perpetrator be unattractive? Did he have to wear clothes that showcased all those hard planes and sharp angles on his body?

"Nina? Why don't you tell Greg what just happened?" Wanda prodded through tight lips.

Nina sent her the death stare. The one Wanda and Marty'd labeled her "bully" for. But Wanda flapped a hand in her direction, dismissing Nina's killa, icy glare. "She had a horrible reaction to something. She went into anaphylactic shock. I think . . . Actually, I know that's what it had to be, because I had to chase her down with my epi pen. I'm allergic to bees—thank God I had it with me. There aren't many bees in the middle of winter, but I guess I just never took it out of my purse when summer had passed. Anyway, the shot worked, and I have a bad feeling the reaction she had, had something to do with the blood she drank."

Nina grunted low in Wanda's general direction, but it left Wanda unfazed and sticking her tongue out at Nina.

"Where did you get blood, Nina? I didn't leave you with much last night." Greg's demand didn't sit well with Nina.

"None of your business," she retorted like a two-year-old.

"Oh, Nina," Svetlanna chided with dulcet tones. "You must be careful. Why didn't you just come to us?"

Nina was suddenly mute.

But not Wanda. "She didn't come to you because she's a stubborn pain in the butt. She bought blood off the black market is what she did. Both Marty and I told her she was crazy, but she never listens to us. Most times we just go along with whatever she says, because she threatens bodily harm. And she didn't come to you for help because she thinks you want to turn her into one of your minions. It's a very *Interview with a Vampire* mind-set." Wanda's eyes flashed fire, and she smirked at Nina as if she were daring her to pop her in the mouth for giving her up.

Greg barked a harsh laugh at Wanda's words. "Show me the blood," he commanded, heading toward the kitchen before giving Nina the opportunity to thwart him.

She followed behind him like a contrite child, her footsteps sluggish and reluctant.

Greg's lean tapered fingers grabbed the packet from her stained countertop, eyeing the label and throwing it back with a snort of clear disgust. When he turned back around, Nina was fully prepared for him to detonate.

However, he was eerily calm, and controlled. The strong jaw she so wanted to foolishly tuck her head under, hardened.

Okay, so he was pissed. Big deal.

When he finally spoke, his words were succinct, timed, kinda snarling. "Do you have any idea what could have happened to you, you stubborn idiot? Jesus Christ! Do you know what this is, Nina? This is *positive* blood. We typically drink only negative. Your first feeding was positive, because of the urgency surrounding your appearance at my doorstep. I grabbed the first packet I could get my hands on in the fridge. I noted that and since then I've fed you only *negative*. It's richer in taste and texture, as I'm sure you found when you drank the black market blood. We favor negative because of that. The only thing better is AB negative and that's a rare thing to come by. So now it seems you've built up antibodies to any positive blood as a result of your negative feedings, you fool. That means you can't ever drink *anything* but negative!" he thundered.

Nina crossed her arms over her chest and knitted her brows, fighting not to let him see her wince. He was an awesome yeller. His roar of frustration had this sorta resounding, banging quality to it. Very intimidating. What was worse was, she remembered seeing the label on that second packet of blood and it *had* been negative.

And none of what he'd just said made any friggin' sense to her. But whatever. "Oh, and do you suppose that might have been something you'd want to share with me? I mean, it's pretty important information."

Greg shook his head, the dark chestnut of his hair catching the light overhead, showcasing its healthy gleam. "Do you suppose I thought you'd be stupid enough to purchase blood from an unknown donor on the black market of all places, because you're a stubborn pain in the ass? If you would have come to me instead of foolishly trying to regain your mortality I could have told you all my vampire secrets—like knowing your donors. But no, we couldn't have Nina asking for help from the big, scary bloodsucker, could we?"

Nina squirmed. Point. "So you don't really suck innocent people's necks to feed?"

"Hardly."

Nina still wasn't sure she was buying it. "Look, I was just doing what I needed to do to survive. You were the one who said I had to feed. I fed. All on my own." She smiled smugly. Despite her run-in with an allergic reaction, she'd proven she didn't need his crazy clan or him to feed—which was ridiculous, because she shouldn't need to prove anything to anyone, and she shouldn't be so pleased she had, seeing as it had landed her on the floor with Wanda in a half nelson.

"And I also said you should come to *me* for your feedings. Not go off on your own and buy blood you can probably ill afford."

The hackles on her neck rose. "It's none of your business what I can or can't afford."

"That's not the point. Your chemistry has changed since you were turned, and due to the fact that you're not nourishing yourself at proper intervals, your new body is in an uproar. Were you AB negative in your human form, Nina?"

Maybe . . . "Yeah, and?"

"That explains your reaction. Forget the technicalities and medical explanations. Just remember, never, ever drink anything that isn't negative. If you'd done what most good fledglings do and hung around, I would have been happy to help you. So the point is, it was a stupid thing to do. But I should have expected it. It smacks of *Nina*."

Like he knew her so well to say what she'd done smacked—of anything.

Greg's eyes narrowed at her, pinning her to the wall of her kitchen with an icy stare. "I don't need to know you well to know you can be pigheaded, arrogant, and a bloody rock when it comes to taking someone's advice. For people like *you*, it's like telling you what to do instead of what it actually is—which is merely offering help."

Nina rolled her tongue around the inside of her mouth. People like her, eh?

His hard stare wasn't letting up. It left Nina wilted with pangs of guilt nipping at her.

Oh, fine. All right. She'd made a mistake. She'd never do it again. From now on it was negative blood all the way.

"Make sure you remember that, fledgling."

"Remember what?"

"To drink only negative blood."

"How the fuck do you know what I'm thinking? Get out of my head, you nutcase."

Crossing the space between them with two swift strides, he loomed above her. "With pleasure," he ground out. "No one should be in it for long, because it's a dark, scary place."

Poking a finger in his chest—his so hard, so yummy chest, Nina's lips thinned into a line of fury. "Look, *Gregori*, I'm just trying to get by until I can figure this out. I didn't ask you for help because I don't want your help. You people don't want me to be human again, and I know it. It only furthers your cause if I stay a vampire. Strength in numbers and all. So get off my back, go find your mother, and take her home."

"My cause," he drawled, low and gravelly.

Her chest grew tight as he looked down at her. Though she couldn't feel much these days in the way of hot and cold, his stare sure as shit made her warm and tingly all over—especially when he invaded her space. "Yeah, your cause, and don't pretend you don't have an agenda. The more vampires in the world, the more likely you'll rule it one day. It makes sense you'd want to keep me a vampire."

He barked a laugh. "Right. Like we'd want someone like *you* in our clan anyway."

Oh. He did not just say that.

Greg's head nodded, and he hitched his jaw in her direction. "I did just say that. Why would we want someone so damned difficult? So we can all have ulcers? Not likely."

"What the hell kind of freaky crap is that anyway? How do you know what I'm thinking?"

"It's just one of those vampire perks. If it makes you feel any better, I don't always know—or I didn't before tonight. For some reason I just started picking up on some of your random thoughts. It's a gift." He offered her one of his specialty items—a smug grin.

Her face contorted with rage, her muscles stiffening along her spine. "Well, knock it the frig off. And isn't your mother waiting for you? She made you come here tonight, didn't she?"

Greg sucked in his cheeks, glaring at her. "Maybe." Clearly this was an admission he didn't want to make, which was perfect because it meant ammunition for her.

"Mama's boy."

"Loud mouth."

"Blood drinker."

"Wannabe blood drinker."

"Children?" Wanda poked her head around the corner of the

kitchen doorway, clucking her tongue. Her cheeks were flushed, which meant she was cranked. "We can hear you, you know. Svetlanna and I are having a perfectly lovely chat, and you two keep interrupting. So break it up, already!" With a huff, she ran a hand over her wrinkled skirt and pivoted on her heel.

Greg returned to the task of glaring at her. "Yes, I only came here as a courtesy to my mother. Nothing more, nothing less."

"If that's what helps you sleep at night."

"Don't do something stupid like that again, Nina."

In light of her face feeling like it had too much air in it, she had to acquiesce and agree it'd been pretty stupid. "Whatever. It's not like I'm going to have to do this for long. I'm convinced you and your bunch of kooks are hiding something from me, and you just don't want me to know I can be turned back into a human."

The crack of his jaw revealed his complete exasperation. He shifted it from side to side, the hard planes of his face tightening. "I think I've made it pretty clear that if we 'kooks' had our druthers, you wouldn't be high on our list of inductees. My clan has no interest in keeping you a vampire or anything else for that matter."

Nina snorted her derision. "Right. That's probably what you say to every dolt before you suck them dry. Whatever. I'm just saying that I won't need your help, because I'm not sticking around."

"There is a God."

"You're very funny. Look, take your mother home. Tell her I said thanks oodles for checking up on me, but it isn't necessary. I'm all good. I don't need your blood. I don't need your clan. I don't need anything but to figure this out so I can go back to life as I knew it." She pressed a hand to his shoulder and gave it a light shove toward the entry to the living room. "Now go away."

Instead of taking the hint, he sidestepped her and leaned back against her fridge. When he jutted his jaw at her with clear defiance, it occurred to her out of the blue that he looked nothing like Svetlanna. Maybe he looked like his father?

And Gawd. He was sick. Sick hot, not sick-sick. As evidenced by the tightening of her fun stuff when she pretended not to peek at him under the cover of her half-closed eyelids. The fleeting thought that if she'd met him under any other circumstances she'd do him came and lingered. It wasn't just one thing that was hot about him either. He was like all over hot. From head to toe he threw off some pretty heady testosterone. If she had to pick just one feature though, it'd probably be his eyes. They ate her up, consumed her when he glared at her all bent out of shape like he was.

Word.

Nina closed her eyes and bade her libido to knock it the fuck off. But his lips . . . firm, but soft and pressed to her own, drawing the kind of response from her she'd never experienced in all of her just-on-the-edge-of-turning-thirty-three years, were killa.

The reluctant memory of their kiss at Lou's reared its head, flashing in her mind's eye. There wasn't a single moment about it she didn't remember like she'd only experienced it moments ago. She tugged at her ponytail with shaky fingers. "Look, can we just do this peacefully? What'll it take to get you off my back?"

"Oh, this has *nothing* to do with me, Nina." He said that like it was preposterous for her to believe he gave a tinker's darn one way or the other what happened to her. "My mother's decided you're her new cause, and she isn't going to let up until she feels comfortable that you're settled. As for me—I did my part. I fed you, apologized to you. That you won't cooperate is your problem."

That Svetlanna was concerned for her left Nina with a stinging warmth curling in her chest. She found herself rubbing the place where her heart used to beat, attempting to alleviate a physical ailment that wasn't really there. From the moment she'd met Svetlanna, she'd liked her, and it softened her urge to shove the pair of them out her door. Her shoulders sagged in defeat. "Okay, what do I have to do to get your mom, who I happen to think is okay, way more okay than you, to go home?"

Greg pushed off her old, avocado green fridge and smiled again, stepping so close to her she had to dig her fingers into her fists to keep from planting her hands on his chest and kneading it through his cable-knit sweater. "Drink the blood she brought and for the sake of my tender ears, shut up."

Nina couldn't move. Thankfully, her mouth still worked. "Bite me, Wing Man."

"Not if you paid me, newbie," he growled down at her, the hum of his voice making her girly bits tingle. "You really are the most exasperating woman alive."

"Well, that'd probably be true, but thanks to you, I'm not alive. I'm dead. That kinda leaves me out of the running."

"Being a vampire has its perks, Nina. It might be easier to simply accept that than to keep trying to find some solution that just doesn't exist."

He was so close she could see a small scar on his chiseled cheek. "I don't want to live eternally and sleep in a coffin," was her feeble, tongue-tied retort.

"Coffins are really uncomfortable from what I hear."

"But I'll miss my soaps."

"There's always TiVO."

Nina laughed. She couldn't seem to stop it. "I guess you'd know, seeing as you've been around forevah."

"And then some."

Her eyes searched his for a moment, looking for what, she wasn't sure. Seconds ticked by with grueling slowness. Greg standing in her space set her teeth on edge, her body to flaming, and left her fighting one crazy emotion after another. Each word he spoke from his yummy vampire lips was like gospel. Every brush of their skin was magnified.

Space. Now. She needed some. Before she examined this rush of girl bullshit any further.

"Gregori?" Svetlanna called from the living room.

His features lightened, showing his love for his mother, whether he liked it or not, and made him finally back away from Nina, easing the pressure in her chest. "Coming," he said, then gave one last look to Nina. A warning look, if she were pressed to define it. "If you can find it in your cold, black, nonexistent heart to do anything, could you at least try being nice to my mother? I won't tolerate disrespect. She has nothing to do with what happened between us."

Nina was ready to shoot fire back at him, but found herself hesitating. Svetlanna didn't do this to her, she reminded herself for the umpteenth time. She'd play nice for Svetlanna. "The only reason I'm agreeable is because I sort of like your mother, even if she is in this with you. So, yeah, I think I can do that," she said over her shoulder, rushing her steps to distance them.

He followed her back to where Svetlanna and Wanda were knee-deep in romance novels. For the love of all things shiny, Wanda was bonding with the kooks.

"I think it's time we go, Mother."

Wanda pouted. "Oh, so soon? Your mother and I were just going over our list of TBRs."

"Your what?" Nina inquired.

"Our 'to be read pile.' Books we'd like to read but haven't gotten to yet." Wanda gave Svetlanna a secretive smile.

Of course.

Svetlanna pursed her lips when Greg held his hand out to her; clearly she was hesitant to leave Nina. "Promise me you'll drink,

Nina. We've brought several packets with us, and you need to pick up the pace if you hope to maintain your health during transition." She held out a tote bag to Nina, but Wanda was the one who grabbed it, jumping to her feet and clutching it to her chest.

"Don't worry. I'll make sure she feeds and that there's no more black market blood."

"Nina?" Svetlanna's question was written all over her beautiful pale face.

"Yeah. I promise. Okay?"

Her smile was genuine and oh, so warm. "Good girl."

Greg took his mother by the elbow and ushered her to the door, whispering in her ear, "I can't believe I let you talk me into coming here. We're clearly not wanted. Now let's go."

Nina's ears burned. She heard each word he spoke as if he'd whispered in her ear. "I can hear you," she warned.

Greg opened the door for his mother, and just as she stepped over the threshold, he smiled at Nina. "Then all's right with the world." He laughed, following Svetlanna out the door.

Her hands clenched at her sides. "God, that man is the biggest asshole!" she yelped.

But Wanda had no pity for Nina as she took the tote bag with packets of blood to the kitchen, putting all three of them in the fridge. "If you ask me, it was you who behaved like an a-hole. Not him."

Nina flipped her the bird, shoving the pile of clothing on her couch away, so she could start looking through some of the crap Wanda had been reading lately. She settled on the couch, crossing her legs Indian style, pulling her hair into a knot behind her head. "They're insane to think it's okay to spend eternity like this. So forgive me if I'm a little touchy about my fate."

Wanda sighed and plopped down beside her, handing her a

stack of romance novels. "You were unbelievably rude, Nina. I like Svetlanna. She's really nice, and she just wants to help you. If you would just try to get to know her, you'd be surprised at what you might learn. Did you know she has her own clothing line?"

Well, that sort of went without saying. She dressed like a movie star. Nina shrugged her shoulders. "I guess that's kind of cool." Clothes and makeup and crap just weren't her kind of thing. Unless Marty forced them on her.

"Know what it's called?"

Nina forced herself to focus on Wanda. "No clue."

"*Fango.*" Wanda laughed as she said it. "Kind of an ironic play on words, huh?"

Yeah. "Very."

"I love their stuff, too. I have two sweaters and some jeans I picked up. Very, very nice."

"Cool," Nina answered distractedly.

Wanda gave her a playful nudge to the shoulder. "See? That's exactly what I mean, Nina. This is an interesting fact about another person—a person who seems to only want what's best for you, and you could care less. If you would just talk to them instead of yelling all the time . . ." She shrugged her shoulders. "I dunno, maybe you'd find they're not so bad."

A moment of remorse, sharp and stinging, assaulted her when she glanced at Wanda. She looked so tired and pale these days, and it couldn't be just from working so hard at Bobbie-Sue. Not if the stack of romance novels she claimed she'd read were any indication of how she spent her free time. Nina gave her a brief smile. "I know, okay? She's a nice lady, and that's fine. Clothes and shoes and purses just aren't my thing, and it still doesn't mean I want to be a vampire. I won't let them suck me in. So let's crack the books and see what we can see. Maybe you missed something important that will help me be human again while you were too distracted by these alpha males you keep talking about."

She needed to find something soon.

She needed to be human again.

Because she'd really dig a can of sardines right now.

CHAPTER
8

Okay, so she'd overdone the blood drinking last night. As the evening with Wanda had worn on, she'd grown hungrier and hungrier. Each divine sip of blood left her guzzling more. It was like a good spinach artichoke dip or a box of chocolates—or she'd venture to compare, like doing Jell-O shots. She couldn't have just one sip.

So she'd done what Svetlanna said to do—fed her inner vampire. Like buffet style.

Nina was sure she hadn't meant her to do it like some gluttonous pig, but that hadn't stopped her, and now she had no blood left. Oddly, the more she drank, the less she gave any thought to how squicked she'd been by it in the first place. In fact, she'd felt so good, she and Wanda had staple-gunned some old blankets to her windows to keep out the sunlight while she slept. A precaution Wanda insisted would be necessary come the summer when the sun set later in the day.

Slamming her refrigerator door with frustration, Nina paced

the floor of her kitchen. A glance at the clock told her it was already seven, and no vampire.

Jackass.

Like it was fair to think he'd show up with more blood after she'd given him such a hard time. She'd only told him a hundred times to leave her the hell alone. He'd finally taken her up on the offer.

Which totally, royally freakin' sucked.

Actually, she soothed herself, this might turn out okay. She'd planned to go see him anyway. She just didn't want to do it while begging for blood, because she'd gotten her oink on the night before. Some blood right now might help her when she sprang her little surprise on him. Feeding left her thinking clearer and her reflexes finely tuned.

She scolded herself for being so impulsive. However, what she'd found last night had to be addressed whether her wits were sharp or not.

Oh, yeah, Greg was all about telling her he didn't want her as part of his precious clan, but what she'd read in *Vampires for Dummies* last night told her every word from his mm-mm good lips was probably just horse puckey. Though obscure, there'd been one single sentence that had kept her riveted until her eyeballs crossed as dawn broke.

According to the book, if she could locate Greg's creator, or sire, as the author had called it, this person had the power to revert her immortality. That was it—just one line, and if she'd read correctly, it was potentially just a myth, but it was enough to give her hope, and she fully intended to take Greg to task on it.

Surely he knew something this important. Which only proved he was full of cow dung when he'd said he had no desire to keep her a vampire and create some super race of night dwellers so they could eventually take over the world.

These freaks could put Pinky and the Brain to shame.

So the question was, who'd created Greg, where was the fuck, and how did she hunt his ass down like so much prey?

Her head took a downward plunge, throbbing with intermittent jabs of agony from behind her eyelids. It was time to feed and feed she would. She'd do whatever it took to hang on until she could find this sire person. Vaguely, she wondered who'd created Greg's sire and if that mattered in the vampire food chain of life with her particular case.

And the 64,000-dollar question—something that had been troubling her since last night. Would it hurt being turned back into a human?

It hadn't hurt turning into a vampire. What if it was like some reenactment of *Alien*? Would the vampire in her ooze out of her belly and . . . Hookay, she had to stop this nonsense and get dressed.

Digging through the rumpled pile of clothes still on her couch, Nina wrinkled her nose with distaste, her eyebrows squishing together. All of a sudden showing up at Greg's with her discount jeans and T-shirts felt cheap, especially if Svetlanna was going to be there. Though she was sure it wasn't Svetlanna's intent, she made her feel shabby with her chic ensembles and perfectly accessorized jewelry, and even Princess Marty couldn't do that to her.

With a cluck of insecurity, Nina headed for her bedroom closet in the hopes she had something Marty'd put together when she'd decided Nina needed not only her color wheel of life revamped, but her stupid wardrobe, too.

The lavender scarf she'd once worn as a symbol she was a newbie and Marty's new recruit at Bobbie-Sue hung haphazardly over a plastic hanger, reminding her she could always go back to selling multilevel cosmetics if all else failed.

And then she laughed at how fucking lame that was.

She'd rather sell breast implants.

Door-to-door.

Naked.

As she sifted through her sparse, and at one time Bobbie-Sue acceptable clothing, Nina tugged on a turquoise sweater that Marty had said accentuated her olive complexion, followed by a dungaree miniskirt she totally hated, but Wanda had talked her into wearing, because she said Nina had hot legs. *Long* and *lean*, were the adjectives Wanda had used.

It couldn't hurt to have long and lean in her favor when visiting with the Wing Man, could it?

For the love of God. That she was even thinking such a thing made her want to bang her head against a brick wall. It didn't matter what the vampire thought. Not even a little, she convinced herself by the time she'd chosen shoes that were totally inappropriate for this time of year, but wouldn't matter because she couldn't feel the chilled winter air and looked übercute, if she did say so herself.

Throwing them on, Nina made her way to the bathroom, hurling some food into Larry's cage as she went to avoid the temptation of actually touching him. At this point, he was as good as a Big Mac in her book, and she just knew once the cravings for dinner subsided, she'd regret the slightest hint of gnawing on Larry.

She'd forgotten that the mirror only gave her a distorted and now rapidly fading image of herself—so a full face worth of makeup wasn't going to happen. She did manage to locate some light pink lip gloss—totally in her color wheel, according to Marty—and glide it over her lips before she deemed herself worthy enough to go see Vlad.

Nina stopped dead in her tracks, frozen with the unbidden thought she'd just had. Wait one friggin' minute. She wasn't dressing to impress the bloodsucker. She was dressing to impress Svet-lanna.

Wasn't she?

The pounding in her head increased, reminding her it didn't matter if she showed up in her birthday suit. She needed to feed.

It was too damned bad she couldn't do that flying thing. The trip out to the Island was going to take forever by train and bus, and there was no way in freakin' Hell she was going to attempt to run from Hackensack to Long friggin' Island. Right now, the idea was just too crazy spooky for her to digest. Besides, there'd come a time that she wouldn't be able to rely on something as nuts as running that kind of distance, because she'd be human again.

Yeah . . . that's right.

FOREVER was an understatement, Nina thought, looking down at her unpolished toes when she arrived at Greg's door hours later. She was bone weary, cranky, and pissed off, but still she hesitated to knock down his door, and it wasn't just because she was exhausted from lack of blood.

Rolling her eyes skyward, Nina sent a plea Upstairs. "Could I get some help here?" What was keeping her from banging down his door and nailing him balls to the wall was beyond her. He owed her an explanation, and she couldn't let herself forget that.

Okay, she had to get her shit together and attack. Her fist rose, preparing to pound out her arrival, when a cold chill ran the length of her spine, crawling in slow increments along each vertebra.

"Huh," she muttered, turning to scan the vast lawns and shrubs of Greg's property. All was quiet in opulence-ville, yet her nose detected the scent of a human. Of course there were humans here. She was smack dab in the middle of upper-middle-class suburbia.

There had to be at least ten families on this block alone—with lots of little humans, too. But this—this smell was different, closer, distinct, and sharp. Like when Wanda had sat next to her on the couch last night, and she'd truly begun to understand how Greg had deciphered Marty was a paranormal, but not a vampire.

Sweet mother, she was smelling people and differentiating their unique odors by species. Cocking her head, she let her nostrils flare. Yep, it was human and a nearby one, too.

Her head banged perpetually, while her skin crawled. She leaned against his door, hoping to find comfort in the cold metal, only to find she couldn't feel it much anyway.

The pocket of her skirt vibrated with a gentle rumble. Nina dug into it, thinking it was probably Wanda checking to see if she'd fed, but the caller ID revealed the number labeled as private.

Flipping her cell open, she tried to catch the call, but it went to voicemail. Damn it, who kept calling her? She shook her head, thinking she'd have to figure it out later.

Nina turned off the sound on her phone before confronting her maker. Whoever wanted her would just have to wait—she had a vampire to take to the mat.

With an angry hand, clenched tight, Nina pounded on the door, eating up more of her energy than she'd planned to expend.

When it jerked open, Nina fell into Greg's tall, imposing frame, stumbling over the sandals she was now wishing she hadn't chosen to wear.

"Look who's come to dinner," he chided, enveloping her in his hard embrace.

Her nose twitched violently against his chest, his scent invading her nostrils, manly and delicious, blocking out the scent of the invisible human. Righting her, Greg took a step back and assessed her with those hard, green eyes. "Hungry?"

There was no point in hiding it. "Yeah. Among other things."

"What happened to the blood we left for you last night? I didn't expect to see you until at the very earliest, tomorrow."

That he expected anything tweaked her gut. "I went a little overboard, I guess," she offered with a sheepish downward cast of her eyes.

Without a word, he strode to the kitchen in the direction of the fridge, the muscles of his back bunching under the tapered white shirt he wore. It grazed the top of his legs, drawing her eyes to the backs of his thighs, then dragging them steadily upward.

Nina licked her dry lips. Sheeit, that ass.

Tearing her eyes from his butt, which was a supernatural feat all unto itself, Nina found herself paying closer attention to the details of the interior of Greg's home. It didn't look much like a castle on the inside. It had a warmer feeling to it, with its throw rugs scattered about, mahogany furniture that gleamed, and vases in various heights and shapes, sitting atop shelves. It bore a woman's touch, and that brought a shadow of a smile to Nina's lips.

Her reluctant feet trudged behind him, salivating when he poured the blood into a glass and shoved it in her direction. Nina's belly growled, and she pressed it against the island countertop to quell the noise.

At least he wasn't razzing her for coming to him to get her daily blood supply.

He braced his forearms on the counter and leaned in so they were at eye level. "So, you finally decided to give in, huh?"

Scratch that. He wanted her at his mercy. Nina eyeballed him angrily. "Yeah. Well, it wasn't like I had a choice. So here I am being a good vampire and nurturing my inner Dracula."

"Headache?"

"So?"

Greg's expression softened for a moment, albeit brief. "I remember them well."

"It sucks," she replied, draining the cup with a voracious gulp.

"I remember that as well."

"Yeah? Do you remember how much you didn't want to be a vampire, too?"

Greg's eyes became distant. Something flashed in them before he focused on her again. "I do."

"Good. Then you'll understand when I tell you I think you're all full of shit. I found something last night. Something that just might fix this whole fucked-up mess you made and prove you bunch of whack jobs are liars."

"Your mouth . . ." he muttered, his eyes going smoky.

"My what?"

"Your mouth. It amazes me that such a pretty thing can spew such ugly words."

He thought her mouth was pretty; her nipples tightened at that . . .

Stop that right now, Nina. Immediately. "There's more where that came from."

"Such a surprise."

"Look, I don't care if you like my colorful language or not. I found something last night, and I want some answers."

His look grew bored. God, she hated when he dismissed her with just a caustic glance. "Wikipedia again? Or wait, one of those romance novels, right?"

"I think I've told you once, don't discount what some of those sappy books say. Some of those writers aren't so far off the mark. And no, it wasn't the romance novels, or Wikipedia. It was *Vampires for Dummies*."

"Interesting title."

She ignored his sly reference to her IQ. "Turns out, I can get my mortality back."

"Do tell," he drawled, cocking an eyebrow in his very accomplished disdainful way.

"There wasn't much, but it said if I can find the nut that created the freak that created me, I can be turned back. And I want me some of that."

"Me being the freak, of course." His mouth twisted as he spoke the words.

Okay, so that was harsh. He wasn't a freak. Just a liar. "That would be you."

"Didn't I warn you about some of the stuff that's out there? Contrary to what your romance novels say, there's plenty of misinformation."

"They're not mine, they're Wanda's, and if that's true, how come I can't look at a crucifix without my eyeballs burning? If what you say is for real, why is it that I feel like a slab of bacon when the sun's up or that I can't keep my eyes open during daylight?"

"And you read that in the romance novels."

"I didn't. Wanda did."

"That still doesn't mean everything you read is true, Nina."

Which only strengthened her belief that Gregori Statleon was hiding something. All of this "let me help you feed" shit just might be hiding a deeper ulterior motive. What, she couldn't fathom. What if the more she drank, the more vampiric she became? Like the more she drank the juice, the more poison seeped into her system . . .

But Svetlanna encouraged her to drink, and though Nina couldn't pinpoint what it was about Greg's mother that lent to trust, it was something she couldn't ignore and was rooted deep in her gut. Maybe Svetlanna had no idea her son did this kind of shit.

Keeping her a vampire, as unwilling as she was to be one, was crazy. Yet, she *did* need Greg in order to feed, and he wasn't offering up other solutions for blood donors, but he'd claimed he didn't feed on other people. Maybe her dependency on him supplying the blood was all just a part of his diabolical plan to keep her coming back for more. Though he'd just said he remembered what it was to *not* want to be a vampire, leading one to believe he'd been turned against his will.

This web was one seriously tangled weave.

Refusing to reveal all of her suspicions, she decided overlooking some things in favor of the bigger picture might garner better results. "How about we don't nitpick? The basic facts Wanda's read are mostly true. So I don't see why what I read can't be, too. Unless you like keeping me a vampire against my will."

"Oh, there's nothing I'd like more than to get you off my back, believe me."

Nina took a different path, attempting to play on his sympathy. "How did you become a vampire, anyway? I mean, didn't it piss you off? If vampires can't procreate, then you sure weren't born one—which leads me to believe you were turned against your will. Unless . . . you said you're almost five hundred. Dude, that puts your birth back in the fifteen hundreds. I did a little research on that, too. Surviving back then had some pretty shitty odds. Becoming a vampire would definitely up your chances for survival in a time like that, right?"

"You could look at it that way, I suppose."

Oh, the mysterious, evasive facade again. "How about you tell me what way to look at it?"

"I think it's far more amusing if I just let you tell me what's what. Your supposition tickles my funny bone."

"What's the big secret? How old were you when this—this vampire shit happened?"

He pushed off the counter, his lips a thin line of deafening silence.

So it pissed him off, then. If it pissed him off to talk about what'd happened when he was turned, why the fuck was he being so closed-mouthed about it? You'd think he'd want to share his anger with her—bond over it or some psychotic shit. Maybe, if he helped her, he could be reverted back, too. But he couldn't possibly want that, now could he? Gregori Statleon didn't seem like the kind of guy who didn't get what he wanted, and that led her back to her original thought. He was a part of some sick crap, though he may not have wanted that in the beginning of his immortality, and now he wanted as many people as he could sink his fangs into to be a part of it, too. He'd bought into the cult—he'd been brainwashed.

Omigod—this was too much like the multilevel sales of Bobbie-Sue. She hadn't fallen for it then, and she wasn't falling for it now.

Nina cornered him, sticking her chest out and spitting her words like hard gravel up into his face. "How old were you when you were turned?"

Greg's hands clamped onto her shoulders, holding her away from him, like she had the plague. "What difference does that make to you?"

"Call me curious."

"It was a long time ago . . ."

"Answer the freakin' question."

"Twenty-three."

Nina snorted, recalling what she'd read about the sixteenth century. "That's a pretty decent life span for back then. Food was scarce, living situations were even worse. From what I read, you didn't last much past your forties, unless you were of some prominence. Did your family have money?"

"We managed."

"Where were you born? I'm guessing Romania, because it

seems like that's where all good vampires come from, and your last name is pretty ethnic."

"Yep, in what is now known as Bucharest. Not Transylvania, like most would assume. Though we immigrated to England when I was a child."

"Why don't you have an accent?"

"Because 'thou doth drive me to ale' just doesn't quite cut it in the twenty-first century like 'you could drive a man to drink'."

A giggle almost escaped her lips, but she fought to contain it. "Quit foolin' around."

"I've acclimated over the centuries. I had to. I pay close attention to trends, slang, the news, etcetera. Can you imagine how the neighbors would talk if I wore a doublet, a cape, and tights?"

"What the hell is a doublet?" Nina shook her head. "Never mind. You're still avoiding the question. How did this happen to you? Did this vampire bite just you or your entire family? I mean, Svetlanna's a vampire, and she's your mother. Where's your father in all of this?"

His reply was cool. "My father's dead, and Svetlanna isn't my mother. Not biologically anyway."

If words were bombs, those very fuckers he'd just spoken would be spinning around, hissing violently before they exploded. Nina's shock was evident. Confusion came only after the concern and sadness she felt, knowing only too well what kind of loss that equaled. "I-I'm . . . sorry. I didn't know. You guys look nothing alike, but I guess I just thought you looked like your dad." Her frown eased, and her eyes softened.

Greg tilted her chin upward. "I like a contrite Nina. She's much sweeter. My biological mother's been dead a very long time." His voice was tinged with sadness; though restrained, it was there. "Svetlanna was turned just before me. She sort of adopted me, and together we learned how to adjust."

"So you became vampires together?" Now we were getting somewhere.

"Yep."

Or not. "And that's all you have to say?"

"What else would you like me to say, Nina?"

"How about you quit yanking my chain? We're beating around the bush, and it's pissing me off. I want you to tell me who created you, and I want to know now. I deserve to know who this shithead is, so I can find him and beat the information out of him. Stop with all the secrecy and spill, or I'll be forced to freak."

His laughter rankled her. It was crisp, harsh, and bordered on mocking her. "It wasn't a he. It was a she, and I have no idea where *she* is."

Shut. Up. A woman had done this? Somehow, in her mind, only the male counterparts were smarmy enough to do this kind of thing. She'd always just assumed men were the troublemakers when it came to turning folks. "A woman turned you?"

"Damn feminism, huh?"

"Who? Who was she?"

"A woman . . ."

"Damn it, Greg! What was her name, and where did you last see her? The annual blood drinker's ball?"

"Actually, I think it was Christmas 2005."

Nina wrapped her fingers in his freshly pressed shirt and pulled him to her. Which was a mistake, if her body had anything to say about it, but she plowed on despite it. "What-is-her-name?"

Greg surrounded her wrists with his hands, clamping them so tightly she lost the grip on his shirt and reared back, but he didn't let them go. "Lisanne. Her name is Lisanne." He said her name between clenched teeth, like it literally had to be pulled from his jaws.

Finally. An answer. Nina sagged against him for a moment, drawing an uncanny strength from his presence and another one of those unwilling responses from her body. A body that, since she'd fed, was now very aware of everything, including the rigid line of his crotch. His eyes told her she'd gone way far. Maybe too far.

She couldn't reconcile his anger about this woman Lisanne, if he liked being a vampire so much. The question still remained, had he been turned willingly, or had he gone down with a fight? His statement of sympathetic understanding and his anger led her to believe he hadn't been willing. His reluctance to tell her who his creator was—a stark contradiction. If he hated this woman, why wouldn't he give her up with much less pulling of the teeth? Why would he protect her identity? Was she mean? Could he get in trouble for giving this bitch up? Oooooh, maybe some crazy punishment was involved if he told her.

This was a WTF moment, fo sho. As in, what the fuck was going on? Nina decided he was already riled enough. She'd clearly opened some wounds and poured salt on them. Letting go of the how and why of Greg's origins seemed wise at this point. Not that she was afraid of a good old-fashioned verbal spar or anything, but contrary to popular belief, she did know when to can it and . . . He. Was. A. Vampire. 'Nuff said. "Okay, so why don't you tell me how to find this chick?"

"I did tell you."

"Nah, you gave me some shit about how you haven't seen her since Christmas 2005. I don't think I believe you. If she's in charge of this clan crap, then there must be a way to contact her. Surely you clan-eese keep in touch, talk from time to time?"

"Um, no, and no one said she was in charge of anything."

"If she made ya, she's in charge."

"No, she's not. She may be my faction's creator, but many of us have branched out, broken off, and created our own clans. Yes, she's the person responsible for my creation, but she doesn't own me."

Wow, talk about all het up. His face hardened when he'd said Lisanne didn't *own* him.

"Jesus, effin'. There are more of you than just this one clan?"

"Hundreds of us. Thousands, I'd venture to guess. Our clans are much like the politics of humans. They're many and in all varying degrees. We have zealots, pacifists, conservatives, and rebels, too. Though, I'm sure you'll be relieved to know my clan's take on things is probably by far the least likely to offend a human."

Holy Hannah. How did these people go unnoticed? "Who's in charge of your clan?"

He presented her with another overconfident smile. "Me."

Greeeeaaat. "Does this mean you're the boss of me, because you turned me?"

His chuckle was thick, vibrating through her ears and reaching far into her chest. "Yeah, it kinda does."

"Fat chance."

"Your *only* chance."

Fucknuts. She wasn't going to get into who was the boss of whom. If she could find a way to return to her mortality again, it wouldn't matter what he bossed around. "Does this Lisanne have a phone number? An email address? Something? Any way to find her?"

His face clouded, his eyes darkening. "You know what boggles my mind, Nina?"

"What?"

"If you think I'm diabolical enough to want to keep you a vampire, what makes you think Lisanne would be any less likely to want that as well? No matter whose clan you're a part of, you're still a vampire, and if you think that's what I secretly want, then we all must want that, right?"

Um, well . . . she was reserving judgment for now. "Forget it. I don't care what anyone wants. I only know that *I* don't want to be a vampire and if there's a shot in hell of me regaining my mortality, I'm going after it. This is my life we're talking about here, and one less vampire in this kooky scheme won't be the end of the world. Got that, Bat Boy?" She loosened a finger from his grip and wiggled it under his nose.

He nipped it, letting his incisors elongate. The act itself was primal, enticing, and made her want to lick them. "Loud and proud, baby."

Nina shuddered. The visual of his mouth on hers returned with a vengeance. "Put your teeth away. So how do I find her?"

His shoulders shrugged, the rise and fall of his shirt brushing the longer lengths of his milk chocolate hair. "I have no clue. We don't do the Secret Santa thing at the office much."

Exasperation finally got hold of her, and she screamed her rage, "Arghhhhhhhhhhh! You do so know, and what I want to know is why you don't want me to know!"

"Huh?"

Enough pussyfooting around. "If you don't tell me where this chick is, I'm going to—"

"What, Nina?" Greg ground the question out, hauling her to him with a rough jerk, fusing every inch of their flesh together. "Don't threaten me," he whispered against her ear, leaving a hot shiver in its wake.

Her eyes flashed a challenge. "I just did."

His lips whispered across her sensitive skin. "I can promise you the tactics you use with everyone else won't fly with me. I'm not much intimidated by your loud mouth or your Bruce Lee take on life."

Her comeback hitched in her throat. She wanted to tell him she'd show him just what going kamikaze on his ass was all about, but dayum, he was mad-hot when he wouldn't take her shit. She'd never encountered a man who not only rose to the occasion, but virtually dared her to bring it.

And she had to stop and begrudgingly admire that.

However briefly.

"I'd take my hands off of me, if I were you." It was the best she could summon while she warred with the notion that his hands on her, his body slapped up against hers, was a total contradiction to how she felt about this whole hot mess.

Greg's chuckle slid from his lips in satiny ribbons of mirth. "Or you'll what?"

Well, she'd—she'd . . . she couldn't think when he was in such close proximity. She was so lost in the hunger she felt from deep within. Lost in the crazy craving to consume this man, lap up every last lickable inch of him, drive her own body closer to his, until they were one tangled entity of flesh. His teeth elongated again, and Nina watched in rapt fascination as he lowered his mouth to the spot on her neck, grazing the tender flesh with the lightest of pricks. The rush of warmth gathering at the apex of her thighs and the beading of her nipples was so close to unbearable it made her weak, leaving her clinging to his shoulders for support.

A crazy visual raced across her mind's eye, making her arch her neck as she envisioned him drinking from her.

Fuuuuuck. This just couldn't be. Wanting him to take a hunk out of her was ludicrous, preposterous. There were other "ous" words, too, but she couldn't think of them when he was so close, wedging a hard thigh between her legs and taunting her with his hot lips.

Her back bowed, allowing the full weight of her spine to fall on his forearm, thick and muscled. Nina scrunched her eyes shut, gulping. No, no, and no. Only her will of iron kept her from succumbing to the powerful pull his body seemed to have on hers. She walked her fingers up along his chest, ignoring the low moan he emitted and grabbed back onto his shirt.

Her words were ragged as she hauled herself upward to look

him in the eyes. "Let's get one thing straight. You-are-not-the-boss-of-me."

Greg's chiseled face glowered down at hers, his teeth fully visible. "Oh, but I am, and struggle over that all you will, Nina, but I'm in charge whether you like it or not."

Ohhhhh, nice display of some serious bad-ass. And if she were a smart girl, which she prided herself on being, she'd pause to remember that he'd been a vampire for a long time. If the books were correct, the longer you were a vamp, the stronger you became. It was like some crazy video game where you built up life force points or something. Now if she chose to venture any farther over this line between them, she might reach the point of no return when it came to his patience.

Ugly. Things could get ugly very fast.

Options?

Get the hell up out of his shit and let it go.

Yes, that was definitely the safest route to take in light of all that fire and brimstone he was shooting at her with his eyes and easier than admitting she was having a momentary lapse into the realm of the pansy-assed.

Nina let her body go limp in feigned submission. "Let me go."

And he did, just seconds before he pressed his lips to hers and then whispered, "I think you're getting the hang of this."

Her nostrils flared in reignited anger, only to catch a scent she was familiar with. A scent that made her want to scream with longing for her old life. "Oh, my God, you ate a Ring Ding just before I got here, didn't you? How could youuuuuuuu?"

He grinned, that boyish grin he reserved for a good neener, neener. "Yeah. I did, and I was hungry."

Growling out her anguish over not being able to eat junk food anymore—or anything for that matter, Nina clapped her hands on his shoulders and pushed him away from her. "Fuck you, Gregori

Statleon. You bloodsucking, mortality stealing, junk food eating jerk! I'll figure out where to find this Lisanne. If you won't tell me, maybe I'll look some of my fellow clan members up and ask them!" She strode over to the fridge and reached in to grab several packets of blood, juggling them as she headed for the door.

"And don't go thinking I won't do it either," she yelled her threat.

She put a package of the blood between her teeth just so she could slam his door behind her for effect.

So, yeah. Take that shit and—and . . . hoo, boy . . .

Nina looked down at her hands, the blood still between her clamped jaw. Now here was a dilemma. Exactly how in theee hell was she going to explain all of this blood to the people who rode public transportation?

God, why didn't she ever think before she reacted? Her hot temper had always been her downfall. She just didn't know when to shut it. She had to win and win at all costs. Always have the last word.

Fuck, she was having one of those moments Marty was always yammering about, where you discovered you were caught up in an endless circle of the same result.

The door popped open behind her, and Greg's face, partly shadowed by the streetlight, appeared. He stuck his hand through it and let a plastic grocery bag flutter to the ground. "Thought you might need one of these," he said teasingly before quietly closing the door.

CHAPTER
9

"So Nina was here." His mother made her way down the staircase, gliding her hand along the mahogany banister with a glib smile on her face.

Greg turned his back on her, striding to the living room to hide the smile on his face. "As if you couldn't hear her. I think South Jersey heard her."

"You like her," she accused, coming up behind him and tapping his shoulder, forcing him to face her.

He let his head dip to his chest, clenching his jaw. "I want to strangle her."

"Which is a clear sign you like her."

"You've concluded this how?"

Svetlanna scoffed, rolling up the sleeves of her sweater. "You couldn't care less about the women you bring home. You purposely find women who don't want to stick around any more than you want them to. They know the score going into a venture with

you, and you know it, too. You certainly don't care enough about
them to want to strangle them. Nina infuriates you, and it makes
you boiling mad. Wanting to strangle her is a sure sign she's gotten
under your skin."

He had to fight an ironic smile. "Who could possibly like someone like Nina, Mother? She's not remotely likeable. She's rude,
she's pushy, and to top things off, she wants to find Lisanne." *She's
also hot in a tomboy sorta way, she has killer eyes the color of black olives,
and a mouth that you have dirty thoughts about, Statleon.*

Svetlanna blanched, her pale skin going gray around her eyes.
"That's not good. Lisanne isn't someone Nina can handle on her
own, never mind the fact that we have other matters to deal with
when it comes to that viper."

The "other" matters should hold precedent for him, but he
shoved them to the back of his mind, because Nina, slender and
sloe-eyed, held court there.

"I heard you tell her you didn't know where Lisanne was."

"Which is the truth."

"I know."

He almost hated to ask, but his sense of honor made him. "Do
you know where Lisanne is, Mother?"

"Hardly. And even if I did, I don't know that I'd tell Nina. She's
raw right now, Greg. Finding that bit . . . er, Lisanne would only
make things worse, and this crazy quest Nina's on to get back her
humanity just isn't possible. But we have bigger things to contend
with if we're to stay in the moment."

"Like?"

"Like your attraction to her. Don't bother to deny it, Gregori.
I know you almost as well as I know myself, and Nina's a real kick
in the pants for you."

More like a fucking kick in the gut. The very idea that a woman
as brash and as loud as Nina could turn him on was making him

nuts. He hadn't been able to stop thinking about her since she'd first passed out on his doorstep. "Her mouth is like the Grand Canyon—wide and cavernous. I've never been even a little attracted to a woman like that, and you know it, Mother." With the wave of a hand he dismissed Svetlanna's statement and wandered to his desk, pulling out his chair and dropping his tired ass into it. A round with Nina was like twelve with Evander Holyfield.

"That may well be, but it's her opinionated take on life, her less-than-dazzled-by-you attitude that's keeping you up at night. That's new and refreshing, I'd suspect, given the women you usually consort with. There aren't many women out there, human or vampire, who don't fall at your feet because of either your power or your money. Nina wants neither. It would seem all of your charm and persuasiveness just doesn't fly with Nina." Svetlanna cast him a sly grin, clearly pleased she might have hit the nail on the head.

He shifted in his chair uncomfortably. Goddamn his tooth and that stupid dentist's office.

"And the guilt you feel for biting her isn't the only reason you can't sleep. So don't try and snow me."

For the love of Pete. Not only did his mother know him, she had no qualms about using her knowledge as a weapon. He continued his silence, knowing it only solidified her suspicions, but he damned well wouldn't openly admit it. Yeah, Nina's too-skinny frame made him hotter than Hades, and yeah, those lips of hers were hard not to get lost in even when she was spewing foul language. And okay, all that dark hair that she tied up in a ponytail was of endless fascination to his fingers, fingers that itched to sink deeply into the silken threads. It was all he could do last night not to show up on her doorstep.

First, because she needed to be taught a lesson about biting the hand that fed her. Had she not shown up, he would have sought her out later in the evening. He wasn't some monster who'd let her turn to dust, whether she liked to believe that or not.

He'd apologized, and he was doing everything in his power to make his mistake right by offering her nourishment and guidance to the ways of his clan. Yet Nina wasn't giving him an inch. Yes, he'd done something irreversible. Yes, he'd changed her life totally in a matter of seconds, but his intention was never to involve an innocent—that just wasn't his thing. But with no way to fix this, other than to move on, they had to live in the here and now. And right now, she needed him. That he was taking a perverse pleasure in that was beside the point.

Second, because he needed the distance from her. Simply being near her made him want things he'd never considered in almost five hundred years.

And he didn't like it, for Christ's sake.

She just wasn't the kind of woman he typically took pleasure in bedding. The women he hooked up with knew where he stood in the mating game, and he never dwelled on them once they were gone. Not like this anyway.

Yet here he was, unable to get this skinny, cranky wench out of his head. When she'd arched her neck at him so temptingly tonight, it was all he could do not to sink his fangs into her and drink her rare, sweet blood. And rare it was, having been, of all the damned things, AB negative. Stopping himself from drinking from her was that much harder because her blood was one of the rarest.

"I don't want to keep repeating myself, Gregori," his mother's voice interrupted his dark, wanton thoughts about Nina, "but she could be the answer to our . . . *my* prayers."

His smile of irony over this predicament with Nina hardened. "The hell she is."

"Don't be angry with me, mister. You're the one who's spent

all of these centuries playing around. Sometimes you have to pay the piper."

He didn't need his mother to remind him of the severity of his pending situation. What he did need was to get Nina out of his system. Steepling his hands under his chin, Greg paused to get a clearer perspective.

What he came up with was simple.

This wasn't good.

And it wasn't just the urgent issue with Lisanne.

"HEY, you okay?" Marty's lips moved against Nina's ear so she could hear her over the caterwauling of karaoke night. Her voice sounded like a bass drum in her head, pinging around and leaving behind an echo.

Nina pulled back and eyeballed her. "I'm a vampire," she hissed back. "No, I'm not okay." Thankfully, the loser who was trashing a perfectly good Tom Jones song finished and the karaoke MC took his ten-minute break.

Wanda sat on the other side of Nina at the bar, twirling the big, looped pink straw in her virgin daiquiri. She looked better tonight than she had in a while in her hip-hugging jeans and tank top, with a short green sweater that fell just under her breasts. Yet, even in her misery, Nina still thought she looked thinner. Wanda poked her arm. "Did you feed?"

Nina's response was edgy and tense. "Yes, Wanda. I fed."

Wanda folded her napkin in a neat square with prim fingers. "Don't get huffy. What kind of friend would I be if I didn't at least check? It seems all I do these days is check to be sure you're doing what's necessary to keep you on this plane. My apologies if I don't want you to turn to dust."

Nina let her head fall into her hands, leaning her elbows on the sticky bar and allowing the curtain of her long hair shelter her from the packed space. While she'd fed, and plenty, she still felt distracted and jittery. Like she was going to jump out of her skin any second. Nothing felt comfortable or familiar anymore. She couldn't eat a basket of Buffalo wings—which was typical for her on karaoke night—because she'd yark. She couldn't chugalug a few brewskies—because she'd yark. She couldn't feel the temperature outside, but she could feel the frenzy of heat Greg evoked in her.

She couldn't, she couldn't, she couldn't.

She couldn't even karaoke.

A sob welled in her throat. She wasn't much of a cryer, but this was heinous. She loved to karaoke. She loved to karaoke to Barry Manilow. But tonight, not even that had the power to soothe her. Not even her beloved Barry Manilow. Oh, God. What was the world coming to if not even Barry could make things right? This was like death by lack of "Can't Smile Without You."

"I can't believe you forgot the words to 'Copacabana'," Marty chided, popping open her purse to dig out her compact. Because Marty just couldn't be anything less than perfect at all times.

"I was distracted," Nina said from the basket she'd made of her fingers, letting her forehead fall into it. Not that she could believe it either. It was, after all, Barry. There wasn't much she loved more than him. Yet trying to get her sing on with a good round of karaoke just wasn't working tonight. The only thing she could think of was trying to find this Lisanne and get her life back.

Oh, and it'd be peachy if she could stop thinking about Greg and his yummy neck. That'd be an added bonus.

Wanda stuck her head under Nina's hands. Her worry touched Nina and aggravated the shit out of her all at the same time. "But it's *Barry*, Nina. You never forget the words to *anything Barry*," she said in a hushed, reverent tone usually reserved for places of worship.

"Wanda?"

"Uh-huh?"

"Get the frig out of my face. I'm not exactly on my game, and if it's okay with you, I'd really like it if you dropped it."

"Nina?" Wanda asked, pinning her with her soft blue eyes.

"What?"

"No."

"No?"

"Yep. You heard me. I'm sick of you wallowing. Boo-hoo, I'm a vampire. Wah-wah, I have to get blood from the hottest guy on planet Earth. Cut it out already, Nina, and get on with the business of living . . ." she paused, "or not living. But for the love of all things shiny, stop acting like the end of the world has happened. You can have a life, even if it involves many, many lives. That makes you lucky, if you ask me."

Her face clouded over for a moment, and it made Nina pause with momentary concern. What was going on with Wanda? If someone as insensitive as Nina could pick up these odd, but subtle signals Wanda was giving off these days, she knew she had to be missing something of great importance. She'd been so wrapped up in herself, in typical Nina fashion, she hadn't had time to question Wanda about it.

And Wanda obviously wasn't going to give her the op. "Look at Marty. She adjusted, and so can you. In fact, I would have thought you were scrappier than she is, but I guess I was wrong."

Nina didn't even have the get-up-and-go to care that Wanda was presenting a challenge in the will department between her and Marty. She just wanted her old life back, and in her yearning, she forgot all about any troubles Wanda could be having. "Well, Wanda, I'll tell ya what. If this ever happens to you and you're left broke, with no job and nothing on the horizon for future employment except maybe a position as the Wal-Mart greeter, I'll offer comfort, because you have a light at the end of the tunnel. A hot guy with some blood."

Wanda grimaced. "Okay. I'm out. When you find your big girl panties, you just let me know." Sliding her head out from beneath Nina's chin, she grabbed her drink and sauntered off to the dance floor, inviting Marty to go with her.

But Marty had one last parting piece of wisdom, shooing Wanda away with a smile. "I just have to say this, Nina, and then I'm not saying anything else, because you really don't have your listening ears on—even with your new, supersonic hearing. I know this is hard—this adjustment. *Nobody* knows better than me, and at least that much you can't deny. I know you have no job, but there are alternatives. Wanda and I have only told you a million times we'd find something other than cosmetics sales at Bobbie-Sue for you, but you just won't budge. We would never let you just be thrown out on the street.

"You have friends, Nina. You have *us*. Friends who take a boatload of crap from you and still keep coming back to try and help. I know all the blood drinking and living forever stuff has you freaked out, whether you'll admit it or not, but my life is good and every time you knock being a paranormal with your jokes, you kinda knock my way of life. A way of life I've come to love. A lot. What happened to you—it was an accident. If you'd lost a limb, it'd be almost the same thing. You'd have to learn to live without it. I'm not saying it was an easy fate for me to accept, but once I was at Keegan's, I knew I had no choice, and then I tried like hell to fit in—even with all the human haters in his pack."

Marty sucked her cheeks in while Nina remained silent, slinging her purse over her shoulder. "Maybe what you and Wanda read in that *Vampires for Dummies* is true, but maybe not. What if Greg really is telling the truth and you can't be turned back? So until you know more, you're a vampire. Get over yourself. End rant." Marty rose and pushed away from the bar, her cute butt prepared to sashay away. She stopped momentarily and turned back around. "Oh, and, Nina?"

Jay-seuss. "There's more?"

"Just one more thing." She smacked her lips, rubbing them lips together to make sure her lipstick had complete coverage. "You're even crankier as a vampire than you ever were as a human."

Ba-dump-bump.

Nina pressed her thumbs against her temple, rotating them over her eyes. God, she really was a bitch. Hadn't it been her who'd called Marty a whiner because she'd been so distressed over her lycan state?

Wasn't she behaving far worse by not only whining, but acting out against everyone and everything?

Uh, yeah.

Though Nina hated like hell to admit it, Wanda was right. Her big girl panties needed some tailoring. Squaring her shoulders, she sat up and shook off the heavy cloud of bad mojo she'd been beaten down with since she woke up and made a conscious effort to start figuring out what to do next.

To start, she needed to find this Lisanne. A job she was qualified for, unless it was at the local 7-Eleven serving up slushies on the midnight shift, was out of the question until she could go out in daylight hours again. The root of this began with her reverting back; the rest would have to wait until she was human. It just couldn't wait long, because she needed cash. Like bad. Her rent was due, and so was her cable bill.

So Greg claimed he didn't know where Lisanne was, and he'd also claimed he was the leader of his clan. Who were the members of this clan, and where did she have to go digging to see what they knew? Would they keep a lid on any Lisanne info if Greg ordered it? Could he order it—more to the point—would he?

"Are you Nina?"

Her thoughts were interrupted by a pudgy, moonfaced man with a flat nose, dimpled chin, and thick lips. She'd seen him eyeballing her when she and the girls had first entered the bar, ignoring his apparent interest. For the love of dick. Clearly her "not if you had *two* schlongs" vibe hadn't been conveyed properly.

And how the frig did he know her name? "Do I know you?" Suspicion rang crystal clear in her question.

He wedged in between the swarming bodies at the bar and smiled, revealing small, white teeth. His plaid flannel shirt did nothing to hide the paunch hanging over his tan Dickies. The thin wisp of his reddish-hair, brushed over his balding scalp, left him looking out of place with the trendy, thirty-something crowd.

His silence blocked out the noise of the bar.

"Do I know you?" she repeated, narrowing her eyes.

His affable expression didn't change. "No, but you might want to."

Nina grunted, pushing strands of her hair over her shoulder. So not what she needed tonight. Every guy that had ever come on to her with his slick one-liners thought she wanted to "know" them. "Look, if you thought you were gonna get lucky with me, you got another thing coming. Your luck just ran out. So scurry off back to your hole." She circled her two fingers around the circumference of her face for emphasis. "This is my not interested face." Then she promptly turned her attention back to the grimy surface of the bar, officially dismissing him.

He leaned an elbow on the bar and cupped his chin. The round moon shape of his face pointing in her direction. His eyes were watery and blue, with more bushy hair for eyebrows than he had on his head. "No, you misunderstand."

Christ on a roller coaster. Couldn't he see she was trying to think? "Oh, by all means, do enlighten me," she said distractedly, plotting her next move with Greg.

Placing his hand on her arm, he gripped it lightly. The spot where he rested it suddenly felt hot and uncomfortable. "If you'll just listen to me, I'd be happy to explain."

"So explain," she demanded, fighting the wave of nausea a tray of burgers passing under her nose brought.

"I believe I have something you want."

Out of sight. "Like?"

"Like something big."

Lord, men were predictable. He was talking package. She'd sigh if she still had the ability to. All men thought they had one to rival a blue whale, and in their zeal, they thought sharing that with women who were strangers was copasetic. Blech. Why was it that men thought the most important thing to a woman was dick? Well, to be fair, it didn't hurt, but it wasn't everything. "Dude, take your something," she swiped her index fingers in the air, "big and go away." She gave him that killa glare she was such a pro at for follow-up.

His smile never left his face. He wasn't fazed even a little.

Huh. So had she lost her cower power when she'd become a vampire, too? Men usually backed right off when she gave them the "look," but this guy was anything but unsettled.

"No, no. you're misunderstanding me, Nina. I'm not trying to pick you up. You're not my type. Not at all." His smile faltered when he said that, wrinkling his nose briefly. Then his placid smile returned. "Tell me, would you like to know where Lisanne is?"

Nina's stomach dived. She might not have intestines that worked anymore, but you could have fooled her, because they were jumping around like grease on a hot griddle. Her cautious glance gave way to some internal questions. How could anyone, other than Greg and maybe Svetlanna, know she wanted to find Lisanne? "Who the hell are you?"

The shrug of his sloped shoulders was casual. "Who I am doesn't matter. *What* I am definitely does."

The hell? Nina's mind raced to put this together. He had to be some kind of paranormal something, if he knew of Lisanne's existence . . . what next? Fairies? Witches, warlocks? She let her nostrils absorb his scent, flaring them to detect a hint of paranormal or human. Fuck, who could think with all these smells? "Okay, so *what* are you?"

He leaned into her, his flannel shirt grazing her fingers. "I'm a vampire. Just like you. I've been trying to call you for days." His reply was cheerful, the serene smile still plastered on his face.

Hackles rose along her spine, chasing each other up to her arms, even though she knew they were only a product of her imagination. Were these damn vampires like everywhere and humans had just never been the wiser? Yeah, this guy was pale, but he didn't look nearly as imposing as Greg did. In fact, he looked pretty harmless.

Nina flared her nostrils again. Though she was beginning to decipher scents, like Marty was an AKC wannabe and Wanda was definitely human, she still wasn't fully capable of sniffing him out completely. He didn't smell human, but that didn't mean her olfactory senses weren't snafued—situation normal all fucked up. So she decided to play dumb. The less said the better. And was he really the one who'd been trying to call her? "A vampire?" She gave him her best beguilingly innocent look. Which wasn't easy, considering she mostly just frowned. She had no practice in the art of flirt. "I have no idea what you're talking about."

Marty'd warned her about being careful who knew what she was, and for once, she was going to take heed. He could be some crazy poser who just *thought* he was a vampire. She'd seen that all over the Internet. But that didn't explain how he knew Lisanne. Although, in his favor, "I'm a vampire" wasn't your standard pickup line.

"I can prove it to you," he assured her.

Nina gave a snort filled with sarcasm. "Oh, really? Like how? Wait, never you mind. You're nuts. Go stalk someone else with your something big."

His smile wavered just a little and began to border creepy. "Oh, Nina. I'm not crazy at all. If you want to find Lisanne, I can help."

"So help."

"Not here."

"But I like *here*."

"Here's crowded."

"I like crowds."

"I don't."

"Tough shit."

He sat silently beside her, a stoic calm in not just his body language, but also on his face.

This was a fast train to nowhere. Maybe if she just tested the waters without showing too much interest . . . "Okay, so I take it you're not going to go away. Why would you want to help me find this Lisanne, if I was even looking for her, and I'm not saying I am. How do you know anything about her? And if you've been trying to call me, how did you get my cell phone number?" Smooth. That was pretty smooth and not too interested. If he wasn't just some crazy, he'd have an answer.

"I have my ways. Word gets around in our circles, if you know what I mean. Like clan circles. Like *Statleon* clan circles."

Well, there went the bells and whistles in her head. Okay, so he knew Greg, and he'd used the word *clan*. How many people in this day and age used that word to refer to a group of people?

Nina sensed his impatience, his growing agitation with her.

"Look, do you want to know what I know, or are you going to continue to kid yourself into believing you'll only be roaming the planet for the next fifty years instead of eternity if you don't find Lisanne?"

Hmmmm. "All right. Tell me about this Lisanne."

He shook his head, the thin wisps of hair on his scalp bobbing gently. "Not here."

Her antenna went back up. "Why the fuck not here? Here's just fine with me." The hell she'd go off with this cracker. She was staying right here where it was well lit and her friends were off behaving like they were booty-licious on the dance floor. No go.

"Because I can take you directly to Lisanne."

Nina shut her trap—even though she was tempted beyond reason. If he was a vampire, he'd probably been around a lot longer than she had and to wander off with him meant risking ending up vampire meat. Greg himself had said not all vampires were nice. Nothing about this guy seemed right, yet he had all the right answers.

He reached into his pocket and pulled out a small, spiral notepad. "Look. Here's an address where we can meet. Take some time to think it over, then if you're willing, meet me there tomorrow night. I'll bring Lisanne. I'll call you tomorrow with the time, but you have to keep this quiet. There are members of the clan who wouldn't take too kindly to me bringing you to her. No questions asked. Just be there."

"Wait, why don't you give me your number, and I'll call you."

"Because it doesn't work that way." He shoved the slip of paper at her and disappeared in a blur of flannel before she had the chance to question him further.

Nina looked down at the paper. Surprise. No name. Just an address located in the business district of Hackensack. She jammed it into her jeans pocket just as Marty came up behind her, out of breath from dancing. "Still scaring men away? Who was that?"

Suddenly, everything was too much. The noise of the bar, the stench of human food, the swirl of conversations being held around her, garbled and muted, left her overwhelmed. "He was just some jack-off looking to get laid. I dunno. Look, I think I'm gonna blow. I'm a total drag to hang around, and I'm sorry."

Marty's shoulder-length blonde hair bobbed when she cocked her head at Nina, her eyebrows at an upward tilt. "Did you just apologize? Shut. Up. You really are off your game, eh?"

On impulse, Nina grabbed her and gave her a quick hug, finding the scent of her Bobbie-Sue perfume comforting. She closed her eyes for a second and absorbed it, then let her go clumsily.

Marty's head fell back limply, her mouth forming the shape of the letter *O*.

Nina placed a hand under her chin and pushed up. "Close your mouth, Marty, and tell Wanda I'm sorry, too." She waved her fingers over her shoulder as her feet carried her out of the bar.

Outside, she leaned against the brick of the building, her hand finding the outside pocket of her jeans. She rubbed it, taking comfort in the fact that she had a lead. A small one no doubt, but one nonetheless. She still wasn't sure if she was going to hook up with him or not. Human men she wasn't afraid of. Vampire men, if he in fact really was one, might be cause for hesitation.

So now what? She'd done the right thing by leaving Marty and Wanda because she was shitty company, but she didn't want to go home either. Not with all those stupid romance novels piled on her couch, a stark reminder of her current conundrum.

Nina made her way past the clumps of people bundled in their winter clothing and spotted a neon marquee for a dollar discount movie theater. Discount movies were right up her alley because she was now officially dirt poor. Fishing around in her pocket, she found two bucks' worth of change and plunked it down in front of the cashier.

The stench of urine, stale buttered popcorn, and sweat greeted her. With the exception of one middle-aged guy, guzzling from a brown paper bag, the theater was empty. Sliding into a seat, she covered her mouth to keep from gagging. This particular new-found superpower she could live without.

As the credits began to roll, Nina realized she didn't even know what the hell she'd paid to watch. Slumping down in the seat, she decided it didn't really matter. It was a distraction, and it was dark and quiet.

An hour into the movie, Nina was thoroughly disgusted with herself. *Beaches.* She paid two bloody bucks for *Beaches*, and she was attempting tears that just wouldn't flow. She was crying, sorta, at a chick flick. How sissi-fied. It must have to do with the topsy-turvy condition of her life right now. She never cried. She never even came close to feeling like crying. Nina hacked into her hand, swiping at her eyes that refused to shed tears.

"Well, well, well. Is that an emotion other than pissed off I detect? I didn't think you had it in you, Nina." The sultry sounds of her favorite vampire tickled her ears with a direct hit.

Christ, he was like *Visa—everywhere.*

Nina's spine went ramrod straight as Greg nudged her knees, squeezing in front of her to sit in the seat to her left. Though the contact was limited, it sent a wave of heat along the back of her neck. His dark profile, silhouetted by the light of the screen, held a hint of a satisfied smile.

"Jesus, how did you find me?"

Greg pointed to his nose.

Of course. "Why are you here?"

"You're like a fly to one of those bug zappers. I just can't keep myself from going into the light." He'd said that without a trace of sarcasm, but another emotion Nina couldn't pinpoint.

"Well, I fed, if that's what you're worried about. I'm still a vampire against my will. So you can go do your night thing in peace."

He turned to look at her, the glow of his green eyes somehow calming in the dark, smelly theater. "I think I'll just stay here with you."

She was incredulous. "And watch *Beaches*?"

Greg nodded affirmatively, his face serious. "And watch *Beaches*."

"I don't need a babysitter. I think it's pretty obvious I can't run off, because I'm broke. So if you were worried I was going to escape your evil clutches, quit."

His laughter wound its way to her ear in a sinful thread of amusement. "My clutches are hardly evil, and you can go wherever you want, Nina."

Her body was tense, pressing into the seat to avoid contact. "Yeah, that's what all people who have a clan say. You don't want me to be human any more than I want to be a vampire."

"And why is that again?"

"Because you want everyone to be a vampire. You know, the Dr. Evil, maniacal plan thing."

"Oh. Right. How about we set aside my maniacal plan for now?"

"Can you do that? Just set aside something as big as taking over the world," she joked. Her belief that he wanted to keep her a vampire, which she was clinging to by her new fangs, was beginning to sound dramatic even to her.

"For tonight, I say we truce. Besides, I've been thinking . . ."

"About what? Moving on to a new profession of women to bite? Maybe some innocent nursing students?"

His chuckle slid into her ears, making her shiver. "Um, no. I was thinking there are some things you ought to know about our clan. Now yours, however briefly."

"Like?"

"Like, we have a strict no turn policy. I'm sure you don't believe that, but it's true. We buy our blood from various sources. We don't grab onto the first neck we see and bite it to feed. I know I've said that, but I felt like it needed to be said again. It's your choice to believe or not, and if you bite someone, you're on your own. I couldn't live with myself if you ate your guinea pig. And don't tell me you didn't think about it."

"Poor Larry," she mumbled.

"It's understandable and an urge you'll be able to control, given time."

"So you really expect me to believe you don't hunt people down to feed from them?"

"Uh-huh."

Oh, how she wanted to believe, and she didn't even know why. Wait, yes she did. She wanted to believe, because the closer he inched to her in the chair, the more attracted she became to him, aroused by just his arm pressing against hers, and Nina was hoping she couldn't be this hot for someone who sucked big, fat man hooters. "So I was just an unfortunate incident." That sat much better with her, although she still thought it was wishful thinking, not fact.

He chuckled again. Probably the most she'd heard him chuckle in any one encounter they'd shared. "Among other things."

"So why don't you suck necks? I thought that was a vampire's staple."

"Because those of us who belong to my clan want to blend in with everyone else and cause as little trouble as possible. We were once where you were, too."

"Where I was?"

His tone lowered, ominous and dark. "Of the unwilling."

Hookay. Her anxiety lessened a little more. "So you didn't really want to be a vampire to begin with?"

"Ah, no. I don't think anyone really wants to be one, except maybe a few nuts and the rebels who've decided to take their anger out on the world by turning everyone and everything they can sink their incisors into."

"So there *are* vampires who want to rule the world."

"Just like there are humans who want to rule the world. We just have an unfair advantage."

Nina paused. That definitely wasn't far off the mark. There were plenty of zealots who bombed shit and started wars because of it. How interesting that these paranormals had the same sorts of political issues and the superpowers to go with them.

"My clan may not go out of its way to interact with humans, but we don't want to harm them either. I won't bite anyone or anything. Unless it's out of pleasure." The last he said with a flicker of a smile, sending a ripple of awareness throughout her body.

"And how do you know everyone in your clan feels the same way?"

"I don't. No more than you can believe a politician who stares you in the eye and says he wants world peace, then does the exact opposite once he's elected. I can tell you, we've never had a biting incident in over four hundred years in my clan. Had we, and I was privy to who'd done the biting purposely, hell would ensue, of that you can be sure."

Unfortunately, Nina wasn't sure of anything anymore, though he was damned convincing when he threatened the ensuing of hell. "Wait, if your clan is four hundred years old and you're almost five hundred . . ." That meant she'd caught him in a lie.

He turned to her with a grin, the white of his teeth catching the light from the screen. "It just took time for me to gather the masses and find people who wanted to carry out my evil plan. I floundered for the first hundred years, but then I got my act together, interviewed as many evil freaks as I could, and now, here I am. A clan owner. Who knew?"

Nina giggled. "I don't get the clan dynamics at all. You're allowed to create your own clan?"

"*Allowed* should be used loosely here. We're not disallowed, but
we're not encouraged to leave our creators either." He held up a
hand when he saw she was going to confirm that's what she'd been
saying all along. "Before you get all crazy over that statement, hear
me out. No, we're not encouraged to leave who created us, but you
can if you're willing to stand on your own two feet or if you disagree
with a group's politics. Some vampire rules are hard and fast—some
not so much. Anyway, there are those that feel as I do. No one should
be forced into this way of life. I'd like to think the clan I've created
is a haven for those beliefs. We are where we are, and we've found a
way to accept it. We just want to live out eternity in peace."

Shit, he was making her waffle. She wanted to believe he was
callous and freaky, yet he sounded soooo credible. "So because
Lisanne created you, that was an automatic entry into her clan?"

He nodded, but said nothing, the muscles of his neck flexing.

"I'm guessing you didn't like Lisanne and her clan?"

The air between them changed, losing the relaxed feeling Greg
had set when he'd first sat down. "No. No I didn't."

That sounded like an end of statement, and tonight, Nina
didn't want to fight. Her emotions were seesawing too wildly.
She'd hugged Marty, for God's sake. The world had tipped on its
axis, while she clung to the edge of it. "Did you belong to any
other clans after Lisanne's and before you created your own?" She
glanced at him out of the corner of her eye, watching as his face
hardened for a moment.

"I did."

"And you didn't like it?"

"Nope."

His one word answer meant it wasn't open for discussion.
"Why have a clan to begin with? I don't get it."

"Vampires are bestowed with certain gifts, Nina. Like flying and mind reading. Each clan member has strengths and weaknesses. As a whole, we're far stronger together than apart. We're all connected mentally to one degree or another. It's strength in numbers. An all-for-one kind of deal."

"Very Three Musketeers," she teased.

"I felt differently than the majority of clan members when I was turned. I decided I couldn't be the only one who felt that way, some were just too afraid to speak up. I figured, what could I lose by giving them a voice? And so I did. I'd be damned if I'd live in fear of anyone's wrath. We gathered in numbers, rebelled, and here we are four hundred years later. Because our beliefs are much the same, it helps to keep out the riffraff."

"What do you people do for work? Does everyone work the graveyard shift? Wanda told me about Svetlanna's clothing line, but what about the rest of the people? How do you survive?"

"Most of us have been around a long time. We've invested wisely. Some better than others. We just look out for each other."

Hence the "come join the clan" deal. "So what else do I need to know to be a part of the clan?" Hellafino, had she just asked that? She didn't want to be a part of his friggin' clan.

"Not much."

"Are there rules?"

"Yep."

"Got a handout?"

"Ah, no."

"One more question?"

"Shoot."

"What's the deal with like hot and cold, not being able to feel pain and the ever-crazy healing yourself?"

He smiled, the dimples on either side of his mouth deepening. "You're the living dead now, Nina. It's rather like being preserved in a lifelike state. So while your organs no longer work and you can't reproduce or lose a lung—which in your case might not be a bad thing, with that mouth of yours—you still function. As to temperature and pain, all I can tell you is this is the way it's always been. There are some sensations that are magnified and some that are dulled."

Yeah, like that all over hot thing that happened when he was slapped up against her. Hookay, next subject. "So what are these people like? I mean, the people in your clan?"

"You should come by sometime when you're not fired up and find out."

Yeah, thus showing him and everyone else she was willing to participate in vampire games. Not. Even if she was being swayed to the notion that Greg wasn't evil, she didn't do crowds well. "Do you have like picnics and crap?"

"We have meetings from time to time. We gather, yes."

To do what, was the question. "Well, I don't want to stay a vampire, so I don't see the point."

"But for now, you *are* a vampire, and it wouldn't hurt you to find out how you can benefit from the various resources the clan has to offer. Maybe hone a skill or two."

Nina still wasn't comfortable with blood drinking. Flying was a whole other Pandora's Box. "The skill or two shit still freaks me out. Like the way you disappear. Or the way you break into my apartment."

He smiled with a smug lift of his lips.

"Are they going to hate me?"

"Who?"

"This clan of yours."

"Why do you ask?"

"Well, you know my friend Marty, right?"

Greg nodded, making his hair move, filling her nostrils with the scent of his shampoo. She clung to the chair's arms, sticking her fingers into the plastic cup holder provided by the theater to keep from tugging a lock. "She's a werewolf."

"So I smelled."

Nina smiled in spite of herself. "Her now husband's, then boyfriend's, pack hated her guts. They didn't want to have anything to do with her, and they treated her like shit."

"Fear of exposure." His statement was simple and knowing. Clearly he'd experienced some of his own brand of discrimination.

"Yeah, but there was other stuff, too. Pack politics or something. Her husband, Keegan, was supposed to mate with some other werewolf, and it pissed the pack off that he didn't want to."

Greg's body language changed for a blip of a second, making him shift in his chair and cross his legs before his profile relaxed once again. "That happens I suppose, but I'm not a werewolf. I don't know the intricacies of a pack."

"Do you have crazy shit like that going on in your clan? Are they all going to hate me because I was once a human?"

"We were all human once. In a lycan pack I imagine it's much different. They can have children and create more werewolves. The pack itself is probably so old, not many were originally human— most were probably born lycan. As a result, I'd imagine they want to keep the bloodlines strong, and their hesitation over your friend, in some jaded old-guard minds, makes sense. But vampires can't have children, Nina."

When he let those words go, she felt a stab of fleeting sorrow. Not that she'd planned to have children anyway—or even get married, but the option had been there, and now it wasn't. Or might not be, if she couldn't get the results she'd hoped to from Lisanne. After letting that process in her head, she said, "I wouldn't have been a very good mother, anyway. I think Lou told you I didn't have the best example."

"You're not like your mother, Nina."

Her chest immediately ached from his words. "She wasn't all bad. Not always. She had some moments."

There had been times when she'd come through for Nina, and those were the memories she chose to keep. Not the ones where she'd show up at their screen door, unwashed, unkempt, and reeking of alcohol, begging her father to let her come home with the same old refrain, "This time'll be different, Joe. You'll see. We'll be a family." And they were for a week, sometimes as long as a month. Once for almost two months. Nina's head dipped to her chest, and she squeezed her eyes shut.

Greg's hand found hers, wrapping her smaller fingers in the coolness of his. "No, I'm sure she wasn't. I don't doubt she loved you. She just had a weakness that not even *you* could cure."

Such a simple statement made it all almost seem okay coming from him. Again, she found her throat closing up, and for a moment, she allowed her hand in his to give her comfort. It was big and secure and sending vibrations of soothing calm. Her inclination to lean her head against his broad shoulder grew, but just then the lights of the theater popped up, glaring and uncomfortable to her sensitive eyes. Neither of them moved, and Nina couldn't even hazard a glance at him.

"You made me miss the ending of *Beaches*," she said, keeping her eyes at her feet.

"My deepest apologies."

Slipping her hand from his, feeling an instant sting of longing, she said, "I have to go."

"Plans?"

She placed her hands on her thighs and snorted. "Yeah. I have so many of those. No, it's just late, and I'm sure you have better things to do than babysit me. I fed. Promise. I'll keep feeding until I can figure this out, too. So you don't have to keep checking on me."

"I'll walk you home."

She rose, zipping out of the seat and along the aisle. "You don't have to."

His hand found the small of her back, making her nipples respond by becoming sharp, tight beads. "But I want to," slithered from his lips. He held the door of the theater exit open for her, allowing her to pass through first.

Nina decided to let him walk her home. She found herself reluctant to leave his company, and that was dangerous and stupid and well, dangerous and stupid. But she didn't stop him when he casually slung an arm over her shoulder.

Their footfalls were soft along the pavement, in sync with one another as she followed the path back to her apartment. His arm brushed her shoulder, distracting her from absorbing what he'd said in the theater about clans and rules.

Greg's claim that he had a no-turn policy didn't ring false, if these new emotion-o-meters she had were accurate, and his clear denial that he hadn't wanted to be a vampire in the first place didn't feel like a lie either.

But that still didn't explain why he seemed so uncomfortable when she talked about finding Lisanne. If the motive wasn't to keep her a vampire, what was it?

She couldn't think when he was this close. When they came to the intersection, she decided she needed a moment. "I'm going to take a detour, so I'll drop you here."

"What's here?"

Nina shrugged her shoulders. "Nothing really. I just need some space."

He stopped, turning her to face him. "You okay?" Greg's eyes sparkled, but it wasn't the arrogant glint she'd become accustomed to. There was concern there.

Her gaze was solemn. For the first time since they'd accidentally met, she wasn't into snarking him because he'd done this, and she had nothing left in her to banter in their typically loud fashion. "I'm all right. I just need some time, okay?"

His hand, cool and large, cupped her cheek for only a moment. "Yeah, I understand needing time. Be well, fledgling," he said, low and husky, placing a kiss on her forehead before spinning on his heel and heading off in a blur in the other direction.

Nina shoved her hands into the pockets of her jeans and crossed the street, making a sharp left and stopping in front of the cemetery her mother and father were buried in. The rows of headstones stood out like eerie white soldiers, threading in straight lines as far as the eye could see.

Thankfully, because Lou hadn't been able to afford much, her parent's headstones were located in a secluded, not-so-desirable corner, far away from the other gravesites that potentially might bear crucifixes. Another thing to be thankful for . . . as religious as Lou was, she hadn't been able to afford fancy headstones with crosses on them either. Just being a few hundred feet away from some of the other graves and on hallowed ground made Nina's skin tingle, but for now it was bearable.

Her parents were buried side by side. Joe'd wanted it that way. Lou was right when she'd said he wasn't the same after her mother had died. It was as if he'd been biding his time, never aiding his death, but never quite fully participating in his life or Nina's, either.

Nina sat down on her haunches and ran a finger over the words of *In Loving Memory* on her mother's headstone. Her eyes grew grainy like they had in the movie.

Shit.

"So, I'm a vampire," she said into the black velvet of the night. "I was bitten the first day at my new job. Just my luck, right? I was suctioning this guy with a chipped tooth. He asked for anesthesia, because he said vampire's teeth are sensitive. Um, I mean, he didn't say that at the office. He told us afterward. But he reacted pretty badly to it. He got all loopy and disoriented. And bam, he clamped down on my hand.

"But I guess you probably already know that if what they say is true and you can still see me and all. Can you see me, Mom? Dad?" she asked, her voice hitching, wobbling in sadness. Anything was possible. If vampires and werewolves existed then it wasn't so far out of the realm of possibility that her parents could see her—maybe even hear her, was it?

Plopping down in front of her mother's and father's graves, Nina crossed her legs Indian style. The ground beneath her was frozen, but she couldn't feel anything other than a vague awareness of it. If she focused, the burning sensation that flooded her skin really could be managed. Huh. Greg was right.

The leaves crunched beneath her as she settled in, crisp and brown now from the winter winds. She toyed with the laces on her sneakers, wrapping them around her trembling fingers.

She came here once a month to show her respect. She might not have had a relationship with her mother in life, but whether Janine liked it or not, they had a one-sided one now in her death. Whenever she was stressed or afraid, she came here to talk to her parents.

"It was an accident, you know—his biting me. Or so the guy who did it says it was. His name is Greg. Statleon. Exotic, huh? It's Romanian. Well, I don't know if that's where it originated, but he comes from Romania. Anyway, I behaved really badly when I found out what was wrong with me. If you can see me down here, then you already know I really got all up in his face . . . at first . . . because I didn't believe a word he said. I thought he was like all the vampires I'd read about on the Internet and that he wanted to keep me a vampire to ensure his kind would live forever. Creepy, right? But I hafta tell ya, now I'm starting to wonder if he's telling the truth."

Nina groaned at her admission, covering her mouth with her hand, as if that would stop the words from becoming real. She was liking the side of the vampire she saw at the movie theater, and that was no good. She didn't want to be like him. She most definitely didn't want to like him.

"I wonder what you'd think about all this, Mom. It's pretty crazy—like off the rocker crazy."

Maybe there was truth in what Lou said about her visiting their graves. Nina could talk to them without fear of disapproval or retribution. Lou might be right this time. But there was no way she could tell Lou what was going on, and her friends, while with good intention, were just frustrating to her because they were always offering solutions. She didn't so much want a solution from them, only an ear she could gripe loudly into.

"So, do the two of you have any thoughts on this? I mean, I'm now part of the living dead. Maybe some tips, pointers on where to go from here? I know you guys are dead-dead, but I thought you might have some useful input, seeing as you get the dead part—no offense intended."

The wind whistled, stirring the oak tree in the center of the graveyard, the hustle of cars and people just muted enough that when they'd chosen this spot for her mother, Joe'd said Janine wouldn't hear the call of the streets anymore, a call that was like a siren's song—she'd be deaf to the chaos that beckoned her, chaos Janine just couldn't seem to stay away from.

Nina hoped that was true for Joe, too. He deserved some peace after the life he'd led with her mother. She tried not to hold grudges and that was when she'd decided to come see them—to talk—sometimes rant—sometimes just sit and listen to the silence. Have someone to bounce ideas off of and know, no matter what she said or did, she was loved.

Very June and Ward Cleaver had been her first scathing thought. But not having those very things in life left an impact. Marty and Wanda thought nothing affected her, but that wasn't true. She just didn't say much about it.

No, you act out about it much, though, her conscience reminded her.

Guilty. She didn't know how to interact with people who cared for her, because, while her father had cared, he'd cared more about her mother. Or maybe Janine had just consumed so much of his energy he'd had nothing left for Nina. She'd learned to keep her trifle shit to herself, because Joe had so much on his plate. She'd walked on plenty of eggshells as a kid, and she'd learned to do so with stealthy feet. When she stopped doing that, she became em-powered. Maybe way over-empowered.

Cultivating friendships with anyone was always difficult because she had a hard time doing that sharing thing Marty so encouraged, and, well, if she was honest, her mouth got her into trouble. She was a smart-ass, and she always had to prove by way of that mouth, that she didn't need anyone.

Why that was so important had lost its meaning these days, especially since she'd acquired Marty and Wanda as friends.

It used to make her uncomfortable that Marty and Wanda wouldn't quit coming around, but when they wouldn't quit show-ing up, she came to find a peace in that, learned to enjoy their humongous differences. She'd learned, period. Not just about color wheels and how to be a friggin' girl, but what it was like to have someone if you needed them—anytime—anywhere. She'd learned the joy of Thursday night bingo with a bunch of senior citizens from Wanda, who volunteered at the nursing home, and hanging out at Hogan's on Sunday for brunch—how to put stupid eyeliner on properly, and whether she liked it or not, she'd learned what it was to bond with people of the same sex.

Girlfriends hadn't been her thing growing up, because girls had mothers who wanted to know where your mother was, and if you told them she was dead, they felt sorry for you, wanted to "help" you. Nina didn't want that kind of pity. The eyes of many mothers on mother/daughter day at school had looked upon her with sympathy brimming in them, leaving her embarrassed and ashamed. No one knew about her mother's drug problem, but she knew, and it was like wearing a big ole sign on your chest.

Jesus. She stopped short.

She was wallowing.

God, she hated a good wallow. It was pathetic. Nina shut off the introspective side of her brain. She'd never been one to over-analyze things, but tonight she was like an episode of *Oprah*. She returned her attention to the headstones. "So nothing? No advice?" she asked wryly. "That's okay. I don't know what I'd say to some-one who told me they were a vampire either. I don't blame you for being speechless. I was, too. Not for long, mind you, but I was.

"I'm having some trouble adjusting, I think. At first the blood-drinking thing grossed me out, who wouldn't be grossed out about it? But I got over that when I got a fuc . . . er, really bad headache and had no choice but to drink it. I admit, and only to you guys, it's pretty good. It isn't like chicken wings or anything, but it's good, and it beats turning to dust. Yeah, there's another problem for me. If I don't nourish my immortality, I'll turn to dust—so I don't have a choice but to feed. That's what they call it—feeding.

"So here I am. Bet you didn't think you'd get this kind of update from me, did you? I thought by now I'd have horror stories about my new job. You know, crappy kids with rotted teeth from too many Gummi Bears. Patients with gum disease . . . In the scheme of things, this must sound way more adventurous than my dental hygienist gig I suppose, but . . ." She trailed off, biting her lip and fighting that damned tightening of her throat again.

"I-I-think I'm scared." Jesus effin', it felt so good to say that out loud. Relief flooded her from head to toe.

"I had enough trouble being a human—I don't want to be a vampire. I've been saying that a lot lately. In fact, I might have a T-shirt made up that says so, too. So Wanda's been helping me research this undead stuff, and I found something the other day in a book about vampires. It said I might be able to be human again, and I've been clinging to that ever since. Greg says it's all phooey, and even though I want to believe he's a liar, I don't think I do. But he won't tell me where to find the person who created him. Which is fishy, huh? But then he says he doesn't know where she is, so he couldn't tell me even if he wanted to. I waffled over whether I should believe him. I was still waffling tonight when he came and found me at the movie theater. Now I'm not so sure . . .

"But I met a guy in a bar tonight. No, it's not what you think, not *that* kind of meet a guy. He came and found me. He told me he knew things about the Statleon clan. That's what a bunch of vampires in one room is called, I guess. A clan. Like I said, he says he knows them. How could he know I want to find this Lisanne, unless he really does know her?

"It was weird, and he freaked me out, but he says he knows where this person who created Greg is. I don't know who to trust anymore—who to believe. The worst part about this whole thing is, this guy Greg is cute. I mean, really cute, and I think I'm attracted to him. Jesus, I can't believe I just said that," she moaned, running a hand over her face and up into her hair. "Forget I said that. I'm going to try to forget I said that. In all of this mess it seems so crazy to be drawn to the guy who did this to me, doesn't it? Even if it was supposedly an accident.

"Anywhoo, I wish I had better news this month, but I'm sorta in a pickle right now. So would you guys do me a favor?" Her eyes lifted upward where dark clouds gathered, the deep purple and ebony of the sky littered with them. "Just help me to figure this out. Or I dunno, send me a sign. If there are really vampires and werewolves, I told you about Marty, right, that she's a werewolf? Whatever, if those kinds of things exist, maybe angels do, too, and I could use being touched by one 'bout now."

Nina rose, sadness filling the empty cavity where her heart once beat. Brushing her jeans off, she placed a hand on the headstone and whispered, "I'm sorry I dumped all this on you. I'm really, really trying to figure this out. So you guys take care, okay? And don't worry about me, if you do worry, that is. I'll be okay."

Her footfalls crunched their way back around the corner and out of the cemetery, and she tried to leave not just her troubles but also her fear of what was to come behind her.

CHAPTER 10

Greg waited in the silence of Nina's apartment. Tonight, in her vulnerability, he'd felt a connection to her. One he hadn't felt with another female in a very long time. When her hand curved in his, allowing his comfort, he'd felt a shift from within he couldn't deny.

He didn't want this.

Not now.

Now wasn't the time to play around.

She'd been right about one thing: He couldn't stay away from her. It had almost nothing to do with making sure she fed either, but it had everything to do with the reaction his body had to hers when she opened that big mouth of hers to yell at him. Or even when she flipped him the bird.

An ironic smile lifted his lips. How completely fucked up that this woman, this cranky, opinionated, outspoken, rude, foul-mouthed woman, could have him turning to his hand in the shower for relief. When she spewed fire, he wanted to kiss her luscious lips. When she stormed from a room, he wanted to rear up behind her and do some downright wicked things.

He didn't want this.

He shouldn't want this.

Yet here he was.

Wanting this.

She'd rag on him when she found out he'd broken into her apartment again. That made him smile, too. Maybe his mother was right. Maybe he did like someone who could give as good as he gave.

He had no business liking anything about Nina right now.

None.

But she liked him, too. He could smell it on her, feel it coming off her in wave after wave.

So why shouldn't two people who were mutually attracted to one another spend some quality bedroom time together?

Because now wasn't the time.

When he'd left Nina to go off to wherever she was going, his keen emotional senses had picked up a million different vibes, one of which was confusion and the need to find some kind of solace. He just couldn't let that go, and if she was going to keep him up another day, it might as well be with the comfort that he'd checked on her one last time.

Liar. You want to ogle her ass.

Well, there was that, too.

Mostly he just needed to know she wasn't going to go off the deep end. Some newly turned, rare though they were, suffered from the vampire version of post-traumatic stress disorder. Nina hadn't taken to her turning well, but she hadn't exhibited any signs of giving up until tonight. Tonight she'd been calmer, less agitated, more willing to talk reasonably versus sling insults—he grimaced. That alone should scare the hell out of him. That Nina was willing to converse with nary a single *fucktard* spewed in a sentence should instill fear in the hearts of many.

It had his radar on an all-points bulletin.

And the guilt that he'd done this to her weighed heavily on his shoulders. He was as shocked as she was. He'd never turned anyone in all his centuries. He spoke the truth about his no-turn policy. That was a personal rule he never broke, and wouldn't allow anyone in the clan to break either. He took it very seriously. He expected the same of his clan members.

However, his clan found it highly amusing that he'd fucked so royally up, according to his friend Clayton's email anyway. It might be funny, if it weren't so tragic, and if it had been anyone other than Nina.

He wouldn't wish this life of eternity on anyone, especially not someone he was thoroughly enjoying sparring with, someone he was coming to care . . . Greg halted his thoughts, firmly clamping down on anything warm and fuzzy.

Nina's entry thwarted the good talking-to he'd planned to give himself for going where he'd just been about to go.

She didn't bother to turn on the light, yet she didn't move toward him either. She hovered by the end of her couch. "Why are you here?" Her voice was tired, and he sensed, defeated. The cloud of black hair that covered her head hung in windswept curls down over her small, pert breasts.

Fuuuuck. No breasts.

Greg cleared his throat. "You just weren't the Nina I've come to know tonight. You didn't call me a fucktard once, and that's unthinkable. I wanted to be sure you were okay." *And look at your ass, but whatever.*

"The Nina you've come to know is worn out and doesn't want to fight with the Greg she's come to know." Her fingers toyed with the pillow on the couch.

"Look at me, Nina."

"No."

"I said, *look at me.*"

Her eyes lifted with obvious struggle and hesitation. Her chin jutted forward with that defiant gesture she'd used with him a thousand times before. She stared at him, piercing him with the gaze he used so often on her. Her dark, almost black, almond-shaped eyes set his cock on fire. The fall of her long, curly hair made him fight a grunt of sexual awareness so acute, he had to clamp his teeth together.

Fuck again.

He slid to the end of the couch and grabbed her hand, pulling her down next to him.

In hindsight he'd remember that had been his first of many mistakes.

WELL, if she didn't have nerve endings anymore, you sure could've fooled her. There wasn't a square inch of her body that wasn't on fire when Greg yanked her down to the couch. The press of their thighs, fully clothed was almost intolerable. It made her ache, yearn, long for him to touch her.

Suddenly, him naked was all she could think about. Nina honed in on it, licked her dry lips over it, had a thousand battles in her mind in seconds against it.

Sitting down, Greg was more than a head taller than she was, leaving his neck at eye level. That yummylicious span of corded muscle mesmerized her, beseeched her. Her incisors, even though she'd fed, began to elongate.

Jesus Christ Superstar.

She pointed to her teeth. "Why is this happening?"

"You really want to know?"

"No, I probably don't, but yeah, tell me anyway."

He chuckled. "You're aroused."

Harsh. Humiliatingly harsh. "So this is like the female version of a vampire hard-on?"

His voice grew thick like honey. "Yes."

Delightful. "Well, then, I guess there's no hiding it, is there?"

"Um, no. But in time, you'll learn to teach them to behave."

I don't want to behave. I want to relieve you of your clothing and ride you like the Tilt-A-Whirl at the Hackensack County fair.

Greg lifted her chin up, cupping it and letting his thumb graze her bottom lip. "Could you try not to think so much?"

Her lip quivered at his touch. "Why?"

His green eyes were sheepish, the flash of his white teeth brief. "Remember that reading your mind thing?"

Mary. Mother. Of. God. "Y-yes."

"I'm doing it right now."

"Then you know."

"I know."

He *knew*. Good, good, good. Yippee and skippee.

"I think I'd better leave, Nina," he said, but his voice, turned husky and dark, was saying something different.

"But you don't want to."

"Have your mind reading capabilities suddenly developed?"

"No. I just know."

His finger slipped between her lips, tracing the inside edges of them. His hiss was audible when she flicked her tongue out to graze the calloused digit, the taste of his skin exploding in her mouth.

Somehow, their heads tilted into each other, their mouths but a hairsbreadth apart Nina's gulp was hard when Greg said, "It's dangerous to do this."

"Is there some clan rule about doing this?" she husked out, nearly choking on her words.

"No," he murmured, sliding the heat of his tongue between her lips, groaning into her mouth when their flesh connected.

The sizzle of heat exploded in her mouth, making it hard to concentrate, but there was one thing she had to know. Nina pulled back a bit, yet the flesh of their lips still whispered against one another's. "Is this dangerous because you have a girlfriend?" She didn't play like that ever. She might be a big mouth and not at all embarrassed by her need for the occasional wonking, but she didn't do some other chick's guy.

"No," was all he offered, his eyes holding hers.

Relief was followed on the heels of another wave of lust. Her nipples grew tight, beading uncomfortably; a mad-hot heat built between her legs. The need to have him take her and take her this second consumed her. This overwhelming desire to indulge all her senses in him was new. It took her aback, left her confused, leery, but not enough to stop him when his arms wrapped around her frame and he pulled her to sit astride his lap. The rustle of her T-shirt falling to the floor made no impact on her. The scrape of their jeans when she straddled his lap, stopped all coherent thought.

The fire that coursed through her body was like an onslaught of one vibration after another. Her skin burned, her muscles ached, tensed, and strung tight like bows. The curtain of her hair fell against his cheek, and Greg lifted a hand to throw it back over her shoulder before tracing the outline of her mouth, letting his fingertips glide over the surface.

Greg's slow exploration was wickedly carnal, primal on a level so deep she had to close her eyes to fight the groan threatening to escape her throat. The rigid press of his cock seared the space between her thighs, brushing against it when she dipped her lower body to relish the feel of a hard man wrapped in her embrace.

And it was the single most intense experience she'd ever had.

She'd wanted a man before, but never this deeply, wildly, and so urgently she thought she might pass out from the need. Her hands clenched locks of his hair, her words, when she finally spoke, were ragged and harsh to her ears. "What is *this*?"

Greg's hands came to knead the muscles of her back; knitting his fingers, he pulled her closer. His answer was husky, feral. "It's arousal, Nina. Vampires experience it on a far deeper, more powerful level than humans."

Oh, sweet Jesus, just his hands on her back made her writhe against him, bucking her hips to meet the rhythm he stirred beneath her. Cobwebs formed in her brain, tiny obstructions that kept her from thinking clearly. Yet she had to make something clear, had to explain her hesitation. Even as she splayed across his hard body, her palms frantically moving along his chest, her legs, fighting their way into the couch to wrap around his waist, she knew she had to say it.

Instead, Greg did it for her. "I know in my head we shouldn't, Nina," he rasped against her ear, licking the sensitive spot, suckling it until her neck arched backward. "So tell me to stop. Tell me *now*."

She couldn't. She didn't want to stop, yet logically, she knew plowing ahead was impulsive—reckless.

But she couldn't stop.

Nina lifted her head, taking in his smoky gaze, biting her lip before she said, "No regrets, how's that? I won't hold you to anything, and the same goes for you, but I think, if you're still reading my mind, you know I don't have a lot of willpower left."

Greg's eyes burned her, his gaze dark and intense. "I know."

Her gulp was visible. "Okay, once more with feeling. No re-grets?"

"No regrets," he murmured, dragging her to him and sliding a hand under her ass to scoop her up and rise from the couch. Her legs fell loosely as she hung onto the trunk of his body, helpless. Greg's hand slid under her bra, shoving it away with an impatient hand before lifting it and grazing her nipple with his thumb.

The jolt of awareness was like no other. It spread outward, claiming every part of her, eating a path of scorching, white heat along the way. Nina's hands fisted in his hair, pulling at it to keep from screaming out her pleasure. But there was one more thing.

One very important question that, while dull and distant, needed answering.

"Wait." Oh, God, she didn't know if she could wait. "Just one more thing . . . if-if we do thisssss . . ." She hissed the last word when he tugged at her nipple. "Will . . . will w-we be mated for liiiiife?" she groaned.

The vibration of his laughter rumbled against her chest. "Wiki-pedia again?"

Her thoughts were blank but for the circles he made around her nipple with his tongue. "I can't remember anymore."

Greg carried her into her bedroom, kicking the door shut and pushing her up against it. The grind of his hips against hers made her clench her teeth together in blissful agony. "No, Nina. Not for life."

Well, okay then. Okay.

The last bit of her reluctance scurried off to the dark place she called temporary amnesia, and she gave in to the all-consuming desire licking at every available place on her body.

Clothes flew, shoes thunked against the floor, the tear of silk was audible, when Greg didn't bother to slide her panties off, but took a shortcut by yanking them from her body and shaking them to the floor. She climbed her way back up the hard planes of his body to once more wrap her legs around his waist, lean and flanked with the sexiest indentation along each hip.

Her chest heaved, her eyes rolled to the back of her head, when his mouth slid along the column of her neck and down to her breast, taking a nipple between his teeth and twisting it. Nina reared up against the heat of his mouth, lifting her breast so he wouldn't miss a single patch of skin.

Greg's moan came from deep in his chest, a muffled growl of pleasure. His hands cupped her ass, driving her against his rock-hard cock, letting it slip between the folds of her sex to rub her clit with a delicious friction. His fingers reached from beneath her, slipping between her thighs to stroke her swollen lips with feather light passes.

Her nails dug into his back, her teeth clenched, as lust clawed at her, piercing her sharply. The first orgasm came with a sharp sting to it, driving into her pelvis, racing to every carnal place on her body.

So unexpected, so without warning, it tore every last ounce of energy from her, so she hung from his arms, limp and weak. But the momentary relaxation in her muscles didn't last long when he unwrapped her legs from his waist and steadied her on her feet. Her back was flush with the bedroom door, her spine sinking into the hard surface for balance.

Greg loomed over her, his chest hard against hers, her nipples boring holes into it. He pulled both her hands up, cuffing her wrists in his palm, forcing her breasts to jut forward.

Nina didn't flinch, refusing to squirm beneath his scrutiny. She was no bodacious babe, and she knew it, but she was lean and well-toned and proud that for all the chicken wings she'd consumed in her lifetime, she was still in decent shape.

Greg's smile was decadent when he saw she'd watched him assess her without averting her gaze.

Eyes, green and smoldering, scanned her body from head to toe before following the path his eyes had taken with his mouth.

Greg devoured her, pressing open-mouthed kisses over her collarbone, down along the slope of her shoulder, against her rib cage, laving her nipples until they burned. The sweet scent of lust filled the room.

His lust.

Mingled with hers.

Nina found that deliciously pleasing, invitingly erotic. Greg abruptly let go of her hands and sank to his knees, lifting one of her legs to rest on his shoulder. He paused there, at the apex of her thighs, laying a cheek against her abdomen. Nina's hands automatically sank into his thick head of hair, clenching fistfuls of it, waiting until she felt her stomach tighten and her teeth clench.

When he spoke, it was strained, tense. "You smell so sweet, Nina, so damn sweet."

She tightened her grip on his hair in response, rolling her hips with impatience.

His thumbs parted her flesh, exposing her to the cool air of her bedroom, sending hot chills along her thighs. When his tongue snaked out to stroke her clit, her knees buckled, but he held fast to her, reaching around her and cupping her ass.

Each pass he took was long, silky, hot, and wet, the strokes of his tongue even and measured. She felt every one as if it were a thousand, the heavy weight in her belly growing harder to bear. When he opened his mouth, enveloping her, then drove his tongue upward into her passage, Nina's will to hold out crumbled. She came again, riding a hot flash of fire, rotating her hips until her thigh muscles almost gave way.

Greg rode out her orgasm, fluttering kisses and quick flicks of his tongue against her sex until she settled, the tension seeping from her all at once.

Rising, he slithered back upward, each inch of his exposed flesh rubbing against hers, creating a new wave of desire only one thing could cure. His finger ran the length of her arm until he reached her hand. He entwined his fingers in hers, and for the first time, she took a critical look at his body. She'd been so lost in the lust that rose and fell in such furious waves between them, she hadn't taken the opportunity to hope her imagination met her expectations.

There was only one thought when her eyes fell on his nude form. Christ, he was beautiful. His skin was pale, but not the milky white one would expect of a vampire. It had hues of ruddiness to it, darkening where his muscles bunched together. His stomach was hard and tight, but he didn't have the kind of abs that suggested nothing else but working out. Yet there was that indentation by each hipbone that made her crazy.

Greg let her have her fill, and when she reached out to touch the tip of the head of his cock, rigidly jutting from the thatch of dark pubic hair, he hissed, his eyes closing for mere seconds. Nina drew her index finger over the veins that ran along his length, a length that wasn't outrageously long, but thick and hot. She clamped a hand around him, pumping his shaft with a slow stroke, allowing the space between them to give her room to prepare for what was to come. It was like catching the breath she no longer had.

Greg gripped her hand tighter as she caressed him until he hauled her to his side and pushed her onto the bed. Nina's back met the mattress with a soft whoosh, and when Greg settled between her thighs, she suddenly knew exactly what ecstasy was.

As his body sank onto hers, fusing them together, she moaned from the sweet pressure his heavy weight brought. Her thighs instantly opened to him, inviting him to enter her with an urgent, impatient lift of her hips.

He chuckled against her ear. "Patience, fledgling," he whispered, floating a hand between them to caress her sides. He rose on his hands, bracketing her head, looking down at her as his cock poised at her aching entrance.

Nina let her eyes slide shut, bracing her hands on his pecs, biting her lip at the first nudge of his pulsing shaft. He entered her slowly with agonizing increments of hot silk. She was surprised at how slick she was, something she didn't know could occur anymore. But, God, she was wet with the need for him to take that final thrust, and when he did, she clamped onto his chest, gritting her teeth to stop the scream of fulfillment from leaving her lips.

He stretched her, filled her cervix, stroked her G-spot with leisurely thrusts, until her stomach contracted, leaving her wanting to beg him to drive into her more deeply. She found the muscled hardness of his ass, gripping the flesh to encourage him to drive farther into her.

When he sank into her, balls deep, Nina saw bright flecks of color from behind her eyelids, and she couldn't stop that crazy wave that rolled over her, only now it was faster, hotter, sharper in clarity. Her knees lifted and she dug her feet into the mattress, pushing upward so hard, her clit rubbed against the springy hair surrounding his cock.

The last deep plunge he took grabbed fast to her sanity, holding it suspended, as she waited for the impact, and when it hit, it tore a shallow scream from her mouth that soared upward, clinging to her ears.

Greg, too, lost control, arching his neck, the muscles of his arms straining and bunching together, then letting go as his hips increased their tempo with a final crescendo of shudders.

Her entire body shuddered with his, each muscle tight, then weak from the strain of orgasm. They collapsed against each other, Greg letting his body go slack, sinking back into hers with a grunt.

Reality came in small doses, fighting to surface.

She avoided it for as long as she could, but women, even her, always overanalyzed a good stomp of the mattress, and, well, that—that had been . . . she searched for a word . . . *stupendous*.

Yeah, that was a good one.

Holy. Fucksticks.

Omigod, omigod, omigod. Flat out, that was the best toss in the sack she'd ever had.

Word.

Her eyes popped open.

Be very, very quiet, Nina, lest you reveal exactly how flippin' fantastic he was in bed.

Damn, damn, damn. She had to stop thinking—immediately—or he'd hear her.

Shhhhhhhhhhh. Shut up, fuckwit.

She clapped a hand over her mouth, as if that would help stop her thoughts.

Nina slanted her eyes down in his general direction with caution. Clearly, vampires didn't vary much from human men in the after-the-sex-was-done department. While Greg might not breathe, he didn't appear to be awake. He was slack, his body slumped against hers, unmoving.

Wee doggie. Maybe he hadn't heard her.

"Well, I can't hear you clearly, if that's what you're worried about. It's like a radio signal, and right now there's a lot of static," he said from the muffled confines of her neck.

Lawd. How did you turn off your thoughts?

"You think of other things."

"Get the hell out of my head, Greg Statleon. Now."

He rose up on his hands and smiled down at her. "Now that's the Nina I know."

"Stop reading my thoughts. It's like mental rape or something, and to boot, it's grossly un-fucking-fair. I can't read your mind." But boy, if she could, she'd wonder if he'd had the same angels-singing-from-on-high experience she just did.

Ugh. She had to stop that. Nina peered up at him with hesitation, but if he'd heard her, he let it go.

"I don't always do it on purpose and I did just have sex. Surely you know what that does to a man's brain-cell reproduction."

"Your brain doesn't produce anything anymore, and don't do it at all, on purpose or otherwise."

"If you spent more time cultivating your vampire skills instead of bitching about wanting to be a human again, you'd be able to read a mind or three, too."

"Really?"

"Yes. Really." He rolled off her, taking Nina with him to nestle her against his chest. Her head fit right under his chin, burrowing beneath it, leaving her feeling secure and sheltered. "I really don't invade your head on purpose, Nina. Sometimes it just happens before I realize it has. I think it has to do with spending all this time with you. I've become attuned to you and your whining and raging."

Nina laughed, tired and far more comfortable than she should be against the hardness of his side. "I'm not whining, I'm just not giving up on becoming a human again. Is it so bad to want that, Greg? I mean, what skin would it be off your nose if I did become a human again?"

He stilled the caress he'd begun along her arm. "None, Nina. I just don't believe it's possible. But if it's any comfort to you, I want what you want. If for no other reason than I won't have to hunt you down every night at dusk to reassure myself you've fed."

What did she want?

The only thing that was ultra clear to her was she wanted more of what had just happened. She'd promised no strings, and she'd meant it.

Hadn't she?

Was making love even worth it with anyone else ever again, if nothing could compare to this?

Greg stirred against her.

Fuuuuuuuuuuuck. Had he heard that? Jesus, she couldn't even think alone anymore.

He placed a kiss on the top of her head. "The sun'll be up soon, Nina. Rest and let everything else go now."

Her hand drifted to the sheets under her. "Don't we have some clean-up to do?"

Greg laughed. "Another perk of being a vampire. No wet spot."

But . . . "Didn't you, you know . . ."

His hand cupped her chin, lifting it so he could look her in the eye. "Hell, yeah, Nina. I came, but for vampires it's more spiritual than physical. We don't reproduce, remember?"

"But I was, well, I was . . ."

"Aroused? Yep, you were. I told you sex as a vampire was a whole different ball of wax. It has its contradictions. Now sleep. Your constant chatter's holding up a good nap."

Spiritual . . .

Oh, it had been many, many things. Adding spiritual to the list of the many, many things it was, was just icing on her sexual cake.

"Sexual cake," he muttered with a half smile, before his eyes drifted closed and he slept.

Damn the sun and its power to draw her into sleep. She wanted to mull this over, understand it, but she was nearing exhaustion.

However, that didn't stop the last vestiges of disbelief from re-minding her of what she'd just done.

She'd just boffed a vampire.

As a vampire.

Of all the goddamned things.

CHAPTER
11

Awakening was as easy as it always was for Nina since she'd become part of the undead. The hand she reached across the bed to find Greg wasn't there? Not so easy to swallow. Like she should have expected him to stick around. She'd offered him the milk— not the cow. She shouldn't be allowed to have one moment of self-pity.

Yet, she found she was hoping he'd only be in the bathroom or something.

Her sheets were tangled around her legs, but she fought her way out of them to sit up and scan her bedroom. Her ears perked.

Just her and Larry.

Larry sat up in his cage, sniffing at the plastic with the probable hope she might actually let him run around in his exercise ball again sometime this millennium. His beady eyes sought hers with longing.

God, she'd been a negligent pet owner, and Larry deserved

better, really. Taking the sheet with her, Nina felt it was safe to handle him. She had some blood in the fridge if she got desperate and began to wonder what guinea pig à la mode was like.

The moment she opened the top of his cage, he scampered toward her hand, jumping up into it. She cuddled him to her chest, stroking his soft fur. "Dude, my apologies. It's just been a little crazy around here, ya know? How about a nice run in your ball and then a carrot? I think I still have some."

Larry didn't protest when she popped open the ball and placed him inside, immediately taking off on the floor in a blue flash of plastic the second she set him down.

The moment had come to ponder last evening's festivities.

She'd had sex with a vampire.

The best sex evah.

Seriously, like evah. She'd had her share of sex before this, and nothing had ever been as hot or as satisfying as Greg's hands and mouth on her.

Maybe it was just because she was a vampire that it seemed to have such magnitude? Greg had said it was intense.

She went to the kitchen to pick up her phone and dial Wanda. Wanda would know how to help her come to terms with this. Wanda was sensitive and a kind soul.

"Nina? Are you okay? I know you were mad at us last night, but we're only telling you what we think is the best advice we have to offer. We didn't mean to upset you."

"I'm not upset, Wanda."

She paused. "Is this Nina Blackman? The one who's a new vampire Nina Blackman?"

She smiled, oddly filled with serenity and goodwill. "Yes, Wanda. It's me."

"But it can't be—you're way too calm, way too nice. The Nina I

know yells and swears. Did the pod people come and swap bodies
with you or what?"

"No, but they may as well have."

"Now what happened? Do you have to do something else that's
too high on your ick factor?"

"No. There was nothing icky about this." Nada icky. Like
Nada.

"Oh, God, what have you done?"

"I had sex with a vampire."

"Oh, Jesus Christ in a miniskirt, Nina!" Wanda burst out, and
that she was swearing was a sure sign she was disturbed. Then the
panic in her voice subsided briefly. "Wait, did you have sex-sex or
did you just cop feels—mutually masturbate or something?"

Mutually masturbate? Okay, this cheesy reading hobby had
taken Wanda to places Nina never thought she'd go. "Wow, Wanda,
who's been replaced by pod people? We had sex-sex, for sure."

Her gasp was sharp, cutting. Not at all sensitive or kind of soul.
"Do you know what you've done? Now you're mated for *life* with
him! Have you lost your mind?"

Nina tsk-tsked into the phone with a light chuckle and thought
about how much she was going to sound like Greg. "Knock off the
romance novel crap, Wanda. Some of it *is* true, yes, but just because we had sex doesn't mean we're mated for life. So find your
calm and chill out."

The long silence between their connection told Nina Wanda
was disapproving, but appeased for the moment. "Oh. Well, okay
then. But you've only known him for a little while, Nina, and hated
his guts for almost all of that time."

"In the new millennium, Wanda, some people have sex on the
second date and never see each other again. I'd say we set some
kind of record for longest vampire courting."

"Oh, don't go preaching about the ways of dating these days to me. I'm only thirty-three, and I might be out of the dating scene, but I'm not old and dried up. I watch TV. I'm just saying you couldn't exactly call yourselves dating. So how'd this go down?"

The age-old explanation might be trite, but it definitely applied here. "It just happened."

"Uh-huh. That's usually the way of a one-night stand. What I meant was, you thought he was a creepy guy who wanted to turn you into some monster. Thoughts like that don't typically lead to a slap and tickle."

Had it been a one-night stand? Fuck. Now was when the insecurities would set in, and that just wasn't her thang. But the question still remained—was it a one-night stand? "He can be all right if you let him."

"*All right?* Hold on a second, Nina. Wasn't it just last night that Marty and I were extolling his virtues and you were still whining he was a jerk who wanted to take over the world one dental hygienist at a time?"

Yeah. That'd been her. "Um, yes. That was me."

"And this has changed how?"

"I dunno. I went to a movie last night, and he —"

Momentarily distracted, Wanda cooed, "Oohhhhhhh, whadja see?"

"*Beaches.*"

"Shut up. You saw *Beaches?*"

"So?"

"So, it wasn't *Die Hard* or *Full Metal Jacket*, and that just proves the point I was going to make. You're not right in your head. If you sat through *Beaches*, the Apocalypse is coming. Of that I'm sure."

"What I saw wasn't the point, Wanda. The point is he came and found me—"

Wanda breathed a sigh filled with romantic inflection. "In the movies of all places . . . oh, that's soooo sweet."

Her hand ran through the tangled strands of her hair, fighting exasperation. "Wanda, just be quiet and let me finish. Anyway, he came to check and see if I'd fed and we talked." She paused, unsure exactly when her ginormous change of heart had happened. It was somewhere between seeing the remorse on his face for having been turned and talking it out at the cemetery. "He told me things about his clan, and we actually had a conversation instead of screaming at each other."

Wanda's comment was dry. "I'd bet that was like Christmas for poor Greg, but one decent conversation a sexual encounter does not make."

Nina wrapped her arms around her waist, cradling the phone against her shoulder, her smile wistful. "I guess for us it did."

"You know what it is, Nina?"

"What is it?"

"He doesn't take your crap, and you find that sexy as hell. You can't just send him on his way because he's pissed you off. He won't let you."

Yeah, that she couldn't ruffle his bat wings turned her on—definitely. Not that she'd admit it to anyone.

"I can't even believe I'm asking this. So was it . . . you know, good?"

Good was like crazy downplaying it. That was like saying winning the gold medal at the Olympics was just "good." It was too mediocre a word for what had happened last night. "Um, I think I can say with all honesty it was the best sex I've ever had in my entire life, and while I'm no slut, you know I've had some sex in my time. It was so many adjectives I don't think I can list them all."

"Holy frijole—"

Shit, her doorbell was ringing, interrupting their conversation. "I gotta go, Wanda. Someone's at the door."

"But—waaaaiiiiit. I want to hear about the best sex ever," she squawked, her voice drifting farther away, as Nina clicked the off button.

Nobody rang her doorbell. Certainly Greg didn't. She tightened the sheet around her, hopping over Larry who was zipping around like Speed Racer. Cracking the door, Nina's eyes narrowed.

Her landlord.

Who she owed almost two months rent to.

Motherfucker.

His fist hit the door when she didn't immediately open it. "It is I, Unmesh from India, Ms. Neena. I am needing you."

Unmesh was a decent guy—even if he had the odd practice of announcing where he came from every time he rang her doorbell. He loved everything American—especially Kentucky Fried Chicken and Twinkies.

He'd given her a break a time or twenty this past year, and she didn't want to jeopardize his goodwill by telling him she didn't have the rent.

Which meant she was going to lie, and that meant she had to think fast.

Her excuse was at the ready as she threw the chain off the door and poked her head around it to find Unmesh of India, raven-haired, dark complexioned, and wearing his native garb. She called him U because it was so much easier to remember.

When he saw her, he flashed her a white-toothed grin, leaving her confused, because he should be pretty pissed. "Look, U, I'm sorry I didn't get the rent to you last week, but I promise I'll go to the bank and get—"

Unmesh held up a hand. His eyes, the color of ripe black olives, were twinkling. "You are not needing to explain, Ms. Neena. I come wid a message for you."

Baffled, Nina cocked her head. "You didn't come for the rent?"

His grin widened. "It is paid."

By who? The fucking rent fairy? "By?"

"No, do not say good-bye, Unmesh is not finished."

"No, U, I meant by *who*. Who paid the rent?"

"Ahhhh. I see. It is tall man. Native to dis country, I tink. He is vedy, vedy white."

Greg? Greg had paid her rent? "Was his name Greg?"

Unmesh smiled the smile of the wicked. A smile that suggested he knew some big secret and shrugged. "I am not knowing. I do not ask question. I only know he pay de rent for one year." U held up a single finger for emphasis.

Nina's mouth dropped open. Oh, no. No, no, no. She didn't want his money.

"I come to tell you someting." He leaned in toward her and whispered, "It is okay if you want to, what is dis word? Have party . . ."

Party . . . "What? U, you're not making any sense to me. I don't have parties, and you know it. The biggest party I can remember was when Wanda's house was being painted and she needed a place to have her Bobbie-Sue recruit meeting. Remember the gaggle of women? That's the only party I can think of." God, what a mess of giggling, lipsticked broads that had been.

He winked one big, black eye at her. "Dis is not what I am meaning. I am meaning a party at night."

What. The. Fuck. "A party at night? I still don't get what this has to do with the rent, U."

Umesh rocked back on his heels and clucked his tongue, still smiling. "I tink you know what I am knowing."

Nina didn't know what he was knowing, and she wasn't sure she wanted to know what he was knowing. Ya know? "U, I have no clue what the hell you're talking about, and I have to go." She had a vampire to ream a new one.

He prevented her from closing the door by putting his hand against it. "You can have secret man party at night, but," he held up a stern finger to shake at her, "you must be *vedy* private."

Something in the way he said *private* put the pieces of the puzzle together for Nina. Suddenly, she got it. She shook her head vehemently, her tangled hair falling in her face. He thought . . . oh, hell, he thought . . . "Oh, no, U. It's not like that—"

He snapped his fingers together creating the shape you made when you were making the head of an alligator in the shadows on the wall, motioning her to quiet. "You are not needing to tell me, Miss Neena. It is our secret. But you must be quiet. If de police find out, it could be vedy, vedy ugly."

U thought she was hooking for cash. At night. With Greg as one of her clients.

Christ on a cracker.

So how was she going to explain this? "No, U, you're misunderstanding—"

He did the thing with his hand again. "Ack! No needing to tell Unmesh from India anyting." He chuckled wickedly. "Ahhh, Amedica de land of de free. Good place, Amedica." He waved to her as he sauntered down the hall.

What the hell had she been thinking? This—this was what she got for overanalyzing what should have been left characterized as a good schtup. Nothing more, nothing less. That she'd been all warm and fuzzy over it disgusted her. She was never warm and fuzzy about anything.

The bastard felt guilty, and so he'd decided to assuage his guilt by buying his way out of it.

How dare he interfere in her personal affairs?

He was all up in your personal affairs last night, girlie.

Son of a bitch.

Welllll, he had another thing coming if he thought he could just buy her off like some cheap tart. Nina stomped into the kitchen, scooping up Larry as she went. She'd feed, and then she'd drag her ass back to the Island to tell him he could keep his money.

She yanked open the door of the fridge and almost dropped Larry.

He'd stocked her refrigerator with packets of blood. Rows and rows of it. Her eyes told her it was the right kind of blood, too. All negative.

Was this his way of saying thanks for the lay, ciao, baby? Like buying the woman you slept with a pretty trinket so she wouldn't bawl her eyes out when you dumped her? Or was he feeling guilty because as of right now, her only option for work was the graveyard shift? She didn't want his money. She'd make her own, even if she had to find a job at a twenty-four-hour bodega.

Ohhhhhhhh, when she got her hands on him, she'd—she'd . . .

You'll what, Nina? Go a couple rounds with him? Think vampire, moron. Stronger, faster, as in he can totally take you. He has the technology.

Now what?

That he was stronger than her hadn't stopped her before. The only thing she did know was things were going to get vedy, vedy ugly.

NINA kicked the leaves scattering Greg's walkway as she strode up to his door. At the rate she'd traveled tonight, with delays and such, she could have *walked* faster than public transportation had taken to get her here. She'd vaguely wondered if she really could walk faster than public transportation, then dismissed it as being too Bionic Woman for her.

The ride into Long Island hadn't cooled her anger. It seared her gut, burning a hole in her stomach. That she'd fallen for his bullshit tweaked her beyond words.

And she always had words.

Her phone chirped, warning her she had a message. Not only was the ride long to get here to Posh-ville, it apparently didn't get a cell phone signal either. Her phone had been on the entire trip. Punching in her code to retrieve her voicemail, she frowned.

It was a message from the supposed mystery vampire from the bar. Fuck, she'd totally forgotten about him because she was off losing her brain cells one by one while boinking the vampire. And that this mystery vampire had her cell number freaked her out. She definitely hadn't given it to him, but he'd said he'd call to set up a meeting just before disappearing. In fact, if she recalled their conversation right, he'd said he'd been trying to call her for days.

Bizarre and probably a question she didn't want the answer to.

And he still wanted to meet. He'd listed a time and a location then hung up. She checked her calls received, and the number came up unknown. Looking at her watch, Nina decided she just might have enough time to chew Greg a new one and make her meeting back in Hackensack with the creepy guy.

If she managed her time wisely.

Whether it was wise or not, she didn't allow herself to ponder for long. He might be her ticket back to mortality, and some things weren't achieved without great risk. For now, she'd set aside her anxiety and focus on Greg.

Her eyes narrowed with another rush of angry thoughts. But before she went pushing her way in, she needed to gather her thoughts. Nina had two things in mind and two things only. The third, their blistering sexual encounter, would go unmentioned if she could help it. She'd show him she knew how to fuck and run, too.

Soooooo she had to demand that he take back his money and

pressure him to tell her where Lisanne was, because if he didn't, she had a kooky vampire to meet. Not much freaked her out, but his odd smile and unwavering pleasant demeanor did.

That alone made her angrier. Dude was weird, and that she had to go to these lengths, potentially risking her life by meeting some stranger on so little information to get anything she could find on Lisanne, made her want to throw down with Greg.

Her fist clenched, tight with rage, and she pounded on the door, calling his name and making as much ruckus as she could muster. The hell she'd let him pay her rent and think that'd make her forget she had no job because of this whacked lifestyle.

The hell.

The sudden rustle of the bushes, subtle to a human ear, she supposed, alerted her to use her nose. It was like her antennae and her antennae smelled *human*. Only this time, she was sure it wasn't just some human down the road or in the house next door. This human was so close she could hear his blood coursing through his veins.

Her head whipped around, and Nina found herself staring at an elderly gentleman. He wore a bathrobe, crushed velvet and royal blue with an *F* monogrammed on the lapel. He had a thick head of white hair, and something he toyed with in his age-spotted hand. The wrinkles of time lined his face in a zig-zagging pattern, well worn and hard earned.

Nina waited for him to speak, but his silence grew heavier while she waited. Maybe he was looking for his cat? The elderly at the senior citizen home Wanda volunteered at loved her cat, Menusha.

The odd look in his eyes and his eerily calm face sent a warning signal out to her. Senility? Dementia? Alzheimer's? Was he lost? Her immediate instinct was to help him. It had to be maybe thirty degrees, and his brown, slip-on slippers couldn't be warm enough in this weather. Suddenly, beating the shit out of Greg took a back-seat to helping this stranger. "Are you okay? Can I help you find something?"

His weathered voice was cautious. "Are you just like him?"

Nina ventured closer. "Him? You mean Greg?" She thumbed a finger over her shoulder.

His right leg limped, as he drew nearer to her, holding his one hand behind his back.

Nina grew unsettled. While her senses were becoming keener, she still couldn't pinpoint what he was feeling. "Who are you?"

"Jim. I'm Jim Finch. The neighbor."

"Hi, Jim. I'm Nina. Care to explain what you mean?"

"I said are you like him?"

The term *like* was relative here. "Like who? Greg?"

"Like the devil," he spat with clear venomous disdain.

Two things happened at once: Jim hurled something in her direction, yelling shallowly, and a big arm snaked out from behind Greg's door to drag her inside just before it hit the door with a watery splat. Disoriented, Nina fought against the arm that held her. "You must be Nina," the possessor of said arm whispered low.

Jim Finch pounded on the door, yelling he knew what Greg was, and he wasn't going to let this go on. Something about Neighborhood Watches, patrolling the streets of Long Island to keep out the riffraff and devil worshippers.

Devil worship?

Nina spun around to see who'd grabbed her and found a tall, sandy-haired man dressed casually in pleated trousers and a dark, pullover sweater. Her eyes grew instantly skeptical. Another vampire who had the bone structure of a Calvin Klein male model?

"It's okay, Nina. I'm Clayton. Or Clay to a woman as lovely as yourself."

"Well, Clay, who was that, and who are you?"

Jim's relentless pounding on the door reverberated through the high-ceilinged entryway, but that didn't stop her from wanting to know who this Clay was and what he might be able to tell her.

"I'm a friend of Greg's, and I have to say, it's a pleasure to meet you. Greg's told me a lot about your, er, situation."

Greg had friends? Friends he talked to about her? Interesting. Her suspicion piqued. "So are you a part of Greg's clan?"

His smile was slow, seductive. "I am, indeed."

Aha! Maybe he knew where Lisanne was. Nina cornered him, her eyes narrowing, while Clay looked down at her with amusement. "So then maybe you can tell me where I can find this—"

"Nina?" Greg screamed down the stairs to the front door and gave it a good pounding with a heavy fist. "Knock it off, Jim, and go home to Ruth right now," he hollered.

"You're the devil!" Jim bellowed from behind the door, his voice agitated with a high-pitched fervor.

"Go home, Jim," Greg yelled back, pulling open the door and staring down Jim Finch. "Go home right now. It's freezing out, and Ruth will be concerned if she wakes and finds you gone. What would I say to her if she found you on my doorstep frozen like an ice pop? I'd never be able to live with myself." Greg kept his tone even, humorous, and light, but with a hint of authority to it that brooked no discussion.

Jim backed away, a very real terror clearly in his eyes. His white hair whipped violently in the wind, as he shivered. His hands shook when he pointed an accusatory finger at Greg. "I know what you are. I know!" he bellowed before he stumbled backward and took off across Greg's lawn.

Greg turned to Nina, his face in full scowl, his eyes blazing fire. "Do you see what you've done, Nina? Didn't I tell you we have to look out for ourselves? That you can't be too careful?"

Fury rose from the pit of her belly. She stuck her neck out, circling it in a threatening manner "Oh, like I knew he thought you were the devil, you shit! I thought he was some old, senile guy who'd lost his way home. This is your fault, Dracula. If you'd told me your neighbors thought you were the devil, you know, sort of a heads-up, I *would* have been more careful!"

Clayton's laughter filled Greg's entryway, rich and resounding. "Wow. You two're something to watch in person. I've only heard about these infamous fights from Svetlanna. To witness it is like watching *Ultimate Fighting* without the sweaty, grunting men, and Nina's much prettier. And on that note, I think I'll let you two hash it out—I'm outta here."

He took Nina's limp hand and kissed the back of it. "Nina, you're all Greg told me and more." Then his eyes turned to Greg. "My friend, I wish you the skill to battle this fierce she-warrior. Call me, and we'll hit the green. I found a great place in Florida that's primarily deserted at night but for the chipmunks. Until then, later." His back turned on them both, and then he was gone in an instant.

"She-warrior?"

Greg's nostrils flared. "Clay was turned back in the times of Vikings."

She waved a hand at him, not interested in anything other than clearing this shit up and going back home. Sometimes the information he fed her was just too much. Seeing a guy who was once a Viking, walking and talking, was a lot to take in, even on a girl's best day. "Whatever. I don't care anymore. You and me, we got a beef."

His anger seemed to evaporate, replaced with a mocking smile. "No. Way. Really? I'd have never been able to tell from the way you were pounding on the door, punkin. Speaking of the door . . . do you have any clue what you just avoided?"

"An old, delusional man?"

"Holy water."

"What?"

"Holy water, you pigheaded, impulsive, anger management-needing fool! Jim had holy water, that's what he threw at you. Do you have any idea what that could have done to you and your 'I don't want to be a vampire' backside?"

Nina was stunned. So stunned she couldn't even cowgirl up enough to defend herself and her anger management-needing ass.

Greg took hold of her upper arms, glowering down at her. Hookay, he was truly pissed. "It could have killed you, Nina. Your wish to not be a vampire just might have come true tonight, because you just can't keep your big mouth shut. Jim Finch suspects we're demons. He isn't far off the paranormal mark, and anyone who comes here—especially making as much of a racket as you did—is subject to his suspicions."

He raked a hand through his hair, sending her an ice-cold swish of his eyes. "I can only be grateful for his wife, Ruth, who thinks he's bordering senile and thanks me—*thanks me*—for putting up with his crazy ramblings. She bakes me cookies. But here's the thing—Jim Finch isn't crazy, and there's been a time or two he's seen some things I wish he hadn't. I've lived here for quite some time, and I like it, and I won't let you jeopardize it because you have some bug up your ass. If Jim could find a way to convince just one person what he says is the truth, he could fuck us all for good, and right now, that includes you, too, mouth."

Nina's stomach fell while she watched him glare down at her. She'd just done everything Marty had warned her against.

Her bad.

And he wasn't done. "And did it ever occur to you that because you're always like some bull in a china shop that you're not just risking your own life by revealing us, but others as well? Other vampires who had nothing to do with what happened between us."

Hellafino. No, it hadn't. Shit, shit, shit. It wasn't just Greg she'd risked either, it was Svetlanna, too, and like it or not, she dug Svetlanna. Remorse and guilt had just become close bedfellows. "You're right."

"I'm what?"

There was no hesitation in her reply. No snide remark, no sarcasm dripping from her words like ice cream melting on a hot July day. "I said you're right. It was foolish and impulsive of me, and if anything happened to Svetlanna, I'd be very upset."

He eyed her with clear suspicion. "Did you just say I was right? I know I have supersonic hearing and all, but just confirm that for me one more time."

Nina nodded her head, letting her hands slide into the pockets of her jeans. "I did. You're right and even if you'd turned out to be a fuckwit who wanted me to be his vampire slave for eternity so I could carry out your evil plan to take over the world, Svetlanna probably wouldn't be a part of that, and I would never want to see anything happen to her, just because I want to slap the shit out of you." There. The truth in a nutshell.

His chest rumbled with laughter as he gathered her up in his arms and planted a kiss on her cheek. "Well, thanks, Brain. You had me worried you were some imposter."

That was the second time today someone had said that to her. Had she changed that much? Become that soft? Peeshaw. Despite admitting to her egregious error, she had a mission to complete, and it didn't entail being this close to him.

No matter how it made her now failed intestines twist into a flock of butterflies. Nina squirmed out of his arms, shoving aside the enticing rub of her breasts against his chest. She backed away from him, refusing to let herself be sucked in. "I have a bone to pick, and that's why I was so angry. Not only does it take me a hundred years to get here to pick it with you, it takes many forms of disgustingly filthy buses and trains to do it. So surely you can see my upset."

"A bone, huh? How many more bones do we have to pick?"

Nina didn't waste any time—she went right for his proverbial throat. "Why did you pay my rent—for a year? A year, Greg. That's just crazy."

"Wasn't it you who said I'd ruined your life? Prevented you from working because your qualifications require a day job? Wasn't it you who staunchly refused to come here as a part of the clan? Yep. That was you, and I just didn't think I could live with myself if I was the one responsible for you having to bunk at the local home-less shelter and work the midnight shift, slinging burgers in some diner off the turnpike."

Guilt. He felt guilty, and he thought paying her rent would absolve him of the catastrophic event he'd created. "How about we call it like it is and not candy coat it. It was guilt. You were paying me off to ease your guilt and shut me up."

"To shut you up for whom, Nina? Are you still on the 'join my evil clan' kick?"

Good question—one she hadn't given thought to for a couple of days. She was only in the business of flinging insults at the mo-ment. Whether they had any truth to them was neither here nor there right now. Moving right along. "How can you possibly af-ford to pay my rent for a year? It's almost nine hundred dollars a month."

He nodded vaguely. "Money isn't much of a concern for me."

"Well, duh. You live in a castle, but castles have to be expen-sive."

"I'm going to tell you a little something about my castle, Nina. I've lived a very long time, and in that time, I've invested wisely. Not only have I invested wisely, like in Svetlanna's pet project, Fango, but I've acquired some skills along the way. Skills that take time and effort, but are well worth it. Like this castle. Do you re-ally think anyone would let me build a castle in Long Island in the

suburbs? This"—he swept his hand over the room—"is all an illu
sion. Sort of like mass hypnosis, if you will. I can influence people
to believe whatever I want them to, if I choose. I'm just careful about what and how I go about influencing those around me.
This house was selfish on my part, and it isn't *hurting* anyone. I
just missed my childhood home. And before you get all excited,
thinking you're going to take over the world with these new powers, this particular kind of magic is learned and comes with a responsibility to those around you. It should also prove to you that I
can make you do things you don't necessarily want to do with my
power of suggestion. I just don't." He gave her a crooked smirk.
"And I don't, because I live for a good challenge."

"Okay, David Copperfield, now I know you're nuts."

He hooked his thumbs in the loops of his jeans and shrugged
his shoulders. "Call me what you will, but if I ceased to exist, so
would my castle. Many of the things I've acquired over the years
are simply things I've created in my imagination. If my immortality ended, so would a lot of my stuff. I have to believe we were
given this whatever you want to call it because to live in the human
world and survive, make a living and do all the things you once
called normal, wouldn't be easy. So whatever-whomever, in some
misguided way, was looking out for those of us who're immortal.
I call it compensation. I might not be able to have a beer, but I can
have a castle."

"Got any more skills I should know about, Oh Great and Powerful Oz?"

He winked one delicious eye. "I think I've covered them all."

Nothing was real anymore. Nothing, and as she descended further into this quagmire of vampire-ness, she decided reality hadn't
been so bad. She'd been broke and always living on the financial
edge, but she didn't have to drink blood and learn how to fly.

Though admittedly, a nice little house in north Jersey by the shore might not be a bad gig.

Nina twisted the ends of her hair with nervous fingers. "I don't think I can take many more surprises—so let's just address the issues at hand before I begin to question everything around me while I not so quietly lose my mind. Do you know what your paying my rent did to my reputation?"

His eyes suddenly held understanding. "Uh, no, but I'm feeling secure I'll hear about it."

"My frickin' landlord thinks I'm hooking for cash! Like I'm a kept woman. Me, of all the people in the world. Do you have any idea how embarrassed I was when Unmesh came to my door tonight?"

Greg cracked a smile, then snorted, and then began to laugh— hard. The gurgle in his throat turned into the laugh of a hyena. "Sss-ooo-rrr-yyy. I-I-Iiiiiiiii . . ."

"You what? Think it's impossible someone thought I could make money hawking my wares?"

He doubled over, putting his hands on his thighs to support himself, while he laughed hysterically at her. Rubbing his shoulder over his eyes, Greg gathered his wits and said, "You can't have it both ways, honey. Either you're insulted to be considered a lady of the evening, or you're insulted because I find that particular accusation damned funny." He began another raucous round of laughter.

Nina nudged him in the shoulder, pulling her fingers away quickly to avoid the feel of his flesh beneath her greedy hands. "It isn't funny. I might not have much, but my reputation is important to me. I won't have some shitheads in my building talking to that gossip Unmesh and thinking I'm sleeping with you for rent money. I won't. I don't do drugs, and I don't sleep around."

Greg's sudden seriousness caught her off guard, as he stood back up and ran a finger down her nose. "Honey, I know you don't sleep around, and I'd be happy to make up some story for this Un guy if you want. My intention wasn't to make you look bought. I was just trying to help. Sure, I feel guilt over what I did to you, but not enough to insult you, and shutting you up is the last thing I'd want to do."

Warmth she shouldn't be feeling crept upward to her chest. Oh, no. He wasn't going to influence her anymore with his crap. How he had the ability to make her waffle on something she was dead set on just twenty minutes ago baffled her. Didn't he just admit to being able to influence those around him? No more swaying of the convictions. "You did it to get me off your back about wanting to be a human again because you think it's crazy, and I don't need you to stock my refrigerator with blood. What was that anyway? The vampire equivalent of wining and dining me so you could say thanks for letting me get in your drawers? I agreed to the terms of our schtupping—no strings and no little thank you presents required, thank you very much."

In an instant, Greg's face turned to stone. Hard as granite and masked with a quiet, eerie fury so real it was palpable.

Hoo boy. She'd gone too far. It shouldn't bother her that she had—no one could ever accuse Nina Blackman of being afraid to push the envelope. But it bothered her when she could visibly see it, because it meant she was in too deep and he was going to let her have it. She just never knew when to stop. Her way of poking around and testing his emotions was to hurl accusations before thinking about what came out of her mouth—even if now, in the heat of the moment—they seemed absurd. And she was going to get an ass whooping for it. She sensed it, yet anger wasn't the only sensation she was picking up. He was insulted . . .

The line of Greg's mouth tightened for a moment as he crossed his arms over his chest. "I have a question now."

Her answer was hesitant. Something she didn't do well normally. "O-okay." Or was it?

Greg loomed over her, his body tense, tight with a whole new level of rage. "What the hell is it with you, Nina? You come here to my home to give me hell because I turned you into a vampire. I'm not saying that isn't a big deal and maybe I should have fallen at your feet and begged for mercy if you had your druthers, but that isn't ever going to happen. I'm all about the here and now, and I've told you on at least three occasions, I have no knowledge that you can ever be turned back—so I try, in my Cro-Magnon way, to help you so I can make this huge mistake right. I chase you down and bring you blood. I put up with the insults you fling like sharp arrows, I listen to your constant yelling, crazy accusations, and now I'm supposed to stand here while you accuse me of banging you and casting you aside with some blood? *Blood?*" He shook his head with disgust. The grooves on either side of his mouth were deep, the furrow between his eyebrows cross.

His disgust for her made her cringe. How totally fabulous that now, all out of the blue, she could pick up on all these emotions— *after* she'd fucking stepped in a quagmire of shit.

Greg's simmering anger was palpable in his next words. "You're some piece of work, Nina Blackman."

Nina gulped. Way to make her feel like shit. And she'd accused him of using her.

Greg opened the front door with a hard yank, the wind rushing in to catch her hair with a sharp gust. "Oh, and just for the record, Nina, sometimes it really is okay to just accept the help you're offered without thinking there's some kind of ulterior motive beyond what's staring you in the face, and now I do believe this conversation is *over*."

Nina stared at him in incredulous disbelief. Was he dismissing her? Just like that?

Take that, bitch.

Her phone vibrated angrily against her thigh. Shit, the night dweller meeting. Her hand immediately went to her pocket to quiet her phone, while Greg glared at her with a question in his eyes.

Of all the times. But really, what else was there to say?

Well, if dignity is something you treasure, Nina, you'll leave and do it fast. Go on with your bad self and strut outta here like the world is your oyster and he's just some guppy who amused you along the way. Because you've blown it.

Her feet wouldn't move, and while she knew she had to go if she hoped to get back to Hackensack, she felt like she had to say something. Anything. If this was it, really it, shouldn't they have a "thanks for the memories" moment?

Greg's stony expression didn't exactly inspire a warm parting. His eyes gleamed with fire, just daring her to say something smart.

Defeat settled in her chest.

Nina gave him one last glance, a mixture of confusion and apology, before she placed one hand on his chest and let the cotton of his shirt leave an imprint on her hand. "I have to go anyway," she said, fighting to keep regret out of her voice.

She left minus a sharp retort and with a chest that felt like a ton of bricks had just landed on it.

CHAPTER 12

Okay.

The Hackensack business district at two in the morning sucked wankers. Absolutely no one was around, so if she found she needed help with this mystery vampire, she was certifiably fucked.

Nina checked the street sign again out of nervousness to make sure she'd gotten it right from the message he'd left her on her cell. Snow had begun to fall in fat, wet flakes. Flakes that were merely a distraction to her vision instead of cold and bothersome.

Lifting her face skyward, she let them fall on her cheeks, like she had when she was a kid.

No sharp sting of cold meeting warm, flushed cheeks. No thrilling chill for the first real snow of the season.

There was just nothing. Which she still found hard to believe, considering she'd been hotter than lava over Greg.

Greg.

She'd fucked that up, hadn't she? The farther she'd distanced herself from him, the more she felt like maybe she'd dealt herself a final blow. And that would suck. And that it sucked meant she liked him—which, too, sucked. No one had ever booted her out of anywhere. Especially not some man. She was the booter. He had some seriously clanging set of cajones.

And goddamn it all, that was hot.

Leaning up against a tall, brick building, Nina scanned the street. Where was this motherfucker anyway? She sniffed the air, hoping her bionic olfactory senses would pick up something. She'd know the mystery vamp's smell, unique only to him.

Movement from the building to her right caught her eye. Her bionic one apparently, because it'd only been a quick movement of shadow, but she could see it as though it moved right in front of her face.

Well, it was now or never.

Nina stepped out onto the sidewalk and planted her hands on her hips.

Very Clint Eastwood, Nina.

The snow fell more heavily, blanketing her until she saw only a tall shadow, elongated by the muted streetlamps. It drew closer, coming directly at her. The scent she picked up was anger, and that didn't sit well with her. It made her defensive. Why should he be angry with her if he was the one who'd contacted her? It made no sense, but the smell that made her nostrils flare was definite.

Rage.

What if it wasn't the guy from the bar? What if it was some freak out looking to whack some chick off because his mommy didn't make him buttered toast and cut it into fun shapes when he was a kid?

His dark outline against the white backdrop of snow was almost directly in front of her.

If she were the panicking kind, she'd feel almost stalked, and the hell she'd let him think he could scare her—even if he claimed to have the 411 on Lisanne and even if she was just a little hesitant. Yeah, *hesitant* was a not so pussy word. She was *hesitant* and what did one do when they were hesitant? They came out swinging, and the hell with the consequences.

So she did what she did best.

Reacted.

No questions asked, screw the outcome, his supposed information be damned.

When he was but a foot from her, the heavy snow leaving her almost blind, Nina steamrolled the imposing figure, knocking him down with a solid plow to his chest. Her first, vague thought was if this was the guy from the bar, he packed some serious muscle under that flannel shirt. She was assuming he was male, from the hard wall his chest presented to the top of her head.

It happened so fast, her on top of him, she didn't have time to think. Nina felt the movement of muscle in her limbs, she just couldn't keep up with it.

Very, very impressive, she mentally patted herself on the head. It was so Kung Fu and Rambo all at once she couldn't help but be awed by this ability to move around in a wild momentum of motion.

Until whoever had her decided she was far better off facedown on the pavement with his chest on her back. The solid weight of the body was definitely male, she decided.

Nina grunted before wrapping her hands around his head and preparing to crack it on the sidewalk by her shoulder. The elongation of her incisors was welcomed, yet horrifying, but her anger, vampire anger she guessed, for being thrown down on the wet snow, had her in its clutches. Nina saw Marty's infamous color wheel of life flash before her eyes, and all the shades spinning on it were red. She grabbed for his hand, ready to sink her teeth into him.

"I'd put those away, if I were you, before someone gets hurt," her attacker muttered against her ear, thrilling and further inciting her all at once.

He pushed off of her, only to flip her over on her back and cuff her wrists above her head.

The rush of adrenaline Nina had experienced began to fade, replaced by surprise.

Wing Man.

Jay-suess. *What was he doing here?*

"Looking out for your impulsive, rude butt. I think the real question here is, what are you doing here?"

Nina struggled from beneath him, tearing her hands from his strong grip. God, that Amazing Kreskin thing was a little too far this side of crazy. "I went for a walk."

"Oh, the hell you did. You're lying."

Don'tthinkdon'tthinkdon'tthink. She repeated the phrase over and over in her head to keep from revealing what she was really doing in downtown Hackensack in the wee hours of the morning.

Pulling her arms around his neck, Greg hauled her up eye level. "So?"

"So, get out of my head and knock it off."

"I wasn't in your head. Your question was written all over your face, and that you're lying is as plain as that cute nose on your face. So what are you doing?"

"Taking a walk, or I was before you came along. I might have flown, but if you'll recall, I don't have the gift of flight."

The line of his mouth grew grim. His expression said doubtful. "Nope. I'm not buying that. Are you buying more blood because you're too proud to drink what I left you because I'm some scum-sucking pig who buys women off with immortal treats?"

Dayum, he kinda had her tagged. Hearing her accusation out loud made her feel petty. Now the guilt was all hers, clawing at her stomach. "No," she said honestly. "I'm not buying blood. I just needed to clear my head."

"Did you learn anything tonight? Anything at all?"

"Do you mean that 'I'm a big mouth thing'?" she quipped, letting sarcasm lace her words, because it was easier than saying she was a sorry shithead. Or for that matter, that she was just plain sorry.

"No, Nina. I mean being very careful who you consort with. Hooking up with the wrong person could be deadly. It's clear to me that your scent for tracking another vamp is weak at best. By now you should know my scent. Every vampire has a unique scent."

She'd totally forgotten to use that in the rush to best what she thought might be the enemy. But she *had* smelled his anger. Score one for the newbie vamp.

"And your teeth . . ."

Her hand went to her mouth, touching her incisors, now shortening back to their normal size. "What about them?"

"You were ready to use them in self-defense. After all your carrying on, I don't suppose, had it not been me, you'd like to thrust this lifestyle upon someone else, would you? You didn't know it was me, Nina. You just went in both fists flying. You can't ever be too careful, fledgling, and that hot head of yours is going to be your end."

Jesus Christ in a miniskirt. Guilt swelled in her chest. How reckless and foolish. Yeah, she'd been ready to gnaw his hand off like it was a T-bone.

His anger still simmered, evident in the hard stare he kept her under. The snow had plastered his hair to his skull, droplets of moisture sliding from his forehead. "So why don't you tell me the truth about why you're here, two miles from your apartment in a snowstorm?"

No matter how remorseful she was about their fight, there was no way she was going to tell him she'd come to meet some guy who'd promised her she could have her mortality back. It was like telling him she'd gotten an email saying she'd won the lottery in Zimbabwe, and she was off to catch the first plane to collect. Um, no. His staunch belief, whether real or misguided, that there was no going back wouldn't lend to his belief that she'd met someone, in a karaoke bar no less, who claimed he could help her find Lisanne. The impression Greg left her with was he didn't want her to find Lisanne at all. Whether it was because she was dangerous to fuck with or a motivation she was now having trouble justifying, the idea made him jiggy. That much she was confident of.

She used her hands to shove off his chest so she wouldn't be so close. She wasn't much of a liar, and it would show if he could read her eyes. "I told you, I took a walk to clear my head. I don't know why you think I need a keeper."

Her dry response made him smile with a cocky lift of his eyebrow. "At the very least, you need a babysitter."

"Bite me," she yelled up at him, fighting the driving wind and wet snow dripping from her hair and onto her shirt.

"With pleasure," he yelled back.

She rolled her eyes, wishing away the temptation to tell him to go right ahead and take a piece of her. A piece of her neck. "Why did you follow me anyway? Wasn't it you I just left all pissed off?"

"Oh, you're damn right I'm pissed, Nina, but it doesn't change the fact that someone needs to look out for you, or are you forgetting the last time you struck out on your own with the blood guy?"

Yes, yes, yes! She'd made some mistakes. Okay. All right. For crap's sake, enough with the constant harping on her shortcomings and persecuting her for them. "I'm going home."

Before she was able to make a very dramatic display of a good huffy, pouty, stomping-off exit into the night, Greg grabbed her upper arm. "You do that. The world is a safer place if you do," he growled at her, disappearing into thin air with a scowl on his face. The snowy, opalescent night swallowed him up, leaving her to deal with her increasing frustration.

Nina kicked at the snow, trudging home with a whole new barrel of problems. First, she was lying to Greg. Why that disturbed her wasn't worth the time it would take for more introspection. It just did, and if she could get it to quit the fuck nagging at her, she'd set it aside.

But it rankled, gnawing and relentless the entire way home.

The most important thing here was her finding her way back to mortality, and if she wasted one more second liking Dracula, worrying when he was angry with her, being turned on by him, and in general just thinking about him, she'd lose her focus.

Second, why did this asshole keep calling her if he didn't intend to help her? Maybe this was some kind of vampire initiation—like swallowing goldfish—and he thought it was funny to string her along.

If that was the case, she wasn't laughing. It was time to find the wayward vamp or bust.

The tard.

THE next night, Nina threw her phone down on the couch with an angry yelp. The hell? According to her cell phone provider, no calls had been made to her at the approximate time she'd reported to customer service, and there was no record of calls from anyone other than Marty and Wanda. It was right in front of her eyes—it said private caller and listed the date and times he'd called. And to make her sound like even more of a lunatic, there was only one message in her voicemail—from the electric company, telling her if she didn't pay her electric bill she'd have to pay to have it turned back on. After they of course turned it off, because she was two months behind.

And it was Thursday.

She considered calling Lou and canceling simply because she had so much on her plate. Thursday's seemed to come round faster and faster these days, and she'd put Lou off plenty. Lou'd let it go, snickering her encouragement for Nina to spend time with Greg.

When she'd spoken to her yesterday, Lou'd sounded tired, but not too tired to remind Nina to bring back her handsome young man, because he seemed to enjoy her pot roast.

Nina thwarted Lou's notion that Greg would come with her in favor of telling her he had a last minute work thing. After their argument last night, she was going to fly low under the radar, and the hell she'd invite him to Lou's for dinner.

Mulling over what he'd said, while it pissed her off to no end, she realized he was right. She was taking the kind of risks that would have her turning into a job for a dust mop. Her impulse to use a good right hook before she gave anyone a chance to explain was second nature to her, and curbing that could only be wise in this vampire game.

Typically, she'd be willing to risk going down in a blaze of glory, but Greg had a way of hitting some hard truths home to her, and though she didn't like it, his advice was well warranted.

Slipping some jeans and a sweatshirt on, and twisting her hair into a knot at the back of her head, Nina headed off to her grandmother's, trying to let her argument with Greg and their ensuing scuffle go. She needed peace in her head for just a little while, while she figured out exactly how she was going to avoid her eyeballs burning over Lou's crucifixes and how she'd eat Lou's pot roast.

When she rounded the corner, she saw Greg, sprawled out on

her grandmother's front porch with his elbows holding him up. Her stomach tumbled, butterflies taking flight deep in the pit of it.

There wasn't a thing about him she didn't think was mad-hot, and that it was becoming her primary focus made her worry— maybe even more than being a vampire forever did. His jeans fit snugly across his thighs, the muscles bulging enticingly. He wore a pullover sweater, black with splashes of multicolors across the chest, stretched tautly across his stomach as he leaned back. His profile seemed relaxed. The sharp cut of his jaw showed no hint of an oncoming clench, and his arms draped over his abdomen loosely, crossed at the wrists.

The sight of him waiting with a bouquet of flowers in hand brought Nina so much relief she almost couldn't speak.

Confusion, relief, confusion, and more relief wove together, intertwining and making it harder for her to think.

She took the steps two at a time and stopped at the top step, looking down at him, then flicking the bouquet of assorted flowers with a light finger. "I'm going to make a huge leap and guess those aren't for me."

He smiled, warm and inviting, the dimples at either side of his cheeks deepening. "Hell, no. I want to give them to someone who won't wilt them with her evil eye."

Nina laughed, strangely receptive to his teasing tone. "How did you know . . ." She didn't wait for an answer. "Never mind, you hunted me by scent or some hound dog thing, right?"

His eyes twinkled with amusement. "I figured it'd been awhile since you'd seen Lou, and, well, she did like me. Just a feeling she might wonder where I was."

"Either way, I appreciate you coming."

He cocked his head in question. Raising his eyes to meet hers, they gleamed, devilish and carefree. "Again, who are you?"

Nina plunked down beside him, letting their thighs touch. She rested her hands on her legs and said, "Look, Lou likes you, and you're right, she wanted you to come tonight, but I told her you had a last minute work thing. So that you showed up was nice. Nothing more, nothing less."

"Ah, well, then I guess it's a good thing I got that work thing all cleared up in time, huh?"

A smile played on her lips. "Yeah, an übergood thing. Here's the deal. I don't want to fight with you, okay? Not tonight. Lou sounded kind of strange when we talked on the phone last night, and I sort of just want to focus on her for the moment."

He placed a palm on her chest, right where her heart used to beat, and she fought not to squirm from the pleasure it brought. "Wow, sugar lips, you really once did have a heart."

Rising, she snickered. "Yes, Vlad, where Lou is concerned I have a heart. She's all I've got."

Greg grabbed her hand, pulling her toward the door and ringing the bell. "I know that feeling well. I feel that very way about Svetlanna."

Her stomach went all mushy at this side of him. Like in the movie theater, it spread a warmth throughout her that she couldn't fight. "Good, then we have an understanding? I won't accuse you of keeping me a vampire against my will tonight, and you get off my back about accepting my inner night dweller, 'K?"

Greg squeezed her hand, sending warm currents along her arm. "Done."

Lou threw the door open, smiling at them. She'd gussied up, wearing her best burgundy polyester suit and leaving the curlers out of her hair. "C'mere," she said the moment she saw Greg, cupping his face and pulling his head down for a kiss on his cheek.

Greg held out the flowers to her, and she sighed. "For me? You sweet boy. I thought you had some kind of work thing to attend to?"

Greg winked. "I'd clear anything up for you, Lou."

Lou bear-hugged him again and chuckled.

"Er, Lou? Remember me—you know, blood relation?" Nina teased.

Lou's husky chuckle greeted her ears. "Well, I might remember you, if you came around more." She held up a hand to keep Nina from protesting. "I know, I know, you did call, and I can forgive you because you had your young man to tend to, but my pot roast missed you."

Nina hugged Lou, enveloping her weathered frame in an embrace that filled her nose with Lou's dime-store perfume. Lou shook a little, then set Nina away from her to look into her eyes. "How ya been, girl?"

"I'm good. Just busy is all. Sorry I haven't been by," Nina said, following her grandmother into the living room. Lou's movements were slow, slower than usual tonight, Nina noted. The steps she took in her white, sensible shoes seemed labored.

But her focus changed when her eyes settled on the crucifixes littering every available space. Nina fought a groan, forgetting everything but the sting of the religious figurines. She rubbed her eyes, now watering and burning hot, with the heels of her hands.

Greg came up behind her, turning her to face him and lifting her chin with his lean fingers. His eyes held what she'd definitely label as concern.

Lou poked her head around Greg's shoulder. "You two get comfortable. I'll go check the pot roast." Nina wanted to tell Lou to relax, she'd deal with dinner, but she could only think the words.

"Focus on me," Greg whispered. "Count in your head while you do it. I know it's hard, but try."

Nina honed in on Greg's face, forcing herself to keep her mind elsewhere. When she was finally able to speak, she joked, "You know, if you keep this up, I'm going to start believing you like me."

His surprised chuckle filled her with a sense of calm, as he rubbed mindless circles over her spine. "I don't even like you a little, Nina Blackman. You're mean and scary—"

The crash of plates, abrupt and sharp, coming from the kitchen tore them apart, sending Greg sprinting to find out what had happened. Close on his heels was Nina, shoving him out of the way to find Lou, lying on the floor, pale and breathing shallowly. "Lou!" she yelled with alarm, dropping down on her knees and grabbing her grandmother's hand. Her eyes watched in horror as Lou's chest stopped rising and falling with a sudden, harsh gasp.

Nina grabbed frantically for her gnarled hand, wrapping her fingers around her wrist and finding no pulse. "She has no pulse!" she screamed, her terror so thick it rose to lodge in her throat.

Greg dropped down beside her, shoving the shards of Lou's Corning Ware away and pressing his ear to her chest. The line of his mouth was grim when he reached for Nina.

She pulled away sharply, leaning over Lou and wailed. "No, no, no!" Bracketing Lou's shoulders, Nina hauled her to her chest, putting her lips to her grandmother's ear as she hung limply from her grasp. "You listen to me, Lou Blackman, there is no way you can leave me now! I need youuuuu. Oh, God, you have no idea how much I need you!" Her mind raced—call 911, give her mouth-to-mouth, start chest compressions?

And then it hit her, full on with the brutal force of a Louisville Slugger. Greg could save Lou.

He had the power.

Nina's head whipped around, her frantic eyes meeting Greg's. "Turn her," Nina yelled with a plea in her voice. "Do it! You can save her, if you turn her. I know you can. I read it in a book. Turn her," she roared, her voice shaky, and though no tears fell, Nina knew a river would flow from her eyes if she could still cry. Her incisors lengthened; the push of them from her gums surprised her in the midst of chaos.

Greg shook his head no.

It was absolute.

Definitive.

Greg's words were tight, precise and oh, so final. "No, Nina. I can't do that. I can't. It's not fair to Lou," he said in a soft, but firm tone, his eyes set in stone.

Lou hung limply in her arms for what seemed an eternity. Nina's panic, fear, and indescribable grief raced in waves. "Yes, yes you can! You have the ability to save her. Please, Greg. I'll do whatever you want, I swear. I'll join your crazy clan, be a good vampire, drink blood, learn to fly, make castles in fucking Hoboken if you want, but please, I'm begging you, please don't let her die!" She heard her voice, beseeching, raspy, terrified, and she didn't care. Lou couldn't leave her now. *Not now.*

Seconds ticked by, precious seconds that could be devoted to saving Lou.

His face was so resolute, so eerily set, she cringed. "Nina, I need you to listen to me. Lou didn't choose eternity. I can't be a party to that. You hate this lifestyle. Imagine how Lou, someone who's so religious, would feel. I won't do it. *Please*, Nina, just come with me." He held out a hand to her, his eyes searching hers, silently demanding her to let Lou go.

But Nina was beyond reasoning. Lou was the only real family she had. The one person who'd come through for her always. If she could save her, especially now when she felt so alone, then it had to be done. "Then I'll do it," she cried, tearing her gaze from Greg's to look upon Lou's ashen face.

She'd do it—even if she could just barely manage to say the word *vampire* without wanting to scream, even if she had no clue how to do it, she was going to try.

"Nina, *stop!*" he roared, grabbing at her with hands that pulled at her shoulders, keeping her from critical moments in saving Lou.

"Stop! You don't know how. If you do one wrong thing you could leave her far worse off than she is now. If you take too much blood, she'd be nothing more than a zombie."

Her sob was wrenched from deep in her throat. "I don't care! I have to try. I won't let her go," she wailed back, bending her head to place her incisors at Lou's neck. How hard could it be? She'd just sink her teeth in, right? And then it would be okay. Lou'd be pissed as all get out, she'd curse Nina from here to a literal eternity, but she'd have her here—on Earth.

But Greg stopped her, prying Lou from her arms, gathering her to his big frame, his head bent, positioned at Lou's neck.

And then the world stopped turning, all motion and sound blurred, and her frantic thoughts careened like a skidding pair of tires on an icy roadway.

Nina knew in her gut what Greg was going to do—for her.

His fangs gleamed in the glow of the kitchen light, the hiss as they emerged piercing her sensitive ears. He opened his mouth wide, his eyes hazing over, the energy he created sending an eerie vibe along Nina's spine.

Her fists clenched, gouging crescent shapes she could no longer feel in her palms. Her eyes zeroed in on nothing but Greg's dark head and Lou's waiting flesh.

And suddenly, without rhyme or reason, Lou gasped. A long, shrill gust of air filling her lungs—one after the other they came, weak and labored, her chest heaving in an upward battle for breath.

"Call 911." Greg's order was an urgent yet collected demand. His body was tense, as he held Lou and stroked her forehead, murmuring words Nina couldn't focus on. His features, a stark reminder of what he was—they were—returned to normal.

Nina popped up, racing for the phone, punching in the numbers, then dropping back on her haunches to grab Lou's hand, clinging to it for all she was worth. "Just hang on, Lou. *Please*, just hang on," she begged, her throat so taut she could hardly speak, her words watery and garbled.

Greg rose at the sound of the shrieking ambulance's siren, rushing to the door to let the paramedics in.

Two men carrying a stretcher surrounded Lou, crowding Nina out. "Let them do their job, honey," Greg said, ushering her to a corner of the kitchen, holding her in his embrace, lending quiet support. Nina shuddered, burying her face in his sculpted shoulder. Her eyes still burned, but not because of the crucifixes. They burned from unshed tears.

As the paramedics carried Lou away, tubes and gadgets attached to her, Greg put his hand at her back, kissing the top of her head. "Go with her, Nina."

It was true that when disaster struck, crazy things popped into your head. Nina's was a list of things she hadn't done before she'd left home. "I haven't fed Larry," she stated simply, like that mattered when Lou hovered on the brink of death.

"I'll feed him," he offered, his eyes rimmed with sympathy, and so softly green it made her chest ache. "You go and call me the minute you hear something. Do you have my cell number?"

After all this time, Nina realized she didn't. Mostly because she'd been too stubborn to ask for it. Nina shook her head, worry eating her from the inside out.

Greg held out his hand, the hand that had comforted Lou. The hand that had held hers in the theater. The hand that touched her and left a burning trail of fire in its wake. "Give me your cell," he murmured.

Nina struggled to remember where it was, then traced the outside of the pocket of her jeans. She jammed a hand into it and handed it to him. Silently he put his number in, and when the paramedics asked if she was ready, he said low and husky, "Call me, Nina. I need to know she's all right and that you are, too."

Nina gulped. This Greg was so different than the Greg she sparred with on a regular basis. Their steady diet of battle was familiar to her. This Greg—even more different than the Greg in the movie theater—the one who was so obviously worried, not just about Lou, but about her, too, made her feel things she didn't understand.

Nina gave him one last glance, a glance filled with gratefulness, an apology, and a hundred and one questions. "I will. Promise," she whispered back, following the burly paramedic out the door and into the ambulance, where she sat beside Lou and prayed harder than she'd ever prayed before.

CHAPTER 13

A cardiac episode was what the doctors claimed Lou had had. Further tests would be done tomorrow, when she was rested and stronger, to clear up any other possible issues. Nina wasn't sure she was satisfied with that answer. The doctors hadn't seen Lou stop breathing.

She had, and as long as she lived, which just might be a lot longer than she'd planned, she'd never forget that moment. The mental image of a lifeless Lou sprawled over Greg's arm was suspended in her mind's eye, and she couldn't get it out.

Nina sat beside Lou's bed in the coldly painted, sterile hospital room. A white, institutional blanket rose and fell over Lou's chest, and each breath she took was like euphoria to Nina. She couldn't stop touching her to reassure herself over and over that Lou was still here.

The color had returned to her face, and her skin was now warm to the touch, according to the nurse anyway.

Nina could see the rapid improvement just by looking at her. She was afraid to leave, and as she thanked whatever—whoever— had saved Lou, she tried to digest what Greg had done.

He'd been prepared to save Lou—going against that strict moral code he claimed had a no-turn policy. Did that make him a liar or a saint? If what she'd let herself believe all this time was true, then Lou would just have been another notch on his wings. But the niggle in her gut said differently—despite the fact that it appeared he wanted her nowhere near Lisanne. Okay, so maybe she'd clung to the belief that Greg wanted to keep her a vampire for his own evil reasons too long—guilty as charged. Yet believing he'd do something so utterly selfless meant she had to reevaluate where they stood with each other.

As if Lou'd read her mind, her voice, riddled with shaky breaths, startled Nina. "I like your young man. Apologize to him for me, will you?"

Nina smiled, gulping her relief, running her hands over Lou's arms to reassure herself she was still there. "For what, Lou?"

"I invited him to dinner and look how well that turned out." She squeezed Nina's hand with trembling, aging fingers.

Nina laughed softly, her eyes once more burning. "How do you feel?"

"Tired, child. I think it might be time to take that retirement they're always bugging me about at the plant."

Lou's job at a paper mill was all she had, and offering to give it up was monumental for a die-hard blue collar who believed in hard work, God, and meat and potatoes. "I think you need to slow down period, Gram, and if I have anything to say about it, you will, and I'd better not find out you've been smoking again." Nina's warning was stern.

"Nope, haven't touched one in months. That patch really worked."

Nina caressed her forehead, pushing the wisps of stray, wiry hair from it. "Good, 'cause I don't think I could take that kind of scare again. So knock that crap off, okay?"

Lou's smile was slow. "Your young man helped an old, pathetic woman, I assume?"

Her brows knitted together in question. "What makes you say that?"

"I can't say for sure. I remember hearing him—not his words so much as a lot of yelling, but you were there, so I wasn't surprised, and then he had those big arms around me. I can see why you like him so much." Lou wiggled her eyebrows, closing her eyes once more with a weary sigh.

"No one said I like him *that* much."

"Yes, you do, Nina. Don't be so stubborn. It's nice that you like him, seeing as you're not always so likeable."

She chuckled wryly, pulling the covers higher over Lou's chest. "Gee, thanks, Lou."

"I only speak the truth, girl. You're like a porcupine, sticking your quills out when anybody gets too close. But he's unusual, that Greg. You mark my words, he won't put up with your crap."

No. Shit. "No kidding," she mumbled.

"You go home now, honey. Poor old Lou is plum worn out."

"I'm not leaving you. I'll stay right here." And fry when the sunlight comes pouring into the windows, come morning. Now that was a dilemma.

Lou twirled a lock of Nina's dark hair around her finger and tugged. "You have a job, Nina. A new one at that. So go on now and come see me tomorrow. I'll put on my lipstick for ya," she said, yawning and taking another deep breath.

The nurse came in just then to check Lou's pulse. Efficient hands held fast to Lou's wrist, and hawk-like eyes timed each beat to her watch.

"She's still okay, right?"

The nurse nodded, checking her watch once more, then laying Lou's wrist gently beside her. "We'll know more tomorrow, but for now her pulse is strong, and her heart beats like a twenty-year-old's."

Lou cackled, keeping her eyes closed. "If only my ass was like a twenty-year-old's."

The nurse patted Nina's shoulder, her soft voice soothing and low. "I think it'd be okay for you to go home now, Ms. Blackman. You look awfully pale. From the scare, I guess. But I promise we'll call you immediately if anything changes. For now, everything is just fine."

"Right as rain," Lou chirped.

Dropping a kiss on Lou's forehead, Nina knew she had to go. If daylight crept up on her, she'd be in a buttload of trouble and no good to her grandmother. As long as Lou was stable, she couldn't take the chance she'd turn to bacon in front of her grandmother's eyes. "Okay, Lou, but you behave. You're under strict orders to never do that to me again, got it?"

"We all have to go sometime, girl."

Do we? If people only knew.

Nina pressed a kiss to her hand. "Well, how 'bout you not be so dramatic next time, 'K?"

Lou'd dropped back off to sleep, making Nina smile with relief. "I'll be here tomorrow night. I love you."

Her grandmother stirred but sank back peacefully into the bed. Nina took one last look to reassure herself of Lou's stability, then exited to the long sterile corridors, passing the nurses' station, giving a grateful smile to the people who'd settled Lou in.

Nina burst through the doors of the hospital, letting the cold blast of wind caress her face. Tonight she found she didn't much miss not being able to feel it, though she knew it was almost below freezing.

Tonight there were other things on her mind. She didn't want to waste time crying over spilled vampire. She was no closer to her humanity this evening than she'd been since this began.

What still amazed her, left her without words, was the sacrifice Greg was going to make on her behalf.

He'd been prepared to turn Lou for her, to save her because Nina was so bereft at possibly losing her. Would he have done it, if Lou hadn't gasped for breath? After what she'd seen, she'd have to err on the side of her gut and say, yeah.

And were either of them right here? Her for wanting Lou at any cost and him for doing something Nina herself had called heinous—had tortured him about from day one?

Her feet carried her toward the Island.

Nina knew what she had to do.

Greg's sacrifice wouldn't go without mention.

Not tonight.

GREG hugged Svetlanna hard, thanking the gods she was with him. "What was that for?" she asked, the lilt of her voice light and teasing.

"For just being here and being you."

Svetlanna knew him so well. "Oh, Greg, is everything all right?"

He told her about Lou and what he'd considered doing in those frantic moments when she'd hovered between life and death. When he'd found himself at Lou's neck, the seconds that ticked by were excruciating for him morally. Life and death were things you just shouldn't fuck with, but when Nina, raw, vulnerable, and terror-stricken had pleaded with him to turn Lou, he knew in that horrifying moment, he'd do almost anything for her.

And he didn't like this out-of-control shit one bit. He never messed with whatever fate's plan was, but he'd been so close tonight.

So close.

Because of Nina.

Would he have really done it? Turned Lou? The moments flew by so quickly, he couldn't remember if he would have or not. What he did remember was hating seeing Nina suffer. The pain of watching her so distraught had literally been physical, and that wasn't something he could remember happening since he'd been turned—feeling pain, emotional or otherwise.

Svetlanna rubbed her knuckles against his cheek, smiling with sympathy. "Is Lou all right now? Have you heard from Nina?"

Greg glanced at the clock—it was almost two. "No, not yet, but if I don't hear from her in another hour, I'll go find her."

Svetlanna hugged him once more before passing on some sage advice. "That you're where you are, at a moral crossroads so to speak, says volumes about Nina, dear. I know you don't want to hear it, but I'm only going to say this much, and then I'll let it be. She needs to hear some things from you, and you know it. It's only fair. You like her, and you can't tell me you don't. So I think it's time for you to ante up before this goes any further. Now if she calls, please give her my best and tell her I'm here if she needs me." She swept his face with one last worried glance and departed for the kitchen.

Fuck, fuck, fuck.

Yeah, he did have some things to tell her.

Like they absolutely couldn't see each other anymore. Not with what was about to occur in his very near future.

And fuck again.

NINA was as quiet as she could be when she finally made it to Greg's door. She looked down at her feet. Her bionic feet. She'd *jogged* here. Friggin' jogged from Hackensack to Long Island without thinking twice about it.

Caaa-razy.

Ringing the doorbell and hoping Jim Finch wouldn't pop out of nowhere, Nina rocked from foot to foot with nervous anticipation. Svetlanna answered, surprising her.

"Ohhhh, Nina," she cooed, pulling her into the foyer and enveloping her in her floral-scented embrace. "How's Lou and, for that matter, how are you?"

"She's okay. Thanks for asking, and I'm okay, too," Nina responded, ignoring the hitch in her voice. God, tonight had been so close it brought her to the verge of nonexistent tears each time she went over it in her mind. "Is Greg here?" A lump formed in her throat just thinking about seeing him after he'd been so tender with her and Lou. That he was some callous blood drinker just didn't mesh for her as much anymore.

"He's upstairs. Do you want me to tell him you're here?"

Nina put a finger to Svetlanna's lips and shook her head.

She responded by curving her lips upward and whispered, "Third door on the right."

Nina brushed past her, letting her fingers graze Svetlanna's shoulder as she raced up the stairs. She didn't bother to knock; dawn would break soon, and he was probably preparing for bed.

Dark curtains in a heavy material adorned the span of windows she encountered when she pushed the door open. Thick carpeting in a dark burgundy left her feet silent.

Greg sat in a chair covered in rich beige brocade in the corner. He was shirtless and somber. His pecs flexed, drawing her eyes to the patch of hair between them and compelling her to follow the path that hair led to just above the top of his jeans.

She eyed his big bed, with its rich, deep tones of green and royal blue, and licked her lips. "So, where's the coffin?"

Greg didn't laugh. In fact, he didn't say anything, leaving her unnerved but not daunted. His frame, so big and so imposing, made her mouth dry. He was that spectacular to rest one's eyes on. The thick muscles of his arms flexed when he gripped the arms of the chair.

"I-I . . . I came to . . . because . . ." Christ, she was stumbling over her words like it was her first time wearing those stupid high heels Marty loved so much. This shouldn't be that hard, but it felt like she was making an attempt to explain Stonehenge. "I came to say thank you," she blurted out, moving closer to him.

When he spoke, his voice was low, gravelly. "How's Lou?"

"Better, sooo much better." The relief she felt was still evident, even to her ears. Her legs were like butter from it—weak and trembling.

"And you?"

"I'm okay. Good. Really fine." Really pathetic. Expressing herself with wisecracks and anger was usually the best she could do. This—this showing Greg how glad she'd been that he'd been with her when Lou'd collapsed was hard shit.

He spoke but one word. *"Good."*

She came to stand before him, kneeling down in front of him, and on impulse, probably the only impulse that might not bring her some kind of trouble, buried her face in his chest. Greg was stiff and unyielding, yet she didn't care. She burrowed deeper until she finally felt his arms wrap around her body, giving in to the need she surely reeked of.

"I was so scared," she whispered, letting her lips touch his cool skin.

His hand stroked her hair, dragging his fingers though it. "Yeah, so was I."

Him, scared? That just didn't compute. "You were?"

"I don't know any lifesaving techniques, Nina. Yeah, I was scared for you and for Lou. I like Lou."

She had to know. The question consumed her. "Why would you do what you were going to do?"

"Because you'd have nagged me into the afterlife if I hadn't."

Her head shook back and forth. "No, no that's not it, Greg, and right now I don't care what it was, but that's not what it was. I'm sorry I made you question your beliefs. I'm sorry I asked you to do something because I'm selfish."

"Well, well, someone learned a lesson today." His words were meant to be teasing, yet sounded strained to her sensitive ears.

"You can joke all you want, but I'm as serious as a plate of chicken wings would be for me right now. I asked you to step in and potentially change fate. Not only that, I did it without thinking about how Lou would feel. I'm sorry. So, so sorry."

Greg's embrace tightened for a moment, then he let her loose. "It's done now."

She clung even tighter to him, draping her arms around his neck and bringing her lips but an inch from his. "Thank you," she murmured before she pressed her mouth to his, digging her hands into his thick hair.

He was despondent at first, like something held him back, something Nina sensed, but didn't understand. He let his lips remain slack until she slid her tongue between them.

Then all bets were off.

Nina groaned when he slid his tongue between her lips, sipping from them in gentle, fleeting gestures. Her hands stroked the smooth skin of his chest, tweaking a nipple, making him moan. Their kiss deepened, tongues tangled, dueled, until Nina could no longer stand the heat rushing its way to the space between her thighs. His pleasure at her touch inspired her to trace a path to his belly, tugging at the buckle of his belt and popping the button at the top of his jeans.

Shaky hands dragged his zipper down, reaching inside and pushing his underwear down to find his cock, rigid, hot, pulsing.

Greg gripped her shoulders, holding her away from him. "Nina, we have to *talk*." Ragged words came from his lips, but Nina wouldn't acknowledge them.

She said nothing, letting her eyes go smoky with desire and taking his mouth against hers once more. She sucked at words. Nice ones anyway. She'd show him what this had meant to her. That maybe this wasn't just sex anymore.

Dragging her mouth from his, she leaned back and tugged at his jeans, pulling them over his bare feet and tossing them aside. The head of his cock peered out from beneath his boxer-briefs, making her lick her lips with anticipation.

His jaw clenched down hard. The words coming from his lips were said with restraint, yet his body responded with a shudder. "You make this so damned hard, Nina. We have to talk."

Nina yanked his underwear off, spreading his thighs, roaming her hands over the firm flesh, running her fingers through the hair on them, laying her cheek against the springy patch of curls that lay at the tip of his shaft. Her hands roamed his thick legs, kneading the sinew and muscle of them, tracing paths that drew closer to his cock until she'd taken hold of him, bringing him to her lips.

Her tongue snaked out, stroking him, laving the rigid length, until Greg's hands found her long hair, pulling it tightly behind her head, winding it around his wrist. Nina enveloped him with her mouth, taking as much of him as she could, wrapping her hands around his cock, pumping it as she took long passes up and back down.

His sharp hiss spurred her on. The warning in his tone when he called her name rang in her ears, pleasing her with its deep, feral vibrato. Nina cupped his balls, rolling them with light fingers, as she ran her tongue over the head of his shaft, dipping into the slit to tease him.

Greg's howl brought a curve upward of her lips from around his cock. He let go of her hair, tearing at her sweatshirt, hauling it up and over her head, then he slipped his hands under her arms, dragging her from his cock until she leaned into him. Skin to skin, Nina let the electric touch of the flesh of his chest tease her nipples, the friction luxuriously decadent.

Their lips touched once more, his hands grazing either side of her body, finding the button on her jeans and expertly popping it open.

Her jeans were off before she knew it, and Greg settled her on his lap, the swipe of his cock between her legs making her rock against him, moan with need. Nina spread her thighs wide, until they almost ached straddling him.

Hot and sharp, the pangs in her belly throbbed, simmering, anticipating his entry. Nina lifted her hips, putting her arms around his neck for leverage, hissing her pleasure when his lips and tongue grazed the tips of her nipples. She sank down on him, taking him into her, reveling in the thick heat of him. His shaft rubbed against her clit, swollen, aching, sliding in and out of her. Her neck arched as she threw her head back and Greg drove upward, bringing her close to his chest, rasping a tongue over each of her nipples.

The sweet swell of orgasm crept up on her, her gut clenched, her eyes rolled to the back of her head, her hands dug into his shoulders, and she bucked against him, welcoming the release.

Hot flashes of red stroked her clit, pushing her higher until she exploded, calling out his name in frenzied time with their rocking hips.

Greg drove into her furiously. The slap of their flesh echoed like sweet music to her ears, and when he came, he roared his pleasure into her neck.

As they each slowed the tidal wave of sexual currents, Greg gathered her to him, sliding to the edge of the chair and hoisting them up to make his way to the bed. Her eyes were too heavy to open, so she let her legs fall away from his waist, allowing him to lay her on his bed.

Lou's cardiac episode coupled with the soft mattress, Greg beside her, secure, muscular, safe, had left her weak.

Greg's strong arms encircled her, his hand caressing the skin of her shoulder while she pondered the rightness of this moment, and then she remembered he'd said they needed to talk. He'd seemed pretty serious when he'd said it, too.

Whoever'd said talking was overrated was totally right.

Wonking beat talking every time, because talking always led to something she wasn't sure she wanted to hear. She was okay with the way things were right now.

Really, really okay.

Maybe too okay.

But, whatever.

CHAPTER 14

Nina popped one eye open, trying to remember where she was. Then she smelled Greg, his scent on her body, and flashes of last night came and went in her mind's eye. *Tumultuous, harried, slow,* and *sweet* were words that popped into her brain, making her smile.

She rolled over to find he still slept beside her, but as she did, her toe hit a lump at the edge of the bed.

Nina sat up, taking the sheet with her.

"Morning, Glory, or should I say evening?" A woman, wearing a midriff shirt and hip-hugging shorts, sat at the edge of the bed, eyeing Nina with interest. Her blonde hair was scraped back in a chic ponytail to show off flashy, gold hoop earrings. Her skin, while pale, was lightly made up with a makeup job that was so perfect, Marty'd weep tears over it. Her violet eyes, so odd in color, were amused.

Greg sat up, too. Bolt upright, as if he'd never slept. "Lisanne," he drawled, letting his gaze drift over her with cool detachment.

This—*this* was Lisanne? *The* Lisanne? Nu-uh. "*You're* Lisanne?" Nina crowed, shoving the tangled mass her hair had become while she slept out of her face. Her black eyes narrowed.

Lisanne's smile was winning and perfect. "That'd be me."

"I'm Nina Blackman, and oh, lady, do I have a bone to pick with you." Nina scurried to the end of the bed, taking the sheet with her, forgetting Greg's nudity.

Being naked didn't much seem to bother him—not even in front of this very blonde creature. He swung his legs off the bed and strode to the chair where his clothes still lay, jamming his legs into his discarded jeans.

"A bone?" she inquired with a saccharine sweet tone Nina couldn't miss.

"Yeah, a big-ass one, too. Lady, I gotta tell ya, would it hurt to leave a forwarding address, so that if someone, say like me, needed to get in touch with you, I'd be able to find you?"

"What could your concubine possibly want with me, Greg?" Her question was punctuated only by the slide of her ass against the sheets when she slipped from the edge of the bed, completely acting as if Nina wasn't even in the room.

Concubine? Did that mean . . . she'd read that somewhere. Wanda's romance novels? And then it hit her. "Does she mean hootchie?" Nina directed her question at Greg.

He nodded curtly, the hard planes of his face once again like granite. "She does, and because of that, I've no doubt she's going to get a taste of your mouth in about, oh," he glanced at the clock on his tall armoire, "two seconds. Go get 'em, tiger," he encouraged Nina, grinning.

Oh, she so had not just said that . . .

Rage swept over her. Concubine this! "Who the flip do you think you are, calling me a concubine?"

Lisanne's shoulders lifted, her expression bored. Her violet eyes, the strangest color Nina could ever remember seeing, settled on her. "Well, darling, Greg never has anything beyond a one-night stand—what else am I to think?"

Nina's fury escalated as she hopped off the bed and wrapped the sheet around her. How the frig did she know what Greg had? "Look here, you fucking nut. I don't give a rat's fuzzy ass what you think about me. You and me, we got something to talk about."

"Got something to talk about? How interesting. What could Greg's playmate and I have to discuss?" She tapped a pink nail against her matching pink lip.

Nina cornered her, forgetting that if push came to shove, Lisanne could probably throw down like a pro. She was centuries old. But that didn't thwart Nina. Not today. Not after all this. "Listen closely. I know you have the power to turn me back into a human, and I want you to get your ass in gear and do it. Like now. I don't know what you have to do, but I want it done. I don't want to be a vampire. This was all a mistake. Greg didn't mean to bite me, and I didn't mean to become some freaky bloodsucker. So fix this. Today."

Lisanne sent Greg a look of amusement when he came to stand beside Nina, placing a hand on the slope of her hip. "Nice execution, babe. Very direct, very succinct," he muttered. "And you choose now, of all times, to finally believe I don't want to make you join my evil plot to rule the world? Your timing, as always, is impeccable, snooky."

Nina made a face at him, but ignored his remark. They could talk about that later. Her eyes narrowed in Lisanne's direction. "So let's do this. Hit me with the human whammy."

The look Lisanne sent winging Nina's way, littered with disbelief, made her feel as if she'd just told her the Pope was really Amish. Lisanne's laugh was subtle at first, building until her fit of giggles made Nina want to rip her head off and shit down her throat. "Oh, you silly, silly fool. Is this why you sent word you wanted to see me, Gregori? And here I thought you wanted to help plan the mating celebration." Lisanne pouted prettily. "Such a shame you just won't participate."

Greg had looked for Lisanne? Nina didn't know what to think. "You really *did* look for her for me?" Nina's voice grew soft.

Greg's eyes held hers for a moment. "I did."

Ohhhhhhhhhhhhhhh. All the girly, mushy shit Marty talked about when she spoke of Keegan flooded her chest, and to make matters worse, she'd beat him up every chance she could by accusing him of wanting to keep her a vampire. "Well, fuck, Greg. Why didn't you just tell me? Do you have any idea at all the war you could have saved me over you?"

He cocked an eyebrow of disbelief at her. "Uh, let's be honest here, honey. No one can tell you *anything*, and I wasn't sure I'd be able to find her anyway. I didn't want to get your hopes up. Then I doubted you'd believe me anyway, because, you know, the evil plot to rule the world thing. Plus, I knew she'd show up eventually because—"

"I hate to break up this sweet exchange, but here's the scoop. There is *no* turning back. *Ever*," Lisanne interrupted with impatience. The look of hatred she sent flying Nina's way was über-creepy, überaggravated.

Stunned, Nina gripped Greg's wrist to keep from getting all up in Lisanne's shit and potentially losing a limb that with her luck, even being a vampire, wouldn't grow back.

Greg leaned down and whispered in her ear almost smugly. "I did tell you, honey." He squeezed her hand to soften his neener, neener.

"The fuck you say!" Nina bellowed.

Lisanne cast an even more bored than she was before look at Greg. "I have little time to waste with your new plaything, Gregori. I'll say this just once and slowly in case you're troubled by so many words at the same time, uh, Nina, is it? There is no turning back. *None.* I have no magical powers to give you back your mortality, and neither does any other vampire here on planet Earth that I've ever run into. Understand?"

"You're a liar," Nina rebutted. There had to be a way. She'd read it, and even if Greg didn't want to keep her a vampire, from the impression she got of this Lisanne chick, *she* definitely would. She clearly had no qualms about turning people, because she'd turned Greg.

"Oh, I'm many things, darling, but I'm not lying about this." She waved a hand in Nina's direction, dismissing her and turning to Greg. "Now tell your sleepover date it's time to go home. We have business to discuss?"

Business? Didn't Greg say he'd left Lisanne's clan because he didn't like her? Or something like that? Why would they have anything to discuss? Suspicion reared its ugly head again. Just when she'd thought it was safe to believe Greg was a decent guy.

The clench of his jaw tightened. "The hell I have anything to discuss with you, Lisanne."

Better, much better. Cool disdain on Greg's behalf made Nina feel muuuuch better. Okay, maybe he was still a decent guy.

"We have plenty to discuss, Gregori. It's business. Your birthday's in a week."

"I've made my position clear to you, Lisanne. There's nothing to discuss."

Nina couldn't take any more. "What kind of business are you discussing?"

"Marriage business," Lisanne said snidely.

Um, whoa. Nina tilted her head back at Greg and gave him the "look." "Um, your turn, *honey.*"

Greg rolled his tongue along the inside of his cheek. "It's not open for discussion, Lisanne. It's not going to happen."

Nina fidgeted. "*What's* not going to happen?"

"Gregori foolishly believes he won't have to marry me."

Nina whipped a hand into the air. "Yo, hold up, you loons. You're supposed to marry her? *Her?*" Oy and vey. "You said you didn't have a girlfriend! This is your fiancée? You piece of shit!"

"I don't have a girlfriend, honey, or a fiancée."

"But you just said you had to marry her!"

Greg's face held contempt, bitter and rife. "On my five-hundredth birthday. Yep, that's the plan. All part of the crazy mystical, magical life of a vampire."

Christ on a cracker. "And the reason for these nuptials?"

"If I don't marry her, I'll turn to dust."

Niiiice vampiric touch. Dust. All these threats all the time. So unattractive in a clan. "Uh, why?"

He shrugged his shoulders as if it didn't matter—like this was no big deal. "It's a vampire law, passed down for centuries. When you reach your five-hundredth birthday, if you're not already mated, you must mate with a female from your bloodline or mate with your sire. That is, if your sire isn't already mated. As you well know, Lisanne is my female sire—or my creator, so to speak—and I don't like anyone in my bloodline well enough to marry them. But there is package B, option C—I can mate with someone I've created, and we both know you're the only one I've done that to."

Lawd, did she ever. Nina's level of astonishment was matched only by the archaic bullshit of these clan rules. Funny how'd he'd forgotten to mention this little detail when he'd said there were rules to being a vampire.

"How did she get to be so *old*," emphasis on old purposeful, "and not have a mate? You can't be the oldest vampire in her kooky clan, and she definitely looks older than you." Nina shot a snide wink in Lisanne's direction. She didn't know how long Lisanne had been around when she'd turned Greg, but she'd definitely been a vampire longer than him.

"No, I'm definitely not the oldest, but everyone else has mated. I'm the only one who's turning five hundred in a week, though."

Hold the fuck on. "So you never found a single female in your bloodline you wanted to mate with enough to keep from turning to dust?"

"Um, nope."

Nina smiled, wide and proud, but that smile turned to worry. "And you're telling me Lisanne's never had to live by the same rules? What kind of shit is that? If she's like old hag vampire, shouldn't she have found someone to mate with by now, too?"

One eyebrow rose in clear contempt. "Ahh, Lisanne's had several mates who went the way of the dinosaur with no explanation, and as time passed, and two more people took themselves out of the running, my luck has apparently run out."

This was insane, infuriating, bloody fucking bananas! "Who in theee fuck makes this shit up? What kind of rule is that—having to marry someone when you're five hundred? Why not five hundred and one, and how do you *know* you'll turn to dust?"

"Oh, I've seen it. On two occasions. Both involving Lisanne," Greg said, giving Lisanne a cold, smug glare.

"Who cares who you friggin' marry?"

"Apparently, whoever cosmically rules a vampire's existence. If we don't mate, thus keeping our clans tight-knit and ever-strong, we turn to dust. Our powers combined keep us safe from those who want to harm us. I did tell you there are those who want to harm us. For whatever reason, vampires are much stronger mated. We sort of infuse each other with our powers. By the time you're five hundred, if you've learned your vampire lessons well, you've honed your skills, and you're one bad-assed force to be reckoned with." His hands came up to push the tangle of her hair from her shoulder.

"I'm next up on the chopping block. I'd really hoped this guy named Gus would end up Lisanne's mate, but he opted out at the last minute. Something about he'd rather be staked in broad daylight and strung up with ropes of garlic. To which I say, go figure." He directed the last to Lisanne, who narrowed her eyes to slits at him.

Nina's mouth dropped open.

Greg cupped her jaw, rubbing his thumb over her lips. "You met me at a really unfortunate time, Nina. I was going to try to tell you that last night, but, well, things got a little out of hand."

Warmth wisped over her, despite this crisis. For real.

Nina thought frantically back to something Marty had told her. Marty'd had a similar experience, because Keegan had refused to mate with some viper named Alana, but they'd only threatened to boot him from the pack, not annihilate him. Jesus.

Lisanne wedged her way between Nina and Greg, planting her back squarely in Nina's face. "So, darling, any special requests for our pending nuptials? Any particular vampire you wish to be present to witness our mating?"

Nina tapped her on the shoulder. "Hold on there, you vampire eater." Her eyes sought Greg's, hoping he'd go along with her. "Did I hear right when I heard you say you could mate with someone *you'd* created?"

She caught his glimpse of confusion and sent him a message with her eyes that said shut up. His answer was slow. "You did."

Nina brushed her hands together. "Aha! Then I'm your girl." She craned her neck around Lisanne's shoulder to address her. "So then, Lisanne of the extinct husbands, you can hit the road, sistah."

Nina felt the fury seeping from Lisanne's pores, oozing in angry waves. "I'm sorry?"

"Oh, you're definitely sorry, you power-hungry bitch. I'm your girl, Greg. I'll marr—er, mate with you." *Pick me, pick me.*

He gave her a warning glance followed by the tone. "Nina . . ."

"What? You just said you could marry someone you'd created, and I'm the only one you've done that to. So Lisanne, who can't turn me back into a human, can go home now." The turning to dust thing was far outweighing her mortality troubles, and why that was, she couldn't say. She only knew there was no way, not even if she were presented with the ability to again eat chicken wings until she puked, that she'd let Greg turn to dust—or mate with this viper.

Nope.

Lisanne pivoted on her wedged heels. "You'd mate with *this*?" She thumbed a finger at Nina.

Nina snapped. Fury, anger, pride, fear for Greg, and resentment for this woman, who'd begun all this trouble in the first place, bubbled to the surface in hot lumps. All of a sudden the possibility that Greg might not be around after next week left her feeling emotionally empty. I mean, who'd torture her to feed? Who'd yell right back at her when she went off? He'd looked for this dried-up, bitter bitch knowing—*knowing* what he had to do come next week. That he'd become food for a Swiffer was out of the question.

She gave Lisanne's shoulder a shove. "'K, here's the deal, you heifer. Greg's mating with *me*, not you. So go on back to your bat cave. You're not needed," she said between clenched teeth, tightening the sheet around her chest in case things went like that. Violent and all.

Greg's hands went to her shoulders, gripping them. "Stop, Nina."

"Don't you tell me to stop, Gregori Statleon! I'm not afraid of her, and I'll be fucked and feathered if I'll let her come in here like this and throw her weight around. He's *mine*, honey. So back off, and you," she turned and pointed a finger at Greg's chest, "just shut the flip up." Then she planted a kiss on his lips to silence him, softening her harsh words.

"Oh, Nina," Lisanne chided, clucking her tongue. "You should be *very* afraid, but I'll leave you two to duke it out, because I'm sooo over this. Gregori? I'll see you in a week. Nina? Good luck with the crazy notion that I'll let you anywhere near Greg." And poof, Lisanne disappeared without another word, her cute round ass, poured into her hip-hugging shorts, gone, just like that.

Nina sank to the edge of the bed, trembling from the tension in her limbs. Greg sat beside her. She gave him a narrowed, angry look, flicking his arm with two fingers. "Do ya think maybe telling me this sooner would have been a good thing? What the hell is the matter with you? How could you not tell me something this important? I thought you were trying to keep me from her for evil intent, you pain in my ass. Were you just going to disappear without a trace and not say a word? What kind of load of shit is that?"

Greg gave her a sheepish grin. "I didn't think you'd miss me. You are the one who tells me to go away at regular intervals, aren't you?"

"Yeah, that's me. But I don't want you to go away forev . . ." Oy. *Shut the fuck up, Nina.*

He rubbed his shoulder against hers in a circular motion. "That's nice to almost hear," he teased.

Nina laughed, despite her deep fear for him. "Okay, so all we have to do is what? Mate on your birthday, right?"

Greg brushed her hair from her face, tucking it behind her ear. "Honey, I'm not going to let you do that."

She brushed his hand away in irritation. "Don't tell me what I can and can't do. I owe you. You were there for Lou. I can't think of anyone besides me who would have done what you were prepared to do, whether you did it or not. We're mating, and that's final."

"You owe me nothing, Nina, and you have no idea what the mating ritual means. None."

Her look was pensive. "It's going to hurt, yes?" She winced.

"No, honey, it doesn't hurt."

"You've seen it?'

"Yep. It doesn't even sting."

"Then what's the problem? Let's do this, unless you dig the idea that you'll be food for a *Hoover*."

He took her hands in his, entwining their fingers. "Honey, listen closely. If we mate at midnight on the night of my birth, we'll be mated for life. This entails many rules as well."

Fan-fucking-tastic. More rules. "Why is it that you people have so many rules that involve dust and death? Everything is so damned dire—so final all the time. Whatever happened to simple stuff like thou shalt not lie? So much less dismal than marrying someone you don't want to marry."

"Listen to me, Nina—it is what it is, and nothing changes it. The mating ritual is very serious. It means you'll never be able to mate with anyone else, as in, have sex with another person, ever, or you risk the chance you'll be shunned. Trust this vampire when I tell you, you *never* want to be shunned. To be sent out into the world without any kind of vampiric support is beyond harsh, due to the fact that we rely on each other heavily for many resources. And by the way, the impulsive 'no one gets the best of me' twit that you are needs to remember one thing."

"Which is?"

"Vampires, barring garlic, crucifixes, lack of blood, and wooden stakes through the heart, live *forever*."

There was that final thing again. Everything was always so flippin' final with these paranormals. So she'd have to mate with Greg for who knew how long if she went through with this. She could live into the next millennium and beyond.

Now *that* was commitment.

Dude.

"LISANNE!" Svetlanna shrieked, grabbing her by the arm and whipping her around to face her. The cold mask of fury Svetlanna wore was only a fraction of the hatred she had for Lisanne. "I'll see you in Hell before I'll let you force Greg to mate with you!"

Lisanne threw her head back and laughed. "I think we both know how foolish that notion is," she hissed, pulling her arm from Svetlanna's grasp. "Are you forgetting the last time we did this, Svetlanna? As I recall, the circumstances were rather similar."

Her expression grew pained. Svetlanna remembered all too well. As if it had happened just yesterday. They'd gathered at Gregori's family's home to celebrate her pending nuptials to Greg's uncle Aiden.

God, she'd loved Aiden. Even now, mated as she was to someone she loved just as much, the memory of that horrific, scream-filled night still haunted her.

Aiden and Lisanne had been a couple for a time. When he'd met Svetlanna and they'd fallen deeply in love, he'd broken off his affair with Lisanne, though Aiden had been unaware of Lisanne's vampiric origins. None of them had been aware until it was too late.

Lisanne had gotten wind of Svetlanna and Aiden's engagement, and no one left Lisanne. No one. She did the leaving, if Svetlanna remembered her final words correctly. She'd been so infuriated by their potential union, she'd stormed Greg's home during the celebratory dinner in a raging, screaming fit of maniacal, bloody hysteria.

Almost no one had survived that night. Lisanne had drained Greg's mother, father and sister dry. That Greg had survived the turning was only because of carelessness on Lisanne's part—that and she thought he was pretty.

Aiden was left in a crumpled heap at Svetlanna's feet, lifeless and cold. But Lisanne's plan for Svetlanna was to make her suffer for eternity, because she'd taken Aiden from her. Instead of killing her, she'd turned Svetlanna, and thus, her and Greg's journey as vampires had begun.

They'd picked up the pieces, fought hard against the rules of Lisanne's bloodthirsty clan, and found others like them. Others who were doomed to roam the Earth for eternity, but refused to participate in Lisanne's deadly games.

Svetlanna's anger boiled. "I'll kill you myself," she seethed, gritting the words out between tight lips.

Lisanne smiled wickedly, so self-assured, so blatantly pompous. "Um, sure. You get right on that. In the meantime, I'll plan our coming mating. Don't you see, you fool? It doesn't matter what happens to me, Svetlanna. The end to Greg's immortality is imminent, whether I'm around or not. If he won't have me, I'll kill this Nina, and he'll end up dead anyway. So it seems I'm his best shot at survival."

Damn this bitch to Hell for ruining them so thoroughly. The swift rise of her anger caught the better of her, and her hand swiped out to strike Lisanne's cheek, leaving behind a red-hot slash that quickly faded. "Damn you, Lisanne, I'll find a way, and when I do, Hell will look like a pretty room at the Four Seasons compared to my hatred for you!"

Lisanne shook off the blow and smiled once more, sinfully depraved. "Isn't that exactly what you said about Aiden?" she cooed, then laughed as she disappeared, filling the large foyer with her twisted brand of glee.

CHAPTER 15

"You know, vampire, I've been thinking," Nina said as they left the hospital after a visit with Lou. She was improving with leaps and bounds and was due to be released within the week. Thankfully, Lou's insurance covered a nurse who'd come in daily and cared for her. Though Lou'd squawked about it, when Greg had insisted she listen to the doctors, her grandmother had melted.

"I don't know if that's a good thing or a bad thing," he said, chuckling and draping an arm around her shoulder. In the past four days, the peace between them had been oddly blissful for Nina. They fed together, hung out, and went to visit Lou every evening. The frenetic threat of Greg's pending death was always just beneath the surface, though, and the more he refused to mate with her, the more determined she became to make him.

Tonight she planned to do what she did best. Bully the fuck out of him and bend him to her will. If she knew nothing else, she knew how to bully like Paris Hilton knew hair extensions.

Nina nudged his side with her elbow. "How can you laugh at a time like this? I can't find a single thing funny about it. Your head's on the block, and that you can find anything—anything funny about it is pathetic. Now knock it off and listen. Marty told me when she had all that trouble with Keegan's pack that they could appeal to a council or something about her and Keegan mating. Why can't we do that, too?"

"Because there's no one to appeal to, Nina. Our higher order is fate. Our laws have been in place since the beginning of time. There is no changing it."

She made a face at him, pissed all over again at all of the brick walls they kept crashing into. "There would be if you'd just stop being such a shit and mate with me." Nina had made up her mind, and if she hadn't been convinced a couple of days ago that she was willing to do this, she was now. There were pluses to mating with him. Sex with Greg for an eternity couldn't be such a bad thing. Okay, so they fought a lot, but she'd watch Dr. Phil or some crap—or maybe take anger-management classes at the Y, and it'd be all good.

Greg stopped along the sidewalk, facing her under the sign for the emergency room. "I can't let you do that, Nina, and you know why I can't. You'd be mating with me forever. That's huge—especially when you have at least four hundred years of freedom due you until you have to even consider it. Besides, I just don't get the impression you're the forever type."

Nina was aghast. Pot meet kettle. "Oh, and you are? You've had four hundred and ninety-nine fucking years to find someone to mate with, and oh, look—no mate. Only a man would spend so little time organizing his eternity the way you have." God, he was so stubborn.

And you're easygoing? Okay, okay, so she could be difficult, but this was his undead-ed-ness they were talking about here.

Greg pursed his lips. "I just never found someone who interested me enough to risk eternity with, but I can tell you this, I'd rather turn to dust than mate with Lisanne."

Nina snorted. Just the thought of her encounter with Lisanne made her want to knock the broad's pearly whites out one by one. "Yeah, she's some piece of work, and I can't blame you for that. What I don't get is what the big deal is about this mating thing. What happens when you mate for eternity?"

"It's a bond. Bloodletting is what we call it. It's that spiritual stuff again. A witness is present and so on. Not too dissimilar to a human wedding—except there's no cake."

"Is there a Chicken Dance?"

He barked a laugh. "Uh, no."

"The Hokey Pokey?"

"Nope."

"Does it involve the color yellow?"

His eyes were confused. "Not that I'm aware of."

"Cool, then we're good to go. Let's do this."

"We can't just do it, honey. The bloodletting has to be done at midnight on the night of a vampire's five-hundredth birthday. In this case, mine."

"I should have known it involved blood. So what's the deal with it? Is it like being blood brothers?" She remembered the childhood pact and had to laugh if all they had to do was prick their fingers and rub them together in order for the cosmos to consider them mated.

"No, it's not quite like that. One or the other drinks from the neck of their intended, thus sealing the mating. *Forever*."

Again with the forever. Her mind took another path suddenly, and she looked up at him with a pensive gaze. "Can I ask you something?"

"Shoot."

"Why did Lisanne turn you?" Nina saw him immediately stiffen, but she deserved an answer. "Don't go getting all bent on me. I'm asking a legitimate question, and it's only fair you tell me what happened, so I can grudge on her properly after you've turned into a pile of dust in the middle of the living room floor and all."

Rolling his head on his neck, he cracked it before speaking. As if just saying the words were difficult. "Lisanne is a spiteful, greedy bitch. Svetlanna became engaged to my uncle shortly after he'd left Lisanne. My uncle Aiden was at my family home, celebrating his and Svetlanna's engagement when Lisanne found us. She hated Svetlanna and vowed she'd be cursed to roam the Earth without Aiden forever."

"So Lisanne turned her to pay her back for what she considered stealing Aiden, but why you, too?"

She saw him replay the memories of that fateful night in his head and regretted stirring it up again. His look of remorse, the pain that set in his eyes, made her cast her own eyes downward. "I was a casualty of Lisanne's rage. The engagement party was at my parents' house. Aiden was my uncle and very close to my father. Lisanne's fury was like something I've never seen in my life. She wiped out everyone and everything in her path. My mother, my father, and my sister—she drained them dry and threw their life-less bodies on top of one another." So many emotions flickered through his eyes, there were too many for Nina to count. Rage, grief, horror, all there for her to see.

"But that still doesn't explain why she didn't kill you, too."

Greg's jaw clenched, grinding back and forth before he spoke with disgust in his voice. "She thought I looked like my uncle Aiden. So she decided to keep me around. She called me pretty."

Nina shivered in revulsion. "Okay, that's just creepy. It gives me the willies, and so does Lisanne. Why didn't you kill her? You've been around a long time. Your powers have to at least be close to matching hers, don't they?"

"Because then I'd be no better than she is, would I? I began my clan with other vampires who shared my philosophy that we could get by in a human world, minus the bloodshed and abuse of power."

All this nobility and integrity. Had it been her, the shit would've flown. But then, therein lay the difference between her and Greg. He was a thinker—she was a beat the shit out of them, ask questions later.

He interrupted her anger on his behalf with, "Promise me something, would you?"

"Sure."

"When I'm gone, stay the hell away from Lisanne. Clayton'll look out for you. He's next in line to rule the clan, but I need to hear you tell me you'll keep that fresh mouth shut where she's concerned. You have no idea what inciting her will do. And learn, Nina. Learn how to be a vampire. Svetlanna will help, but don't let pride keep you from asking for help."

Her stomach sank. He really didn't intend to mate with Lisanne, and he wouldn't even consider her—which hurt. More than she'd like to admit. She teetered between relief that someone as fabulous as Lisanne couldn't appeal to him because he had morals, and cringing that she herself didn't appeal to him enough. "I'll promise you this much, I'll be very careful. That's as good as it's getting. I have a big mouth, and I know it, and sometimes it just can't be contained. Lisanne pisses me off—and you know how it goes if I'm pissed."

His look was grave. "Oh, I know how it goes."

"You know, something occurred to me. Svetlanna . . . isn't she the same age as you? If you were both turned on the same day, and we're working with vampire years here, anyway, isn't she required to mate on her five-hundredth birthday, too?" Cheerist. She didn't know how she'd help if Svetlanna needed a man. She was all outta single white vampires.

Greg's smile was genuine. "Svetlanna did mate. Almost one hundred and ten years ago."

So Svetlanna had a man. It comforted Nina to know she'd eventually been able to move on after the vicious death of her fiancé and that there wasn't another person needing saving. "And where's he?"

"He's in Seattle, working on some rain forest project. Garth's a good guy and he's made her very happy. After my uncle Aiden died, she deserved some happiness."

"Well, that must have been a big fuck-you to Lisanne, huh?"

"I suppose, in a way, Svetlanna turned lemons into lemonade, and yeah, I'd guess that pissed Lisanne off. But she was on her third mate by the time Svetlanna and Garth mated. She was otherwise preoccupied driving mere vampires to the brink of insanity."

"What happened to all these mates that are supposed to hang around for eternity? Where'd they go?"

He raised an eyebrow at her. "Would you want to be mated to Lisanne for eternity?"

'Nuff said. "Point."

They walked in silence a bit farther, Nina chewing on what he'd told her in slow bits. "Did those other vampires before you really opt to turn to dust rather than mate with she-bitch?"

"Yep, and it was too bad. Like I said, I liked Gus. He was a good guy, and while he was too afraid to leave Lisanne's clan, he did as little turning as possible. His end saddened us all, but I can relate."

"Okay, one more question."

He pulled her closer, and she let her head rest on his shoulder while they walked. "Go."

"Why won't you, even just for a second, consider me as your mate? I'm the key to keeping you around. I mean, who's going to razz the shit out of me and keep me in line if not for you?" she asked as they approached her apartment.

When they reached her front steps, Greg pulled her into his embrace and hugged her hard, planting a kiss on the top of her head. "We've been over this a hundred times in the past four days. Up until just a few days ago you believed I'd turned you because of some malevolent plan to rule the world."

Yeah, yeah, yeah. Slap some cuffs on her, she was guilty of the charge of misconception of a vampire's intentions, but she didn't feel that way anymore. She didn't. She'd been waffling for a while now, but gradually she'd come to believe him. She was a tough sell. She knew it. "I can't help that I'm suspicious and thick-headed. Sometimes it takes more than the average amount of proof to make me see what's right in front of me. I jump to sometimes ridiculous conclusions. I yell. I accuse. But what difference does it make now? *Now* I believe you."

He leaned back from their embrace, looking into her eyes, so clearly seeking understanding. "It's just proof that you don't know who I really am at all, Nina, and there won't be a chance to get to know me much more before . . . look, it's not like I'm asking you to loan me a couple hundred bucks you may never see again—I'd be asking you to spend eternity with me, and I won't let you sacrifice that for me." The set of his mouth, a grim line, was resolute.

It didn't have to be like this. It didn't. Maybe it was crazy of her to think it didn't, but it wasn't like she was marrying him so he could get some damned green card. This was his life. *Life.* And that led her to believe the idea of being mated to her for life was too horrible for him to consider. "You know, I'm beginning to think it isn't just Lisanne you'd rather die than mate with—maybe it's me, too." Wow, where the fuck had that insecurity come from? And she'd said it out loud—it'd just slipped out. Christ, she'd like to slink into a hole and never come out.

"Nin—"

She put her hand up with a flash of her palm. Embarrassment and utter humiliation made her react in the fashion that was like a warm, comfy blanket. "I get it. No need to explain. You'd rather *die—die*, you fucktard—than mate with me. Candy coat it however you like with all this self-sacrifice bullshit on my behalf, but I see it clearly now. I'm a big mouth, opinionated, and rude. Spending eternity with me'd be like your own little Hell on Earth. So, okay. I get it, and this is where I say buh-bye." She didn't give him the chance to say anything more. Her throat was clogged, and her eyes burned, but when she walked away from him, seeing him for what might be the last time, she did it with her head held high and her dignity in tact.

God love her dignity.

"WHERE have you been?" Wanda sniped around the chain lock on Nina's door, her eyes filled with concern and ire.

Nina popped the lock with a limp hand and traipsed back over to the couch where she'd been for the past day and a half with only a break in between to see Lou. Hiking up her pajama bottoms, she curled a pillow into her chest and sat down.

Wanda stalked in behind her, yanking the pillow from Nina's grasp and glaring at her with eyes that weren't so softly blue tonight. "You look like crap."

"Yeah? Well, thanks, and just for that, I hope they cancel *Oprah*."

Wanda's eyes widened when she gasped. "That was mean, Nina. Very mean. What is going on with you? You don't answer your phone, and I've only called twenty times in the past four days since you called about Lou. Last I knew you were looking for Greg's sire and having wild otherworldly sex. Now I find you here on the couch like some bum with your messy hair in a ponytail and pajamas that I'd wholeheartedly suggest you burn." She stooped to the coffee table, picking up an empty bag. "And what is this? What are all these bags?" She held them up and examined them closer, wrinkling her nose.

Nina grimaced. So she'd thrown back a few plasmas in a fit of pity? Okay, a ton of plasmas in the night dweller's equivalent of Death by Chocolate Häagen-Dazs, since she'd last seen Greg. "It's blood," Nina answered with disinterest.

Wanda shook a bag in her face, wrinkling her nose. "I see that. Tell me, is this the equivalent of a vampire pity party?"

Nina shrugged her shoulders and yawned. "Well, I may as well get used to it, 'cause I ain't goin' back."

Wanda's face immediately changed from irritated to sympathetic. "Oooooh, honey! How could you have found out you're going to be a vampire forever and not have told us? When did you find this out?"

"When I found Lisanne, or rather she found me." Nina yanked the pillow out of Wanda's hands and put it back under her arms, hugging it to her.

"Omigod! You found her? What's she like?"

"She's a horrible bitch, and don't go lecturing me on not giving people a chance until you hear the full story."

"Okay, so I'm all ears. Move over and take your filth with you. Oh, and Marty'll be here in just a few. We decided an intervention was in order." Wanda shoved aside the litter of empty blood packets and sat down beside her.

Good. Just what she needed. Marty and her Rebecca-from-Sunnybrook-Farm-with-color-wheels approach to life. Where to begin? "So Lisanne showed up at Greg's."

"Are you two still—*involved?*"

Wanda meant sexually, because she whispered the word like her mother might hear it. "We were, are . . . were. Never mind, forget that. Lisanne showed up and informed me that there really is no turning me back. My mortality is shot—gone—kaput. I'll never eat another chicken wing again."

"Greg did try to tell you."

Nina rolled her eyes in exasperation. "I know, Wanda. And he was right. So I'm a vampire for good." And that was that. No more chicken wings. No more Starbucks White Chocolate Mochas, no more of Lou's pot roast. Just no more.

"Wow. Well, that explains your depression, but you do know that wallowing is only allowed for like three days, and then you have to be done. It's a girl rule or something. I can give you an extra day because this is way bigger than a guy dumping you, but I think four's the limit." She chuckled.

"It isn't just that, Wanda. There's more."

The doorbell rang, and Wanda patted her knee reassuringly. "That's Marty. I'll grab it, you carry on. Wallowing, that is."

Wanda sashayed over to the front door, pulling up the pants of her mint green sweat suit, one she'd bought when she'd forced Nina to go to the designer outlet malls with her only three months ago. And already, it looked too loose. Wanda was pale and looked so tired all the time, and now her clothes were sliding off her ass. It worried Nina.

But she lost her train of thought when she heard Marty's voice.

Nina sank farther into the couch, waiting for Marty to fly in, in a blaze of perfume and perfectly color-coordinated clothing. God, she just wanted everyone to go away and let her be.

Wanda hugged Marty, then pulled her aside to whisper in her ear.

"I can hear you, Wanda." Nina pointed to her ears. "Or have you forgotten? Supersonic hearing."

Wanda made a face at her. "Sorry, I was just telling Marty—"

"She was just telling me you're still whining. Get up, Nina," Marty demanded, planting her hands on her winter-white jacket-clad hips. "If I can take being a werewolf, you can take being a vampire. Knock off the pussy bullshit and get off that couch." Marty jabbed a finger under Nina's nose.

A flash of anger, the old Nina's bread and butter, stung her into action. She slid to the edge of the sofa. "Don't you wave that perfectly manicured finger under my nose, Marty Flaherty, because I will kick your ass from here to kingdom come."

Marty and Wanda smiled at each other and nodded. Marty stuck her tongue out at Nina. "There's the Nina we know and abhor. Now get up."

"I don't want to get up. I'm happy here. I have everything I need." Blood, blood, and more blood and late night TV. Who knew they had a channel devoted just to reality television?

Marty unraveled her deep blue scarf from around her neck and hung it on the rack by the door. Her coat soon followed. She smoothed her blonde hair back into its chic ponytail and straightened the edges of her eggshell colored sweater. "Where's Greg these days? The last thing Wanda told me you two were boinking."

Nina groaned, burying her face in the pillow.

Wanda yanked her head up by her ponytail. "What have you done now?"

"Wanda, let go of me, or I'll knock you from here to eternity." Ohhhhh, *eterniiiiityyyy*. What had made her use that word—of all words? Her angry expression fell flat, fizzling with no desire to follow up her threat.

Wanda held fast and peered into her face. "I'm not afraid of you, Nina. Now, what-have-you-done?"

"Why is it always me who has to have done something?"

"Because you don't know when to quit, that's why," Marty answered.

"Then you'll be thrilled out of your knickers to hear it had nothing to do with me," Nina said, slapping at Wanda's hands.

Wanda let go of her ponytail with a jerk of her wrist. "So tell us what's wrong."

"Greg is going to die." There, she'd said it—out loud, and then she cringed.

"What?" both women yelped.

Crap. How did you explain something like this? It was too bizarre even for Marty, who was paranormal. "It's a long story, but here's the gist of it. Greg is turning five hundred in two days. On his five-hundredth birthday, according to some cosmic, fucked-up vampire rule, if he hasn't mated with someone of his bloodline, that means people like that freaky bitch Lisanne has created, or his sire, or," she paused to keep her words even, "someone *Greg's* created, he turns to dust. He flat-out refuses to mate with Lisanne, who, as you know, is the vampire who created him, and I can't say as I blame him 'cause the heifer's a total bitch. I'm nothing compared to her, and that's saying something. So that's it. If he won't mate with her, he's done for."

Their collective silence made Nina feel far worse than she had to begin with. This was some ominous shit. It showed in their reaction. She could see them both stop breathing at once.

Marty blew out a breath first. "Whew, and you call us lycanthropes fucked up?" She shook her blonde head, the shimmering strands perfectly smoothed back. "Okay, so let me get this straight here. If he doesn't mate in less than two days, he's meat?"

Wanda slapped at Marty. "Don't put it like that! God, can't you see Nina's in pain?"

"I'm sorry, Nina. But this is crazier than any lycan law I've ever heard of. So what exactly does this have to do with you? Is it because he has to mate with someone else? Are you jealous?"

"I'm not jealous. I told you, he refuses to mate with Lisanne."

Marty pursed her lips. "Okay, so, yeah, he's a nice guy, and no one wants to see a nice guy hit the highway to Heaven, but . . ."

Nina sat silently, casting her eyes downward, refusing to look either of them in the eye.

Marty was the first to finally burst out with, "Ho—ly—shit! You like him. Oh. My. God. Nina's fallen for someone, and she didn't even meet him at a truck stop! You like him, and the fact that he'll bite the big one is killing you, isn't it?"

Nina sucked in her cheeks. "You know, Marty, I'm glad you find this some kind of payback for me being so crappy, but this isn't just about laughing at me for getting a taste of my own medicine, this is about Greg's life," she squeaked, biting her tongue for sounding so friggin' weak.

Marty sat on the coffee table in front of her and took Nina's hands in hers, instantly contrite. "I'm sorry. I just never thought I'd see you like this over *anyone*, especially the guy you thought turned you into a vampire because he was evil incarnate. Tell me what I can do. Whatever you need, I'm in."

"Me, too," Wanda added, her soft eyes sympathetic.

Nina choked on a cough, using her shoulder to swipe at her eyes. "There's more."

Wanda heaved a sigh. "More?"

Nina nodded. "I offered to mate with him. Because—because I just can't imagine . . ."

"What life was like before him—even with all the mean shit you've accused him of," Marty finished for her.

"Yes," she nearly sobbed.

Wanda cupped her cheek. "And I'm guessing, from your command at pity central on the couch, he turned you down?"

"Yep." Nina closed her eyes and tried to forget what he'd looked like when he'd so determinedly refused to mate with her.

Marty closed her hands tighter over Nina's. "Did he say why?"

"He said he couldn't let me mate for life with him, because life with a vampire is forever. It's not like fifty years or something, and you can't just get a divorce. If either of us even considered having sex with someone else, we could risk what he called a shunning. I didn't ask details, but it can't be good, if it has the word *shun* in it. Anyway, he said I had four hundred years of freedom to go before I needed to even think about it, and he wouldn't let me do something so drastic."

"That's because he's a good guy, Nina. I sensed that from the start, but when you get on a roll, there's no changing your mind. I wish you'd trust me sometimes. These lycan senses of mine have become pretty keen."

"Marty?" Wanda interjected. "This *is* life we're talking about, and in Nina's case, many, many lives. I know this is going to sound skeptical and totally mean, but most of the time they've known each other Nina's cracked on him for turning her to do his evil bidding? I almost tend to agree with Greg."

Nina eyed her with disbelief. "This from the woman who reads romance novels? All that soul mate bullshit and kissy face garbage is like your mantra these days."

Wanda's fiery look made her eyes glisten. "It's *fiction*, Nina, and even I, sentimental fool that I am, know the difference. I don't read it because I believe any of it's real. I just like being given the possibility to believe."

"Yeah, Wanda, but think about all the junk that you read that *was* true in those books." Marty's bangle bracelets clacked together when she patted Nina's hand. "You were right on the money in most cases. I'm not saying that Nina offering to partner up with Greg for life isn't a hasty choice, but it's a side of Nina we've never seen. And to me, that means something. Nothing makes our dear friend do anything even remotely schmaltzy. She's considering getting married, Wanda. *Married.* Need I say more? This is a huge leap, and to me it's a sign Greg's gotten to her in a way no one else ever has and maybe never will. The Nina we know doesn't do anything drastic but threaten to knock your teeth out. She's cautious, always with the wall up—always waiting for a kick in the gut. This—this kind of sacrifice is *drastic*, and eternity's a long time to miss someone and wonder whether the choice you made was right."

Wanda finally nodded her head, this time with tentative agreement. "You're right about that. It definitely shows some real deep something if she's considering keeping him forever." Her face grew thoughtful, and then she said, "Greg's definitely more capable of handling her than anyone I've ever seen. But does she like him enough to live with him for eternity?"

Nina waved a hand at them, shaking her head. "You guys don't understand. There's still more. Do you remember when I told you what happened with Lou last week?" God, just thinking about it again made her ache all over.

Both women nodded, and Marty added, "I went to see her tonight on my way over, by the way. She looks great."

Nina smiled her thanks at Marty for visiting Lou. "There was something I didn't tell you. Greg did something that night that changed everything for me with him." She rubbed the heel of her hand over her eyes. Maybe she couldn't cry anymore, but every time she talked about that horrible moment with Lou and what Greg had been willing to do, she got all stupidly verklempt.

"And that was . . ." Wanda prompted.

"Lou was dead, or at least as far as I could tell. She had no pulse, and I didn't hear her breathing. I begged Greg to turn her, because I knew he could save her if he did, and I don't mean I just said please either. I begged—literally." She looked them both square in the eye so they knew how serious she'd been that night. Nina begged for nothing and no one, and her friends knew it.

"At first he said absolutely not. He'd told me he had a strict no-turn policy. That he didn't believe anyone should unwillingly live like he does—we do. He said I was taking Lou's options into my own hands, and she'd have no say—that I was messing with fate. So I told him I'd do it. In my panic and fear, I would have done anything to help her."

Marty's blue eyes welled, shimmering with tears, and Nina swiped at them with her thumb. "Don't start caterwauling before I finish." Marty gave her a watery smile and flapped her hand at Nina.

"Anyway, everything got kind of crazy then. I was begging, and he was saying no, and then, he grabbed Lou from me, and just when it looked like he was going to sink his teeth into her, she took a breath. After everything I've said to him, accused him of, he was going to do something that went against everything he believes in for *me*. Honest to God, I've never been so afraid in my life. If I'd lost Lou . . ."

Wanda's voice was husky when she spoke. "So now you think because Greg was willing to do something so magnanimous for you, you should do something for him in return that's almost as big?"

Nina shook her head. "It isn't just that, Wanda. I *do* like him. In between all the arguing and accusations I've hurled at him I like him, and I'm going to admit something right now I didn't think I'd ever admit, especially in front of the two of you, so gird your loins, girls. It turns me on that he's not intimidated by me. He just won't take my shit. Seriously, have we ever encountered a guy who isn't intimidated by me?"

"I think it's a sign, Nina," Marty said finally. "I think what happened with Lou was the universe's way of making you sit up and pay attention. You don't listen much, you know—not to reason, not to anything. You're tough as nails, and no one's going to tell you otherwise, but you have a good soul whether you like it or not."

Nina made a face at her. Soul schmoul. Vampires didn't have souls—or did they?

But Marty wouldn't be thwarted. "Don't make faces at me. Just listen. You sacrificed your pride for Lou's life. Yeah, maybe it was selfish of you to consider a life-altering change without giving her a say in it, but who isn't selfish when it comes to the people they love? What wouldn't you do to keep them safe and here with you? I can't say I wouldn't have done the same had it been Keegan. Loving someone can be just as selfish as it can be a sacrifice."

Nina's shoulders slumped. "Look, you guys. I'm not saying offering up my entire eternity to save a guy I've mostly beaten up doesn't sound crazy, but it's what feels right. Like right here." Nina pointed to her gut.

"Do you love him?" Wanda asked.

Nina hesitated before answering. "Before we go any further, I gotta say this. If this shit ever leaves this room, I'll kill you both."

Two heads, polar opposites in color, nodded consent. "Pinky swear?" Marty asked, sticking out her finger.

Nina held up both hands for each of her friends. "Pinky swear."

Oh, Jesus, she was going to say out loud what she'd been thinking for the past day and a half. But who better than Marty and Wanda to reveal it to? She clenched the pillow tighter to her stomach. "Okay, no I don't know if what I feel is love, because I've never been in love. I only know that for the past day and a half, not seeing him has been like having bamboo stuck under my fingernails." She closed her eyes to focus on keeping her voice from shaking.

"Sure, part of it is that we have a dire situation here and I may never see him again, but part of it is that I just miss him being around. Even on the nights when he didn't show up to bring me blood and I thought he was trying to keep me from getting my mortality back, I wondered what he was doing and who he might be doing it with. I battled between angry for what he'd done to me and attracted to him for what he does to me."

Marty giggled softly. "I'd definitely say you're on your way, and that's nice. Really nice, seeing as I never thought you'd ever meet someone who you wouldn't scare away." She paused for a moment, obviously hedging her words, then shook her head definitively as if deciding she was just going to speak her piece.

"Look, I'm just going to say this, and if you threaten to pop me in the mouth—remember I have big teeth."

Nina laughed. "Yeah, me, too."

"But mine have *lots* of practice. You've been a slacker."

"Shut up, Marty. If you don't knock off the crap about how you can take me—"

Wanda popped up off the edge of the coffee table. "Could we just have this moment?" she intervened, giving them both her best stern expression. "Nina, shut it. Marty, knock off the one-upmanship and just say it. It needs to be said."

Nina looked at them both, bewildered.

Marty blew a long breath out. "You know you do that, Nina. Scare people away with your tough talk. I know all the crap about being a product of your environment applies here, and you're tough for a reason because you grew up in the Bronx. But if you push people away because of what your mother did to you, it's time to stop. If this is like one of those subconscious tests where you treat us like garbage and wait and see if we'll keep coming back, cut it out. You dole out a lot of shit to us, and we do—come back, that is. Every time. We didn't reject you, Nina, and I believe with all my heart, you're mother didn't either. She got lost, like seriously lost, but drugs made her lose her way. It had nothing to do with you not being worthy of her love."

Wanda's head bobbed furiously. "And don't hand me that we've been watching too much *Oprah* nonsense. It's true, you're difficult and confrontational and we accept that about you for the most part. It kinda cracks us up, but it can also wear thin—especially when you do stuff that jeopardizes your well-being," she said, offering a tired smile.

"Not to mention, you have one helluva time accepting our advice or help—any help for that matter, but we're always here for you anyway. You don't make it easy to be there for you. Everything is a fight. It's taken you forever, and only because Greg's life hangs in the balance, to decide maybe Greg's okay and it might be all right to trust him. Do you always want to be in this position, or is it safe to say you might wanna let up a little? You can never jump in the deep end if that's how you want to play it, but you might miss a mighty fine swim if you'd just test the water."

"I fucking hate to swim," Nina joked.

Marty clucked her tongue. "I think what we're trying to say is this, sometimes people do stick around, Nina. Greg did, and he didn't have to. We do, and we don't have to. So if you're going to pursue this thing with Greg, we just want you to keep that in mind."

Nina sat back on the couch, exhausted from all this revelation, defeated and with a gnawing sadness in her breast. "I know I'm difficult, and I'm going to say this just once, but if you ever even mention it again, I'll knock your teeth out."

Wanda and Marty smiled at each other. "Go."

She tugged the end of her ponytail. "I know I have trouble trusting people, and I'm sorry. It isn't intentional. It really is just how I grew up. You didn't ask questions where I came from. You just assumed everyone around you was a piece of shit and behaved accordingly, because if you gave someone a chance just once, there was always the possibility you'd end up with the life beat out of you. I did that over and over with my mother. Trusted her. And she let me down every time. I'm not just tough because of where I grew up—I'm tough because of my mother. Yes, I do the rejecting first so no one else can beat me to the punch. Okay? There. I said it."

Wanda bobbed her head. "Because you don't want to be disappointed, and that makes perfect sense. But life is full of disappointments. I think after a time, you have to choose to either jump in or keep running scared."

Nina agreed with a curt nod. "I never knew when my mother was going to show back up, but I waited like an ass anyway, and when she didn't anymore, I guess I decided I wasn't going to let anyone humiliate me like that ever again. So I push people away and try not to let them get too close. I can't be disappointed if I don't count on anything. I had me to count on and Lou. But Lou worked a lot. She couldn't be around to baby me. So I keep people at arm's length, and I know I do. It takes a long time for me to be comfortable enough to open up, and even then, it's really uncomfortable for me. I guess behaving badly is easier." She pressed the pillow to her face because her eyes were beginning to burn again.

"But there's hella trust involved in mating for life, Nina," Marty reminded her. "Maybe Greg took that into consideration when he said no."

Nina said nothing. What could she say? Marty was right. She'd have to trust Greg. She hadn't done such a good job of it so far.

Wanda's next question really gave Nina the smack in the head she needed. "But you know you can trust us, don't you? I mean, by now I think we've proven that. I just don't want to have to keep proving it to you—or feel like I am, anyway."

It had to be a tiresome task. "Yeah, I trust you—in my own way.

But it isn't just the trust thing. You guys freak me out with your makeup and clothes and shit, and I guess sometimes I wonder why you'd want to be my friends, when I'm so different from you. I really don't care about whether my lip gloss matches my shoes."

"Your skin tone, Nina," Wanda teased.

"Whatever. You know what I mean."

Marty patted Nina's hand and grinned. "You grew on us—on me anyway. During the thing with Keegan when you came all the way to Buffalo to check up on me, I knew you had a good heart. That like it or not, you cared about me—us—and that you needed us as much as we needed you."

Nina shrugged, forcing an indifferent front. "Well, Keegan did offer us a private plane ride and the pilot *was* hot. Who'd turn that down—even if it did involve listening to you whine."

Wanda giggled, swatting Nina's thigh. "Like you would have done it if you didn't want to. No one makes you do what you don't want to do. You've done other stuff, Nina. Like stick up for Marty with that nasty bitch Linda Fisher at Bobbie-Sue when she was stealing Marty's accounts and even when you help me on bingo night at the senior citizens' home. You're a good person, just a cranky one, and we only want you to listen sometimes before you put your guard up. Okay?"

Nina wished she could sigh to relieve the pressure in her chest for what she was going to tell them. "It doesn't matter anyway. When he told me he wouldn't mate with me was where we left it the other night. Haven't seen or heard from him since."

"And you didn't wrestle him to the ground and make him scream uncle until he bent to your will? Who are you, Nina Blackman?" Wanda teased the question. "I don't know about you, Marty, but the Nina I know would have hacked off Greg's limb for having the audacity to say no to her, then beaten him with it."

"Or at least gouged an eyeball out," Marty chimed in.

Wanda leaned into Nina and hugged her, then stood up and chucked her under the chin. "You know what? I think we're going to let you have some time to think about this. We love you, and I hope you know we just want you to be happy. If you need us, we're here, but now it's time for you to think really hard about what we said and what your next move is going to be. You're a smart woman, Nina. I know you'll find a way to make whatever you want to happen happen."

Marty was apparently in agreement. She hugged her, too, and pinched Nina's cheek. "Yeah, you're smart. Go do what smart girls do, blood drinker."

Nina watched their backs as they exited her apartment, knowing what they'd said was as honest as it got, and maybe part of Greg's reluctance to mate for life with her was because she never knew when to shut up and take a chance.

Well, she'd fucked this up but good, and because of it, she wanted to scurry off to a dark, secluded cave and never come back out.

Her cell phone rang, and when she leaned forward toward her coffee table to see who was calling, hoping against hope it was Greg, she frowned, then flipped the bird at her caller ID, deflated.

It was the mystery vamp, more than likely. No one else showed up as private caller or caller unknown but that fuckwad.

Well, she knew where Lisanne was now, so he could take his happy, clappy vampire attitude and his supposed information and shove them up his undead ass.

Fuck him and fuck Lisanne.

Nina reached for a bag of blood with one hand and the television remote with the other.

At least she still had cable.

CHAPTER 16

"Have you seen Nina?" Clayton asked.

"Nope."

"My friend, this is a sad day indeed. A beautiful woman offers to mate with you, and you turn her down in a grand show of chivalry, I might add. Does the word *dead* mean anything at all to you?"

Greg gripped the arms of the chair he sat in. "I know what I did, Clay."

"Do you?"

"Yeah, I do. I won't let her give up her freedom to save my hide. Period. And let's not forget the difficult, opinionated mouthy part either."

They sat in Greg's study, one day away from his birthday, while Clayton tried to convince him turning down Nina was a dumb-ass thing to do.

He'd stayed away from her because seeing her again would be his undoing, and he couldn't promise he'd be able to keep turning her down if he spent any more time with her. Yet he would have liked the chance to say good-bye. He'd hurt her when they'd parted, and he'd never have the chance to apologize for it.

"You have way too much pride for your own good, bud," Clayton said, sipping the last of his blood from a beer mug.

Greg cracked his jaw. "It isn't my pride that's keeping me from accepting, Clay, it's the sacrifice involved. How could I live with the idea that she'd have no choice but to always be chained to me?"

Clay chuckled grimly. "I think I could live with it, if my intended looked like Nina. Though I will say, she's nothing like the animals you usually hunt for sport."

No, Nina was nothing like the women he'd toyed with for four hundred and ninety-nine years, three hundred and sixty-four days and counting. He knew she was different, and while he'd tried to deny his attraction to her, after they'd made love, the intrigue had turned to something deeper—something he wanted to have time to explore, but time wasn't a gift he'd have bestowed upon him after tomorrow. "She's definitely different," was all he'd offer.

"But not different enough to mate for life with?"

"Get off my back about it, Clay. It isn't going to happen."

Clay rose from his place on the sofa. "I'll say this once more. I think you're making the biggest mistake of all your centuries."

"I'll keep that in mind. You know all you need to know when you take my place in the clan?"

"I promise to honor your efforts, but this isn't something I want to do." Regret laced his tone, worry lined his face.

Greg nodded curtly, fending off the dread involved in their meeting. "Let's not drag this out." Greg rose, too, extending a hand to his friend of so many years.

Clay took it, gripping it hard and pulling Greg against him with a sharp slap on the back before he searched Greg's eyes one last time. "So this is the last I'll see you?"

"I think so. Godspeed." He set his jaw in a tight clench.

Clay turned away with the good-bye he didn't have to speak, leaving Greg alone in his study and even more alone with his thoughts. He made a choice just then.

He had one last thing to do.

He could lie to himself all he wanted, but he had to see Nina.

Just once more.

He appeared in Nina's bedroom with the stealth of a cat, creeping along the edges of her bed to find her deep in her vampiric sleep. Her long, dark hair splayed out on the pillow, a stark contrast to the white of the sheets. Her limbs were tangled in the covers, and a single foot dangled off the side of the bed.

Greg traced a finger along her jaw, then up around the shell of her ear. He wanted to drag her into his arms, pin her there, keep her near him until he'd spent himself.

But if he touched her for too long, lingered, he'd have to leave her and whatever had drawn him to her in the first place would only magnify his sense of loss tomorrow.

He rested his head against her cool cheek for a moment, closing his eyes to take in her scent and remember it to tide him over until . . . well, just until.

Greg placed one last kiss on her forehead, dropping a package on Nina's dresser before leaving as quickly as he'd entered.

NINA woke with a sense of impending doom.

Today was the day, and it sucked big, fat man hooters.

But that was okay, because Wanda's words had stayed with her long after she'd left. All while she'd guzzled blood like it was booze and way into the wee hours of the morning when they played the stupidest, crappy, sappy shit on some channel called Oxygen. Long into the much-needed shower she took and well into her dreams, which were jagged and fractured.

Nina knew what she had to do, and she picked up the phone to call her friends to tell them. Friends who'd hung around when they should have ditched her bitchy ass long ago.

During her big old pity party, she'd finally come to terms with something. She was never going to be human again, and though she might always want that, it wasn't going to happen.

Now that she'd come to acceptance, she also knew she didn't want to live out this thing called immortality without Greg's guidance.

And nobody was going to damn well stop her from making that happen.

Wanda had asked why she hadn't wrestled Greg to the ground for having the audacity to say no to mating with her, and it had stuck with her all night long.

Yeah, why hadn't she?

Probably because his will was as strong, if not stronger than hers. And if he didn't at least like her as much as she liked him, why should she beg so they could spend an eternity with him not liking her? Fear of rejection was her answer. Reject him before he rejected her. This way, she'd never be humiliated again the way she'd been with her mother. It had taken her a long time to come to grips with the fact that no matter how much she'd loved her mother, needed Janine in her life, her mother loved drugs more than she even loved herself. She hadn't rejected Nina as much as she'd rejected life.

As a kid, she'd spent a lot of time steeling herself, preparing for her mother's eventual departure. It hurt every time Janine left, and her hopes were dashed so many times, she'd learned to protect herself in her own, harsh, brash way with others who showed any interest in the way of any kind of relationship. If she didn't let anyone get too close, they couldn't leave, now could they?

But this wasn't about some guy not liking her or the humiliation because he'd rejected her mating wish—Greg would die if he didn't mate with her, and no amount of pride could be allowed to get in the way of that happening.

Even hers.

Her stomach fluttered, hollow and filled with fear. Before she could let her thoughts go to a deep, dark place she shouldn't allow them to, she picked up the phone and dialed Wanda.

Wanda answered on the second ring. "Nina? You okay?"

She nodded resolutely. She was more than okay. "I'm fine. Is Marty still with you, or did she go home to the dog?"

Wanda's laughter was light. "Now I know you're okay. Yeah, she spent the night at my place. What's up?"

"Tell her to get her color wheels spinning—we have a mating to prepare for."

Wanda breathed into the phone for a moment, then said, "So I see some introspection was had since we left you?"

"Just get over here. I need help getting ready for my big, fat vampire wedding. I'll leave the door open for you." Clicking the phone shut to the tune of Wanda's gasp, she dropped it on the couch and looked at the clock. It was just six—if she hurried and Marty and Wanda got here soon, she'd have plenty of time to make her twelve o'clock mating.

She scurried into the bathroom, dropping some more food into poor Larry's cage as she went. "Sorry, dude, it's just been really nuts lately, but I promise we'll have more quality time soon." Nina patted the top of the cage and ran for the bathroom, stripping her clothes off and turning on her shower.

While she soaped up and as she washed her hair twice, she

fought the insecurity that Greg would refuse her even at the eleventh hour. She couldn't let that happen, not if she had to duct tape his ass to a chair and latch onto his neck by force. He'd get over the eternity thing, because she said so.

Toweling off, she heard Marty and Wanda from her bedroom, whispering in frantic, hushed tones. As she threw a nightshirt on she also heard their worry.

Nina poked a head out of her bedroom door. "Um, vampire here. I can hear you and quit bitching. I'll be fine."

Marty wore a soft gray knit dress with a wide black belt. She toyed with the buckle of it with nervous fingers. "We just want to be sure you're doing the right thing."

Wanda, looking very tired today, fretted out loud. "Are you sure, Nina? I mean, really sure?"

Nina paused for a moment, uncertain how to express to her friends that this was as sure as she got. "Yeah, I'm sure. If I had to spend eternity feeling the way I did these past couple of days, then I'd rather do death by garlic or something equally as horrible. Yeah, I'm sure." She turned her back on them to race to her closet to find something suitable to wear. What the hell did you wear to a mating? Probably something that didn't stain if the bloodletting got out of control.

She went to her dresser to find some undergarments, when something caught her eye, a flat, square package, wrapped in newspaper. Her fingers trembled when she tore at the paper, dropping it to the floor, revealing a DVD.

Greg had been here.

He'd been here.

But why? When?

Oh, God, he'd been here. Her throat did that clenching thing while her hands shook. She could barely muster a whisper. "He was here."

Marty came into the bedroom with her lavender Bobbie-Sue makeup case. "What are you mumbling?"

Nina held up the DVD. "He was here."

Marty laid the makeup case on Nina's bed, her blue eyes confused. "Huh?"

Wanda gave a breathy sigh from the doorway, holding a plastic covered bag in her hand. Her eyes were watery, and her lower lip trembled. She said but one word. *"Beaches."*

Nina gulped hard. "Yeah. *Beaches.*"

Greg had left her a DVD of the movie *Beaches*.

"Not *Full Metal Jacket*," Wanda said as if in a trance.

Marty clapped her hands to get their attention. "Uh, does one of you want to tell me what you're talking about?"

Both Nina and Marty rushed to explain, stumbling over their words and interrupting each other.

Marty sank to the bed, running her red-tipped nails through her hair. "I think we need to hurry."

Wanda hurled the plastic bag at Nina, wiping her eyes.

Nina caught it. "What's this?"

"It's something appropriate to wear, because God knows you don't have a suitable ensemble to get married in. I just don't think a sweatshirt and some holey jeans will work."

Nina unzipped the bag, her eyes falling on a simple cream linen dress, square at the neck and slim fitting. "Yours?" she asked, looking at Wanda.

"Yes. I wore it to one of my customer's bat mitzvah's last year. I'm a bit bigger than you in the chest, but I figure you'll make up for it in the booty."

Nina laughed, throwing her arms around Wanda's neck. "Thanks."

Wanda disentangled herself from Nina and gave her a mocking look. "You'd better knock it off, or I won't believe this is really you."

"Girls!" Marty shouted. "Look at the time. If we don't hurry up, we'll miss our midnight deadline."

"We have four hours," Nina complained.

Marty cocked a skeptical eyebrow at Nina. "Do you have any clue the amount of time it's going to take to whip you into shape? It'll take at least an hour to pluck those eyebrows, not to mention figure out what to do with that rat's nest on your head. This is a task I'd compare to conquering world hunger—so we need to get on it—like now."

Nina rolled her tongue along the inside of her mouth, approaching Marty. "You know, Marty, don't make me show you that vampire beats werewolf every time."

Marty cocked a skeptical eyebrow at Nina. "Well, Wanda, so much for our Nina intervention."

Wanda pushed her way between them, putting her arms around them both, smiling. "Some things never change. Now cut it out, and let's do this and quit fighting. Marty, you find some eye shadow in your power pack of makeup. I'm calling Smoky Mountain Grey with Deep Foliage Green as an accent. Nina's eyes are so damned black, it'll make them dark and seductive. Who could resist her if she's got sexy, smoldering eyes? Oh, and grab the Passive Pink lip gloss—it's almost sheer, and it'll perfectly play up her cheekbones."

Three hours later, Nina was a lot further in than she'd first thought she'd be.

"God, Nina. You look incredible. I don't think I've ever seen you look so beautiful." Wanda dabbed at her eyes with a tissue.

"Knock it off, Wanda." Nina's embarrassment was showing.

"No, I mean it. Doesn't she look fab, Marty?"

Marty nodded her head. "I gotta say, Wanda's right. You're gorgeous." She swatted at Nina's cheek with the makeup brush. "Stop licking your mouth, you'll wipe off your lip gloss."

Nina scoffed. She had enough lip gloss on to stick her to a wall, for Christ's sake. She'd been buffed, plucked, yanked, and tortured by this thing called a plunge bra—which really should be called chain mail—to within an inch of her life. Yet, there was a small part of her that wished she could *see* what she looked like.

Wanda's hand went to her mouth. "I forgot, you can't see what you look like clearly, can you? Want me to describe it?"

"Not a lot," Nina said dryly, knowing full well that was a lie.

Wanda rolled her eyes. "Oh, you do, too. Okay, here goes. Your hair is pulled back in a ponytail, but waved all over your head, and you have soft curls that surround your face. It falls down along your back at least two inches past your bra. It gleams from that shine and texture stuff Marty put in it. She threaded some kind of ribbon around it, too. Your eyelids are a smoky gray, they look like bedroom eyes. That's what my grandmother called it, and your lips are pouty and subtle, but the best thing about you is your cheekbones. God, you have perfect cheekbones."

"The dress fits you better than it ever did me. It's simple, but sophisticated and shows off the waist I never knew you had."

Nina looked down. The nylons they'd stuffed her into were scratchy, and her feet hurt already from the low-heeled beige pumps. But she was grateful. They hadn't just stopped everything they were doing to help her, they'd made it a special affair. She was getting married, uh, mated under the craziest of circumstances, and yet they'd made it seem like it was a mating between Brad Pitt and Angelina Jolie.

"Um, thanks. I know I don't say that often, but you guys sorta rock."

"Sorta?" Marty tilted her head.

Nina laughed. "Just a little, not a lot."

Wanda rose from the bed and planted her hands on her hips. "So, girls, are we in?"

Nina looked at Marty who smiled wickedly. "In," they re-peated.

"Let's just hope Greg's in," Nina muttered.

Marty gave her a playful shove. "Like you'd let a little thing like him saying no stop you? Puuullllease. Now let's go and hope there's no traffic."

Nina gave one last glance downward at the fall of her dress, catching a glimpse of her shoes. Christ, her feet were killing her.

If Greg wouldn't mate with her, she'd take off these damned torture devices and fucking stab him in the eye with the heel of her shoes.

Yeah.

It was like that.

CHAPTER 17

"Shhhhhhhhh," Nina hissed at Marty who was fussing with her ponytail from behind. "It's fine. Leave me the fuck alone already. Stop princess-orizing me to death and be quiet."

Marty threw up her hands. "Fine, far be it from me to want you to be perfect on your wedding day."

She pulled up short, each of the women behind her knocking into each other. "Would you shut up?" Nina barked.

"Why do we have to be quiet?" Wanda whispered.

"Because Greg has this old guy, a neighbor who suspects—"

Marty tapped her on the shoulder. "You mean him?"

Jim Finch popped out of the bushes by the front door in a firestorm of limbs, waving a bottle around. He wore a dark green bathrobe this time, and his lined face held awe and fear. The clap of his slip-ons sounded like hard thumps of a hammer as he pounded down the decorative pavement at them.

Fuuuuuuck. Nina took a firm stance a few safe feet away from him, planting her legs apart and giving him the scariest Nina look she had in her arsenal. She shielded Marty and Wanda with the spread of her arms. "Jim, go home!"

"You're one of them!" he yelled so loud porch bulbs around the neighborhood began to flash on like blinking Christmas tree lights. "You're the devil!"

Nina caught Marty's mouth drop open from the corner of her eye. "Uhhhhh, trouble?"

"Holy water," Nina whispered harshly.

Wanda squeaked, "Hoo, boy."

Nina rocked from one foot to the other, trying to dodge him to get to the front door. Time was at a premium here and a run-in with Jim was the last thing she needed right now. "Go home, Jim!"

But Jim had grown braver since her last encounter with him. The bottle he held had a chain wrapped around its neck, and he swung it like it was a pair of nunchakus. The air snapping around it made short whipping sounds.

Fuck, fuck, fuckity, fuck. His rapid approach wasn't unsteady this time, and if he nailed her with that holy water, she was done for, and that meant so was Greg.

Fear and crisis seemed to be a motivating factor when it came to her incisors making an appearance. Nina felt the stretch of her gums as they elongated and decided it was now or never.

She opened her mouth wide, hissing at Jim, flashing her teeth and narrowing her eyes with menace.

Jim's shriek and his sudden plunge backward into the bushes made Marty and Wanda gasp, running toward him just as Svetlanna appeared at the door. "Nina?"

Nina pushed past Marty and Wanda who'd dragged Jim behind the bushes, laying him on the ground, then rushed to Nina's side.

Nina searched Svetlanna's eyes. "Where is he?"

Her eyes looked tired, and her face was drawn. "He's in his room. What's going on?" She scanned Nina from head to toe, shaking her head, disbelief evident in her gaze. "Oh, Nina. You're beautiful . . ."

"Yeah? Thanks, and I hafta say, I don't know how you do it all the time. My feet are killing me, and this fuc—um, stupid makeup feels like goo all over my face. My hair is like an Aqua Net festival gone awry, and I can't breathe in this contraption I'm told is a bra. But forget me, is the heifer here yet?"

"Lisanne?"

"Yeah, her."

"No," she spat, distaste written all over her face. "What are you doing here?"

"What I do best. Bully people into doing what I want them to do."

Svetlanna threw her arms around Nina, sobbing. "Thank you. Thank you," she whispered earnestly.

"So where is my unwilling groom again?"

"In his room—you have to hurry, time's running out. It's already eleven thirty."

Nina took the stairs two at a time, silently hoping she wouldn't trip on them in Wanda's shoes, then raced down the hall to Greg's bedroom.

She burst through the door, scanning the room for Greg. It was empty. But the heavy drapes at his window rustled, and someone stepped out from behind them.

"Hello, Nina," a vaguely familiar voice said with cheer in the greeting.

When Nina was able to make the connection from voice to face, she was at first confused, and then she understood. Whatever deemed it possible for her to get the big picture, deemed it should be so at the absolute worst moment.

Go figure.

Wee doggie—she was fucked.

LISANNE appeared out of thin air while the girls waited downstairs for Nina. Her smile was sly, her posture confident when she strolled through the wide foyer.

"Omigod, are you Lisanne? The *Lisanne*?" Marty threw her head back and laughed, strolling over to the infuriated Lisanne and eyed her outfit with contempt. "Tell me something, would you?"

Lisanne cocked an eyebrow in question.

Marty scanned her dress with disdain. "What—out of all the colors on a color wheel—made you choose *that*? It's so wrong for you on every color level that exists. I mean, really, who picks your clothes?'

Lisanne's face went hard. "Who is *this*?" she asked Svetlanna.

Svetlanna had to find a way to stall her. If she got to Greg before Nina did, she'd overpower her and for all the havoc Lisanne had wreaked, she'd have a wooden stake in her heart before she let that happen. But Marty didn't give her time to answer Lisanne.

Marty stuck her face in Lisanne's and smiled brazenly. "I'm the bitch that's going to make things very difficult for you, and I warn you, if I break a nail doing it—I'll get überupset and then, well, then you have to *die*."

NINA felt the rise of fear in her chest, and a chill of foreboding swept along her spine in a cold blast. Why had the mystery vamp shown up tonight, of all nights? "What are you doing here?"

He smiled, that same pleasant grin that had left her creeped out the last time she'd seen it at the bar. "We have some things to discuss."

Discuss. Everyone was always discussing things in this crazy clan. Talk, talk, talk. Maybe they all should stop discussing shit. "I'm not discussing jack shit with you, you dumb ass. Where have you been? I went to the place you said you'd meet me, and you never showed up, you asshole. You've called me at least three times since this began, but you don't leave messages with your number. That's very, very irritating. And you were full of shit anyway. There is no turning me back. So what's your beef with me?"

He took his hands from the deep pockets of a long, brown trench coat and folded them together. "Your boyfriend showed up that night. I told you not to bring anyone with you, didn't I?" His voice had risen an octave, sending off alarms and whistles in Nina's head.

"Oh, puuhllease. I didn't bring him with me. He followed me."

"It won't matter in the end, Nina."

The end? Huh. Was there going to be an end she was sorely unaware of?

He wasn't as collected as he'd been a moment ago. His eyes were shifty, and his movements agitated. He slunk closer, advancing on her in measured, precise steps. The threat in his eyes, that evil glint, had her head spinning.

Nina backed away without thinking, her mind racing to find a way out of the room. Her hands touched the far wall from behind her, and that was when she realized she'd made a grave mistake.

Never, ever let the enemy back you into a corner, fuckwit. Don't you remember what happened with Atwood Goldstein in sixth grade? They'd been fighting over her lunch. Atwood, in all of his stupidity, had foolishly thought he could take away her—*Nina Blackman's* lunch— and not have the snot beat out of him. She'd had a reputation at Sternson Middle School for making boys cry, but every once in awhile some hero came along who thought he could throw down with her just because she wore the label "girl." She'd been about to show Atwood who could take who, when he'd cornered her. She'd been too cocky, and with the incentive of the crowd, she'd grown even more confident, forgetting her position.

That was when she ended up against the chain link fence with chocolate pudding all over her head. Atwood had outsmarted her, and this weird-ass mofo was doing the same thing. He'd used her surprise to his advantage.

Her mystery vamp was up in her face in a matter of seconds, just like Atwood had been, leaning into her and pressing something with a sharp tip to her abdomen. His flat features still held the smile he wore, but his eyes scared the bejesus out of her. They were glazed and shiny, wild and unafraid.

Nina struggled to push him away, but he was rock-solid. "What the hell do you want from me? I don't even know who you are!"

"Here's the problem in a nutshell. I know who *you* are. Greg created you. If he mates with you tonight, that leaves me next in line to mate with Lisanne, and that's just not going to happen. I'll never mate with that hag." His eyes slanted, changing colors. "If you're out of the picture, Greg has to mate with Lisanne, and I'm safe."

Oh, if only he knew how completely delusional he was. She struggled to tell him he was anything but safe, because no way was Greg mating with Lisanne. "Wait a minute. Who said I was mating with Greg?"

He grinned. "I saw you together, and I heard you with your friends tonight."

She was stunned. "You were spying on me?"

His grin widened. "If you'd taken Greg's advice and cultivated your magic, you'd have smelled me watching you all this time. But it doesn't matter now, Nina."

She didn't like the sound of that. Hold on one fucking second. Did he intend to kill her? Her? Whoa, whoa, whoa. "So I'm going to take a stab here and guess I'm on your list of things to eliminate."

"You got it."

Gnarly. Without allowing herself to think, Nina shoved him so hard, whatever he had in his hand ripped her dress, the sharp tear of it sending a spike of anger, that despite her position, made her react. "You ripped my goddamn dress! This isn't even mine, you fucktard. How am I going to give this back to my friend like *this*?"

His surprise at her outburst lasted but a millisecond before he was moving in on her again, and she was finally able to identify what he had in his hand.

A wooden stake.

Ya know, this here was a fucking predicament if there ever was one. Had she spent a whole lot less time kvetching about being a freakin' vampire and far more time honing her superpowers, she might have stood a chance at taking this guy—but seeing as she'd been such a whiner—it wasn't gonna happen today.

Good planning.

He brought his forearm up under her chin, muscling her back against the wall. The power of the impact on her back made her head slam against the hard surface.

"Owwwwwwwwwwww—that hurt, you freak! Get the hell off me." Nina shoved him again, but this time he'd dug his heels into the thick carpeting, and trying to move him turned into trying to move Mt. Olympus. Her chin was high on his forearm, her legs nearly immobile. She'd never been stupid enough to kid herself into thinking she had the upper hand when she didn't. So it was time to find a different route. If she stalled him, maybe someone would wonder where she was. Her eyes caught the alarm on Greg's nightstand. It read eleven forty-one. "Wait!"

He stopped putting pressure on her chest for a short moment. "I'm going to kill you, and you want me to wait?"

"Yes! Yes. I have vital information." She grasped desperately at the last of her imaginary straws.

He cocked his head. "Do you? Do share."

"Greg won't mate with me." Crap that hurt to admit over and over. It was like some kind of broken record and karma kept playing it to remind her where she stood.

She saw him stop to think about that, watching the wheels grind in his head. "I don't believe you." He raised the stake, holding it at an angle, aimed at where her heart once beat.

Nina pressed her hands against his chest, clinging to his trench coat. "No, no, wait! He won't and, P.S., if you were a better spy, you'd have heard us the other night. He hates Lisanne—hates her *guts*, and he said he'd rather turn to dust than spend an eternity with her." Nina nodded as a follow-up. "He did, I swear."

For the first time, his smile faded.

"Don't you see? It won't matter if you off me. You'll still have to mate with Lisanne." So hah!

He shook his head as though he were clearing cobwebs, tightening his arm across her throat. "I don't believe you. That just leaves me next in line to mate. Greg wants you, I know he does. He told Clayton."

Shut. Up.

She'd hang on to that for ammunition if she ever found out where the fuck Greg was. What the hell was he doing? "Well, I got some news for you. He sure didn't tell me that. So I say we let me go, and we'll go talk to Greg, and get this all cleared up. Whaddya say?"

"Noooooooooooo!" he roared into her face, raising the stake high above his head. His voice bordered on hysteria now, and if her gut was right, her eternity was going to be cut short like real soon.

"Waitttttttttttttt!" Nina shoved at him again, lifting her knee to knock him in the crotch, but he was prepared, grabbing her by the material at the neck of her dress and whipping her to the floor. He was on her in the blink of an eye, while she thrashed beneath him with a totally hopeless effort. "Stoppppp! Stopstopstopstop!"

"Would you shut up? Jesus, Greg's right, you're a loud mouth."

"Wait," she rasped. "I have another quesssssstion!" Her hysteria was rising now, her legs aching from digging her heeled feet into the floor, her fingers throbbing from gripping the lapels of his coat.

"This better be your last," he threatened, tightening his hold on the stake.

Her lips moved fast, spitting out words without thinking. "What's your name? I don't even know your name, and I think it sorta sucks that you're going to whack me and I don't even know your name. Don't you think everyone should know the name of the person who kills them? It's only fair. You know my name, but I don't know yours. I mean, I'm going to die here. *Die!* That's bad, like really bad. Death—sooooo final, ya know? Like over, done, gone. Have some mercy here, huh? It would be cruel to kill me and not tell me who you are—"

He clamped a hand over her mouth. Clearly he planned to indulge her. "It's—"

"Melvin!" someone thundered from above them.

Greg! Oh, thank God it was Greg.

And Melvin? What the fuck kind of name was that for a vampire?

Hands tore Melvin from her prone body, throwing him across the room in such a spectacular feat of fast-forward motion, Nina might have missed it if she hadn't been scrambling to get back on her feet.

The impact of his body slamming against the wall ripped through the room. The imprint of his body left a dent in the plaster. Sheetrock rained in dusty bits everywhere, falling to rest starkly against the burgundy backdrop of the carpet.

Greg went after him, tearing across the room in a flash of muscle and blurred flesh. His words came out in a roaring demand. "Get up, Melvin!"

Melvin cringed in the corner, covering his head with his hands and pulling his knees up tight to his body, whimpering.

"Get up, you piece of shit, and tell me what the hell you think you're doing threatening my woman!" Greg hovered over Melvin, his jaw clamped tight, his fists clenched.

Nina's eyebrows rose. His *woman*, eh? She tapped him on the shoulder. "Um, question?"

Greg craned his neck around, his mouth a single line of tension. "Now?"

"Uh, yeah."

He rolled his eyes. "What is it, Nina?"

"Your woman?"

"That's what I said."

"Um, another question?"

"Whaaat?"

"Wasn't it you who just a couple of days ago said," she lowered her voice a couple of octaves, "I can't let you mate with me, Nina. You don't know me at all. I won't let you give up your freedom for me."

"Yes, that was me."

"Then how can I be your woman?"

"Nina?"

"Greg?"

"Remember how I also told you, you have a big mouth and sometimes you don't know when to keep it shut?"

"Uh-huh."

"Do that for me now, would you, honey?"

She made a zipping motion with her fingers across her mouth. "This is me being quiet."

He smiled his gratitude, then returned his attention to Melvin, who whimpered when Greg dragged him up to his level. "Wanna tell me what you were doing?"

The friendly grin he typically wore was long gone, replaced by frightened eyes as wide as double moons and quivering cheeks. "I won't mate with Lisanne," he sobbed. "If you don't, I have to. Do you know what she's like? She's despi-pii-cab-l-le . . ." he stuttered with hysterically fractured syllables.

Shoot. Maybe Nina hadn't given Lisanne enough credit. She was bringing vampires who were hundreds of years old to their knees.

Greg took Melvin by the neck and shook him hard. "If you ever come near Nina or anyone in my family again, I will kill you. Got that?"

Melvin nodded with a violent bob of his head. "Y-eeee-ssss."

Greg seethed his next words. "Call yourself lucky I don't bring the clan together for a good old-fashioned shunning."

Melvin shook, head to toe, his body trembling.

Dayum. What was this shunning?

"Get out, Melvin, and never darken my doorstep again." Greg dropped him like so much trash with the flick of his wrist.

Melvin scrunched his eyes shut, his crumpled form fading out with a shimmer of his brown trench coat.

Nina turned to Greg, shaken but as determined as ever. "You know, you people are like a day in the psych ward. Fun, fun, fun."

Greg's lips lifted upward, but just barely.

And here they were at the crux of this whole matter.

"Where were you? For God's sake, you were going to turn to dust all alone?" She heard the desperation in her voice, and she didn't much dig it, but Jesus, the drama since she'd met him was going to drive her out of her mind.

"Eating a Ring Ding in the hedge maze. You know, like the last meal thing." He had the nerve to give her a cocky grin.

"So, here we are." Nina spread her arms wide. "It's ten minutes to twelve on a Saturday night, and this vampire I know has
nothing to do. I'm all dressed up with nowhere to go. I mean,
look at me, would you? I hear I look really, really good. 'Course,
I wouldn't know, because there's this guy, kinda cute, a little arrogant, and way pushy who turned me into a vampire, and I can't
see my reflection very well anymore. Sucks, huh? You know . . .
this vampire? He's very, very stubborn, and he has this problem.
If he doesn't mate with someone by the stroke of midnight on his
birthday, he's fried. Like done for, because vampires are crazy and
they have stupid rules. Anyway, this guy, he's such a stupidhead, he
can't see a good thing when it's standing right in front of him." She
curtsied, nearly tripping on her heels.

"He's so stupid, in fact, he'd rather let this good thing spend an
eternity maybe boinking a bunch of other vampires instead of him.
Dumb you say, yes? Don't answer that. I know the answer. He's an
idiot and so this good thing's giving this arrogant, pushy, sorta cute
vampire one—last—chance before she throws him to the ground
and gnaws on his neck whether he likes it or not—"

Greg grabbed her around the waist and pulled her to him.
"It's eternity, Nina. For—ev—er. Not just ten years or until you
tire of me. This is a lifelong commitment. Permanent. No going
back—"

She pressed a finger to his lips. "Or the shunning. I know. I get
it, okay? We can't ever break up. But did you really think I'd let you
turn to dust? Not a chance. How the flip do you expect me to do
this vampire thing if you're not here? I think it's your obligation,
seeing as you got me into this mess to begin with, to stick around.
Who'll teach me how to fly? Who'll help me build my own
Castlevania with my mind? Who'll remind me what an utter bitch
I can be? Who'll . . ." she stuttered, her throat doing that odd tightening thing again. "Who'll watch *Beaches* with me?"

His lips found hers, kissing her so soundly, so completely, her knees buckled. She pulled away, her nose detecting a very familiar scent. "For fuck's sake, you did have a Ring Ding!"

He gave his shoulders a sheepish shrug. "Actually, it was a Ring Ding *and* a Chocobliss. I told you, last meal and all." Greg planted his mouth back on hers.

They might have stayed that way but for the shrill yelp coming from below.

"Ninnnnnnnaaaaaaaaaaaa! Get down here now!"

Ahhh, judging from the tone of Wanda's voice, Lisanne had arrived.

Game on.

CHAPTER
18

Greg flew down the stairs, dragging a tripping, stumbling high-heeled Nina behind him. When they hit the foyer floor, Nina saw the shit had hit it, too.

Marty lay unmoving on the floor, Svetlanna was in a heap beside her, and Wanda was beneath Lisanne, trying to scream for all she was worth. Lisanne's long fingers rested at her throat.

Nina's incisors immediately lengthened, poking out from her gums with fury. "Gird your loins, Lisanne! If you don't get off of her, I'll fucking wipe the floors of this castle with your ass!"

Wanda clawed at Lisanne's hands, her eyes bulging as she gasped out the words. "Midnight—hurryyyy!"

Nina's frantic glance caught the grandfather clock in the corner of the foyer. Two minutes. She had two minutes to keep Wanda from the same fate Lisanne had bestowed upon Greg and his family.

Greg was the first to react, fastening his hands on Lisanne's

shoulders and tearing her from Wanda with a whoosh of air. She
landed with a hard crash against the front door, but immediately
scrambled to her feet.

Wanda sat up, choking and coughing, her face bright red, her
skirt almost up around her waist. "Sharpen your fangs, Nina," she
bellowed in a harsh breath as Lisanne came at her again with a
scream so bloodcurdling, Nina knew she'd never forget it. It left a
chilling, shrill howl in its wake.

"I'll kill her if you do this, Nina!" Lisanne screeched.

Chaos in its cacophony of color and sound erupted.

Greg literally flew across the room at Lisanne with a roar, eerie
and resonant.

Nina ran for Wanda who struggled to breathe.

A tall, slender man appeared out of nowhere in the long hallway that led to the kitchen.

The front door burst open with a loud crash.

Svetlanna roused, rising to her feet to scream, "Look out!"

The moment before Greg reached Lisanne, Marty, in all her
furry lycanthropic-ness had shifted, bisecting Greg's pending
tackle and landing on Lisanne with a smack. Her wolven nails clat-
tered on the hard flooring as she held fast to Lisanne.

Wanda shook Nina. "I'm okay. Go. Hurry before it's too late." Nina
hauled her up, then ran for Greg who'd vaulted back to his feet.

The first chime of midnight sounded on the grandfather clock.

"You're the devil! You're both the devil!"

Oh. For. Fuck's. Sake.

Jim Finch staggered at the couple, winging his bottle of Holy
water in wild arcs.

Two chimes, Nina thought frantically. Yes, it'd been two.

Wanda yelled to Nina over her shoulder. "I've got this, Nina.
Hurry!"

Three bloody chimes.

Nina heard Wanda chide Jim Finch. "God forgive me for doing this because you're my elder, but shut the fuck up!" She punctuated her demand by clocking him one with a solid right hook Nina caught out of the corner of her eye.

Now four.

Chime number five rang out, as Svetlanna rushed to them, dragging them by their hands to the slender, solemn-looking man in the hall. "This is a clan member, here to witness the mate bond. If you're doing this, do it *now*. You have to hurry!"

Six chimes, and Greg was giving her that look like he was going to start with the eternity crap again, and after all this, she just wouldn't have it.

Her eyes narrowed, black and glistening. She pushed her hair from her face, ready with whatever it took to do what needed to be done. Her voice rose in a tone that wouldn't allow him room to speak, words tumbling out of her mouth at high speed. "Don't even go there, Wing Man. No, I didn't trust you. Yes, I have trouble trusting anyone. Yes, I thought you wanted to turn me into some brainwashed zombie. No, I don't believe that anymore. Yes, I'm a pain in the ass. No, we don't know a lot about each other, but we'll have plenty of time, and if I went to all this trouble to princess-up and you turn me down, I'll find a way to make your after-afterlife a living hell! Now stop being a killjoy and hold the fuck still."

Nina didn't give Greg a chance to protest. When the seventh chime sounded, she jumped up, threw her legs around his waist, and sank her teeth into his neck with a yowl.

And if she'd once thought drinking blood from a cup was this side of Heaven, she'd have been mistaken.

The direct rush of blood, coppery, sweet, and sinfully delicious was far, far better. The sensation of her teeth in Greg's neck ripped through her, touching every inch of her skin, making her eyes roll to the back of her head, leaving her weak and clinging to him.

This—this beat chicken wings and sardines hands freakin' down.

Greg used a gentle hand when he finally pulled her teeth from his neck. They left his skin with a pop. He rubbed the spot where they'd been with a swift hand. "I think we're good, honey."

Nina's head fell back on her shoulders, her body like melted butter, and she listened, her ears finely tuned to the grandfather clock.

No more chimes.

Thank fucking Christ.

Her head popped up, and she looked Greg square in the eye with a grin. "Done."

Greg rubbed the tip of his nose to hers, returning her smile. "Indeed."

Nina slid from his waist, still hanging on to him for fear she'd topple over. "Now that is better than any blood in a bag. Why didn't you tell me?"

Svetlanna's light laughter tinkled when she hugged them both. "Thank you, Nina. You'll never know how grateful I am for this."

"Um, newly married—uh, mated—uh, whatever, people?" Wanda called from across the room, looking down at Jim Finch who lay on the floor at her feet. "I think we have some carnage. I swear, I didn't mean to hit him so hard. But he's still breathing if that helps any."

"Don't worry. I'll have someone get him home," Svetlanna assured her, then turned in the direction of Marty and Lisanne, her gaze cold and hard. "For now, I have a little something I have to take care of." She patted Wanda on the arm and smiled. "By the way, that was some right hook."

Wanda smiled coyly. Then her eyes followed Svetlanna's, taking her attention from Jim.

Wanda stomped across the floor to stand over Marty. "Marty,

stop that now. It's not nice to toy with your prey before you kill it. Where are your manners?"

Marty had a prone Lisanne nailed to the floor, her four paws surrounding her body while she licked a startled, stunned Lisanne's face. She swiped a large, blonde and chocolate paw at her, nudging her jaw with her muzzle.

Wanda reached down and admonished Marty in her pointed ear. "Marty Flaherty, cut it out. The mating is over, and we have to go. I'm tired. I mean, everyday with the two of you is like some paranormal marathon. I really, really need to rest, and I need a facial." She nodded. "Yes, that would be refreshing, seeing as I've aged a hundred years between the two of you."

Marty sat up on her haunches, pride written all over her werewolf face, and ran her tongue over her muzzle. Nina raced for a blanket from the couch in the next room, knowing what came next. Marty had ripped her clothes during a shift again, and if Nina knew Marty, she'd never hear the end of it.

Wanda held up the blanket to cover Marty's nakedness when she returned to her human form, scrunching her eyes shut and frowning. "I can't watch."

Lisanne, clearly shocked, sat up and rose to her feet. Her gaze went to Greg, clearly knowing she couldn't touch him, now that the mating had been done. Her fury was silent, her rage palpable, leaving her unprepared when Svetlanna appeared behind her. Yanking Lisanne by the length of her hair with a vigorous tug and forcing her legs to crumble, Svetlanna dragged her to the front door.

Lisanne struggled with a sharp screech, digging her heels into the floor and grabbing blindly at Svetlanna's hands, but Svetlanna's anger, sizzling like a current of electricity, was stronger. She looked at both Nina and Greg and spoke through clenched teeth. "You two go honeymoon. Lisanne and I are going to stroll down memory lane together, right, Lisanne?" She hauled the vampire who'd caused her so much pain so many years ago up hard, tearing open the door and hurling Lisanne out in front of her. The clatter of heels flying and a grunt made Nina cringe.

Nina turned to Greg with worried eyes. "Do ya think your mother might need some help?"

Greg's smile was wry. "Um, no. I think my mother can handle this. Years of rage can be potent, and if anyone owes Lisanne, it's my mother."

"Is this the shunning thing?"

"Uh, no, honey. This is the end of Lisanne's immortality thing."

A shiver coursed through her. Svetlanna, serene, calm, collected, was going to finish Lisanne off. And Nina wouldn't allow herself to think any further than that. Lisanne had created havoc so many years ago and had used her power to tear apart a family, killing them in the name of something as nutty as the green-eyed monster. That Greg hadn't done her in thus far was a testament to the kind of man he was.

"So we don't have to worry about Lisanne anymore—or for that matter, some new, kooky rule you crazy night dwellers might have forgotten to share with me that'll come back to slap me in the head? Like one that says we're not really mated after all that drama?"

Greg chuckled. "Nope. We're golden."

The collective sound of relief spread from one person to the next.

"So we're a couple now," Nina said, grinning at Greg.

Greg crossed two fingers together. "Just like this. Eternally. Forever. Centuries of commitment—"

Nina looked up at him, making a face. "I said I get it. Besides, I'd be more worried about you than me, Dracula."

"And why's that, honey?"

Nina pointed to her mouth. "For eternity you'll be forced to listen to my big, potty mouth. I swear all the time. I have a lot of opinions, I'm not ashamed to express them, I'm cranky and bossy, and I love a good fight—"

Greg captured her lips. "Whaddya say we go do couple things and I'll shut that big mouth up?"

Nina cocked a saucy eyebrow at him and sauntered to the bottom of the stairwell. "After you."

Wanda and Marty crowded them with hugs and good wishes before they hit the stairs, and this time Nina was in the lead. She shoved open the bedroom door, turning to face him with a smug smile while crossing her arms over her chest with an "I win, you lose" attitude.

His return smile was hesitant, but tempered with amusement. "You don't know me, Nina."

"Nope. I don't know what your favorite color is or what your middle name is, or even what you like to watch on TV, but I'll learn."

"William."

"What?"

"My middle name. It's William."

"You're serious?"

"Yep."

"How can you have a first name like Gregori, but a middle name like William?"

"My father had a close friend whose name was William."

"Oh. Well, I'll try to remember that."

The smile that had hesitantly been on his lips before, twitched a little, then disappeared. "You've done something you can't take back."

Her smile grew wider. "Yep."

"You don't even like me."

"You don't like me either," she returned.

"Yeah, I kinda do."

"I do, too."

"You do, too, what?"

"Like you. Sort of."

Greg snickered. "Only sort of?"

"Okay, look, lemme give this to you straight. It wasn't so much *you* I didn't like. I just didn't like the vampire part a lot. Not you being a vampire, but me being one against my will. When I'm forced to do something I don't want to do—I get crazy. I behave badly. I swear. I become confrontational. It comes from where I grew up, and people always trying to intimidate you. It was a tough place, as you know. See? Now you've learned something else about me. Something deep and emotional. Look at us all getting to know one another, and playing well in a team setting."

He chuckled. "Why don't we shoot for something in the realm of the less obvious? All of those things you mentioned are pretty obvious to anyone within hearing distance."

"Mandy."

"Who?"

"My middle name. My middle name is Mandy." She waited for his reaction.

"Um, like the Barry Manilow Mandy?"

Nina narrowed her eyes in warning. *"Do not."*

He put the back of his fist over his mouth to cover his smirk, clearing his throat. "That's so *totally* unfair to ask of me."

"I'll say this once and only once, just so you know how totally jacked up I can get about it, okay?"

He nodded solemnly, only one corner of his mouth lifting in a smirk. "Go."

"I know no one expects someone like me to love a guy who sings cheesy love songs, but I do. My mother loved him, and when she dragged herself home, she played his albums over and over. So never, as long as we live together, ever make fun of Barry Manilow. *Ever.*"

"I'll see what I can work out."

"Do that. If you don't, there'll be hell to pay."

"I don't doubt it."

"*The Bachelor.*"

"Say again?"

"*The Bachelor.* I love that show. It cracks me up when all the girls he doesn't pick cry like a bunch of sissies. I know that's sadistic, but c'mon."

"I'm a *24* fan, myself. I have to wonder how that guy's able to stay up for twenty-four hours, let alone take the beat-down he gets almost every episode, and he's human. I don't even think a vamp like me could keep up with Jack Bauer."

Nina laughed. Okay, this was good. She liked *24*, too. "Green."

"Really? You never wear green."

"That's because it isn't really in my color wheel. Not the shade I like anyway."

Greg cocked his head in confusion. "What *is* this color wheel?"

She smoothed a hand over her ripped dress. "Looooong story, but I know about them because of Marty. She owns a portion of Bobbie-Sue Cosmetics, and color wheels are her reason for breathing. That story, the one with Marty, is almost as unbelievable as ours. Someday I'll tell you all about it."

"Your friends are really something." His voice rang with admiration.

Nina grinned. "Yeah, yeah they are."

"Marty took on Lisanne like a champ."

"I didn't know Wanda had it in her to clock someone like that."

"She's been paying closer attention to you than you think."

Nina shook her head. "I need to spend more time with her. Something's just not right these days, and I can't put my finger on it."

"That would mean you have a heart."

"No. You stole that, remember?"

He chuckled. "Yellow."

"Oh, God. Please tell me that's not your favorite color."

Greg cocked his dark head at her. "It is. It reminds me of the sun, which I mostly can't get out to see anymore and have no problem admitting I miss."

"Then I guess I can forgive that. Just don't wear it, okay?"

"If it displeases you, mistress . . ."

Nina laughed again. "I'm not a girlie-girl. You probably won't see me like this often." She waved a hand along her borrowed dress.

"I've had one too many girlie-girls in several lifetimes. I think I'll manage without the high maintenance," he said, winking.

"Have you then?"

"Have I what?"

"Had many girlie-girls?"

His expression grew sheepish. "A couple."

"Well, I guess those days are over."

"As are yours for pushing men around. I'm not easily pushed."

"Yeahhhhh—that's kinda hot."

"That I won't take your shit?"

"Uh-huh."

"How informative," he drawled, giving her a lazy smile, finally pulling her to him with strong, lean hands firmly clamped around her waist.

Nina sank into him, relaxing for the first time in two days. "See? Look at all this sharing we're doing. In no time flat you'll know everything about me and be bored to death, um, eternity."

"I just don't see life with you as boring."

"E-ter-ni-ty," she corrected, gazing up into his green eyes. "Forever, many, many, many lives.

"I get it."

"Do you? I mean, really?"

"After all this, I'd better."

Her giggle seemed foreign to her ears. Kinda like the ones Marty and Wanda spewed when they were twirling their hair and flirting.

The silence between them grew, Greg's gaze becoming serious, heated.

"So, ya wanna watch *Beaches*?" she teased.

His finger traced the top of her dress, now ripped and stained from the battle to mate. Greg dipped a finger between her breasts, making Nina's nipples turn to tight beads. "Uh, no. I wanna watch you naked," he husked out, splaying his hands along her waist and curving them into her hips.

Nina arched into him, her spine tingling with those magnified rushes of heat. Her arms draped around his neck, molding herself to his body, reveling in the rigid line of his cock through his jeans.

His lips slid over her jaw, his tongue snaking out to caress her neck in hot swipes. "Did I tell you how beautiful you look tonight? Even in the midst of Melvin and company. Did you do this for me?"

"And if I said yes?"

"I'd say bravo."

Nina hid her face in his neck. "Then it was worth all the crap getting there." She kicked off her heels, wiggling her toes to uncrimp them. "And let me tell you about the getting there. Jesus, what a production. My hair feels like cardboard, my eyes are going to glue shut any freakin' moment, my lips are like flypaper, and this damned bra. Who, in all of their friggin' maniacal insanity, thought creating the plunge was a good idea?"

Greg reached down and slipped the dress up over her hips, the sensuous slide of it leaving a trail of shivers. "I say you let me see the product of this insanity, and I'll take a guess." He threw Wanda's dress on the floor, cupping Nina's bra-covered breasts, leaning down and kissing the rounded swell of each one. "I dunno," he muttered against her skin, "this is pretty smokin'."

She silently preened, running her fingers through his thick hair, pulling his lips closer as he inched his way inside her bra with his lips. Unhooking it, he let it fall, sliding it off her shoulders and dropping it to the floor.

Her moan was low, husky, hot. Her head fell back on her shoulders, her hands reaching for Greg's shoulders as he took a nipple in his mouth and suckled. The hard tug sent sharp stings of pleasure between her legs.

Greg tugged at her nylons, rolling them over her hips, pushing them past her thighs until she shrugged out of them. Her panties soon followed in a soft whisper of silk.

Nina grew impatient to feel the press of his skin against hers. Her fingers fumbled, tugging his shirt off, unzipping his jeans, shoving his boxer briefs to the floor, and finally, clamping a hand around the stiff length of his cock.

It was his turn to moan against her nipple. Rising to mesh her length with his, he threw his shoes off and walked her backward. The backs of her knees touched the edge of the bed, and then she felt the soft mattress against her spine.

Greg hiked her leg up around his waist, sliding his fingers between the soft folds of her sex, teasing her clit with long strokes. They found each other's mouths, clinging, sliding tongue against tongue, delving deeper until she was dizzy.

Greg swept his hands over the slope of her hip, turning her to lie on her stomach, rising up over her and letting the outline of his body weigh with enticing anticipation above hers. His hair skittered across her spine as he kissed along her back, over her shoulders, down along her spine, past the curve of her ass to nudge his head between her thighs.

He clamped a hand on the inside of each leg and dipped his head between them. Her hips rose of their own accord, lifting to accommodate him, gripping the sheets at either side of her when he stroked the outer lips of her aching sex. His descent between them was unhurried, parting them with excruciating, deliberate slowness.

The first touch of his tongue to her clit sent her muscles into a tight spasm, making her rear upward, her spine curving toward the mattress, his hum of pleasure making her weak. Greg's large hands crept up to cup both of her breasts, tweaking the nipples into rigid peaks.

As she rested her sex on the heat of his mouth, sliding back and forth with a seductive, slow rocking motion, he lapped at her, making her fingers curl into the pillows above her as the rise of orgasm swelled in her belly. This time it didn't take her by surprise, but took a slow path, wending along each inch of her body until it settled in the depths of her swollen sex.

Nina's cry was hoarse, unbridled, and desperate when she came, pressing herself flush to his mouth until the sharp, pleasurable sting subsided.

Greg slid from between her thighs, moving up to lie beside her. He brushed the hair from her face, dragging her thigh back up around his waist and cupping her ass.

The head of his cock poised at her entrance, but he paused. His green eyes, solemn, smoldering, piercing, scanned hers.

Nina shifted her hips with impatience as she held his gaze, her stomach in a knot, her need to have him inside her fraught with desperation.

Greg's incisors lengthened, and just as he drove into her, his teeth sank into her neck. He plunged upward, stroke after flaming stroke, thrusting into her, while his lips clamped onto the stretch of Nina's skin.

An aching, exquisitely painful wave of carnal pleasure swept over her, consuming her, dragging her to a height she'd never been to. She shook in his arms, helpless to fight the primal, gut-wrenching assault of indescribable sensations. Just as she reached the crest of this harried wave, it dropped her with a suddenness that made her clench her thighs more tightly around him, grit her teeth, dig her nails into his back.

Greg bucked within her, only barely noticeable, she was so lost in this newfound height of pleasure. She came with a short, sharp scream, grinding her hips to his, driving them upward to take every last inch of his cock.

When Greg tensed against her, each muscle in his body letting go like arrows from a bow, he collapsed against her neck, limp.

Her hands cradled his head, smoothing his hair, running her hands over the hard planes of his back.

"Whoa," she muttered against the top of his head.

"A decided whoa," he chuckled back, pushing up to meet her at eye level so their noses touched.

"Uh, that neck thing? Hot, very, very hot."

"Just another little vampire perk."

"It rocks."

"Well, it's a good thing you feel that way because you can't ever do that with anyone else. For *e—ter—ni—ty*."

Nina rolled her eyes at him. "You're really crackin' on me about that. I know what I got myself into, Wing Man. It's you who should start thinking about a hundred years down the road when I've reamed you out for the umpteenth time. I can be difficult at best."

He winked. "Difficult is hot."

"Ya think?"

He kissed her lips, savoring them with his tongue. "I think."

Greg curved her body into his, tucking her beneath his chin.

"Sooooooo . . ."

"Sooooooo . . ."

"Ya wanna watch *Beaches*?"

"Is this what my eternity is in for?"

"I did warn you."

"I think there are other things we could be doing."

"What's better than *Beaches*, for Christ's sake?" she teased.

He covered her body with his, sinking his delicious weight into her. "This," he murmured, capturing her lips with his.

"Ohhhh, that," she muttered against the slide of his tongue.

Well, then.

That beat *Beaches* every time.

EPILOGUE

Four Months Later

Wanda waved the keys to her new sky blue convertible at Nina and
Marty with pride. They'd gathered at Nina and Greg's to celebrate
her most shining achievement. Nina couldn't help but notice how
tired Wanda still looked these days, and she had to hope it was
from all that Bobbie-Sue-ing she was doing. Not something else.
Watching Wanda gnawed at her gut, but she set it aside, because
Wanda's smile was wide and her spirits were high as a kite.

Marty sat cross-legged on the couch across from Nina, who'd
planted herself on the edge of Greg's desk. "I'm so proud of you,
Wanda, even if sky blue is totally *not* in your color wheel."

Wanda laughed, and Nina noticed the lines around her eyes
seemed more prominent, dark smudges beneath them stood out,
despite her makeup. "Well, how about I stick to the convertibles

because I can assure you, vampires and werewolves aren't in *my* color wheel."

Nina's acute senses had begun to pick up the subtleties of her friend's emotions as of late, and she detected sadness in Wanda's words. Maybe she was lonely. "I'd be happy to introduce you to some of the clan members. Of course, you'd have to come to Long Island more often and give up those cheesy romance novels at night."

Wanda's bark of laughter made Nina smile. "I think I'm okay with single, thanks. I was married long enough to know I don't want to do it again. Romance novels are much safer. I mean, where else can you get an H—"

"EA," Nina finished for her. "And an alpha male and a duke and a lord of the manor and a rake and all the sappy stuff that comes with *women's fiction*."

"Speaking of alpha males," Marty interjected. "Where's the bloodsucker?"

Greg poked his head around the corner. "I'm here. Ladies, I hear congratulations are in order for Wanda." He took two strides and planted a kiss on Wanda's cheek, then went to Nina's side, gathering her to him.

The comfort he brought when he put his arm around her always left Nina amazed. No matter what they fought about—and just because they were mated for eternity didn't mean they didn't still throw down—no matter how much she swore and threatened him, at the end of the evening, lying beside him in that big bed made eternity seem like icing on the cake.

"So, all's well that ends well, eh, potty mouth?" Marty chided with a grin.

Yeah, all was well, and that thing called love had hit Nina in one big slap to the head one night a month or so ago when she'd caught Greg trying to hide a Ring Ding he'd been stuffing into his mouth like it was the Last Supper. The look of pure guilt on his face, coupled with his total remorse because he was able to eat something she still couldn't, had been the clincher. She'd said the words as easily as she'd once called him a fucktard, and Greg had returned them, after he'd brushed and rinsed his mouth out with Listerine.

This eternity thing was going really well so far, and the deeper she got, the harder she fell. This mating of circumstance had turned into something bigger than Nina was able to take on with two fists and some cussing.

Though her biggest regret was not having Lou with her when she'd mated. No way would Lou's health have been up to taking the kind of chaos that had happened that night.

Like she could have explained what went down anyway. Lou didn't know they'd mated for life just yet—or even that she and Greg were vampires. She thought they were living together here in Castlevania. She'd stated her desire to come visit once she was up and around. She was recuperating nicely, and in celebration of Nina and Greg moving in together, she'd had her day nurse send a statue of the Virgin Mary—which Greg promptly stuffed away in a cabinet until Lou was able to drop in. There'd be time enough to tell Lou about what had happened her first day on the job.

A job . . . that was something that had troubled her a great deal while she came to terms and adjusted to her immortality. She was working class and always would be. The idea of doing nothing with her eternity but hanging out in a castle just wasn't cool.

Working during the day was out of the question until she'd begun to build up this tolerance Greg talked about. For now, it was an impossibility. But Svetlanna had offered a suggestion that Nina had at first scoffed at, then with the encouragement of Greg and under the tutelage of some very patient coworkers, she'd joined Svetlanna's company Fango—as the head of quality control.

Who better than Nina of the big mouth to bully perfection out of people, Wanda had joked.

And Wanda was right, though her hat was off to Svetlanna for teaching her the finer points of being diplomatic—over and over. But she was conquering her potty mouth, and even if clothes weren't her thing—telling people what to do was.

Diplomatically, of course.

Nina snuggled against Greg, letting her hand rest on his thigh. "Yeah, Princess Marty. All's well that ends well. How's the head dog?"

Marty jumped up off the couch. "Quit calling us dogs, you, you neck gnawer. You only wish you could do the things I can."

"Like shed?" Nina snorted.

"Oh, please, tell me one thing you can do as a vampire that's cooler than what I can do as a werewolf. Go on." Her hands had gone to her hips, and her neck stuck out in a challenge.

"You know, you two are like a never-ending boxing match. Who cares who has better superpowers? I mean, really, who wants to drink blood and shift into a hairball," Wanda said from the couch.

Nina's smile was secretive. "I bet you'd feel differently if you could *fly*, Wanda."

Marty gasped her outrage. "Oh, you cannot either *fly*, Nina. You're so full of horse puckey."

"The hell I can't—ask Greg."

Greg nodded his head. "She's working on it."

"Okay, so I'm not totally there yet, but I have lifted off, and you're just jealous, Marty, because I have cooler powers than you."

"You do not."

"Flying beats shifting every time," Nina crowed.

"Knock it off!" Wanda yelped. "Jeez, could we just have a nice, quiet evening together without whipping around our paranormal weapons with challenges of death by teeth and fur? The two of you will be the end of me someday."

Nina giggled. "And where would you be if you didn't have to referee me and Marty. Your life would be sooooo boring. We keep things interesting."

Greg laughed, nuzzling the top of her head. "That's definitely something we're not around here, huh, honey?" He looked down at Nina, grinning.

"Oh, life is definitely not boring with you, Wing Man," she whispered.

Definitely not.

Dakota Cassidy lives for a good laugh in life and in her writing. In fact, she almost loves a good giggle as much as she loves hair products and that's saying something.

Her goals in life are simple (like, really simple): banish the color yellow forever; create world peace via hot rollers and Aqua Net; and finally, nab every tiara in the land by competing in the Miss USA, Miss Universe, and Miss World pageants, then sweeping them in a stunning trifecta of much duct tape and Vaseline usage, all in just under a week's time. All while she writes really fun books!

She loves people, loves to chat, and would love it if you'd come say hello to her on the Yahoo! group of "Accidental Fans." Join Dakota and friends in the chaos by sending an email to dakotacassidy-subscribe@yahoogroups.com, or visit her website at www.dakotacassidy.com.

Dakota lives in Texas with her two sons, her mother, and more cats and dogs than the local animal shelter, and she has a boyfriend who puts the heroes in her books to shame. You can contact her at dakota@dakotacassidy.com. She'd love to hear from you!